SONG OF THE TURTLE

SIDDIKA ANGLE

BEAUTIFUL PACIFIC PUBLISHING

Beautiful Pacific Publishing, P.O. Box 3986, Berkeley CA 94703-9991

This is a work of fiction. Names, characters, businesses, places, events, and incidents are either the products of the author's imagination or used in a fictitious manner. Actual persons or events have been fictionalized to serve the story.

Cover photograph by Harold Davis

Cover Design by Ezra Barany, Barany Productions

Book Produced by Beth Barany, Barany Productions

Hymns:

"El Dios de los Pobres" ("The God of the Poor"), lyrics and music by Carlos Mejia Godoy. Used with permission.

Here I Am, Lord" (80670) Lyrics and music by Dan Schutte © 1981, OCP, 5536 NE Hassalo, Portland, OR 97213. All rights reserved. Used with permission.

"Be Not Afraid" (80666) (c) 1975, 1978, Robert J. Dufford, S.J. and OCP, 5536 NE Hassalo, Portland, OR 97213. All rights reserved. Used with permission.

Lift Up Your Hearts (80671) (c) 1981, 1993, Robert F. O'Connor, S.J. and OCP, 5536 NE Hassalo, Portland, OR 97213. All rights reserved. Used with permission.

The Cry of the Poor (80686) (c) 1978,1991, John B. Foley, S.J. and OCP, 5536 NE Hassalo, Portland, OR 97213. All rights reserved. Used with permission.

Poem:

"If You Forget Me" By Pablo Neruda, translated by Donald D. Walsh, from THE CAPTAIN'S VERSES, copyright ©1972 by Pablo Neruda and Donald D. Walsh. Reprinted by permission of New Directions Publishing Corp.

1st Print edition ISBN: 978-1-7323421-0-1; 1st E-Book edition ISBN: 978-1-7323421-1-8

"Arise, my love, my beautiful one,
and come away,
for behold, the winter is past;
the rain is over and gone.
The flowers appear on the earth,
the time of singing birds has come,
and the song of the turtle
is heard in our land."

SONG OF SONGS 2:11-12

For C and M and J
and the courageous, inspiring people of El Salvador

PROLOGUE

S he is catapulted awake by a sound like the flapping of wings. Tears are running down her face, and her chest clenches with grief. She tries to gather the strands of the dream but they have already floated away.

A few tatters remain: a table, trees, a glimpse of children.

It is the third time this vision has shattered her sleep.

She turns on her pillow and gazes at the shadows of branches the moon casts on the wall. Suddenly she is seized by a joy so fierce her body can hardly contain it.

Her mind reels.

The same strange dream. These wild conflicting emotions. What in the world is happening to her? What does it all mean?

ONE

1983

The silvery call of a bell opens the silence in the chapel. As the last reverberations fall into a deeper stillness, Jamie Quinn spreads his hands reverently over the unleavened bread.

"Blessed are You, God of all creation,
through Your goodness we have this bread to offer
that earth has given and human hands have made.
It will become for us the bread of life."

Jamie has always loved this central moment in the Eucharistic liturgy when his role is to disappear into the mystery of Christ's presence.

Bread, the humblest and most universal food, and wine, a drink that has comforted and sustained human beings throughout history, now move into a sacred destiny, fulfilling Jesus' promise to be with us always in their simple forms.

He intones the familiar words of consecration, "On the night before he died, Jesus took bread, and giving You thanks, he broke it..."

His heart is full as he repeats the words calling Love Himself into this moment.

The bell rings once more, inviting the congregation to an inner awareness that binds together all who ever have and ever will share in this Christian mystery of transformation. In an earlier era it had seemed like magic. In the age of quantum physics, it might just be the literal truth.

Jamie allows the quiet to stretch out like a loving embrace. The musicians begin a meditative song for those gathered here in the name of Christ and longing to be instruments of his love. Jamie knows many of these people. Most are professors and students from the Pacific Theological Union, a consortium of graduate schools where Christians of many denominations, Jews, Muslims and Buddhists learn together and from one another. It is a vibrant, ongoing interfaith conversation that enlivens the participants and soothes the wounds of ancient conflicts. The afternoon sun illuminates their faces. Jamie can see men and women of varied ages, colors and cultures, come from around the world to study here.

His eyes light on Frank and Vivian Sidwell, a couple in their seventies, white-haired with faces etched by life and time. He notices they are holding hands. At communion, each will take the bread and give it to the other saying softly, "You are the body of Christ." This loving act never fails to move Jamie and elicit a small ache in his heart.

Rabbi David Friedman from the Jewish Studies Center is here. He occasionally attends Catholic ceremonies on "Holy

Hill," as the PTU campus above UC Berkeley is affectionately known, "to pay my respects to our most famous Jewish brother." Jamie had laughed when David explained his reason for attending. He really likes to see the man, now a friend, at liturgy, just as he smiles inside when visiting Buddhist monks slip into the chapel wearing their scarlet robes.

"This is the way religion is meant to be," he thinks.

Later, walking down a steep street to the apartment he shares with Sam, his friend and fellow Jesuit, Jamie stops to appreciate the landscape spread before him: the shimmer of San Francisco Bay with the great Pacific Ocean beyond it, so vast and incomprehensible to the mind that it serves as a powerful metaphor for the Divine. The Golden Gate Bridge hovers over the water like the gate of heaven.

With the stunning beauty comes a familiar sadness as he recalls watching Vivian and Frank leaving the chapel arm in arm. That simple, ordinary closeness between a man and woman is something essentially unavailable to a man like him.

As longing courses through him, Jamie mentally shakes himself, irritated at what seems too close to self pity. He knows just how fortunate he is. He has better shelter, clothing and food than most of the five billion souls sharing the earth, not to mention opportunities and life possibilities they can hardly imagine. Within the security of the Jesuit order, he is even removed from the ordinary problems and challenges of lay people. A friend once joked that while priests and nuns took vows of poverty, unlike the actual poor, they never had to worry about money again.

Making his way down the hill in the golden autumn light, Jamie finds his mind repeating its incessant commentary about the pain he is feeling lately when he considers the relational doors closed to someone who has made the promises he has made.

Most people would think sexual deprivation would be the biggest problem for a healthy thirty-nine-year-old male vowed to chastity, but they would be wrong. He has, after all, survived his twenties, when hormones and desire had surged like the wild and treacherous Crystal Rapids he'd once rafted in the Grand Canyon.

In the early days of trying to live his vows Jamie had brought his struggles with being truly and honestly chaste to his spiritual director, Father Richard. "I can't always control my body with my will," he had complained.

"Look," the older Jesuit told him, "I don't care what the Pope says or what the 'official' teaching of the Church is, masturbation is not a serious sin. I promise you God is much more concerned about your relationship with him and with other people than whether you sometimes take your sexuality in hand, so to speak."

Father Richard's eyes had twinkled as he continued, "The purpose of the vow of chastity isn't to keep you orgasm free. It's to create in you a single-heartedness that will allow you to be totally available to God and the world.

"I think the vow's requirement that you work to subdue your sexuality is something like the fasting Muslims do during daylight hours in the month of Ramadan. They gain mastery over themselves that makes it easier to do the will of Allah in all things. You're going to need that self-mastery to live out your vocation as the years go by, and your youthful enthusiasm fades."

Richard's solution to the dilemma of chastity has shaped Jamie's life. He'd recommended that young celibates develop and nurture their sensuality, cultivating appreciation for the wholesome pleasures they were permitted. He believed the senses, used for God, could be paths into deep spiritual experience, and that music, art and the glories of nature needed to be part of their spiritual unfolding.

Jamie embraced this teaching whole-heartedly. It fit so well with what he'd already learned from his widowed Italian grandmother Angelina, who made a home for him and his sister after their parents were killed in a car accident when he was nine and Ellen was twelve.

His grandparents' farm in southern Oregon originally had been apple orchards. When the Quinn children arrived to stay, their grandmother still sold the fruit from a stand at a farmer's market in the Rogue River Valley. She also provided most of the family's food with a large garden, chickens and a cow.

The property bordered a national forest and was within biking distance of the river. For Angelina, a woman who loved the natural world and had educated herself about its geology, plants and animals, Sundays meant church in the morning and afternoons outdoors, forever linking religion and nature in Jamie's heart and mind. Through rain or shine and occasionally in snow, the three made their way along obscure trails and paths. They explored the river itself in the family skiff. Some of Jamie's best memories were of those Sundays that his grandmother had turned into adventures of discovery.

Childhood had also meant music. Even when their parents were alive, the children spent part of every summer at the ranch. In the evenings after chores were done and it was too dark for games outside, Angelina would play and sing. Other children had bedtime stories; the Quinn kids had bedtime songs. They would fall asleep to ballads like "There's a long, long trail a-winding into the land of my dreams…"

In the months of grief after the accident, Angelina would

bring Mom and Dad into the bedtime ritual by singing their parents' favorites like "The Isle of Capri" or "Ramona." The children might well up in tears at hearing the familiar melodies. Yet it was a comfort too, because for a few moments their parents 'came back'. Their grandmother taught them grief was a rich, beautiful emotion because it was an expression of love for those who were gone. He can still hear her say "Besides, my darlings, when you cry, you know you're alive."

From the first time Jamie's five-year-old fingers had moved experimentally across the keys of the old upright piano at the ranch, he was enchanted. There was magic in the way a person's hands could bring forth beautiful sounds and harmonies from piano keys and later from the strings of a guitar and electric violin.

Now music is his solace and a source of spiritual inspiration. At times, alone in his room or outside, perhaps at the edge of the Bay or in a forest, his hands can draw his emotions and longings from his guitar, allowing him to experience the far reaches of his inner self. He can drop away from distractions and cares into an awareness of being completely present. This is when Jamie feels closest to God.

Lately, however, God seems distant and unavailable. It is certainly different from the early days of his vocation when his love was a bright fire, burning steadily, sometimes flaring into feelings so intense Jamie could hardly contain them. He was incandescent, and people responded with pleasure to a young priest so filled with enthusiasm, a manifestation of its classic Greek root, *en theos*—in God.

Giving his life, flinging it without reservation at the feet of Love himself, leaving all to follow Jesus, was so right and easy then. Yes, there had been years of testing and discernment in the lengthy Jesuit formation process, but all obstacles were manageable in those days. The challenges of a life shaped by vows of poverty, chastity and obedience called forth the hero that every man secretly hopes to find inside. At his ordination to the priesthood, as Jamie lay face down before the altar, the stirring hymn accompanying the solemn ritual was like an ocean wave that swept him into the Great Mystery.

"I, the Lord of sea and sky,
I have heard My people cry.
All who dwell in dark and sin,
My hand will save.

I who made the stars of night,
I will make their darkness bright.
Who will bear My light to them?
Whom shall I send?

Here I am Lord, Is it I Lord?
I have heard You calling in the night.
I will go Lord, if You lead me.
I will hold Your people in my heart."

At that moment, he had felt ready for anything; no sacrifice was too great. He could gladly turn over his will to his Jesuit superiors and allow them to make decisions that would determine his future. He could live without owning anything. So in love with God, he was sure he could transmute his natural desire for love with a woman into spiritual desire for "the greater glory of God," the Jesuit order's motto and purpose.

These days, however, that easy confidence is frayed. His mind and heart feel dull and burdened. At times even the beauty of the earth is muted. It is difficult and disheartening for an ordinarily passionate man to go through days with his emotional thermostat so low. Jamie wonders if he is experiencing what St. John of the Cross called "the dark night of the soul," a time of spiritual dryness that envelops the spirit like a fog, pushing out joy, vitality and meaning to prepare a soul for more profound grace.

Or is it just comeuppance for his arrogant naïveté in daring to make perpetual vows in the first place?

Sometimes in the deepest hours of the physical night Jamie awakens feeling afraid. His chest constricts and his pulse pounds as he asks himself some version of a troubling question: suppose what he's going through is not a spiritual prelude to some inner flowering, but the lack of sensation which comes from putting a tourniquet on a limb too tightly for too long?

When he's honest with himself, Jamie has to admit the constraints his vow places on his relationships with women are forcing him to seal off rooms in the house of his psyche. The areas he can enter in comfort seem to be getting smaller.

Negotiating friendships with women is a minefield for most heterosexual priests. Whenever you share the stories of your spiritual journeys, intimacy happens. When a man finds a woman who seems a kindred spirit, attraction often follows. Then what? It's a dangerous place to be. And a great deal depends on who the woman is.

While most spiritually-inclined women are reluctant to take on a priest as a lover for obvious reasons, for some, a celibate male is an alluring challenge. What could be more romantic than having a man desire you so much he is willing to break his vows for you? Jamie has met his share of women like that. There had been occasions when the invitation was so tempting that Jamie had to flee, with as much grace as possible—usually not much!

Over the years, he has found himself engaged in a weird balancing act with most women. One part of him can be emotionally warm and open, yet another part needs to remain defended. It's frustrating for someone who prizes openness and transparency in the flow of being with another person. He can't help asking himself what this is costing him as a priest and as a human being. It seems absurd to have to guard his "safety" in half of all of his friendships and associations. But that's the reality. Passing a fence close to the sidewalk, Jamie has a sudden urge to bang his head against the wood. He is so damned tired of these thoughts, but they have hold of him and will not let go.

He does have two women friends with whom he can be less guarded. Julianna, an attorney, is the wife of his boyhood friend Mark, a pediatric surgeon. The couple live in Berkeley, and Jamie sees them as often as he can. There is also Rosa, twenty years his senior, who runs a center in San Francisco's Hispanic Mission District. She is like a much-loved elder sister.

Jamie is close to and enjoys many of his Jesuit brothers. He depends on the wisdom and guidance of a few older priests who have become spiritual father figures. Yet men in community tend to hold each other at a distance in ways that women generally do not. Sometimes he hungers for the closeness women nurture and offer. Sometimes loneliness burns through his mind and heart.

Sam, one of his best friends, has been reluctant to discuss Jamie's current angst, uncomfortable with the whole subject. A conversation a week ago ended abruptly when Sam clapped him affectionately on the shoulder. "Come on, Jay, this isn't the dark night. It's just early mid-life crisis. Talk to Richard. Go over and cook at Dorothy Day House. Go for a run. This kind of self-preoccupation can't be good for you."

There is nothing in Sam's advice that Jamie hasn't said to himself over and over to the point of tedium. Richard had recommended deepening his prayer life and more time out in nature. So now he goes camping alone when he can and spends hours in contemplation of God in creation. He's volunteered at the local Catholic Worker house, adding it to his teaching duties in the PTU pastoral counseling program and his activities in a men's homeless shelter and the neighborhood center in the Mission. When lonely thoughts begin, he cuts them off. He runs and exercises daily to get access to all those feel-good endorphins.

Jamie has to laugh; his body is now in great shape but a lot of good that does him. He is reminded of a priest friend's sarcastic comment about the Church's insistence that being a priest required both celibacy and male genitalia: "You have to have it, but you can't use it!"

Although he has done all the "right things," nothing has changed inside. At times he feels depressed—something new for him—and very vulnerable.

TWO

Sarah Caffaro enjoys the surprise on her students' faces as she highlights the importance of a little-known story in the book of Exodus of two Hebrew midwives who defied the mighty Pharaoh and saved their people. "If it weren't for these two women, the nation of Israel would have ceased to exist in Egypt," she declares with a smile.

"Why have I never heard this?" Sister Elizabeth asks. "I've been in religious life for thirty-eight years, and I've taken classes in Scripture studies. Not once did anyone, in church or in class, ever mention the names Shiphrah and Puah."

Around the modern classroom in a building adjacent to a 19th-century seminary on holy hill, the two dozen students open their Bibles to re-read the text their instructor is talking about.

They look again at the verses in which Pharaoh calls these two insignificant Hebrew midwives to appear before him. He commands them to immediately kill every boy baby born to a

Hebrew woman. Girls would be allowed to live because they could be married to Egyptians and assimilated into Egyptian society, Sarah had explained. "Without the males to continue the lineage, Israel as a nation would have been finished."

They read the text again carefully.

"But the midwives feared God and did not do as the king of Egypt commanded them, but let the male children live. So Pharaoh called the midwives and said to them, 'Why have you done this and let the male children live?'

"The midwives said to Pharaoh, 'Because the Hebrew women are not like the Egyptian women, for they are vigorous and are delivered before the midwife comes to them.' So God dealt well with the midwives and the people multiplied and grew very strong."

Sister Catherine glances at her well-worn Bible and smiles. "Imagine these two little women defying the great king of Egypt. Talk about bravery, not to mention chutzpah!" She grins. "Here they are, facing death because they've disobeyed this absolute monarch, and not only do they keep cool but they tell a story that's plausible and almost impossible to refute. Wow."

The students go on to discuss how women also save the day when Pharaoh later decides to drown Israel's baby boys in the Nile after his first plan has been thwarted by Puah and Shiphrah. Risking severe punishment, the mother of Moses first hides him, then—when that is no longer possible—places him in a basket of reeds in the river. Pharaoh's daughter rescues Moses and adopts him, although she must have known he was a Hebrew baby.

"Women are the real saviors of the Exodus!" Monica, another student, is elated. "And now, thanks to Sarah, we know this."

Sarah laughs. She relishes the sense of inclusion and empowerment women experience in discovering their part in the Jewish and Christian scriptural traditions. It reminds her of how women and African-Americans unearthed their own rich histories a decade before in the 1970s. It is affirming to learn the many contributions women and people of color have made to the world despite the severe oppression and limitations both groups have endured for millennia.

For many years Sarah had not found the Bible particularly interesting, although many Catholic and Protestant friends seemed obsessed with it. A single class in Biblical studies she attended with women friends at Pacific Theological Union had changed all that. When the two hours of class were over, she'd shocked herself by thinking, "This is what I want to do for the rest of my life."

Studying the Bible as an academic was like being a detective. It meant peering into the mists of the ancient Mediterranean world to discover as much as possible of the places and communities in which these texts had been written.

It was a formidable task. So much had been lost through wars and natural disasters. The earliest Christian community led by James, Jesus's apostle and brother, had disappeared around 70 A.D., swept away by the Roman-Jewish war which decimated Jerusalem and the Temple. When the smoke of the destruction had cleared, Peter was left, as was Saul turned Paul, a convert who had never met Jesus yet would prove to be his most influential publicist.

Now in a turn of events she could not have predicted in her youth, Sarah is teaching classes in the Bible. Her particular specialty is the role of women in the New Testament and Hebrew Scriptures.

After graduating from UC Berkeley in 1965, Sarah had made her living writing, first for a daily newspaper and later for a left-leaning political and literary magazine in San Francisco. She enjoyed the challenge of investigative reporting but such publications didn't earn or pay much money. To make ends meet, she'd moved into a women's commune, The Free Women's Collective, in the Haight-Ashbury district of San Francisco.

The San Francisco Bay Area in the 1960s and 70s had been perhaps one of the best times and places to be young. Thanks to the hard work and sacrifices of their parents who'd lived through the Great Depression and World War II, her generation had the luxury of exploring new ideas and ways of being in the world. Thousands of middle class kids could afford to "drop out" for a while and dip into alternative lifestyles before returning to the mainstream of a traditional career and family.

Sarah found the Haight community a vibrant, lively place. Imbibing its culture changed her. With the women in the collective she engaged in a feminist analysis of society and discovered a hidden and ignored "herstory" that was new to them and inspiring. She met people from many countries, spiritual and intellectual adventurers. Long hours of conversation in old Victorian parlors, quaint coffee houses and the vast garden of nearby Golden Gate Park turned her into a liberal feminist with deep spiritual longings who despised war, racism, sexism and injustice of any kind.

In the early '70s, Sarah had returned to Berkeley, both because she had decided to attend graduate school and also to be closer to her Aunt Eugenia. Her father's sister lived on the lower slopes of "Nut Hill" above the university where some of Berkeley's early eccentrics had built unusual homes that included a castle and a Greek temple. It was an appropriate location for Eugenia, her Italian family's "free spirit" who was oblivious to the conventions a woman was expected to observe in the America of her youth.

Long after the implied promise of equality from women's suffrage had faded, Eugenia still believed in it. She had worked her way through the University of California and Stanford and held a Ph.D in history at a time when women with doctoral degrees were rare. She'd taught for decades at Mills College in Oakland, the first chartered woman's college west of the Rockies. Her specialty was the history of women in the American West.

Although she'd had what she termed "presentable suitors" over the years, Eugenia had chosen not to marry. She declared frankly that she seemed to have been born without the need to mate for life or procreate, even though she liked children—especially her nieces and nephew—in measured doses.

From the time they were quite young, Sarah, Madeline and Anthony always looked forward to visiting their aunt in her delightful home on a winding Berkeley street. She was a glamorous figure, traveling to foreign countries, going to plays, opera and ballet. And she regularly played host to a fascinating and changing cavalcade of guests who sat around her dinner table long after the meal was finished and discussed diverse topics.

When they were considered old enough to understand some of what was being said, the children were welcome to listen in and thus learned things about the 1950s and 60s they never heard at home or on television, from the Ban the Bomb movement to exposés of advertising's "hidden persuaders" and the abuses of McCarthyism.

Eugenia and her friends also liked to converse on art and literature, films and theater, psychology and world religions. In her aunt's home Sarah first heard of Buddhism, Emily Dickinson's poetry, and the revolutionary visions of Thoreau and Emerson. The children listened to professors in many fields, as well as artists and writers, politicians, social workers, newspaper reporters and a radio disc jockey. The guests relished exploring the universe of ideas that flourished in Berkeley at mid-century.

That table was also where the children discovered how delicious and various food could be. One Sunday a month, Eugenia held an open house for her Mills students who came from around the world. They were encouraged to bring their favorite foods. As a result Sarah, Anthony and Madeline tasted exotic dishes like baba ganoush, sushi, fiery Indian curries and Peruvian ceviche decades before they became common fare in Bay Area restaurants. Far from home, the foreign students loved talking about their families' recipes. The foods triggered reminiscences and stories about the cultures and people of their native lands.

The dinners at her aunt's place were feasts on many levels, and some of Sarah's happiest childhood memories. They also showed her just how rich and interesting the life of a single woman could be.

In 1977 when Eugenia developed breast cancer, Sarah, who was by then working toward a doctoral degree in Biblical studies, had moved in with her. In love and sadness, reflection and laughter, she'd accompanied the older woman on the journey through treatment and hope, remission and return. The last years of her aunt's life had drawn them very close. She'd been privileged to share in Eugenia's process of leaving the life she had enjoyed so much. That was three years ago, but she still misses her every day.

This afternoon, driving home from class in her 1969 Volkswagen beetle, Sarah keeps stealing glances at the views from the Berkeley hills which never fail to lift her spirits. She loves the way the streets suddenly open onto breathtaking vistas of San Francisco and the Golden Gate in daytime or a magic carpet of colored lights at night. Raised in the orchards and vineyards and rolling hills of the Sonoma County, she never tires of the natural magnificence of San Francisco Bay.

Pulling into the driveway of her craftsman home—part of Eugenia's legacy to her—she is suffused with gratitude for her fortunate life.

Fall flowers greet her as she enters through the gate in an adobe wall the color of the desert touched with the rose glow of dawn. Every time she steps into the walled yard, Sarah feels like Mary Lennox in the Secret Garden. A gnarled olive tree ringed with wild impatiens and tuberose begonias stands in one corner. The flagstone path is bordered by chrysanthemums, gladiolas and asters.

The front porch is large enough to hold a hanging redwood swing, a rocking chair and a stately urn filled with ferns and flowers. As a girl Sarah treasured the times she spent there alone or with her aunt, listening to the birds and observing the fascinating activities of the insects that lived in the front yard. Her innate interest was guided by Eugenia's knowledge of the natural world.

Her aunt and paternal grandfather Oreste were the chief catalysts for Sarah's joy in nature. While other little girls held tea parties for their dolls, she had roamed her family's ranch in the Valley of the Moon like an explorer.

The creek that ran through the property was her personal Wonderland and Narnia. Her grandfather had brought her there for the first time when she only three or four. Stealing an hour from his demanding ranch work, Oreste would sit under a tree, reading a book and watching as his little grand-daughter crawled through the bushes or waded in the creek. He was there to keep her safe but not interfere with her sense of adventure. Frequently, Sarah would be oblivious to him, lost in a new world of fascinating beings with secret lives she wanted to know. The child could hardly contain the excitement she felt watching the shimmering dragonflies and surface-skimming water boatmen, the little fish, the tadpoles, frogs and the burnt orange salamanders.

She learned to sit quietly in the tall grasses or under a tree or grapevine keeping company with the birds and waiting for the appearance of jackrabbits, the occasional deer and a small brown resident fox.

A favorite memory was of one spring morning when a rabbit hopped very close to her. Either it had forgotten she was there or had grown accustomed to her presence. She reached out to touch it as it nibbled grass. "Hello, Bunny! How are you?" As she spoke, it looked up, hesitated, then took off running. At first she was disappointed and realized she had frightened him. She looked at her grandfather, as if to say, "Did I scare him away for good?" But Oreste just smiled, as if to say the bunny would be back. And in fact he did return often, becoming tame enough that Sarah could occasionally pet him.

In 1907 when he was twelve years old, Oreste Caffaro had traveled alone from his native Tuscany to America to join an older brother who'd emigrated to California in 1896.

Although he had only an eighth grade education, Oreste had continued to learn all his life. As a poor young farmer with 40 acres of fruit trees, unpredictable weather and a fluc-tuating or depressed economy, he had obtained a library card. Every few weeks, even during the busy days of "fruit season," he would take his granddaughter to what he called "*la casa dei tesori*,"—the house of treasures—to get books. They would check out one for him, one for her and one they would read together. She never forgot the first time he introduced her to the modest library building on a Sonoma street. Oreste had removed his hat in a gesture that, young as she was, Sarah intuitively recognized as respect. "*Cara mia*," he said solemnly, "this building is small but inside you can find the whole world!" Thanks to him, she was an avid reader with a great curiosity about almost everything.

At the age of nine Sarah fell in love with author Jack London after seeing his picture on a copy of The Call of the Wild. She was excited to discover Jack had lived on his own ranch not far from her grandparents' acres. The first time they visited his Beauty Ranch was one of those childhood days that are jewels we keep forever in the storehouse of memory.

In a house-turned-museum, Sarah had studied a wall papered with the rejection slips Jack received before he became successful. There were indigenous arts and crafts collected by the Londons on their sails to the South Seas. She had been fascinated with the handwritten versions of his books complete with corrections made by Jack himself. She put her fingers on the glass case with a child's longing to be as physically close as possible to the writer.

Dominating the main room was one of the most attractive photos of London pictured at the wheel of his schooner The Snark. Dressed in a black leather jacket, his hair tousled by the sea breeze, Jack's remarkable dark eyes seemed to look directly into hers. Below the photo was his "credo"—written in bold letters—that resonated in her so strongly that she memorized it:

"I would rather be ashes than dust! I would rather
that my spark should burn out in a brilliant blaze
than it should be stifled by dry-rot. I would rather be
a superb meteor, every atom of me in magnificent
glow, than a sleepy and permanent planet. The function of man is to live, not to exist. I shall not waste
my days trying to prolong them. I shall use
my time."

Reading the words out loud, she took her grandfather's
hand. "I want to live like that, Grandpa," she said with
feeling.

"I hope you will," Oreste replied. "It is a good way. And
may you have many years, dear one, to be warmed by
this fire."

OPENING HER FRONT DOOR, Sarah walks into a room lit by
the late afternoon sun through a bank of windows facing
west. The slanting golden light of autumn adds to the natural
warmth of the living room with its symphony of different
woods typical of craftsman houses.

Oak floors gleam with the patina of more than seventy
years of footsteps. Eugenia's Persian rug, a hand-woven
garden in unusual soft pastel colors, is spread over the room.
Comfortable chairs and a cream-colored sofa with brightly-
patterned pillows gather around a fireplace of native stone.

Sarah knows she is truly at home.

A few hours later she finishes dinner on the deck overlooking her small backyard. The overcast skies and cool
breezes of the Bay Area have given way to a warm, clear
autumn evening. As she sips from a glass of red wine, Sarah's

mind drifts in the quiet air, the silence broken only by the calls and laughter of neighbor children.

The yard backs against a hillside topped by gigantic rocks, but there is room for a pocket vegetable garden. An old fig tree shades bright forget-me-nots. Sarah has a special fondness for the fig with its large lovely leaves, certainly one of God's better leaf designs. It reminds her of the fig and olive trees her grandfather and other Italian immigrants planted on their Sonoma valley ranches as reminders of life in the "old country."

Dusk falls over the garden and the sky turns dark cobalt, that period just after sunset the French called *"l'heure bleu."* Sarah feels a familiar longing for someone to share this beautiful moment. Sometimes it's a yearning that pierces her heart. Tonight it's a soft flickering of melancholy. Twilight and the feelings it evokes often bring to mind the Longfellow poem she learned as a child:

"When day is done and the darkness
falls from the wings of night,
as a feather is wafted downward
from an eagle in its flight
I see the lights of the village
shine through the rain and the mist,
and a feeling of sadness comes o'er me
that my soul cannot resist,
a feeling of sadness and longing
that is not akin to pain,
and resembles sorrow only
as the mist resembles the rain."

When Sarah was a girl in the 1950s, everyone—herself included—had assumed she would marry. Unless a woman became a nun, marriage and motherhood were her destiny in southern European Catholic families like hers. Yet by the mid-1960s when Sarah graduated from UC Berkeley, young women were beginning to consider other possible lives. "Travel, work, enjoy your youth," her mother Giulia had advised. "Don't be too quick to settle down." And of course the example of Eugenia's life and its satisfactions was always before her.

Sarah knows she is not beautiful. She is moderately tall for a woman, five foot nine inches, with dark blue eyes and unruly, curly dark auburn hair. Her figure, like that of her Italian mother, is what her father admiringly calls "bounteous." She has what she thinks is a pleasant face, but nothing special. She envies her mother, her sister and brother their large, dark expressive eyes.

There have always been men in her life. In high school it was Mike, the handsome bad boy son of another valley rancher who was in the habit of disrupting classes with his antics, skipping school, driving too fast, and sneaking wine from his father's cellar. With Mike, she was in love with love, and their relationship faded away when she went off to the university and he headed for a backpacking trip through Europe.

At UC, Sarah met Daniel. For seven years they came together and broke apart. They fought and made up with romantic dinners overlooking the Bay or the Pacific, then plunged again into misunderstanding. She was, Daniel told her, "the only woman I've ever loved," but also "a person no sane individual could live with for more than five minutes." He made her laugh and was so handsome she felt beautiful just being his girlfriend. Yet he was also neurotic, someone who hid his inner life from everyone else. Sarah herself believed romantic love necessarily involved about fifty percent action and fifty percent intimate conversation. So the two of them were a volatile combination.

When they finally broke up, their paths diverged, and for a long time they were out of touch until they reconnected a few years ago. While it was pleasant and sweet to be in contact, it was also clear that the romantic fire of their past had burned out. Now they are simply friends.

THREE

A wave of cheerful noise greets Jamie as he opens the door of the storefront community center in San Francisco's Mission District. Lively chatter in the musical Spanish language counterpoints the beat of Mexican salsa tunes pouring from an old phonograph. Children play in a corner of the large room painted in electric colors—sky blue, sun gold, forest green and Sunkist orange. At one table several would-be artists concentrate on translating their visions to paper or canvas. At another, older people play cards.

Noticing his arrival, a small round woman tosses aside a dishtowel and hurries toward him from the kitchen area. "Padre Jamie, we're so happy you could come!" Her broad face and dark eyes shine with welcome.

"Madre Rosa, my heart is glad to see you!" Jamie bends down to hug the little woman tightly against him. Calling her "Mother" is for him a recognition that Rosa is as much a mediator of Christ's love and presence as any priest. If there were true justice in his Church, she'd be the official priest for her community. Hell, she'd make a great archbishop for the entire City.

Rosa carefully regards this man she considers a dear younger brother. Lately, subtle changes in him worry her. His attractive face —usually filled with vitality—looks tired, and there is sadness beneath the smile he offers her now. She's known Jamie for almost eight years and watched him grow into a fine priest, sensitive and giving.

He'd endeared himself to her early in their association when she'd bemoaned her plumpness as they were having lunch together. Without missing a beat, he'd replied, "Rosa, Rosa that is the only way God could find to pack so much wisdom and goodness into such a little woman!"

Who would not love a man like this?

And on the surface he is still the upbeat, fun-loving person who enjoys and is enjoyed by everyone, especially the smaller children who usually run to him as soon as they see him. The kids will not let Jamie alone until he promises to "play" with them before he leaves. Thanks to an unwise decision once made in response to their pleas, this means folding his 6'1" frame to get down on the floor with them. He is expected to be whatever animal or vehicle they ask for, complete with sounds and appropriate movements. Needless to say this generates screams and shouts of childish joy, and it would be hard to say who is having the best time.

"Clerical dignity is overrated," he's told Rosa.

Not that he's a saint. He has a temper, oh indeed, and Rosa has seen the evidence. She remembers going with him to the area police station after the beatings of several young women who made their livings walking the streets to find customers for their one salable commodity. The police investigation has been perfunctory. Addressing the station commander, Jamie had begun his conversation politely enough, but he wouldn't be dismissed easily. A few snide "what-do-they-expect-in-that-line-of-work?" comments from the officer had led to harsh words, punctuated by Jamie's fist pounding on the policeman's desk.

In the privacy of Rosa's tiny office, he has also shared his anger at the ecclesiastical powers-that-be, particularly when the Pope preaches against birth control in poverty-ridden parts of the world or when the hierarchy closes poor churches while keeping open those in affluent areas. Once Jamie had gone so far as to declare that anyone who tells poor women they can't use birth control is himself committing a mortal sin because he is deliberately doing serious harm to innocent people, including children. And Jamie has stated that, as far as he was concerned, the greatest public relations coup of all time has been to convince the residents of this planet that the institutional Roman Catholic Church is the official represen-tative of Christ on earth.

"O Lord!" He'd regarded Rosa with chagrin. "You didn't hear that! It never happened, right?"

"I can't promise you that, Father Quinn S.J., because I wouldn't want to lie to a priest." She'd grinned wickedly, hands on her hips. "Someday I may need to blackmail you."

One bright afternoon as they sat on a bench in Dolores Park watching over a group of children on a field trip, she'd questioned him.

"Why do you stay with the Church? You're still young. You're a psychologist. You could work in the secular world.

"I see how you love children. You could have some of your own."

Jamie looked into her face, and his eyes kept changing like a clear gray river reflecting the lights and shadows of the mind behind them. He was silent for a long time, and their mutual gaze stretched out for what seemed forever.

Finally he spoke in a voice so soft that Rosa had to lean close. "This is what I was born for. To be a priest and do this work is why my life was given to me. I knew this from the time I could think. I will never leave. Even if they kick me out, excommunicate me, somewhere in a hidden place I'll continue to be a priest."

His face flushed, and he lowered his head, embarrassed. "I've never said this to another person. Please don't repeat it to anyone because it sounds so strange...even arrogant...it sounds like I believe I'm someone special, and that's the last thing I mean..." His voice trailed off.

The sturdy little Guatemalan woman put her small hand over his larger one. "No, Padre, it is that you are called by God to do this. Being a priest is essential to who you are, like your blood or your bones."

Jamie regarded her tenderly. "And God has called us to be friends, dearest Rosa, and I can't tell you how grateful I am."

NOW ROSA GATHERS those who will attend the Mass in the "chapel," a room whose windows look out on an alley. Like many of the early California mission churches, the walls are painted with flowers and vines and other images from nature. The altar has been fashioned with talent and devotion by two local woodworkers. Around the top is a frieze of wheat and grapes joined by flowers and grasses, so skillfully carved that it is a small masterpiece.

There are also the paintings by local artists that reflect Christ, Mary his mother and the saints through a lens of the various Latino cultures the center serves. Their dark skin and distinctive features mirror those of many in the room. Jamie always smiles at the one showing the child Jesus cuddling a pet armadillo.

Some thirty people sit on folding chairs. Most are older but there are a couple of young families and two teenagers, although the latter usually attend the Sunday evening "rock mass" whose pulsing music draws young people in from the streets. Lured by the powerful rhythms, they often stay to pray. Jamie and some fellow priest-musicians inaugurated the youth Mass a few years ago. Now local groups and singers provide the music and have even written new Spanish hymns.

A few people have slipped in quietly from the alley. They sit in the back, avoiding notice. The center surreptitiously serves people who are in the country illegally, refugees from the wars and terrible persecutions in Central America. The American government has taken a hard line against these persons and those who shelter and support them. While Jamie is not officially connected with the American Sanctuary Movement, he's promised Rosa to help the refugees in any way he can. Fluent in Spanish, he does counseling, visits the sick and makes himself available for other pastoral ministry.

Looking out over those assembled as he stands behind the altar in a many-colored chasuble made for him by women of the community, Jamie feels a wave of affection, like a son entering the family home after an absence.

"My mothers and fathers, my sisters and brothers, my daughters and sons, *El Señor esta contigo,*" he intones.

"*Y con tu espíritu,*" they reply.

Music begins, a song to gather those who have just blessed one another into the Body of Christ they are called to be.

Jamie wishes there was more freedom to shape liturgy to the moment and the community. He experiments as far as he can but knows it's dangerous. To innovate is to invite trouble from ecclesiastical authorities. One of his Jesuit professors was forbidden to say Mass publicly for months after using corn bread and date wine at a liturgy for African students.

He remembers his friend Larry, a Franciscan priest who died last year. When he knew he was terminally ill and had nothing to lose, Larry abandoned much of the Rome-sanctioned forms and made up the liturgy as he went along, expressing his poetic soul in the prayers and sacred words. While some people were shocked, most were deeply moved and would never forget the humorous yet profound friar who transformed the Mass into a living, breathing organism, evolving moment to moment along with the universe itself and the spirits of those present. Every time he plans a liturgy these days, Jamie says a prayer to the man he thinks of as "St. Larry" whose own funeral Mass had ended with a unique closing "hymn" of Larry's choice: "I'll Be Seeing You in All the Old Familiar Places." By the time the song ended the packed church was filled with handkerchiefs and wet eyes.

Rosa gives her attention to the Mass. As she listens and watches, her concern for her friend deepens. There is something different about Jamie lately; his sunny disposition seems darker. She sighs to herself. "Ah What do these old men in the Vatican understand about the needs and troubles of these priests, their spiritual sons?"

These are the same men who—with their rules and regulations—seem oblivious what it's like to be a person in the Third World where poverty and disease and war stalk families like birds of prey.

Rosa's own story is one repeated thousands of times in the life histories of Central Americans. She was a nurse in Guatemala. Her husband Fernando was a high school history teacher who failed to come home one day, one of countless ordinary people "disappeared" by the country's ruling junta. He was last seen being pulled off his bicycle and pushed into the back of a police van. Frantic inquiries turned up nothing. He was just one of some 200,000 Guatemalan men, women and children who have been murdered in the last few decades by the American-supported generals and their minions. Fernando might have been one small, insignificant person for the powerful, but to Rosa and her two little sons, he was the world. A life that had been sweet disappeared with him.

Because Rosa treated anyone who sought her help, she feared being considered an enemy of the state for giving aid to someone who opposed the cruel regime. If she were killed for "collaboration," her boys would be orphans. Still crying in the night for her beloved husband whose fate she would never know and could only imagine in nightmares, she had come to a decision. She had packed bags and with nine-year-old Diego and six-year-old Miguel embarked on the harrowing journey to "El Norte." It had been hard travel, sometimes frightening because of men with bad intentions they'd encountered on the roads.

Through the kindness and assistance of new friends and strangers, Rosa and her children had not only survived their difficult beginning as illegal immigrants: they had flourished. In addition to becoming a citizen, she had obtained her California registered nursing license and then went on for a degree in non-profit administration. Now she is employed by Casa de Nuestra Señora de Guadalupe, both as a nurse in its medical clinic and a part-time administrator. The work gives her a deep sense of satisfaction.

As the result of her own experiences as a desperate refugee and mindful of the great blessings she has received from kind, compassionate Americans, Rosa is heavily involved in helping those fleeing violence. She keeps that part of her life secret, since it could have serious consequences. Jamie is one of the few who knows.

The first time Rosa met Jamie, she felt kinship. He was a man who listened deeply, from his heart as well as his mind. From his own experience losing his parents suddenly and a profound encounter with a family living at a Tijuana dump when he was a young Jesuit, he had an empathy for all she had endured in Guatemala and in the poverty of her first days in this country.

Once as they walked down Valencia Street and passed a large Spanish-language evangelical church, Jamie had asked her the same question she'd put to him. "Why do you stay in the Catholic Church?" They both knew Protestant congregations often had more vibrant communities and offered members more help and services than many of the City's Catholic churches.

"Ah, *mi hermanito*, it's home... familiar... like a family with all its problems and difficult members, like crazy old uncle Juan Pablo. But when I walk in the door of any Catholic Church, I know this is my place, and I'll meet Jesus here in a way I won't meet him anywhere else. I'm somewhere my soul longs to be." She'd laughed. "See what a serious and thoughtful woman I am!"

Now, as Jamie reverently places the Communion host in well-used hands, she looks deep into his eyes. A sadness arises within her, echoing from the time her husband was wrenched from her and the children, and even beyond that to the sufferings of her people through the centuries. It calls to and meets the pain within the priest. Rosa senses a lostness in him, well-hidden but there nonetheless. "He is suffering but doesn't want us to know it. Dear Lord, if there is any way I can help him, please show me how." She makes the sign of the cross.

FOUR

The tree-lined road through the orchard curves before
it reaches the Italian villa and its garden. They
appear suddenly through the greenery in an attractive vista.
Sarah's grandfather Oreste had planned it with an artist's
eye.

The house is constructed of cream-colored stone. Two
slender Corinthian pillars stand on either side of the front
door which opens onto a covered porch supported by pillars.
A pair of gnarled walnut trees complete the picture of an
Italian country home.

Sarah can't see anyone, but voices, laughter, and children's shouts come through her car windows. Some guests
have already arrived to celebrate her mother Giulia's sixty-
fifth birthday. It's typical of her family's parties: you can hear
them before you can see them. Sarah smiles. Like most
Italian clans, the Caffaros sometimes yell in anger, pout or
give an offender the silent treatment. But they also know how
to have fun together.

She parks at the edge of an orchard, gathers her purse and gift, and prepares to enter the fray.

Twenty minutes later she's pouring pesto sauce over bow-tie pasta, surrounded by a group of women who all seem to be talking at once. Enthusiastic chatter is as much a necessary ingredient to the meal as are the savory fragrances of roasting meat, garlic, zesty tomato sauce and onions sautéing in olive oil.

Taking it all in, Sarah basks in a familiar sense of well-being. Her mother comes up behind her, peers into the bowl and touches her arm. "Don't forget the lemon juice."

"*Certo*," Sarah promises. She puts her spoon down, turns and wraps her arms around the stately woman wearing a gaily-flowered dress. "What would I do without you, Mommy?"

"Well, even though I'm now officially old, I hope I'll be around a long time to tell you what to do far into the future!" Her mother laughs.

A chorus of "Amens!" fills the room.

Behind the house are make-shift tables shaded by the trees. The men are setting places and doing other tasks assigned by the culinary generals in the kitchen. In this family everyone works to get dinner on the table, and a number of the men are skilled cooks. Her Dad's spaghetti sauce, from his own father's secret recipe, is renowned throughout the valley. Franco smiles modestly at praise for his food, only a glint in his eyes hinting at the pride he feels in competing with the strong women in his family and coming out on top in something as important as cooking.

Sarah enjoys the ways her family differs from the traditional Italian family. Her father is the best cook. Her mother keeps the financial records and essentially runs the ranch.

When it comes to religion, the Caffaros are also atypical.

In contrast to most Italian families, the men are the devoted Catholics while several of the women are free spirits who don't go to Mass at all or grace the church with their presence only on holidays. Her father goes to church every Sunday. In winter when there's a lull in ranch work, he often slips away to daily Mass before joining friends around a wood stove in a neighbor's barn for cards and conversation.

Her mother, on the other hand, stopped attending Mass regularly years ago after a very young priest strode into the pulpit one Mother's Day to preach about the failures and sins of modern mothers and then proceeded to inform them how to be "the kinds of wives and mothers God wants."

That young priest's arrogance was the final straw for Giulia Caffaro, who'd been uneasy and increasingly frustrated with the church hierarchy since the death of Pope John XXIII, whom she considers a saint. When it came time to get dressed for church the next Sunday, Giulia instead went to work in her garden "where God really is." While her husband and children trekked faithfully to the local parish each week, she stayed home.

She wasn't thrilled when her only son Anthony decided to be a priest. After much struggle and prayer, Giulia has come to peace with his choice. She respects his sincerity and tries to support him. Assigned to serve four small parishes on the northern California coast, Anthony knows if he says Mass anywhere near the ranch, he can look out to see his mother in a pew with love in her eyes.

Franco's sister Eugenia had limited her involvement with Catholicism to family gatherings at Christmas. She'd loved midnight Mass with its candlelight, nativity scene and banks of winter flowers. When she was dying and her brother expressed concern about the fate of her eternal soul, Eugenia had declared confidently that, if there were a heaven, she believed she'd been virtuous enough to make it. Besides, she'd joked, "I've been a faithful servant of Turan, the Etruscan goddess of love, and she's promised to speak up for me in the afterlife."

Franco, who holds a typical Italian view that an all-loving God is totally incompatible with descriptions of hell and its eternal fiery agony, had been reassured. "Of course if we were Irish, you'd be in real trouble," he'd told her.

Sarah usually attends Sunday night Mass at the Newman Center at UC Berkeley, but she's a very liberal Catholic, particularly when it comes to social issues like women's roles in the church and homosexuality. Lately she's begun to have doubts about some of the things she'd once taken for granted in her faith.

THE PARTY IS OVER, and the birthday lunch is a memory. Toasts to Giulia, offered in humor and love with homemade wine, have been made. The gifts have been opened and exclaimed over. Giuila has confided to her daughter that Sarah's gift was her favorite. It's a brocade journal and a list of thoughtful questions she can answer to share her experience and insights with her children, her grandchildren and other descendants who might be interested: "What have you enjoyed most about your life? What is the best thing about being a woman? What is the wisest advice anyone ever gave you? If you'd been born a man what would you have done differently with your life? What is the most important thing you'd like your grandchildren to know about you? About life in general?" And so on.

"Wouldn't it be something if we had a journal from our great-great-great grandmother answering questions like these?" Sarah says to her mother. "Maybe you'll start a family tradition."

"It's a wonderful present!" Giulia plants a kiss on her daughter's cheek. "I love your questions." They're relaxing in chairs around now-empty tables. The men and older children have done the dishes. The guests are gone, leaving only Sarah who'll be spending the night in her old room. Sarah's sister Madeline and her family have gone home. Anthony is staying at the rectory in Sonoma; the pastor is his friend and mentor. He'll return in the morning to have breakfast with his family before driving to Gualala.

Franco ambles out into the yard, still wearing an apron from the clean-up because he knows his wife gets a kick out of seeing him in it. Years ago, noticing her husband working diligently at the sink after a holiday dinner, Giulia had declared passionately, "Lord, Lord, is there anything in this world as sexy as a man washing dishes?!" Wild laughter had erupted from the women in the kitchen and the remark passed into family lore. Any man doing housework around these women may find himself receiving a jokingly-seductive look or word from a passing female. The Caffaro women (and their men) know when they've found a good thing.

Franco drops into a chair. The sun has set behind the hills but it's still not dark. The leaves of the trees and vines glow vividly green in the special light that comes before night descends. In the garden two large red-orange pumpkins seem lit from within.

A soft breeze touches their faces. A priest once told Franco this kind of gentle air movement was like a tender caress, God's way of whispering, "Here I am."

He looks at Giulia and Sarah with appreciation. Fine women, both of them, smart, strong, good-looking, and with a sense of humor that can smooth the rough spots of living. A wave of gratitude courses through him bringing with it a flash of sadness for those who have gone. It is at holidays and family gatherings that Franco experiences most poignantly their absence. He longs for his father and mother and his sister. "These are the times I sure miss Genia. She was one great talker. When she was around you never knew what subject we'd be pondering next. Every visit was an education." His face is wistful.

Sarah nods. "When I look at her dining room table at home, I can see her presiding over her 'salon.' Because I've kept her beautiful furnishings, she's still very present to me in a very special way. But now the house is mine, and it's like I'm part of the flow of the people who've lived there. Every new householder is a bend in the river, heading in a new direction. I wonder what mine will be."

Franco wonders too. His eldest child is the least settled of their three. Madeline has her husband Paul and three children and is in charge of the business side of their West Wind Winery. Anthony has given his life to God in a vocation destined to last a lifetime. Sarah is a different matter.

When she'd been hired as a reporter for the *San Francisco Examiner*, he thought his daughter had found her profession. Yet she'd left the security of the newspaper for a magazine that was always struggling to stay afloat financially despite its excellent reputation for investigative journalism. Then, for reasons he still couldn't quite comprehend, she'd used an inheritance from her maternal grandmother to attend the Pacific Theological Union in Berkeley. Now she has a PhD in Biblical studies and teaches classes at PTU.

Thankfully, Eugenia provided Sarah with the freedom to live the way she does and pursue her intellectual and spiritual interests. While making cash bequests to Madeline and Anthony, Eugenia had willed her home to her favorite niece, along with an investment income. The money supplements a salary which fluctuates—depending on the number of classes Sarah is teaching. It allows her to live modestly and even do some traveling. But for her father, who's worked hard all his life to support his family from the ranch and achieve a predictable existence, his daughter's life seems unsettled and tenuous.

Franco also hates to think of her being permanently single, deprived of the happiness of marriage. Of course marriage is no bed of roses, as he and every other married person knows from hard experience. But it means that you're important to another human being, that someone is there for you every day. Life with Giulia certainly hasn't always been easy, yet he treasures what they have together and can't imagine being with any other woman. He wants that kind of relationship for Sarah.

Over the years she's gone with several men he'd liked and a couple that he and her mother had considered excellent marital prospects for their complex daughter. Lately she's been seeing a talented and personable architect, and Franco again has hopes. He speaks in a casual tone. "Say, how is Tim? Why didn't he come up with you?"

"Tim's with friends in Carmel." Sarah is brisk, hoping to pass over the subject quickly. She hates seeing her parents' faces fall, though they both try to pretend they aren't disappointed.

Franco looks sad. "It's just that I worry about you, Honey." He puts one of his large, work-worn hand over his daughter's. "I don't like to think of you alone forever. You have so much to give a man."

"Maybe too much." Sarah grins and pats her stomach.

"Don't be ridiculous! You're a beautiful woman. And a little extra means there's just more to love."

"No wonder I'm not married, Dad. What guy could possibly measure up to my father?" They laugh. Each thinks of Eugenia and what a good life she had as a single woman. The moment passes.

~

SARAH'S BROTHER strides up onto the porch where she is drinking espresso and contemplating the beauty of the morning light on the trees and flowers. "So how's life at that apostate school?" There is an an edge to his voice.

Anthony is a handsome man, six-feet tall with dark curly hair and his mother's large soulful eyes. His expressive face can convey many different things. At the moment it's telegraphing a condescension that annoys his sister. Tony is convinced he possesses "The Truth" about God and life and reality. For Sarah what is Ultimate is far beyond the doctrines her brother and the Church proclaim.

"Teaching heresy is just such fun!" Sarah counters her brother's jibe. "Now I know why those heretics were willing to let your side burn them at the stake. They were having such a good time in their doctrinal depravity, they just couldn't stop."

"All right, you two, that's enough," Giulia calls through a window from the kitchen. "It's too early for theology.".

Since the Bible is so important in Tony's life and ministry, Sarah generally gets a kick out of confounding her traditionalist Catholic brother with her superior knowledge of the sacred texts, their histories and contexts. He becomes defensive when she notes that some Catholic dogmas are contradicted or at least called into question by details in the Hebrew Scriptures and New Testament.

Recently, however, Sarah is losing the desire to argue with

41

him and win any debate. A few months ago when they were bickering about religion, she'd seen pain and uncertainty flash across her brother's face, then disappear as quickly as they had come. In that instant, she'd glimpsed his vulnerability as she never had before. It was strange how you could live with someone your entire childhood but never see deeply into his heart.

From the time he was a small boy, Tony has always projected a cocky confidence and know-it-all attitude that pushes his sister's buttons. Suddenly, she'd glimpsed beneath the surface and recognized—on the level of deep feeling—their common humanity. It was a full-blown realization, come and gone in a second, of a person who loves God deeply and has committed his life to the Church, but is suffering from doubts of his own. And she knows at some primal level that her insight is true.

Sarah stands, walks around the table and sits in a chair next to Anthony. She leans over and ruffles her brother's hair fondly. "How are doing, Sweetie? What's the best part about being a priest so far?"

He eyes her warily, suspecting she's mocking him, but her expression indicates she genuinely wants to hear. His face opens and relaxes.

"It's really something to be with people at the happiest and saddest times of their lives," Tony sounds earnest and almost shy. "I'm invited in, and they trust me to help, to do the right thing. Sometimes I'm afraid I won't be up to it. I'm not wise like Dad and Mom or as smart as you. How did I have the nerve to think I could be a good priest? It's crazy. But I love it, Sarah, It's so great being there with people when they need me!"

She throws her arm around his shoulder and draws him close. "Anthony Francis Caffaro, you have such a good heart.

I've known that from the time you were little, and I saw how tender you were with our pets and even with the bugs. Remember how you caught flies in the house with a glass and a piece of cardboard and took them outside so they could fly away? Your heart is why God called you to be a priest and why you'll be a wonderful priest."

A tear rolls down Tony's cheek. He turns and hugs her tightly. "Thanks, Sis," His voice breaks slightly. "I love you too."

FIVE

J amie feels a flash of pride that he isn't out of breath as
he reaches the top of the eighty-nine stairs leading to
the house on Belvedere Island. It's the kind of masculine reaction that amuses him. Celibate males can't hone their
sexual prowess, but monasteries and rectories still reek of
testosterone. Priests and brothers have other ways of vying for
alpha male status—intellectual competition, verbal sparring
or the Sunday afternoon basketball games at Pacific Theological Union. The play draws men from various religious orders
who fight like demons to control the ball. Guys tend to be the
same everywhere.

He's here for his fourth visit to Sallie Olds, a psychotherapist who's teaching him a fascinating framework for understanding human experience. As a teacher in the master's
program in pastoral counseling at PTU, Jamie requires his
students to work with someone whose psychological methods
will be useful in their future practice. Sallie came recom-

mended as a mentor by a fellow Jesuit doing therapy with her. To understand what she thinks and how she works, Jamie is seeing her for six meetings. He's enjoying his sessions with the warm, brilliant woman whose spirit reminds him of his grandmother.

The entrance to the three-story brown-shingled home opens into a kitchen. Sallie is pouring a cup of coffee. She looks up with a smile.

"Jamie, Hi!" No one can smile like Sallie. You feel she's been waiting eagerly just for you. She hugs him and then places a steaming cup in his hands. Jamie follows her into her therapy room, a long narrow space with a banks of windows on three sides. Outside one can see trees and bits of sky through their branches. It's like a peaceful outdoor porch, and it brings up memories of being a boy and feeling hidden and safe in a tree house on the ranch.

Sallie's work is based on psychiatrist Eric Berne's Transactional Analysis, and Jamie is finding the psychological system a fascinating framework for understanding the human person.

She's introduced him to the idea of two distinct ways of being in the world. The first she calls "The Real Self" or "Natural Child," which is the sum of the innate capacities each of us is born with: capacities for love, creativity and deep experience. The second, "The Adapted or Survival Self," is a persona the natural child develops very early to protect its vulnerable center and survive in the world of its family. As she describes them, the two selves are markedly different from one another.

An hour later he's walking back down all those stairs, his mind alight with Sallie's ideas. The concepts are simple yet profound. Already in the few weeks as he's been learning the distinctions between the selves, it's clear to him that just knowing the difference between the two could be a powerful catalyst for personal transformation.

Berne and his colleagues developed the model of the "Real Self" by studying both the capacities babies brought with them into the world and what the psychiatrists called "fully-functioning adults"—individuals whose lives and relationships were happy and fulfilling. Sallie has added her own considerable wisdom to the model.

Take something as basic as feelings, those primary drivers of behavior and inner experience. If asked to name feelings, she taught him, most of us would name many—positive and negative ones. Yet the study of infants indicates human beings possess only five innate emotions: anger, sadness, fear, joy and love (or feelings of connection). All other feelings like guilt, shame, jealously, hurt, despair, hope and the rest are learned, according to Sallie.

If this is true, the implications are stunning. "If so many of our ordinary feelings aren't 'innate,' where do they come from?" Jamie had asked Sallie.

"We see them modeled from the time we're born, and so we learn them," she had replied. "Once learned, they can be brought out in response to anything that happens," she'd continued. "Then our minds will drive a particular emotion and even form our experience of it."

Jamie often struggles with anger, especially when he sees injustice and deliberate cruelty or when someone does or says something that really irritates him. Today he was surprised to learn from Sallie that anger is experienced very differently in each of the selves. For the baby, she asserted, anger is simply a strong sensation that something she needs is missing in the here-and-now: food, a dry, comfortable diaper, someone loving to hold and connect with her. There's no other content to the feeling except the reality of the baby's current situation. Anyone who's ever seen an angry baby easily recognizes the emotion for what it is.

In contrast, she continued, adult adapted anger involves some kind of blame. Real anger is an energy that erupts in the body. Initially it's merely raw energy until the mind comes up with a reason for the emotion: usually the behavior of another person. This kind of anger grows by adding one thought to another. Sallie had smiled at him.

"Even a Jesuit priest must occasionally lose his temper. Have you ever had the experience that you got madder and madder as you continued thinking about whatever it was that set you off in the first place?"

"No, never." Jamie tries to look pious. They both laugh.

As his "assignment" for the next week, Sallie has challenged him to consciously notice when he becomes angry and then drop whatever angry, blaming thoughts accompany the feeling.

"Go with anger as pure sensation like the natural child experiences it, and leave the content behind," she advised with a smile. "No thoughts, just the emotion. Try it and see what you discover. You may be surprised."

Thinking over his own bouts with rage, Jamie finds it hard to envision anger without the fuel of content. But Sallie, who is one of the warmest, most loving and insightful human beings he's ever met, has him intrigued.

It doesn't take long for him to find material for the experiment. It comes that afternoon as he's running along a trail in the Berkeley hills, and it's a familiar catalyst. His mind drifts to a newspaper article he'd read that morning in which Pope John Paul II once again condemned artificial birth control.

The pope warned that married couples who used contraception were too hedonistic. He declared it was contrary to the gospel, and threatened those who questioned the church teaching with grave consequences. He didn't say "eternal damnation," but the hint was there.

As he'd read the words, Jamie's thoughts had flashed back to a summer spent in the slums of Tijuana, Mexico where desperately poor families struggled to survive by picking over a huge garbage dump. It was a common means of survival in parts of the Third World. He had been in the border city with a group of Jesuit volunteers building and repairing houses.

Of many powerful memories, one remains with him in a particularly vivid way. It's the face of a little mother, so gaunt she resembled a concentration camp survivor, as she led her band of five small children in their daily scavenging for the basics of survival. When they were introduced, she'd smiled shyly. *"Buenos Dias, Padre."* She then invited him back to her home, a shack near the edge of the mountains of refuse. It was a two-room shanty composed of wooden slabs, tin panels, cardboard, a few panes of glass and some empty window frames for support.

With grace and dignity, she offered him a cup of water. Her gesture was warm with hospitality. When they went inside to fill the cup from a jug that she'd undoubtedly carried from the local well—if not somewhere even further away, he'd noticed that the only decorations on the walls were magazine pictures of Our Lady of Guadalupe, the Sacred Heart of Jesus and Pope John Paul.

The next day Jamie had returned with bags of food and some money donated by the volunteers. Sitting on two old plastic chairs, the two talked for a long time. Abrilla's story was a familiar small tragedy repeated endlessly in the chronicles of the poorest of the poor.

She'd been orphaned at twelve and married at fourteen to a boy she knew and liked in her neighborhood. With no medical care or contraception available, the teenaged couple gave birth to one child after another until they had five under the age of nine, all "gifts" from *el buen Dios,* according to the local Catholic priest.

When their youngest was four months old, her husband Pacifico had gotten a temporary job burning trash at an auto body shop in the town. After a few months he developed a cough which persisted despite medicine from the farmicia. One weekend he was very sick, congested and running a high fever. There was no money for a doctor. Abrilla boiled eucalyptus leaves so he could breathe the steam. Four days later her twenty-two-year-old husband was dead. She still did not know why. Now the little family had to survive without the money Pacifico had always brought home from odd jobs.

Jamie could not imagine what it must be like for this young woman whose salt and pepper hair and lined face made her look middle-aged, to wake up every morning wondering if she would be able to find enough salable items to keep her children from starving. There were millions like her on every continent. Local charitable organizations and churches did what they could, but need always surpassed resources.

He recalled Abrilla with her worried eyes and shy, gracious manner, trying to exist on her garbage dump, being told by a Pope, who lived in a palace in Rome, that using modern science to shape and plan her family was a sin and an affront to God! The Church's teaching made it impossible for the wonderful Catholic organizations whose mission was to serve the poor to offer birth control to women like this one. He'd met many of these mothers whose only desires were to love "*El Señor*," be good people and take care of their children. He wonders how many the Pope has personally visited and talked with on his well-publicized world tours to address huge, adoring audiences.

Thinking about the papal speech while running, Jamie begins to berate John Paul in his mind, harsh language flooding his mental space. He feels a burning anger.

At this moment he remembers Sallie's suggestion. With difficulty, he stops the thoughts. His mind is now free to observe his bodily reactions. They're surprisingly strong and varied. Blood is pounding in his head, and a headache is beginning. His throat is constricted. His stomach seems full of rocks, and his diaphragm is a too-tight belt. His breathing is rapid and ragged. So *this* is rage in his body.

Letting go of the angry thoughts, he has the sensation of floating in space. Dizzy, he makes his way to a bench in a clearing off the path where he sits almost in a daze. He deliberately slows his breathing and gives himself up to the mental silence. Time passes.

Without warning, Jamie begins to cry. Tears cascade down his cheeks, and his chest convulses. He weeps with an intensity he hasn't experienced since he'd learned of his grandmother's sudden death. He's shocked by what's happening to him. He glances toward the trail, but fortunately there' s no one around to see his breakdown. He tries to control himself and though the sobs subside, he can't stop completely.

Suddenly he's thrust back to a day when he was eleven years old and playing baseball at school on a sunny autumn afternoon. The audience consisted of students, coaches and parents. His team was behind and his best friend Gary was at bat in the ninth inning with two outs. The count was two balls and two strikes. Gary swung the bat hard and missed, striking out. The game ended in victory for the other team who jumped up and down, shouting with glee. Embarrassed, his friend had walked back toward the bench with his head down. Jamie felt for him.

Then Gary turned abruptly and started away down the field. Gary's dad, who'd been watching on the sidelines, moved toward him. He put his hand on the boy's arm, then ruffled his hair affectionately. "Son," he said loudly enough for his teammates to hear. "You've learned an important thing today. You win some, and you lose some. That's just the way it is. I could tell you were doing your best at bat. It made me proud." With that, he'd slung his arm around Gary's shoulder, and they turned and walked away together.

Seeing the father and son, Jamie had experienced a sense of loss so great his body had reacted. He felt like he was choking. His chest was full of pain. His own father was gone forever. He would never feel his Dad's arms or hands on him or see his eyes filled with love and pride. Unable to move, paralyzed by the weight of his sadness, the young Jamie had slammed down his grief down inside himself before he lost control. He thought that, if he cried now, he'd humiliate himself in front of his teammates. God, he'd never live it down! Only then could he stand and head back to the gym with the other boys.

He'd completely forgotten the long-ago baseball game until this very moment. Why in the world has it come now in the middle of his anger with the Pope? Searching for a connection, he wonders if he unconsciously conflates "Holy Father" John Paul with his own father. Is his anger at the pope's uncaring stance toward poor families connected in some way to his being deprived of the father's care he desperately needed as a boy? It seems far-fetched, but his bitter anger *was a catalyst* for that powerful memory and the emotions that accompanied it.

Even more sobering, does his sobbing, uncontrollable grief have anything to do with the painful deprivation he's been feeling lately when it comes to intimate personal relationships?

An idea sends a shiver down his spine. "Am I grieving because, no matter how much I long for it, I can't have a woman to love and be loved by?" He brushes the unwelcome notion away swiftly.

If there are personal elements in his rage toward the Pope, why does the anger turn so quickly to grief? Is anger a mask, maybe even a defense, for sorrow? Calmer now, Jamie asks himself honestly whether he uses anger as a "safe" means of dealing with unresolved personal issues like the loneliness that sometimes pierces to the bone?

He shudders at the thought, afraid that it makes sense. Anger energizes a person. Grief and sadness can sink into depression and drain all energy. Given the choice, wouldn't most of us prefer the stimulation of rage?

He's intrigued by the notion that another whole realm of experience exists below the level of thoughts and ideas. During his years of prayer and meditation as a Jesuit, mental silence hasn't been emphasized. Instead, Ignatian spiritual practices draw chiefly on the power of the senses and the active imagination.

In recent years, some of his fellow priests have taken to Buddhist meditation. Entrance to this mysterious inner place must be part of what attracts them. It's probably time for him to explore the world of silence. At the very least he wants to know more.

How often are the experiences of his ordinary life a

superficial cover for something deeper, a dimension he may not even be aware of? He remembers a line of poetry stating that most people live as shallowly as "the foam on the ocean."

He'll certainly have a lot to talk about with Sallie next week.

SIX

Sitting in the library, Jamie feels like Jacob wrestling with the angel as he forces himself to read the scripture for next Sunday's liturgy one more time. It's one of the most controversial passages in the Bible.

The reading is the story of God creating Eve from Adam's rib, a kind of afterthought because it was "not good for man to be alone."

As a Jesuit who is not a parish priest, Jamie doesn't celebrate Mass every week, and he's dodged this particular bullet in the past. Sunday he'll be at a church in an upper-income Oakland parish whose members' viewpoints range from ultra-conservative to very liberal. No matter what he says, somebody is going to get mad.

However, Jamie is not going to cop out on the Adam-rib-Eve text. He's decided on an educational approach. He'll note the first chapters of Genesis were not meant to be historical documents. They were creation stories, and early Hebrew readers would never have viewed them as scientific texts on how the world and humanity came into being. Instead, they would understand the writer intended to present Israel's God as the creator of the earth and the heavens, and more powerful than any other deity still being worshipped in the recently-conquered "Promised Land."

He will wonder aloud about the strangeness of the story of a woman created from the rib of a man, a complete reversal of how things actually are, since women are the only ones who can give birth. Why would the writer create such a weird scenario?

This will be a good place to mention that Israel's God had serious divine competition in ancient Palestine in the form of the Canaanite goddess Asherah who granted fertility to the land, the animals and its people. In agrarian societies of antiquity, fertility was all-important. If the land and the animals were not fertile, people starved. If the people could not produce sufficient children, the community died out. The cult of the great Goddess would have been powerful and compelling. To enshrine their own God as supreme, the Jews would need to convince the indigenous Canaanites that Yahweh was more powerful than Asherah when it came to fertility.

Jamie will call attention to the many Biblical tales of women who were barren until God "opened their wombs" and they produced male children. He will remind them that Abraham's wife Sarah reportedly was 90 years old when Yahweh promised the couple an heir and she gave birth to their son Isaac. Similarly, in the preposterous rib story, Yahweh is portrayed as powerful enough to reverse the laws of nature and create a woman from the body of a man.

Jamie continues making notes. He'll explain that while men traditionally used the story of Eve's creation to show women were inferior to the male sex, it probably had been intended as a kind of advertisement for the Hebrew God's ability to produce fertility. And he'll point that the first account of humanity's creation in Genesis is much more egalitarian: "So God created the human in his own image...male and female created he them."

"That should be enough to make me a heretic to the conservatives," he thinks. "They'll say, 'remember that heretical Jesuit who told us all that nonsense about the creation of Eve?'

He puts down his pen and rubs his eyes.

This morning in the PTU Library Jamie is alone at the antique golden oak tables that form a rectangle on the stacks floor. Lit by copper lamps in the middle of each table, the furnishings give the illusion one has slipped back into the 19th century.

Usually there are others reading or writing here, and he likes the sense of being part of a community of scholars immersed in their work. Today the place seems empty; he misses the quiet companionship.

Suddenly, as though his wish for company has been heard, a woman appears in one of the aisles between the shelves of books. Glad to have a distraction from his task, Jamie glances in her direction. She's dressed in what looks like ethnic clothing of many colors and textures. Her long skirt is a velvet rainbow, and she's wearing a dark vest and white blouse. She's tall and full-figured, he notices, with a halo of auburn hair. She turns away before he can see her face. Her colorful form is a pleasant sight in the neutral tones of the room, and Jamie watches her with a lazy enjoyment, noting how the blue, purple and rose of her skirt flow around her as she selects a book then moves away, back toward the individual desks that line the walls of the huge room. When she disappears from sight, he feels a vague disappointment.

Restless and in need of inspiration and coffee, he leaves his books and papers and heads up the stairs and out the door. It's one of those perfect autumn days. A bright blue sky hovers over a visual symphony of greens and golds of the trees and plants that soften the buildings on the hill. He walks toward Euclid Avenue and the Holy Grounds coffee shop.

Entering the lively and noisy cafe, he sees students from a popular PTU seminar, Contemporary Trends in Christian Theology, gathered around a large table in the corner, continuing their conversation begun in class. Theology students enjoy arguing. They laugh and insult one another with good humor. Jamie likes the always-changing group. Since Contemporary Trends is offered by the Jesuit School of Theology, the discussions usually include a few of his Jesuit brothers, some nuns and "lay" people, a nice mix of perspectives and life experience.

They greet him warmly and pull an empty chair for him from an adjacent table. Today's subject is a debate over the merits of Medieval scholastic theology and Alfred North Whitehead's process philosophy. Jamie listens to the often-passionate debate, and occasionally adds a thought of his own.

As the group disperses, Jamie walks back to the library through a soft breeze. He gives himself up to the feel of it on his face, along with the sunshine, and the whole sensuality of being alive. He finds himself thinking of the woman of many colors. He wonders if she's still in the library. For some reason he's curious to see her face.

By now there are other people working around the tables. He continues to refine the homily. He decides to end with a personal note, that the Bible's creation account fills him with awe as he contemplates the amazing and wonderful creativity of our God in fashioning a universe so vast the mind can't take it in. And a world of almost infinite beauty and complexity in which every part fits together to support the incredible diversity of life on earth. He'll stress the importance of reading Scripture with our hearts and souls as well as our minds.

Soon he's finished, thank God. Emerging from the ancient world of the Scriptures, his consciousness returns to the large library room and he glances around. There's been no sign of the woman in the rainbow skirt, even though he's kept an eye out for her. Gathering his books and papers into his backpack, he finds himself strongly tempted to walk around the library to see if she's there.

He realizes he's behaving strangely. What is he thinking, stalking some woman he's only glimpsed? Is everything he's been feeling lately pushing him over some edge into a neediness he can't afford to indulge? Anyway, enough navel-gazing! This is his day to help with lunch at the homeless men's center downtown, and if he doesn't hurry, he'll be late.

SEVEN

The ebb and flow of voices draw Jamie down the hallway of the apartment building jokingly called "The Monastery" because so many priests and sisters from PTU live there. It's the annual party for three faculty members whose birthdays in the second week of October give students and professors an opportunity to meet and reconnect after summer.

He knocks, then opens the door to a room full of people talking and laughing with post-vacation energy. "Hey, Jay," someone calls, and several faces turn to greet him with a smile or hello. A nun friend, Joan, comes toward him and takes the bag of bread he's brought. It's still warm, and she inhales the yeasty fragrance of the buttermilk oatmeal loaves.

"Wow," she exclaims, "I love that you bake for our birth-days!" Placing the bag on a table, she turns and envelops him in an enthusiastic hug.

"It's good to see you," he says, tightening his arms around

her briefly. "How was your summer? How are your inner-city kids doing?"

Her dark brown eyes sparkle. "Amazing again! We had sixty-one children, and only two had ever been out of the city before. The lake and the forest were a revelation to them. Jamie, these kids just blossomed in their weeks in the wild. I swear, they left different children, more confident and happier. Every year I see it, and every year it seems like a miracle!"

"Could you find a use for me for a week or two next summer?"

"We always need good guys for the boys to relate to. You'd be great! Please come. We'd love to have you."

"I'll call you next week. Let's make it happen."

She smiles broadly, "Definitely. It's a plan. Now I need go command the kitchen slaves." As he glances toward that hive of activity, someone laughs. It's a laugh that catches his attention: feminine, full bodied and uninhibited. There's music in it too. He looks across the room and sees his friend and housemate Sam talking spiritedly to the mystery woman from the library! He recognizes her halo of auburn hair and colorful style of dress.

Jamie stares, riveted. At last he can see her face. It's a good face, a firm chin, well-defined features, a generous mouth. There's a brightness to her changing expressions, an animation and liveliness. From this distance he can't see the color of her eyes.

In the middle of the noisy party, he experiences a silence gathering around him. A deep peace envelopes him, and a powerful surge of joy. Startled, he stands unmoving and lets the feelings flow through him as he continues to gaze at the woman's face. Suddenly she turns and glances at Jamie. For a moment her eyes widen in surprise. They're blue. Color floods her face. She smiles tentatively, then looks away.

As though drawn by a mysterious force, Jamie starts to make his way to her. At that moment a priest friend, Jack, a colleague in the pastoral ministry program, moves into his path, his face troubled. "Jamie, I need to talk to you for a minute," he says.

"Sure," he replies, feeling a bit dazed. Jack leads him into a bedroom. Jamie sees his friend has been crying. "What wrong?" he asks with concern.

"My Dad's had a heart attack...I just got a call. They don't know if he's going to make it." Tears are running down Jack's cheeks now, and Jamie spontaneously grasps his shoulders and hugs him.

"Oh dear God, I'm so sorry! I know how close you two are." His mind flies to a memory of Jack and his Dad in a boat on an Oregon lake, each holding a fish and smiling proudly for a photo. "Is there anything I can do?"

"I need to leave for Portland right away. Can you take my classes?"

"Absolutely! What do I need to know?"

They quickly leave the party without speaking to anyone. Jamie feels a pang at not meeting the auburn-haired woman but brushes it aside.

In an office, as Jack explains his class syllabus, Jamie experiences a wave of compassion as he looks into his fellow priest's anguished face. His own eyes tear up as he remembers what it was like to get the call that his grandmother—who'd seemed so healthy for her age—had died. They hug again, and Jamie assures him his Jesuit brothers' prayers will be with him, his father and his family. "Please let us know how it's going."

Jack leaves to pack. Jamie thinks about returning to the

61

party but just doesn't have the heart, even with the possibility of meeting his "mystery woman." After all, Sam knows her, so there's no danger she'll disappear without a trace. And besides, he needs to think more about his strange and disconcerting reaction to seeing her face for the first time.

~

THE NIGHT IS dark and quiet except for the occasional rumble of a car passing on the street three stories below. The bedroom window is open, allowing a breeze from the Golden Gate straits to enter. The air is fresh and slightly fragrant with jasmine in a nearby garden. Jamie lies on his single bed. A frightening dream he can't remember had jolted him awake. The illuminated clock dial reads 3:17.

His first conscious thought is of Jack and his father, and he prays they'll know God's peace and healing. He repeats to himself the reassuring words of Christ in a vision to the medieval anchoress, Julian of Norwich. "All will be well, and all shall be well, and all manner of things will be well."

"What a mystery human love is," he thinks, drawing the blankets over his shoulders, "the greatest joy and sharpest suffering. You apparently can't have one without the other."

Some of the feminist authors he's been reading lately challenge the traditional Catholic view that "agape," the dispassionate form of love that manifests in sacrificing oneself for others, is the highest, most perfect form of love. These writers contend love which does not include the erotic dimension of human life is deficient. Poet Audre Lorde argues that erotic love is "the root of our lives' deepest meanings," because it is the source of the intimacy she considers to "love at its fullest."

This is a challenge to Jamie's whole way of life. His

priestly vocation, after all, is built on embracing the sacrifice of agape and sublimating the erotic. Without the distractions and preoccupations of human love he can devote himself completely to serving God and other people. At least that's what the church claims.

Yet Lorde's words have remained in Jamie's mind for months.

In the past he has avoided critiques of celibacy and chastity that claim they are abnormal and unhealthy in an age when understanding of the human psyche has grown and evolved from the earlier times when this way of life for priests and religious was made mandatory by the Church. What good would it do him to go there?" From the time he was four years old, Jamie wanted to be a priest. He knew the terms and made the vow. Questioning that promise will only prove troubling and counterproductive to someone totally committed to his ministry as a priest. However, the feminist authors' assertions resonate with his own experience. This is especially true at times like tonight when the poignancy and importance of family love permeate his heart and mind and the room itself.

Love is everywhere in sacred as well as secular literature, its supreme value expressed fluently and powerfully by saints, poets, philosophers, sages, scientists and Christ himself. In choosing the final words he would speak to those who had been closest to him, Jesus pleaded, "Love one another as I have loved you," defining for all time the essence of his teaching. Even a rationalist like Aristotle called love a single soul inhabiting two bodies. And Teresa of Avila, that passionate mystic, reported that Jesus in a vision told her He would create the entire universe again just to hear her say she loved Him.

Here and now in the middle of the night, alone with

God, Jamie finally can admit how much he longs to expand his own experience of loving and of being loved. "Please show me the way," he whispers into the darkness. "I leave the form of love to you. May I be open to receive it in any way you choose to send it." A picture of his mystery woman floats into his consciousness and hovers there briefly before he pushes it away.

That's the last thing he needs! Fortunately, he doesn't think the Lord would send useless temptation in answer to his heartfelt prayer. Wasn't it Einstein who said God didn't play games?

At that moment he resolves firmly not to try to meet her. He won't ask Sam who she is. It's the most ordinary thing in the world for a man to see a woman and be intrigued. You don't have to turn it into grand opera. You can just accept you're human and put the whole thing out of your mind. That's the power of self control which comes from the last sixteen years of training his will to subdue his sexuality.

He remembers a line from the poet Rilke, committed to memory for times when loneliness seems almost unbearable: "I will yearn for no closer connections and accustom my heart to its farthest reaches." Drifting toward sleep, Jamie feels resolved and confident. This woman isn't a problem, just a temptation on the path. He smiles into the dark and falls asleep before wistfulness can overtake him.

EIGHT

Like a great Mother, the San Francisco Bay cradles the wild, rocky coast and the creatures who make it home. For Sarah too, it is a vast sheltering presence. She comes to it in grief and joy and draws peace and inspiration. She loves this place.

Tonight the Bay is mirroring the sky, an exquisitely beautiful blue. The setting sun is a shimmering path of red-gold light across its surface, beckoning into the distance. Just now its waves are gentle ripples, meeting the shore with only whispers of sound. Swirling skyscapes of white clouds are turning into twilight rainbows beyond the Golden Gate. A lone sailboat glides toward the City.

God seems very near and must be pleased with Her artistry.

As the fading light leaches the blue from the Bay, transforming it to silver, an inner vision comes to Sarah, unbidden, sudden. She sees two eyes seeking hers. And those inexplicable feelings rise again.

At a party on Saturday she and Sam, a Jesuit acquaintance, were talking and laughing about one of the weird stories in the Bible when she'd felt something like an energy reaching toward her. She had looked up. A tall man with silver-gray eyes was watching her with an expression she had never seen directed her way.

Even now she can't really capture or understand the totality of that gaze with her mind. It wasn't simply a look of male-female attraction, though it did contain an element of delight she didn't often receive spontaneously from strange men. There was an intimacy in it, both a knowing and a vulnerability.

It seemed to say to her, "Somehow … I know you completely, and I offer myself to you to be known in return."

Thinking such a thought, Sarah feels foolish. How in the world could one intuit such long and precise communication in a single look from halfway across a room? She begins humming "Some Enchanted Evening," mocking herself. It doesn't stop the flow of thought and feeling.

As their eyes met, in a flash the dark-haired man's face had changed. Sarah still can't interpret the change, but at that moment a powerful tide of peace had washed over her, followed by a wave of joy so strong she had to look away. When she'd sought his face again, he was listening intently to another man.

Sarah had felt shaken and disoriented in that noisy, crowded room and wondered what had just happened. What did it mean? Was this the famous love at first sight? It didn't feel at all like the instant and powerful attraction she'd experienced occasionally with other men. She'd vibrated with such a strong awareness of the man's presence and his being that it was like being swept up into prayer.

When she'd seen him leave the apartment with the other man, she'd pointed him out to Sam. "He looks familiar. Do you know him?"

"That's my housemate, Jamie Quinn. He teaches in the pastoral counseling program. A great guy."

"Is he a Jesuit too?" Sarah held her breath.

"He is. In fact we were ordained together."

"I guess he just looks like someone else I've met." Her voice was calm, but Sarah had found herself about to cry. Suddenly in no mood for a party, she'd excused herself to Sam, made her way to the apartment door and slipped out. She needed the comfort of her own home.

Sarah remembers sitting in her garden that evening, transfixed by a few glowing orange leaves clinging to a neighbor's persimmon tree in the fading light. There was such a poignancy about these lingering, lonely souvenirs of summer. Winter was coming, and the rains would wash them away. Yet they remained when the rest of their kind had fallen. She'd laughed to herself. "I am practically dripping sentiment onto the ground." Sarah knew these thoughts were simply small mental walls to keep her away from what had happened earlier. If she were honest, she'd have to admit the intensity of her encounter with that priest Jamie was disturbing. She didn't know why it should have such an effect on her. And frankly, she didn't even want to speculate. Her chest felt tight when her thoughts moved in that direction.

Yet the memory of meeting those eyes with her own and seeing that face looking back at her with deep emotion has taken hold of her and will not let go. How could anything so fleeting assume such importance? So she'd had some kind of mysterious energetic encounter with a man. What was the big deal? Why is she obsessing over it days later?

This was just a feeling, and what is that, but a bodily sensation that comes and goes? She has countless emotions in a single day. She's been with other men, loved a few or thought she had, and almost married two. She decides what makes this emotion so engrossing and unsettling is its unfamiliarity and the powerful, instantaneous connection.

If he weren't a priest, she'd find a way to meet him and see what happened. But as a teacher at Pacific Theological Union she's aware friendships between single women and priests can lead to trouble. And it's usually the women who suffer. In fact, Sarah has found herself impatient with a few friends who'd become romantically involved with priests, then complained about the pain when the liaisons ended badly, as they invariably did. They had gone into the situation knowing the man they wanted was "married" to "Holy Mother Church" and unlikely to leave that marriage. After her brief encounter with Jamie Quinn, she feels more humble and compassionate toward those friends.

"This has to stop. Now." Sarah makes a decision firmly as the first stars appear in the cobalt blue sky over the Bay. "The last thing I need in my life is an alluring Catholic priest! And the best time to avoid to temptation is as soon as it rears its lovely head. So get thee behind me, Satan!" she exclaims to herself with a laugh and a determined air.

WEEKS LATER, wind-driven rains lash the coast. In this season, Sarah loves the warmth and peace of the PTU Library. There's a certain carrel desk in a corner of the stacks floor she often uses. It has a comfortable chair and a small window looking out on a stately oak tree. Although there are others reading and writing around the room, it's quiet. She enjoys the vibrancy of all that silent mental activity going on around her.

This morning Sarah is walking downstairs from the main part of the library to the stacks. Glancing at the tables in the center of the lower floor, she stops suddenly. The priest, Jamie, is sitting there, reading a book. If he looks up, he'll see her. Without thinking, she turns abruptly and almost runs up the stairs. Her heart is racing. She's tempted to leave immediately, but the materials for her class prep are at her desk. Fortunately, you can reach the stacks by elevator, and if she goes behind the book shelves, he won't see her.

Seated with books and papers spread out, Sarah finds it impossible to concentrate. It's bad enough that she is skulking around to avoid the priest. Now he's invading her mind. He's so close. She shuts her eyes and breathes deeply and slowly, seeking peace in her turmoil.

Someone else in the library is also in turmoil. Jamie had raised his eyes just in time to notice the mysterious woman (who's been finding her way into his dreams) turn quickly on the stairs. He'd recognized her clothing and cloud of hair. Her movements were jerky and awkward, as she'd all but run back toward the top floor. He had an immediate sense she wanted to avoid him. Internally he rolls his eyes. "Yes, of course, it's all about you, you handsome stud! She probably just forgot something."

Feeling ridiculous, he can't stop watching the stairs, looking for her. He still hasn't asked Sam who she is. A name will give her an identity, and Sam will surely add some facts about her. Jamie doesn't want this woman to become more "real" to him than she already is as nothing more than a phantom stranger. Yet every single day he has to fight the desire to question his Jesuit brother.

Ten minutes pass...then half an hour. She doesn't return.

The weird thing is, Jamie feels strongly that she's somewhere nearby. He's so sure she's here, he wants to get up and look for her. Yes, he is definitely losing his mind. "Dear God!" he complains fervently, not sure just what he's complaining about. He gets up abruptly, leaving books and papers behind. His hands are cold. He needs a cup of coffee to warm him.

NINE

A t the edge of Jewel Lake, Sarah watches a tiny flock of
dark-eyed juncos frolic. She smiles as the little birds
ruffle their feathers and dart around, tossing sparkling drops
of water into the air. She likes the humble juncos; they're
visual melodies of earth tones with their black heads, brown
backs and creamy breasts. Their soft trilling songs are a sweet
punctuation to the morning.

When she has the time, Sarah enjoys being in Tilden
Park, the 2,000-acre regional park east of the Berkeley hills.
She has her favorite spot: a glade of trees beside the lake. A
great blue heron often stands nearby, fishing. Turtle families
float placidly on wooden rafts built by park naturalists. In the
spring, mother ducks and their fluffy ducklings will be on the
water. And always there are the insects—flying, crawling,
jumping—creating a soft, musical humming she can tune into
if she listens hard enough.

She likes the park's many fragrances. Sometimes the
sharp tang of eucalyptus trees dominates the "scentscape." At

other times it resembles soft music, one subtle scent following another, tart pine giving way to a mysterious floral which changes to the pungent tunes of the wet mud on the lake shore. And it's interesting to notice how differently the air can feel on her skin in different weathers.

Sarah walks out to park's Wildcat Canyon area several times a week. Today it's warm and sunny but with a crispness of late autumn on the breeze. The western sky is a thick hazy blue with a touch of silver shimmer. She turns to the path and heads out now.

Later, returning from her walk, Sarah sees two runners in the distance. The men move gracefully in an easy symmetry. She glances at them as they pass and is jolted by the sight of a pair of gray eyes that have come to haunt her reveries. She almost stumbles in surprise as he notices her. A startled look crosses his face.

Rounding a corner of the trail, she's glad there's no opportunity to look back. She begins to walk more quickly. Coming to a place where a bench is positioned away from the road, partly hidden by trees, she makes for it and sits down. She has to admit it felt good to see him again and experience a flash of that mysterious connection. Perhaps they're destined to be friends. Maybe she's been making too much of the whole thing in her mind and needs a dose of reality. He's only a guy, after all. Still, Sarah shivers involuntarily. A surge of adrenaline floods her body.

She closes her eyes and feels the warmth of the sun on her face. To distract herself, she begins to think about her class this afternoon on the Gospel of John. They'll be considering one of its best stories: the encounter between Jesus and the Samaritan woman. It's a rich, interesting narrative filled with details and symbols most people never notice. Her mind drifts to the intricacies of what is Jesus' longest conversation in the New Testament.

～

"OK, LORD," Jamie thinks, "Why do you keep putting this woman and me together?" Then he laughs to himself. "Yeah, it's veritable miracle for two people from Berkeley to encounter one another on a popular trail in Tilden Park. Impossible without divine intervention, right? Sometimes, I'm a self-centered fool." Then another thought comes. The One who cares for the birds of the air and the grasses of the field knows how alone and desolate he's been feeling lately. Perhaps God is offering him a potential friend. Maybe she needs a friend too.

Still, his inclination is to avoid a woman he feels so drawn to before they've even met. He'd already dreamed about her, although he can't—perhaps mercifully—remember the details. And he's thought of her way too much in the past weeks.

If only God's will were clear in situations like this. He remembers a nun friend's lament that all too often "God's will is still in probate."

When he and Tom reach the fence that borders the path into the canyon, Jamie tells his friend he wants stay out there for a while longer. He'll make his way home on foot or catch the bus that runs between the park and downtown. He hadn't intended to do this at all. Is it to give the auburn-haired woman enough time to leave Tilden? He doesn't know. He is only sure of one thing: he *does not want to meet her.*

～

SARAH HEARS footsteps approaching slowly through the dry leaves and knows exactly who it is. So when the tall priest looks down at her and asks, "May I share your bench?" she is able to reply, "Certainly," in a normal voice despite the rapid drumbeat in her chest.

Shocked to find himself where he is, when he had been so firmly resolved only moments ago to avoid this women, Jamie pauses, then sits beside her. He introduces himself.

"I know who you are because I asked Sam when I saw you at the birthday party. I'm Sarah Caffaro. I teach Biblical studies."

Sarah. She finally has a name. Despite himself, Jamie savors the knowledge. Then he feels anxiety building in him as he contemplates the precipitous action that has landed him on this bench. What was he thinking? What can he possibly say to her?

They sit without speaking. As the minutes pass, Sarah is surprised at the depth of comfort she is feeling in their mutual silence. Her heart has slowed, and quiet happiness is flowing inside her.

She observes his hands are on his knees. They're large, appropriate to someone his height. They resemble her father's hands, nicked and marked by the scars of physical labor. Franco's hands are blunt; this man's fingers are long and tapered. "A musician's hands," she thinks.

So close he can feel the warmth of her body, Jamie finds himself sinking into that peace he experienced when their eyes first met at the gathering last month. As calm expands throughout his own body, Jamie has a strong sense of being entirely at home. The silence deepens between them, alive with meaning that doesn't yet require words.

First, Sarah notices the sounds; then she sees them. The leafy ground below the bushes is alive with juncos, at least a dozen, trilling as they forage for food. Next, she catches even sweeter sounds. In a tree a flock of song sparrows are dancing from branch to branch and singing. She's never seen so many birds together so close at one time.

"Oh look." Her voice is a whisper.

"It's like a fairytale," There is a note of wonder in his reply. His heart swells at God's music, those divine compositions performed freely and generously always and everywhere.

"Do you feel the connection with me that I feel with you?" Jamie's question is swift and unexpected. A frisson of alarm runs along his spine raising the hair on the back of his neck. Has he actually said those words out loud? Revealed himself so completely? Oh God, is this the way it's going to go?

Sarah is stunned by the priest's honesty and directness. A long moment passes. She decides he deserves an equal candor.

"Yes, yes, I do, and it scares me. I don't even know you and yet..." Her voice breaks off.

She turns toward him and sees he's watching her with an expression both curious and tender. Without thinking, she puts her hand over his. Her touch is feather light. He doesn't move but simply looks at their joined hands. Quickly, Sarah pulls hers away. "Sorry!"

Jamie laughs. "It's a strange life I live."

Then, without thinking, he abandons every decision he has made so far.

"I'd like to spend some more time talking with you." He seems to have no control over what comes out of his mouth.

Now she is hesitant. "Part of me wants to say no and leave immediately," she tells him.

"That may be the wise part of you; maybe you should listen to it. A part of me agrees."

Again they sit without speaking. Finally Sarah says, "I have absolutely no idea what we should do." She looks like she is about to flee.

"We don't have to decide right now, do we?" Jamie is suddenly afraid she's going to go out of his life forever. And may God forgive him, he cannot bear the thought of that. "Why don't we pray and think and feel our way into what comes next?" he asks.

The weight of their dilemma hangs in the air between them.

Then Jamie smiles. "Do you think we're making too much of this? We don't have to turn this into grand opera. So we feel a pretty strong connection. It's not unheard of for a man and a woman to be instantly attracted to one another. Priests aren't immune. We just can't act on those feelings."

She returns his smile. "You're probably right. I'm Italian. We love opera."

"Well, I was raised by my Italian grandmother, and she was crazy about Verdi, so I have the same problem." The silly banter alters the mood.

Now his voice sounds decisive. "I think we should pray about this and plan to meet and talk. If we cut this off without any more contact, you'll be even more alluring in my fantasies." Once again his own honesty shocks him. Sarah laughs in surprise.

The atmosphere is lighter.

"You're right," she says. "We'll pray. We'll talk. Who knows, maybe God means for us to be friends."

She stands up. "I have to go now."

He rises and takes her hand. He gazes into her deep blue eyes. *"Vaya con Dios."*

Sarah returns his gaze. "You too."

She pivots, moving quickly, and starts back along the trail without waiting to see if he'll accompany her. Her abruptness leaves Jamie feeling strangely abandoned.

He watches her swirl away.

"Who am I kidding?" he asks himself. "It's grand opera all the way. And God help us!"

His words are part lament, part prayer.

TEN

Gabriela's face is full of wonder as she gazes at the giraffe mother and her baby nuzzling each other in the African Veldt area of the Oakland Zoo.

These are her first living giraffes, and the pictures in her books haven't prepared her for how large the animals are. "You said he was just born, Sarah, but he's taller than Señor Ortega!" The child's eyes are wide. She laughs as the smaller giraffe, hearing her voice, turns and regards her. "He's looking at me! Maybe he wants to be friends!"

Smiling down at the little girl, Sarah's glad for the sweet moment they're sharing. Their time isn't always so easy or happy.

Gabriela is only eight years old, but already her life has been a hard one. Her parents are dead, victims of the drug epidemic. She lives with her grandmother, Fernanda, who loves her beyond words but also suffers from the extreme stresses of her own situation. In the United States illegally from violent Guatemala, the woman lost her daughter and son-in-law on the same night; both overdosed from unexpectedly powerful heroin.

Now assuming the role of parent, caregiver and breadwinner for her granddaughter, Fernanda cleans houses and does janitorial work in offices to make ends meet. Since she has no green card, the East Bay Sanctuary movement helps her find the jobs with employers sympathetic to plight of refugees. It is a constant struggle and the unrelenting demands of her life don't leave her the time or energy to bring enough fun and pleasure into the little girl's life.

The three had met and immediately liked one another at a picnic sponsored by Sanctuary. When Sarah learned how hard and long Fernanda worked, she'd decided to become an unofficial 'Big Sister" to Gabriela. They meet twice a month to do something together. They go to Fairyland, Marine World and the Little Farm or explore the Bay Area's natural wonders from Point Reyes to Muir Woods. On her "good" days, Gabriela loves learning and seeing new things.

The child has dark days too, when her anger and grief erupt, and she sinks into a place of rage and depression where Sarah cannot reach her. What can you do for a child aching to have parents and their special kind of love that will never be there for her, despite her grandmother's best efforts?

Sarah feels helpless and sad when she has to return to Fernanda a furious, sulking or teary child. Her sense of failure can be acute. A couple of times she's gone home wondering if there is something wrong with her—if she lacks normal nurturing skills. She recalls how sister Madeline had cherished her dolls like real babies. In contrast, Sarah's dolls had often ended up abandoned in trees or buried in an underground fortress or some another unlikely spot after sharing her adventures in the orchard or at the creek.

Fortunately, Madeline and Paul had given Giulia and

Franco grandchildren. Charlie, Bella and little Marco are the delights of their hearts, and the feeling is mutual.

Nine-year-old Bella made her first visit to her "Berkeley Auntie" this year, and Sarah really enjoyed getting to know her quiet, shy niece one-to-one. They spent a day at the Oakland Museum and Jack London square and had dinner on a restaurant overlooking the Bay. She would like to be for her sister's children at least a bit of what Eugenia had been for her.

Sarah never officially decided not to have children. It simply hadn't happened. Now she's 38, and her biological clock might be ticking toward midnight, but she feels no particular urgency. At the same time she's experiencing a sense of unease. There are messages all around that motherhood (but not fatherhood for some reason) offers the ultimate fulfillment in life. Yet she's noticed that society regards actual mothers in contradictory ways. They seem to be cast either as saintly madonnas or psychological destroyers of their young.

A decade ago the popular advice columnist Ann Landers had startled the country. She'd asked her readers, "if you had to do it again, would you have children?" An astounding seventy percent of the 10,000 who responded said no, they wouldn't have kids!

Still, Sarah wonders if she is missing something essential as a human being. Is she stunting her capacity for love by never learning what it is to completely surrender her own needs to the needs of a child? Will she become more self-centered as time goes on?

She remembers the meaning-of-life conversations at Eugenia's table, as well as the deep spiritual reflections in the books and the poetry she's read and the courses she's taken. At the center has often been love, a universe within, the purpose and divine intention for being. In the early hours of the morning, while it is still dark and quiet, and truth slips so easily into the mind, when Sarah allows herself to look honestly into her heart, she fears she is a stranger to love's deeper dimensions.

Of course she loves her family and a few close friends. Yet she has never experienced the intense love between a man and a woman which the poets and song writers seek to express. She has always lived outside that gate, face pressed against it, wanting to enter that secret place and having no idea how to find the key.

She knows a great deal about infatuation, that rush of sensation and emotion that transforms the mundane into the beautiful, the everyday into the miraculous. She knows what it is to feel herself vibrating with ecstasy in the look or embrace of a man. But she also realizes how quickly this can fade into egocentric demands and desires. Rapture can come so effortlessly and leave so painfully.

What is "true love" anyway? How could you be certain you were experiencing it? Her parents are one of the few couples who seem to have kept love alive through the years, the children and the struggles. She'd watched it every day of her childhood in the casual physical gestures of affection, the kind words, the spark of interest between the two in conversation or shared activity. She's envious and has tried to draw each of them out on the subject.

"Sometimes Giulia drives me crazy or even bores me, but most of the time I still enjoy her. I guess true love is when the good times outweigh the bad ones. I can't imagine my life without her." Her father had smiled sweetly.

"When Franco comes into a room, even when I'm so mad at him I want to spit, there's always a feeling something good could happen. Maybe he'll say something that will make me laugh. Or he'll look at me in a certain way that reminds me of our early days together." Her mother's smile was equally sweet.

It a mystery to Sarah why a woman like her, someone who comes from such a loving and demonstrative family, has never fallen into a lasting love.

Looking back, she's certain she had not truly loved her long-time boyfriend Daniel, despite their years together. Initially, his beauty had drawn her, making her feel more attractive just by being his girlfriend. They did have fun together, and his weird and wacky humor could sometimes make her laugh until she cried. Yet she was never satisfied with the person he was, secretive and emotionally unavailable. She never stopped trying to change him, to make him over into the image of her ideal man. Of course he rebelled, and their life together had been one long struggle punctuated by partings and reunions. And on that level of communication below the surfaces of words and actions, Daniel had to know she'd been unable to accept him as he was.

Tim, the architect who is currently fading out of her life, is the latest in a series of men she's spent time with, then recognized the feeling she had for them didn't meet her conviction of what love could be. What in the world would it take to go beyond this? Was she totally unrealistic?

Sarah is convinced she has within her the capacities for deep love and caring that remain unexplored. She's a very emotional person, compassionate, with a sense of beauty. She is able to experience the full humanity of another. Sometimes, seeing a face, she has flashes of awareness that take her out of herself. Then she can recognize and feel the inmost self of that person, their vulnerability and loveliness. She also has a natural interest in other people...what they think...how they feel...how they experience themselves and their lives.

Shouldn't these qualities within her give her a talent for relationship?

However, Sarah also recognizes her many shortcomings. She can be self-absorbed. She has a temper and is easily irritated. She's quick to judge others. She lacks patience with people who engage in monologues and are unresponsive to what another person says. She is often tempted to write people off too quickly. At the same time she's willing to face these negative aspects of her personality squarely and do whatever she can to mitigate them. Recently a friend told her, "Sarah, one of the things I like about you is that you're still trying to be a better person." It's true.

As far as she can tell, nothing about her would seem to preclude a lasting, loving relationship. Yet she's finishing her fourth decade still single.

The paradox is that, despite a longing to be with someone, her life is filled with contentment and joy. The longing itself is not so much to be loved as to have a man to receive the love in her heart. One important lesson she's learned from her friend Millie, one of the wisest people she knows, is that, while being loved is wonderful, loving is even better and more fulfilling. She remembers one of her students saying, "Wow, I just realized that when I love, it's chiefly my experience, but when I'm loved it's chiefly the other person's."

Yet no matter how much she ponders and prays for someone she can love with all her heart and spirit and life, it has never happened.

Until now? Oh, please, God, no, not him!

THAT NIGHT, alone in her garden, Sarah can't help thinking of her encounter with Jamie Quinn in Tilden Park.

In retrospect, it is upsetting. He's a priest for God's sake! She smiles at her pun. He has vows! He's off-limits! Yet something is happening between them.

Any word that comes to mind is trite compared to the reality of what she's experiencing. All the familiar expressions flood into her mind to the point of embarrassment: the feeling of finally being at home...of finding the other half of oneself...of having a soul mate.

"God, help me!" Sarah makes her plea to the dark blue sky. "Please don't let me seduce myself with cliches!" She wants to laugh, and she wants to scream. It would be nice to be able to lie on the ground and have a full-blown tantrum. If she were somewhere by herself in the wilderness, she might do just that for the sheer physical catharsis. After all these years and her parents' prayers, the universe sends her a priest?

She and Jamie have exchanged maybe a hundred words, nothing particularly out of the ordinary, although they both have been shockingly honest and direct. So why should she feel her life has changed? Why—as she walked away from him this morning—had the most ridiculous idea flashed through her mind.

"I will love this man until death and beyond that too."

She can still feel the soft dust of the path beneath her feet and smell the tang of eucalyptus leaves. She can still hear the trill of a bird, and feel the breeze off Jewel Lake caressing her face, and the sun gently warming her shoulders. Strangely, there was not the rush of euphoria she'd experienced in past meetings with men to whom she felt a strong attraction. She had walked down the trail in a state of peace that spread through her being. It was as though the world had turned in a different direction with new vistas opening before her.

There is a simple, quiet bliss in knowing she and Jamie

are sharing the planet at the same time and in the same place. She senses a mutual destiny that will dance them into a future she cannot imagine now. Her mind rightly rejects the possibility of an intimate relationship with him. It makes no sense.

But Pascal's most famous words come to her.

"The heart has its reasons that reason does not know."

Sarah does not need to wonder if Jamie is experiencing a similar transfiguration of his life at this moment. She's certain that he is, and she is very curious about how he'll respond. She finds herself feeling sad for this man, this priest, because whatever happens between them is going to be for him a source of pain and conflict. The last thing she wants is to hurt him. Yet how can she avoid doing just that?

ELEVEN

The hazy peace of Friday afternoon seems to float around the conference room on the hill. These meetings with hospital chaplains in the PTU's pastoral ministry program have a Sabbath feel to them, Jamie thinks. There's a special calm that comes at the end of a busy week that seems to encourage a depth of conversation and shared reflection that touch his heart.

He began the sessions to give his student chaplains an opportunity to talk together confidentially about what was happening in their ministries. The work they do is emotionally demanding, sharing the pain of persons seriously ill or facing death, their own or that of a loved one. A chaplain is willing to experience tragedy and pain so intense it comes to feel personal. Yet he or she also shares in moments of great love and transcendence.

As the chaplains tell their stories, Jamie looks around the room fondly, his glance settling briefly on each familiar face. These are good people willing to accompany others on soul-wrenching journeys. Not everyone could do what they do.

Jamie knows from his own experiences as a chaplain that people's capacities for pure, unselfish love can expand in being fully present with persons facing death. And what is human life, after all, but a school for loving?

Each semester he watches with a kind of awe as his students evolve spiritually. He observes their growing ability to put aside their own egos to listen in ways that enable them to truly hear the hearts and hopes and fears of those in crisis. A good chaplain needs to "hear people into speech," with a quality of listening that gives permission to even the most reticent to communicate what's inside them. Often people can say things to the chaplains they are unable to share with their families or friends. Because of the shortage of Catholic priests, most Catholic hospital chaplains today are lay persons. They frequently find themselves acting as confessors to the sick and dying.

Virginia Luna is a chaplain at Children's Hospital in Oakland. It takes a strong, resilient person to be able to enter deeply into the lives of these gallant kids dealing with life and death when their peers are playing sports and video games or worrying about grades or whether other kids like them.

Virginia is a retired child psychologist who began volunteering with sick children 30 years ago when a friend's son was diagnosed with acute leukemia. The precocious wisdom and bravery of the children she's met are her spiritual wellsprings. She'd been a lapsed Catholic with little interest in religion, but the children led her back to God as they faced death or increasing physical limitations with faith and hope beyond anything she'd ever known.

Today she has very sad news. One of their favorite patients, five-year-old Chloe, had died that morning. The group had come to know the little girl through Virginia's photos and stories. She'd tried so hard to live because she wanted, as she'd put it, "to grow up and be a Mommy and a firelady."

Once, when her room was being cleaned, she'd looked under the bed and laughed about what her Mom called "dust bunnies." The child was fascinated with the idea of mysterious little animals living so quietly and so near. She'd begged her mother not to hurt the bunnies by sucking them into the vacuum. Every few days she'd get down on the floor to check on them.

"I think the bunnies had a baby!" Her happy excitement made her mother laugh.

As Chloe grew weaker and began to talk about "going to visit God," she'd asked her mother to bend down to hear a secret.

"Mommy, part of me will go to heaven, but part of me will be a dust bunny. That way when you miss me, you can visit me under my bed. Okay?" The little voice was a whisper.

The woman had told the story to Virginia through her tears.

"How can I ever vacuum again?"

The chaplains pass around Virginia's favorite picture of Chloe. It shows an adorable gamin with short spiky black hair and dark eyes. She's wearing a stuffed rabbit on her head and grinning.

Those on either side of Virginia hug her gently. Everyone joins hands and closes their eyes. Together they sit in silence, sending the energy of their caring around the circle and out to Chloe, her parents and her sister. It's a simple act they practice each time someone they minister to dies or receives devastating news. There's comfort in closeness and communion, but the meeting ends with an air of sadness.

~

AFTER THE GATHERING, Jamie feels depressed. He'd intended to call Rabbi Friedman and ask to come to tonight's celebration that ushers in the Sabbath. He has a standing invitation for Friday night dinners at the Friedman home. He loves sharing in the sacred meal that was Jesus' inspiration for the Eucharist. It puts his imagination in touch with the experience of the person Jesus. Tonight, though, he's restless and disoriented. He wouldn't be able to bring the qualities of attention and receptivity the graceful welcoming of the Sabbath deserves.

It's as though he's moved into another reality in the last few days. He's met Sarah. Their hands have touched. They've shared a moment of surprising honesty. They've talked of being friends. He'd watched as she walked away from him.

Yet he has to face the sobering fact that she is still with him, quietly present in every moment. Even when he's not thinking of this woman, he's feeling her like a warm current through his life. She arrives in many ways: an inexplicable surge of joy, a memory of a glance alternately bright and tender, the sight or sound of birds. He looks for her everywhere, along the streets, in classroom buildings, in cafes and the library, glad just knowing that at any moment she may appear. Just like old song. There should be fear; if he had any sense, *there would be fear*. Instead she's a tide of happiness enlivening everything he does—even his prayers.

"You're in a good mood again...Hallelujah!" Sam had looked pleased as Jamie whistled his way through dishwashing the night before. "Does this mean the mid-life crisis has passed? If so, thank You, God!"

Jamie had answered with a only a smile. "If you only knew," he thought.

~

HE DOESN'T WANT to confide in Sam or seek guidance just yet. He has an important decision to make: how to proceed with this relationship that has come upon him so powerfully. His Jesuit training requires him to engage in a process of discernment that includes bringing the experience "into the light," in the teaching of St. Ignatius. He should go to his spiritual guide Richard. This is exactly the kind of thing the older Jesuit is meant to help him deal with. He's taking a risk by delaying. Just how much of a risk remains to be seen.

Yet he simply cannot bring himself to share what he's feeling until he explores what's happening to him in the privacy of his own heart. He needs a chance to talk with Sarah and see what she's thinking and feeling.

Putting on his jacket against a cool evening breeze, he leaves the classroom building and makes his way through the streets and paths of the Berkeley hills. Walking is a form of meditation for him. Moving through space outdoors usually helps clarify his thoughts.

The sky is darkening. Lights are coming on in the houses he passes. A brown-shingle house, its form softened by the trees and flowers of its front garden catches Jamie's attention. A warm golden glow shines through its latticed windows into a room with a fire burning in a brick hearth. He can see what looks like family photographs and a vase of flowers on the mantelpiece.

Suddenly pain shoots through him so intensely he feels it

physically. All the desolation of the past months, the sense of being only half alive, the numbness, the crushing loneliness are coming together in this moment. He is on the outside looking in on an ordinary life. He is again the orphaned child, face pressed against a metaphorical window, watching what he can never have. He forces himself to turn away and continue down the sidewalk. He tries not to think or feel and concentrates on his breathing...calming, slow, deep breaths.

But he's like the boy with his finger in a dike. The ocean he's holding back is a sea of longing for connection and closeness. This is what he's begun to experience in his brief contacts with Sarah. It isn't primarily a sexual temptation, although he finds her attractive. What Jamie desires and yearns for is to love and be loved by another human being. That is the truth, and he cannot deny it.

Now, for the first time in his life, he believes he's met a woman with whom such love is possible. Yet what in the world can he do with this gift? He's a priest and that commitment hasn't changed with their meeting.

And what of Sarah and her life? What—except pain and frustration—can he offer to this person who already feels dear to him? He's unable to give her what a woman normally wants in loving a man. If they come together in love, he'll hurt her. He's sure of this. "Please, dear God, help us!" he prays fervently as he walks alone through empty streets.

TWELVE

The darkness wraps itself around Sarah like the warm blanket that covers her as she sits in a nest of pillows and lets her thoughts fade into silence. She's meditated for years but recently her practice seems to be changing. A decade of struggling with the distractions of "monkey mind" is giving way to a deep mental stillness. In the past meditation was hard work, something she chose to do because it was "good for" her. It was a rest from busyness, a time to drop the burdens of the day. And as a child of the '60s who'd experimented with hallucinogenic drugs, she is drawn to exploring the interior world.

These days meditation is more compelling. She feels herself moving into a mysterious, unknown place.

This morning the darkness gives way to Jamie's face. The silence makes room for all the powerful emotions she can put aside in the ordinary course of life. If she thinks about the situation with him, a cascade of thoughts leads to anxiety, fear and even hopelessness. One thought crashes into another, and before she knows it, she's far into the future and all its possible negative consequences. Strange that her mind doesn't even bother to consider any happy outcomes.

That's because there aren't any. She's sure of that.

Yet when Sarah allows herself to surrender to pure emotion, her experience is so different. She's open and transparent, and filled with a love waiting patiently for what will be revealed. It has taken hold of her in a way nothing ever has. It is enough simply to let it have her and flow out to this other being and touch him with tenderness.

She lets her loving grow in the quiet until it encompasses the room and moves out into the garden and beyond to wherever Jamie is at this moment. Now she's beginning to sense something else: she's being loved in return. In the secret pathways by which energies pass through the air, his love is coming to her in real time.

Sarah knows this with a certainty that surprises her. In this darkness his thoughts and feelings are reaching for her in a mysterious way that removes the distance from the physical space between them.

And, as surely as she knows anything, she knows that already Jamie loves her.

Sarah sighs, only a whisper of sound. A single tear moves down her cheek.

THE AUTUMN LIGHT that gilded the East Bay a few weeks ago has given way to signs of winter. Rain hammers the hills and the steep streets. Winds from the ocean buffet the coast.

Days pass, but Jamie and Sarah do not encounter one another. Has God decided they need a time out? While he's eager to see her, Jamie is also relieved not to find her as he makes his way around campus, joins friends in the cafes, runs in Tilden or works in the library. For the time being it's sufficient (not to mention safer) to experience the mysterious connection between them in spirit only.

As a Jesuit he's been trained in a rigorous intellectual tradition. His order is not known for its romantic view of life.

"That's for the Franciscans," he thinks with a smile as he walks past the brick-toned Franciscan School of Theology with its beautiful garden and graceful statue of St. Francis of Assisi, that poet and lover of all creation. Jamie does not consider himself a fanciful man, a person given to flights of imagination or fantasy. So what is happening to him now in the absence of any actual contact with Sarah feels strange indeed.

In all kinds of situations and especially in quiet moments he's experiencing the flow of something between them that he can only define as "the energy of love," crazy as that sounds to his own rational mind.

"Am I having some kind of mental breakdown?" He has asked himself that on several occasions.

Then an inexplicable surge of overwhelming emotion fills him, and he feels sure Sarah is experiencing a similar feeling at the very same time.

More disturbing, it is as though all the loves in his personal history—for his lost parents, his precious grandmother, his sister Ellen, his beloved niece and nephew, his brothers in Christ, his friends and even his love for God are coalescing into a new, deeper love.

And the catalyst for this transformation is a woman he has only met once.

He could dismiss the whole thing as infatuation with its power to create the illusion of love. But at his age, infatuation is no stranger. He might be celibate but he's also a man and he's known what it is to be strongly attracted to women during his years as a priest. He's learned how to deal with it and stop it from interfering with the vocation to which he's committed everything he is and hopes to be.

Jamie looks up at the sky and wants to shake his fist in frustration. It's all so confusing. For one thing, he finds himself changing in ways that seem good to him. He's now much more conscious of the signs of love: displays of tenderness between parents and children, passion in the eyes of lovers, casual gestures of affection among friends. Not only does he notice them; he also feels a part of all the loving that swirls around him. It's as though the awakening love within him is giving him access to a whole new realm of being.

Walking toward home through the breezy afternoon, Jamie continues to be troubled by what their association will do to Sarah. He has no idea of her history with men, but she obviously has one. Without any evidence, he suspects she, too, is experiencing with him something that's new for her and deeper than her past relationships. It sounds nuts, but look at what is happening to him, Father Self Discipline!

Does he have the right to be the one to lead her into this uncharted territory? Isn't it wrong to invite her on a journey that can never have the normal happy ending men and women seek when they set out along the path of love?

IT'S UNSEASONABLY WARM TONIGHT, and the light is so beautiful, it almost hurts. The sinking sun has turned the Bay into a sea of diamonds spreading through the Golden Gate.

Sarah is walking along the old wooden pier at the Berkeley Marina. Only a portion is still open to the public; the rest was left to decay after the ferries it once served ceased operation in the 1930s. The weathered structure is a wonderful window on the Bay, the City and three bridges. Sarah always feels part of a special community when she ventures out here. Fishermen of many nationalities and languages drop lines to lure the perch, striped bass, rockfish and other species that swim in the coastal waters. As she walks, Sarah passes two men in camouflage outfits sitting on folding chairs and sharing beers, their poles attached to the railing. Farther along an Asian family is eating dinner with chopsticks, a picnic on the water. The air is soft and breezy, brisk but warm enough to be comfortable with only a shawl. The community on the jetty thins as she heads out. When she finally reaches the end of the walkway, she is alone.

She stands next to the tall fence that blocks further passage. Beyond, remnants of the original pier lie dark and haunting in their brokenness, part of a vibrant history that is no more.

Gazing out, she is startled to see two dark triangles skimming quickly through the water. Suddenly a shiny body emerges, then dives back. A second sinuous form follows the first. Harbor porpoises! It's very unusual, actually unheard of, to see these creatures so near to shore. They usually stay in the western part of the Bay near the Golden Gate. To see two playing together triggers memories of a dream she'd had a few months before and a subsequent conversation with a woman who reads Tarot cards on Telegraph Avenue. When she'd described her dream of two dolphins swimming towards her, the reader took her hand and studied the palm. She then gave it a friendly pat and smiled.

"My dear, this is very good news for you from your unconscious! It's telling you your deepest dreams are coming for you!" she'd said.

Swimming in tandem, the porpoises have begun to race

toward Sarah and the pier. All of a sudden, she starts to laugh and can't stop. She is laughing so hard the sound must be causing waves in the shallows. Without understanding how, she knows exactly what is about to happen.

"Oh God, you Trickster! I hope You know what You're doing!" she exclaims to herself.

Before Sarah even turns around, she knows he'll be there. And he is, standing transfixed a few yards from her. The look of amazement on his face fuels more laughter. Can the world hold much more joy?

Jamie hears that laugh before he sees her, face rosy with merriment, completely convulsed by something only she knows. What a sight she is, hair disheveled by the wind and glowing crimson in the setting sun, overcome with mirth, apparently unable to control herself. Without a thought, he moves quickly toward her, opens his arms and draws her to him. As her arms widen spontaneously to return his embrace, he begins to laugh too. They are both lost in the wild humor and craziness of it all. When they finally draw apart and look into each other's faces, there are tears in their eyes.

Later, looking back, Sarah will think how fitting it was that their bodies' first real contact came with both laughter and tears.

"I can't believe this; do you come here often?" Jamie asks breathlessly as soon as he can speak.

"Is that the best line you've got? No wonder you're celibate!" Sarah gasps, setting them both off again. When the hilarity finally subsides, they reluctantly drop their arms and move apart. They look at one another, and his face turns serious.

"I love you," he says simply, the truth of his words reflected in the expression in his eyes. "I know this is wrong...I have no right to say that. Please forgive me."

Sarah steps toward him and gently places her hands on his shoulders. Her face is tender.

"I've never felt this way before. I'm just worried that what's between us will hurt you and your life." Her last words are a whisper.

"I'm afraid *for you*! The last thing in the world I want is to hurt you!" He puts his arm around her shoulder and draws her close.

For a long time, they stand side by side without speaking, looking out at crumbling ruins of the path ahead of them. They watch the earth turn toward the sun and color the sky with ribbons of light. It is as though they are being held by great silent wings.

THIRTEEN

S arah and Jamie begin to know one another in an old-fashioned diner on the waterfront with red formica tables, dim lights and a juke box that plays hits from the '50s and '60s. As they'd come through the swinging glass door, the Jefferson Airplane's "Love One Another" was filling the air. Their eyes met, then they quickly looked away before laughter erupted again.

"OK, maybe we've been cast in a cosmic musical comedy." Jamie grins. "Think it's a good omen?"

Over cups of strong coffee refilled endlessly by a seasoned waitress who calls them "Sweets" (him) and "Honey" (her) and bustles about good-naturedly, they talk. Other customers come and go, and now they're the only ones left in the place. Trudy, the waitress, assures them they aren't keeping her. The diner will be open for another two hours, customers or not.

"My parents were madly in love," Jamie says. "The thing is, they were so involved with one another, there was almost no room for my sister and me. We were like an afterthought, something that came with marriage, but not very interesting."

Jamie has only confided these details of his early childhood to a few people: his grandmother, a therapist he'd been sent to after his parents died, his Jesuit formation director and Sallie Olds. It's a painful subject, and now, as he reveals this part of his past to Sarah, his voice is at times rough with emotion.

He tells her how, when the children were old enough to be alone after school, they were "latch-key kids," coming home to an empty house. There were rules about homework, chores and other behavior, and they were strictly enforced.

"My parents spent as much time as possible together. My Dad would pick Mom up after work so they had the commute time with one another. They'd get home, say hello to us, then immediately go into the living room for an hour to 'unwind.' They closed the door. We weren't supposed to disturb them unless it was an emergency."

The family had dinner together—usually prepared by Ellen and Jamie as soon as they were able—but most of the conversation was between their parents. They asked their son and daughter questions about school and their day, but Jamie didn't feel they cared much about their answers. After the meal, the children were sent to their rooms to do any remaining homework and then get ready for bed.

"Mom and Dad would come in to kiss us goodnight, and sometimes one would read us a story. After Ellen learned to read, she usually read to me."

Sarah can see in his face traces of the dear little boy he must have been. Her heart goes out to him.

"Lucky for me, I had my big sister and and friends at school and in the neighborhood. Best of all, we had our Grandmother, my Mom's mother, who thought we'd hung the moon and stars. She loved us and made sure we always knew that."

Ironically, their parents had saved the children's lives by not taking them on the vacation to Canada which led to the fatal car crash in which both were killed. The kids were staying with their grandmother, as they usually did when Claudia and Sean took trips.

"The three of us were playing Clue one evening when there was a knock at the door. It was two policeman. I remember they seemed so big and stern. Grandma immediately told us to go to our rooms and play. Instead we waited at the top of the stairs. We knew something terrible had happened even before we heard Grandma start to cry."

"The saddest thing is that our lives were better after we moved to the ranch with her. Being with someone who made us the center of her life ... " He pauses, searching for words. "Of course we missed Mom and Dad. We cried a lot because we weren't ever going to see them again...at least not until we died too and went to heaven. At the same time our lives were happier, and that was very confusing. There were days I felt so glad to be with Grandma in a place I loved, with all the animals and the trees and the forest. Then I'd remember my parents and feel guilty. Ellen went through the same thing. We were orphans and suddenly—for the first time—we were having a really happy childhood. It was hard to make sense of it all."

Sarah thinks of her own childhood, with its warmth and fun and love. When Jamie asks, she describes her family, feeling—as she so often does—just what a privileged life she has. She is touched by his obvious interest and his joy for her as he listens to her stories of Oreste, Franco, Giulia and Eugenia. He asks many questions in their hours at the diner. It's clear he wants to know as much as he can about her.

Since Jamie had taken a bus to the marina, Sarah gives him a ride home to the building where they'd met. She stops the car and looks at him.

"I feel kind of awkward." Jamie offers her a shy smile.

"I know. I think 'what now?' and haven't the vaguest idea."

Then something occurs to her.

"Are you doing a liturgy anytime soon? I'd like to come. It probably would be good for me to see you in the context of your 'real life.' "

Jamie regards Sarah.

"I'd love to share Eucharist with you. I have one next Monday at noon at the Jesuit school. Please come if you can."

"I will."

They part with smiles, each looking forward to their next time together.

FOURTEEN

Entering the large room that serves as one of the Catholic chapels at PTU, Sarah realizes the liturgy is in honor of the four churchwomen murdered three years ago by a death squad in El Salvador. Someone has painted icons of Ita Ford, Maura Clarke, Dorothy Kazel and Jean Donovan. The portraits are grouped around the altar on easels. Candles and roses have been placed near each picture.

Jamie comes in through a side door. It's strange to see him in the regalia of a priest—a long white alb and the dark red chasuble used for the feasts of martyrs. He wears a stole of many colors and intricate designs of the sun, moon and stars, flowers and birds, clearly handmade and beautiful. He looks around the room, sees her and comes over. He gives her a brief hug and a kiss on the cheek. Sarah feels suddenly shy.

"Don't let the uniform put you off. It's still me in here." It's like he'd read her mind.

It is indeed a moving celebration of the women, from the first hymn, "Here I am, Lord," through the final prayer of St.

Francis that Christ make him "an instrument of Your peace." Four people, one a Dominican nun whom Sarah knows, reflect on the lives of each of the women and read from their letters.

Maura Clarke and Ita Ford had been Maryknoll missionaries in El Salvador. They'd worked with poor families being brutalized, murdered and displaced from their homes in the cruel conflict supported by the United States government. The women were helping refugees find homes, food and medical care, and bury their dead.

"My fear of death is being challenged constantly as children, lovely young girls, and old people are being shot and some cut up with machetes and (their) bodies thrown by the road and people prohibited from burying them." Maura Clarke had written those words to a friend shortly before she was killed.

"One cries out: 'Lord, how long?' And then, too, what creeps into my mind is the little fear, or big, that when it touches me very personally, will I be faithful? I want to stay on now...[The Lord] is teaching me and there is real peace in spite of the many frustrations and the terror around us...God is very present in His seeming absence." The face of the woman reading Maura's letter is grave.

Ursuline sister Dorothy Kazel and Jean Donovan, a twenty-seven-year-old lay woman who had left her family and physician fiancé back in the States to become a volunteer missionary in the war-torn land, did similar work with war refugees at a Catholic church in the town of La Libertad.

A slim man in a Franciscan habit reads from one of Donovan's letters from the country in which she would die.

"The Peace Corps left today, and my heart sank low. The danger is extreme and they were right to leave. Now I must assess my own position, because I am not up for suicide.

Several times I have decided to leave El Salvador. I almost could, except for the children, the poor, bruised victims of this insanity. Who would care for them? Whose heart could be so staunch as to favor the reasonable thing in a sea of their tears and loneliness? Not mine, dear friend, not mine."

On December 2, 1980 Jean and Dorothy went to the San Salvador airport to pick up Maura and Ita, returning to the country from a Maryknoll conference in Nicaragua. Their van was stopped, reportedly by members of the El Salvador National Guard. They were pulled from the vehicle, then taken to a remote spot where they were beaten, raped and murdered. It has been three years and still no one has been convicted or punished for the crime.

As Jamie recites the familiar words and gestures of the liturgy, Sarah is struck by the grace and reverence with which he performs each act. He moves almost with the flow of a dancer as he bows to the altar, spreads his hands in prayer or takes up the chalice and the host. She sees something she's rarely seen: a priest totally given over to what he is doing, so fully present in the moment that he seems to draw something sacred into the room. Yet his actions don't seem studied or self-consciously pious. She knows she's looking at an artist giving his all to his art. Something moves around her heart.

His words in the brief homily had touched her and others as well, from the looks on the faces around her.

"I believe we need a completely new model of heroism, one that has nothing to do with war or power or conventional notions of valor. For too long we've honored as heroes those who have killed whoever was our nation's 'enemy' at the time," he'd said.

"We glorify war. We pretend it's noble, but people I love and respect who've actually been to war have told me stories of the horror and destruction they've seen with their own eyes and sometimes participated in. We send eighteen- and nineteen-year-old boys into intolerable situations and command them to do things that go against everything they've been taught, everything they feel inside them. Young soldiers brutalize and kill children, women and the elderly, and they themselves are maimed psychologically by the terrible things they do and see. We call them heroes to justify what they do. That's how we lure young men into endless war.

"The old understanding of what it means to be heroic no longer serves our world. Today we need a new heroism of love. Our spirits yearn for the bravery of Dorothy and Ita and Maura and Jean who risked their lives because they wanted to help people who were suffering. They all knew they could be killed by agents of the murderous military junta that had already assassinated Archbishop Oscar Romero. But their compassion and their love were stronger than their fear. They followed the invitation and example of Jesus. They gave their lives for their friends.

"There's a quiet heroism too, considered so ordinary that we don't recognize it for what it is. The heroes are women and men—but chiefly women—who offer their lives to the young and the helpless. They give their days and their strength to try to see their children have food and clothing and shelter. Sometimes they die using their own bodies to protect their daughters and sons from brutal men with guns or machetes.

"No one knows the names of most of the heroes of love. There are no songs written for them, no parades or medals. But God knows who they are. And even if we have never heard their names, each one of us is blessed by them and their presence in our world."

As Jamie now stands at the altar, Sarah realizes how easy

it would be to be attracted by the "spiritual glamour" of the priestly role he performs so well. It's good that—like other women in her family—she has some emotional distance from the Church, although she still considers herself a Catholic. And having a priest in her own family, someone whose flaws and personal habits are familiar to her, helps dissipate the clerical mystique.

No, glamour isn't the problem. Priesthood itself is the problem. For the first time in her life, she's met someone she believes she could love with all the love in her, crazy as that sounds after such a short acquaintance. If they continue their relationship, is she ready to accept the limitations his vocation imposes? She's been wrestling with that question since their encounter on the pier.

After the final prayer, Sarah makes her way to Jamie, who is surrounded by several people talking about the situation in El Salvador. As she approaches the group, he immediately makes room for her beside him. They are discussing The School of the Americas at Fort Benning, Georgia that trains counter-insurgency forces for Latin America.

"Our government teaches the soldiers who commit the atrocities," a blond man is saying. "Men trained there tortured, raped and killed more than 800 women, children and men in a single day at a place called El Mozote in El Salvador."

When there's a lull in the conversation, she puts her hand on Jamie's arm and tells him she has to leave.

"I'm really glad I could be here. Thanks for inviting me."

"Thanks for coming. It was great having you here."

"See you soon." Her voice is quiet.

"I hope so." The smile he gives her is warm.

Sarah walks out into the brilliant wintry afternoon filled with questions.

THE STEEP PATH up the hillside winds through a small stand of redwoods and along a ridge. Now Jamie sees only some tiny white flowers, but in other seasons wild iris, pink and white clover and blue forget-me-nots will blanket the canyon walls. As he walks on, the sound of falling water intensifies. He stops as he reaches the waterfall that makes this one of his favorite spots in Berkeley. It's a lovely place to stop, listen and pray. He watches a hummingbird move close enough to sip from the tumbling water before darting away.

Jamie sits down in small meadow and experiences the calm of this place. It's warm for the time of year; soon he's lying in the native grasses looking at the sky. "Dear God, what a beautiful world you've given us," he thinks, gratitude surging in him. He rests there, mind empty, simply looking, listening and feeling. So many colors and forms. So many different sounds, from the rush of the falls and the buzz of bees to the drone of a plane far overhead. A high breeze sets the tops of the trees to murmuring. The air is soft.

Then, as inevitably happens these days, Sarah is with him. He imagines her beside him sharing this perfect moment.

Soon they'll meet and talk again. Jamie feels a thrill of anticipation. Sarah is a country he longs to explore. Yet how can he ignore the tsunami of emotion she's arousing in him? His years of self-mastery with the female sex are not helping him with her.

He's been at war within himself for weeks Part of him insists his "so-called love" is nothing but the fantasy and projection of a man who's been feeling lonely and somewhat depressed for months. Sarah and the "love" are only phantoms created by his psyche to fill unmet needs. The argument makes sense. It fits the situation. It's obviously true, this dimension of himself asserts, even if he doesn't want to face it. Sarah is a solution to his mid-life crisis.

Another part of him is perceiving a truth that doesn't have words or ideas or rules attached. It's an experience, profound and compelling. This part believes Sarah is a gift God is offering him to learn to love in ways beyond his present capacities.

As a Jesuit he's been trained in discernment. Through prayer and self-knowledge, he is called to be aware of his deepest desires and open himself to God's direction and guidance. Now, Jamie drops into a state of quiet attentiveness to the Divine Being, sensing rather than thinking. He asks sincerely to see the choices facing him as God might see them.

He closes his eyes and drifts with the sound of the falls, letting the remembered beauty of the canyon wash over him. "Please help me to do your will," he prays. "Please show me the way you want me to go." The silence of his mind deepens until even the waterfall is muted. The warm sunlight feels like a vast love enveloping the whole world, embracing him and every plant and creature. Time stands still.

He opens his eyes. In the air just above him two monarch butterflies are engaged in an aerial dance. They swoop until they're almost touching, then move away in orbits circling one another. They come together once more. As Jamie watches, they both land on his body, one on his right hand, the other on his arm. He can see the details of their wings, small masterpieces of design in brilliant orange, gold, black and white. They spread and fold their wings in synchrony, like a pair of dancers. Jamie holds his breath. They remain for a few seconds, then float away together like sky flowers.

Jesuits are not supposed to look for signs, according to one of his professors.

"Reason and revelation...that's all you need!" The white-haired priest had told the class of novices. "Anything else is mere superstition."

Jamie begins to laugh. Jesuit professors are not, after all, infallible. He remembers the birds in Tilden the first time he and Sarah actually met and spoke, and the harbor porpoises at the pier she'd mentioned. Signs or not, the creatures are certainly on their side.

FIFTEEN

It is a Friday in mid-December, the last day of classes before Christmas vacation. Jamie clutches folders of student papers as he lets himself into his apartment. He finds a note from Sam. "Jack's father died, God rest his soul. He's pretty broken up...wants to talk to you."

He bounds up the stairs to the third floor of the building, knocks on a door and opens it. Jack is sitting on the couch, on the phone. He motions Jamie to sit beside him and continues his conversation.

"He was doing really well...taking long walks...he had more energy than in a long time. We all thought he was going to be okay. Mom woke up this morning, and found he'd died in his sleep. As you can imagine, she's distraught."

As his friend talks, Jamie remembers times he's spent with the family. John Jablonsky was a friendly, enjoyable man, devoted to his wife and children. His heart attack two months ago had been a shock. He'd always seemed so fit, playing golf and tennis regularly, hiking and biking. The priest puts the phone down and stands. Jamie rises too and grasps his shoulder.

"Oh Jack, I'm so sorry! Your Dad was a great guy. What a sense of humor!"

"He liked you too. Remember after that homily you gave at St. Ignatius, when he said you were 'a hell of a priest?' "

"Yeah, I asked if I could quote him on my resume." Jamie elicits the small smile he hoped for. "How are you, my friend?"

"I'm numb...I just can't take it in. He called the day before yesterday, and he was upbeat, looking forward to a fishing trip to Costa Rica. I'm flying up tomorrow to be with Mom, and Dana's coming from Atlanta. But Dad won't be there, now or ever again. I can't believe it."

"Is there anything I can do? I want to."

"Actually there is. Dad always liked your music. He'd dabbled in guitar when he was a kid, and he thought you were really good. Can you come to Portland and do the music? I'm not sure of the day yet, but it'll be next week before Christmas. Are you free?"

"I'd be honored."

Mark and Julianna have invited him to their cabin near Jenner, but they'll certainly understand if he can't make it. The two Jesuits stand together silently for a time, staring out the window. The death of a parent or sibling seems especially poignant for people like them who will never have families of their own.

"Today I wish I had a wife, someone to hold me all night. Right now I hate not being able to have the comfort only a woman who loves you can give." There is deep sadness in Jack's words.

Jamie frowns, "God, I know! It's so hard. Sometimes it feels inhuman, not more spiritual, just unnatural." He looks at Jack with a wry expression. "Well, now that I given you those words of hope and encouragement..."

The men share a hug. Jamie takes Jack's face in his hands. "You and I are family," he says softly.

His friend looks about to weep. Then he grins suddenly. "I'm sorry for all the times I've mocked your touchy-feely ass."

"Now don't go all unmanly on me," Jamie warns with a grin. "Somebody's got to keep up the Jesuits' masculine standards."

WALKING the streets of Holy Hill, Jamie thinks about Jack tonight, alone in a grief he can't share in the simple physical ways human beings use to comfort themselves and one another. How can it be spiritually beneficial for a person to live without that kind of solace?

A thought intrudes: will Sarah really help him keep his vows? Or will she become, as the old term put it "an occasion of sin." God, he is beginning to love a woman he doesn't even know well enough to be able to answer such an important question. Abruptly, he feels he's spiraling out of the discipline and control he has exercised for years. Fear goes through him. He looks at his hand; it is trembling.

He walks quickly down the hill to the nearest Catholic Church, dedicated, ironically, to Mary Magdalene, Jesus' closest female companion. The sanctuary is dimly lit and empty. Through red glass, a candle at the altar proclaims the living presence of Jesus as Eucharist in the tabernacle. Jamie falls to his knees at the altar rail. Before he can even think about it, he finds himself lying face down on the wooden floor, arms spread out. It's the same posture every priest took at ordination, the powerful physical symbol of the total offering of himself he was making to God in being anointed "a priest forever."

What in the world is he doing? Suppose someone comes into the church and discovers him lying on the floor? How will he explain himself, especially if it's someone he knows? Suddenly it doesn't matter. "Please help me, Lord!" The plea emerges from the depths of his soul. The silence drifts around him like music. From the stillness, he seems to hear the voice of Julian of Norwich's revelation of Christ.

"All will be well," it whispers. "All manner of things shall be well." The frenzied thoughts and frightening emotions depart. Calm flows over Jamie like a blanket spread by a loving mother.

SIXTEEN

The week before Christmas Sarah, in a warm coat, is having tea in her back garden enjoying California's winter flowers, especially her creamy white and deep pink camellias. On Sunday she'll head home to the ranch for a Caffaro holiday extravaganza. Twenty-three people are invited for Christmas dinner, so the cooks' brigade will muster a few days early. Sarah's looking forward to it. All the work and fun with people she loves will take her mind off the situation with Jamie.

She hasn't seen him since the liturgy two weeks ago. How strange to have such strong feelings for a man whose phone number she doesn't know. In fact, she doesn't have any way to reach him, short of ringing the bell at the apartment building where he and Sam live. She wonders what the other Jesuit would make of that. Has Jamie even told his friend about her?

Yet Sarah can feel him with her as she goes about her

days. Sometimes it's as though she can even tune into his mind and emotions. Lately she's sensed a sadness akin to grief in him. She would never admit to this psychic phenomenon publicly. It is much too "flaky" for a scholar and especially a woman teaching in a religious tradition that long doubted that females even possessed the rational minds attributed to the male sex.

When the wind starts up, she goes inside and builds a fire. She turns on the lights of her small Christmas tree and settles on the sofa. She loves the wild beauty of red, gold and blue flames dancing from the logs. Something about fire often takes her into deep inner places. And there, of course—as is usual these days—she discovers Jamie waiting...those silver gray eyes...his melodious voice. She wonders if he's a singer.

A pang of longing for his actual physical presence flashes through her. She wishes he were here, near her, sharing the fire-lit room and its cozy atmosphere. Till right now she's been content to let whatever is between them evolve in its own slow way. Tonight for the first time she's impatient. From the beginning—could it really be only two months ago?—he's moved gently toward her, welcoming her into his life, opening himself to her with a transparency she's found to be rare in most men. The word "love," spoken by Jamie on the pier, is always lurking close by, a powerful, sobering reality that could change their lives.

Sarah recognizes she should stop their association now. It's the only sensible thing to do. Instead, the desire to see him again and explore what is between them is growing in her. If pain is inevitable, well then, she's ready for whatever will come. Isn't she?

Her reverie is interrupted by the phone ringing. "It's Jamie," she thinks with a shiver of fear before she answers and hears his voice. He'd looked up her number in the PTU faculty handbook and hopes she doesn't mind his calling out of the blue.

"Actually, I was just thinking about you and wishing you were here."

"Really?"

"Yes, I'd like to see you."

"I have to leave for Oregon the day after tomorrow. My friend's Dad died, and he's asked me to help with the liturgy. I won't be back until New Year's Eve."

He pauses, and Sarah makes a decision. "Would you like to come here now and have tea or something?"

"I'd like that very much." She can hear the pleasure in his voice.

THE MOMENT SARAH opens the door and welcomes him into the house, Jamie feels immediately at home. The living room with its polished woods and comfortable furniture, art works, plants and shelves of books all work together to create an interesting, charming atmosphere.

"Wow! What a wonderful place!"

"This was my Aunt Eugenia's house and she had good taste."

With her permission, he examines the paintings and prints and reads the titles of some of the books. A glance at their subjects reveals a woman of deep and varied interests.

Soon they are sitting at the opposite ends of the sofa, stockinged feet up on the cushions, sharing a large crazy quilt. They alternatively look at the fire and one another. Instead of the torrent of conversation both had rather expected, their comments have been desultory. Jamie can't remember when he's felt more relaxed. Sarah lets a quiet happiness wash over her. The fire continues to burn like a symbol of what is kindling between them.

Jamie talks of Jack and his father and how touched he is to have been invited to do the music for the funeral.

"You're a musician?"

"Yes. Guitar and piano."

Sarah waves her hand toward the stereo where a cello sonata is playing softly in the background.

"Music's always been important to me. In my next life, I plan to be a cellist or a violinist. What's it like being able to make music?"

"How do you express the deepest part of yourself?" Jamie waits for her answer.

"I write."

"I play the piano or guitar. That's what I do when I can't find words to describe what's going on inside me."

He looks at her.

"I wish I had my guitar."

In response, Sarah stands, walks into a hall. She opens a door, reaches in, then turns back to him with a guitar.

"This is my aunt's. There's an upright piano in the dining room. She used to be kind of famous in Berkeley for her dinners and salons where people discussed and debated everything you can imagine. She kept a few instruments around, so guests could play. She always said musical inter-ludes made for better conversations."

Sarah's face is alight with memories, and Jamie feels something move in his chest.

He takes the guitar from her with care. His fingers test the strings and tune them.

"This is a fine instrument. May I?"

She nods. He smiles at her, closes his eyes and begins to play. She doesn't recognize the composition but its haunting sound fills her with a formless longing.

For a while she observes Jamie, watching his hands draw music from the old guitar. He plays with obvious skill, his whole being intent on what he's doing. This is a man who gives himself to the present moment in a way that thrills her.

The music changes to a Celtic-sounding melody of love and loss. She can sense a deep energy coming from him to her and she returns it from her heart. Though her eyes are now closed, she can still see his face, his hands, his body in her mind. She lets pure feeling take her.

There is in Sarah a profound tenderness for this man, compassion for the losses he suffered as a little boy and the loneliness she recognizes in him. Jamie seems to her a man made for love. He has offered himself generously to God and the service of other people. Whatever he needs from her, she prays she can give it.

"I love you." She tells him without speaking. "There's no other way to describe what's happening in me."

She opens her eyes and sees he's gazing at her.

"I love you too." He says it aloud and smiles, answering her unspoken declaration. She isn't surprised.

"You read my mind."

"I read your face."

Jamie looks away and continues playing for a while. Then he stops.

"Will you please read me something you've written?"

"I'm just working on a reflection on Mary Magdalene's experience as Jesus' disciple, but it's not ready to share. However, I do have a poem I'd like you to hear." She picks up a slender volume from an end table. "Do you know the poet Rumi?"

Sarah was introduced to the 13th-century Persian poet by an old friend and has a couple of volumes of his work in her office at PTU. The small book she holds contains some graceful modern versions of the mystic's poems.

She gives Jamie a mischievous glance. "I think this fits our situation quite well."

"Out beyond ideas of wrongdoing and rightdoing,
there is a field. I'll meet you there.
When the soul lies down in that grass,
the world is too full to talk about.
Ideas, language, even the phrase 'each other'
don't make any sense."

"Please read it again." He listens carefully as she does.
"It's beautiful. Who is he addressing?"

"It's a love poem to the divine. Rumi was a Sufi, an Islamic mystic. The Sufis think of God as Love, Lover and Beloved. He's also speaking of his mystical love for his friend and spiritual teacher, Shams'uddin of Tabriz."

He's quiet, contemplating the poem and the metaphors for God. Finally Sarah says, "Here's another one for you."

"The minute I heard my first love story
I started looking for you, not knowing
how blind that was.
Lovers don't finally meet somewhere.
They're in each other all along."

At first, Jamie doesn't speak. He just looks at her, his expression full of wonder. "It's like that with us, isn't it?"

"Yes, it is."

He doesn't answer. Minutes pass. Then the planes of his face deepen, and it becomes grave.

"Sarah, Sarah, what in the world am I doing? It's like being tossed into the middle of the ocean. I'm here with you, and I can't be. I'll hurt you, and I can't bear the thought of that. This isn't fair to you. There's so little I can give you. I'm being selfish."

Sarah laughs. "I give you absolution for the sin of loving, Go, my son, and love no more. And how about an act of contrition now?"

Jamie grins and crosses his eyes in a humorous expression. "Pretty crazy, isn't it? What's wrong with this picture?"

Sarah turns serious. "I have absolutely no idea how we're going to negotiate this path. How many times have I asked God to open my heart, to increase my love. And I'll just bet you've made the same prayer."

She glances at him, and he nods.

"So this is God's answer?" she says, "The great Cosmic Comedian. Here I am with you, this priest I hardly know but already love. And I haven't a plan or a solution or anything useful in my mind."

For a few moments, they simply look at one another. Jamie likes her face and doesn't believe he could ever grow tired of it. It's a good face, strong and soft at the same time. Her every emotion changes it in subtle ways. It's perhaps the most alive face he's ever seen.

Sarah considers Jamie handsome but it's the openness and vulnerability his face reveals that most attracts her. His clear gray eyes really *are* the windows into his soul. He uses them to show her who he is. At times she can even read his thoughts in them.

"When did you take the vow of chastity?"

"Sixteen years ago when I was twenty-three."

"Have you always kept it?" Jamie blushes, and Sarah's quick smile shows him she's noticed.

"Well in the beginning, there were times I couldn't completely resist temptation. I had my 'private moments.' " He forces himself to continue. "That's been the hardest thing to stop. It's still something I have to struggle with at times."

"So the biggest temptation hasn't been actual women themselves?"

Jamie is a bit startled by her words. He's never thought of it quite that way.

"We're pretty well-trained in 'defensive measures' against having sex with women," he says. "So we're always ready to bail if things get too hot."

He gives a wry laugh. "I've been proud of my ability to make a get-away without offending the other person, so she thinks of me as a nice guy dedicated to his vows rather than a jerk. Right now, it's not the sexual thing that scares me. I find you attractive but I know how to deal with that. What scares me is that a woman is suddenly part of me in ways I've never experienced. I carry you around wherever I go."

"Well that must be exhausting!" Sarah retorts, scared by the intensity in his voice and wanting to lighten the mood.

Jamie's smile does not reach his eyes.

"Discernment in community is an important part of the Jesuit charism. I should be talking to my spiritual director. Instead I haven't told anyone what's going on with me. Except for you, no one knows. And I don't want to talk to anyone in the order, at least not yet."

They fall into the kind of trance that comes when the mind has nothing left to offer. The fire burns; coals dance with light, looking so beautiful that one can almost forget their destructive power.

The clock in the hallway chimes, and it's like a signal.

They stand. Sarah puts her hands gently on his shoulders, feeling Jamie's body vividly alive under her fingers. He leans down and places his forehead against hers in a kind of communion.

"Please pray for us!" James says as they move apart.

"With all my heart."

SEVENTEEN

On her way to the ranch for the holiday, Sarah had actually considered telling her mother about Jamie. Her ultra-Catholic father might freak out. While she knows Giulia will be worried about her, she will likely listen carefully without immediately leaping to judgment.

However, as the preparations and the festivities proceeded at their usual wild pace, filled with laughter, great food and the usual friendly or heated arguments about everything under the sun, the opportunity had not arisen.

Christmas, the moving center of the faith they share, had brought Jamie so near in spirit, that Sarah sometimes felt they were sharing one long, continuous embrace.

Midnight Mass with the beauty of flowers, candlelight, music and prayer had been an uplifting spiritual experience. As the choir sang "O Come, O Come, Emanuel," Sarah held within her the longings of people all over the planet. They yearned for peace, hope and a God who loved them through the gift of His Son. The Christmas story had to be the world's greatest love story.

As the priest raised the host, she had thought of Jamie and wondered where he was and what he was doing. Her thoughts seemed to bring him even closer. She'd sensed some essence of him come to her through that mysterious energy path between them. It was like a warm breeze carrying his love. She'd closed her eyes and tenderly breathed out, sending her love back to him.

Now driving to town to meet Chiara, her friend since kindergarten, Sarah is ready for the first time to tell what she's starting to think of, sometimes almost humorously, as "my secret life."

Chiara is like her sister. As girls they had biked the back roads of the valley together and wandered the hills. They'd attended the same schools, from St. Francis Solano Catholic School to UC Berkeley. They'd dressed together for their high school prom and made peace signs for the first march against the Vietnam war. They'd been roommates at the woman's collective in the Haight.

Even though Chiara lives on the East Coast with her husband and two sons, the women keep in touch. Her friend is a curator at a Boston museum, and her life is ultra busy. Sometimes weeks slip into months between their conversations.

It is probably best that Chiara will be the first person to hear about Jamie. She has very mixed feelings about the Church. She's had her boys baptized, and the family attends Mass once or twice a month, but she views Catholicism mostly as an ethical base for her children. Chiara strongly disapproves of the Church's treatment of women and can carry on for hours about Catholic teachings on sexuality.

Sarah is curious—and a bit apprehensive—to know what Chiara will say about her relationship with a priest. She longs to lay out the whole situation to someone she trusts.

~

"THE LORD IS A TREE!"

Chiara's face appears so shocked it's almost comical. Her exclamation is one the women adopted as their own private expletive when they were in the second grade together. It came from a new Protestant classmate trying to say the Hail Mary, a prayer unfamiliar to her Presbyterian self. Her interpretation, "Hail Mary, full of grapes, the Lord is a tree." Apparently only the two girls had heard this.

It had sent them into peals of laughter that disrupted the rosary the class was saying. They'd practically fallen out of their desks and just could not stop. Sister made them stay after school, but it was worth it to have what they decided would be their own code way of swearing, something that no one else could understand. And truth be told, Sister Louis Marie, when she learned the reason for their outburst, couldn't help laughing out loud herself.

Sitting on a bench in Sonoma Plaza at the center of town, Sarah regards her friend.

"Well, what can I say? Believe me, it's not exactly my dream come true!"

"But a priest, for God's sake! Are you out of your mind?"

"Damn it, Chiara, it's not like I chose this! When I've prayed to find the right person, this isn't the answer I expected. And don't start telling me how crazy it is. I know that! Pain...no future...it's all true.

126

"However, I seem to recall a time years ago when I was awakened in the middle of the night by a certain friend who told me excitedly that only hours before she'd met the man she was going marry and live with till she died. I remember her saying something like, 'Oh Sarah, this is love, the real thing, and I knew immediately. I think he does too.'

"Well, certain friend, *finally* I know exactly what you meant back then, because I've now experienced it myself. You don't have to warn me there's trouble ahead. I *know, for heaven's sake. I know!*

"I've fought the battle all alone in my own brain for two months now. You're the first person I've told. All I ask is that you keep an open mind, even if you can't understand. I want to share this with you. You're the person who knows me better than anyone else. I need your listening and your support. Can you give me that? Even if you think I'm totally nuts, can you just be here for me?"

Chiara looks at her oldest friend. There is a long pause as her eyes search Sarah's. At long last she speaks.

"Look, I'm probably the most opinionated person you know...except maybe for yourself. So when you ask me to put aside what I think and feel strongly, it's hard. It seems so obvious to me that this relationship is a bad idea. But hell, Sarah, even I can't predict the future." Chiara's voice turns soft. "Tell me everything. I'll listen."

Sarah relates it all: the peace, the sweetness, the synchronicity, the kind of person Jamie is. When she's finished, her friend is silent for a while. The breeze blows through the leaves of the large old trees in the square. Finally Chiara takes Sarah's hand with one of hers and gently strokes it with the other.

"It sounds like what you've always hoped you'd feel for a

man someday. I'm just so sad it's come in a way that's going to hurt you, and him too."

"Why is everyone always so concerned about avoiding pain?" There is an edge in Sarah's tone. "Remember what Zorba said in that movie we liked, 'Life is trouble. Only death is not.' Pain...suffering. I couldn't care less right now. If that's what it costs to love Jamie, I accept.

"The thing is, I want to be good for him, support him through my love. How is that possible in our circumstances? My prayer is to have the wisdom to know what to be for him."

"He sounds like a good man." Chiara caresses Sarah's fingers. "I wonder how he'll be able to love you with the vows he's made."

"I don't think either of us has any idea how it's going to go. So far it's just been enough to talk and be together, to experience what's between us.—the feelings, the joy. We're sensing our way moment by moment. What else can we do?"

Chiara grins. "Well, you know how much I liked soap operas when I was a kid? How we used to sneak into the house in the summer and turn the TV on, but so low Mom wouldn't hear? I'll definitely stay tuned for this one you're going to star in! It may be even better than As the World Turns."

It's an old pattern between these two: going for humor when things get too serious. Their laughter rings out as uncontrollably as it did when they were in the second grade.

~

JAMIE SPENT the celebration of Christ's birth in Portland with Jack's family and stayed at their home. Christmas day was laced with memories of John Jablonsky playing Santa Claus and enlivening the holiday dinners with his humor. Amy Jablonsky, her normal ebullience dimmed by the loss of her husband of forty-three years, tugged at his heart. All he could offer was a hug or a listening ear and that special comfort Catholics sometimes feel from being with a priest.

The funeral in St. Ignatius Church was moving and well-attended. John's "communities" had come together to honor him: colleagues in the building trades, fishing buddies, children he tutored in a poor neighborhood, and those touched by his volunteer work in the parish. It was a tribute to a life well-lived and a man well-loved. Jamie was glad to lead the music that included some of John's favorite hymns like the Weston Priory's "All I Ask of You is Forever to Remember Me As Loving You." As always, music had opened the emotions of those gathered. By the final strains of the closing hymn, "Be Not Afraid," there were tears in many eyes.

Now, walking along a trail at the Jesuit retreat center on the Oregon coast where he is spending a few days, Jamie thinks about a conversation with a Jesuit from El Salvador that he has been unable to forget. Diego Rios is in the United States to give talks at churches around the Northwest. He is here to educate people about the brutal war happening in his Central American homeland and to seek help for those suffering from the cruel conflict.

When they met here the other day, the priest had told Jamie of his life and ministry in the Salvadoran town of San Francisco Gotera where he is associate pastor of a church, as well as principal and a teacher at a small school for the children of the region's peasant farmers.

Jamie found Diego an excellent storyteller who created vivid pictures of the small farmers, their families and their predicament. Jamie could almost see their faces and hear their voices. The tales made him think of Abrilla and her children. He's followed the news from El Salvador more closely than most Americans, because Jesuits are a significant presence there, heading a major university and working for social justice. A few have been assassinated. Yet information about actual conditions on the ground is hard to come by. U.S. newspapers, and TV channels don't devote much attention to Central America. Except for the murders of Archbishop Romero and the four American church women, El Salvador rarely makes the news.

Hearing from someone who's been there amidst the carnage and the terror is very different from reading about it. His heart aches to think of the unimaginable suffering of ordinary women, children and men who've done nothing to deserve the horrors unleashed on them by a repressive government and its murderous army and militias.

Jamie is haunted by Diego's tales of fellow human beings murdered or disappeared, villages and lives destroyed. The images of brave and loving people trying to live, keep their children safe and offer them a future have crowded his mind since their talk. When he isn't thinking of Sarah, he's thinking of El Salvador.

Once again, he has found himself considering the direction his vocation has taken and trying to discern if God is calling him to a change in ministry. These kinds of thoughts are not new to him.

In addition to teaching pastoral counseling at PTU and heading the chaplaincy program, he works with local churches to help them use music, art and silence to transform the Mass from a perfunctory rite to a deeply-meaningful experience of worship. He also volunteers at the Guadalupe Center in the Mission, Dorothy Day House and a men's homeless shelter. His provincial has indicated the Society is grooming him to participate in the spiritual formation of young Jesuits when he is older and more seasoned.

However, Jamie is beginning to admit to himself that his current ministries do not meet his vision of what priesthood could be. Surely there's more a priest can offer. Since his Tijuana summer, he's felt drawn to Latin America and particularly to work with the poor and marginalized. He's studied Spanish, including a summer immersion program in the language, and has become quite fluent.

His current work helps people, it's true, yet he has begun to question whether the good he's doing for others as a priest is worth the renunciations he is required to make. His growing feelings for Sarah have intensified his misgivings, but they have been there for some time.

When Diego had suddenly invited Jamie to visit El Salvador to get to know the people and their situation, he had felt an emotional tug so strong it was almost physical.

"Americans need to know what their government is supporting in my country—the killing and the oppression," the Salvadoran had told him. "A small elite holds almost all the wealth and power. The government and the military serve them. They suppress any movements seeking land reform or indigenous rights. They'll kill anyone who gets in their way, priests, nuns, even an archbishop," Rios had said. "Come and see for yourself. Be a witness. Not only that, but we have a serious shortage of priests. We could use more of them on the ground."

"Why me?" Jamie asked him. "Are you inviting other people to visit?" Diego regarded him. "You are the first," he said. "I don't know why you. As we're speaking, I have an intuition you have a role to play, Jamie, perhaps even a destiny."

A destiny. The word is full of portent. Could God actually

be calling him to El Salvador? And how strange that Diego's invitation has come just as his relationship with Sarah is developing. Are the two events connected?

Since the evening he spent in her home, Sarah has been closely-held in his heart, a sweet presence. Walking to Mass on Christmas Eve, the deep blue of the sky with light still shining through it had reminded him of her eyes. At the liturgy, he'd been sure she would have smiled to see nine-year-old Joseph and eight-year-old Mary processing solemnly to the "stable" banked with bright poinsettias. The flowers made the place look more like Florida than ancient Israel, and a Biblical scholar might find that amusing.

The truth is, Jamie wants her with him wherever he is, whatever he's doing. Today he wishes he could share with her this stunning landscape where the Nestucca River meets the Pacific Ocean at the Jesuit retreat center. With giant trees and silence broken only by the sound of waves and bird calls, it is truly God's own cathedral. He aches with longing for Sarah with an intensity that is sobering, even threatening. At the same time, he feels more alive—more attuned to life, to the divine, to other people and to the world—than he has in a long time.

EIGHTEEN

I t's New Year's Eve. The fabled year of 1984 is about to arrive.

Sarah is getting ready for an annual celebration with nun friends in their house-turned-convent in the Berkeley hills. They're interesting and humorous women whose guests can be sure of good conversation and laughter. In the hour before midnight, everyone will gather to reflect on the passing year and offer prayers for the one to come. Sarah looks forward to those shared sacred moments.

She's wearing a long dress of cornflower blue velvet with an embroidered bodice and sleeves of creamy lace. She dons knee-high laced boots and adds final touches: dangly gold filagree earrings and a flower-patterned Turkish shawl in subtle pinks and mauves. Glancing in the mirror, she's pleased with how she looks.

Earlier in the evening, gazing out at her twilight garden, Sarah had felt a stab of longing for Jamie's physical presence. He was supposed to return home today. "I'd really love to see you tonight," she'd whispered into the air, hoping her words would reach him in some mystical way.

"Dear God, if it's your will for us to be together, let us begin this year together," she'd prayed.

"Oh Lord, now I'm asking for a sign," she'd chided herself. Professors of religious studies were expected to be above such magical thinking. Still, she'd been disappointed as the hours passed with no word from him.

Leaving the house, Sarah decides to follow the principle of the Lord helping those who help themselves, so she drives around the PTU campus on her way to the party, hoping she'll see Jamie on the street. He's nowhere to be found. She chuckles wryly. So much for psychic communication and magic.

An hour later she's in a comfortable chair, listening to Joan and Brigit, two Dominican sisters, talking about their upcoming trip to Turkey, a country filled with Christian history. "I'm really looking forward to Ephesus," Brigit says. "Imagine walking in the footsteps of St. Paul."

Joan tells Sarah of the stone house high on a hill near Ephesus where Jesus' mother is believed by the locals to have spent her last years.

"A friend of mine felt a powerful spiritual energy in the little chapel there. She watched Muslims come to pray on their prayer rugs. Apparently they love Mary too. There's even a book in the Qur'an named for her."

As the women speak of Santa Sofia, Constantine's great basilica in Istanbul, Sarah wishes she were going with them.

"Hey, Padre, glad you could come!" The feminine voice is enthusiastic. Sarah glances up. Standing near the door is Jamie. His eyes find hers immediately and light with pleasure. He greets several people, then makes his way to the corner where she and the nuns are. Brigit and Joan obviously know and like him. They happily invite him to join them, asking if he's met Sarah.

"Yes I have," he replies, smiling.

"Well," Brigit stands. "We're the hosts of this party, so we better start hosting."

"We'll be back," Joan promises.

Left alone, Jamie and Sarah look at each other. Jamie bends his head toward hers.

"If I had my way, I would give you a hug and kiss you on your cheek or your forehead, because those are the only facial locations a celibate male is permitted to kiss a female. However, I am going to be extremely professional with you, a valued colleague with whom I am discussing academic matters." Obviously giddy, he can barely contain his glee.

Sarah wants to giggle like a fourteen-year-old and feels the blood rush to her face. She adopts a stern expression and her voice matches it.

"Thank you, Father. I'm grateful you're setting the tone for our interaction. As a daughter of Eve, that perennial seductress, I might be tempted to kiss you on a lips. I've been given to understand lip kissing a celibate male is not forbidden if it lasts for no more than a second."

"The time element is very important, yes, but most of us don't want to take the risk the other person will linger beyond what's acceptable." He is equally serious. "So it has to be cheek or forehead. Or perhaps the top of the head if you don't mind hair in your mouth. It's best to be conservative."

"And don't forget a celibate hug has to be an A-frame," Sarah counters. "You may touch lightly above the waist, but that's it. I believe there's actually a recommended pressure that must not be exceeded."

Jamie grins, then frowns to keep up his sober demeanor. Sarah lowers her voice, and her eyes twinkle.

"You know, I prayed for this. I even tried to communicate with you psychically, so we could be together tonight. Now I believe in magic!"

"That explains the path of golden light I saw when I left home," Jamie tells her. "It was leading into the hills, and I just followed."

Sarah chokes with laughter. With difficulty, she manages to contain her happiness at being with him as the party ebbs and flows around them. Friends and acquaintances come and go, and the conversation moves in many directions. They talk about their holidays and share stories.

The sweetness of being together after almost two weeks apart carries them toward the new year. Jamie enjoys the animation of Sarah's face and the pleasure of her conversation. Sarah loves looking at him, especially his eyes. They are so expressive.

As people talk in the pre-midnight gathering, Sarah is moved by the compassion and simple goodness of these women and men who have given themselves to God and those who need their care. They pray for hearts more open and responsive. They hold up their fellow human beings and all sentient creatures who are suffering tonight and send them loving energy.

In silence they contemplate the year of our Lord 1984. Then each person speaks a few words of prayer for their own journeys.

"The courage to follow my heart," Jamie says when his turn comes.

Sarah asks for "the wisdom to know Your will, dear Lord."

When the clock chimes the first hour of the new year, Jamie leans over and kisses her cheek. His lips linger for a few seconds. Sarah's eyes close. A tide of many feelings sweeps through her. When she raises her face to his and touches his hand, it is as though a covenant has been made and sealed. They have not exchanged a word, yet they both know they will explore this love together.

They rise and go their separate ways to hug and kiss other friends. When people start leaving shortly after midnight. Sarah and Jamie join the exodus. Since he's on foot, she offers him a ride. "It's a good thing I'm still limber," he says, folding his long legs into the Volkswagen Beetle.

"It's how I test my dates for flexibility," she replies. "I don't relate well to rigid men."

They drive slowly, reluctant to part.

"How about a new year's walk in Tilden?" Jamie proposes.

"I like how you think," Sarah tells him.

The moon is a sliver of silver in the sky casting only a faint light on the Wildcat Canyon trail. As their eyes grow accustomed to the dark, they can pick out trees, bushes and grasses along parts of the path. Then it plunges into dense blackness.

At a point so dark one has to navigate by remembering the trail by day, Jamie takes Sarah's hand. The warmth of that ordinary gesture of affection travels through her body like an electric shock. She experiences a thrill of fear at how intimate it feels, yet she can't bear to break the contact. Instead, she tunes into the sounds of the park at night. The wind is rattling the dry leaves of the eucalyptus trees. There is rustling in the undergrowth. The soft, haunting call of an owl comes from a nearby grove of trees.

They say nothing, but communicate by joining the rhythm of their steps, so they move together easily. Ahead they see the shine of Jewel Lake and make their way down to a bench beside the water.

Looking up into a sky, they realize that through some unusual condition of the atmosphere, the light pollution of Bay Area cities is suspended and a million stars are visible. They can even see the sweep of the Milky Way.

"Oh my God," Sarah breathes in awe. "It's so rare to see the sky like this from here. I've only seen it two other times, once at Point Reyes and once from Belvedere Island."

"I've only seen stars like this in the desert," Jamie says. He puts his arm around her shoulder and leans closer and whispers, "I can't tell you how happy I am to be here sharing this amazing sky with you."

Sarah rests her head against his. Undoubtedly it is wrong to sit like this, but it seems so right, their physical connections simply an innocent expression of love. That thought sends a powerful jolt of desire through her body. Perhaps not so innocent after all.

"When you think about us, what's in your mind? What do you see for us?" Jamie asks after what seems like a long silence. Sarah doesn't reply immediately. How honest should she be about what she's experiencing at his touch? At some point, she'll have to tell him, but it's so early.

"I thought about you a lot while you were gone," she says. "I wanted to talk with you about the things that were happening, at home, with my family and inside of me.

"But it's much more than that, and it *does scare me*. I want to share my life with you. Spend time with you. Support you. Listen to you. Be there for you. When I saw you across the room tonight, I was practically ecstatic. I realized how much I'd been longing for you."

Although she can't see his face clearly, he has turned toward her.

"It's the same for me. I was on my way to class in Burke Hall last month when I heard your voice. You were teaching a class on a John's gospel. I stopped just outside the door where you couldn't see me, and I listened. You were talking about the Samaritan woman, and some of what you said was a revelation to me. I'd never thought about her leaving her water jar, the symbol of her vocation, to go back into her city and testify to Jesus as Messiah. All those paintings and stories of Simon Peter and Andrew leaving their fishing boats, all the sermons, and not a single picture or homily on that woman leaving her water jug. It blew my mind and made me want to read your thesis.

"You were so enthusiastic. And your students were responding with intriguing questions and comments. They seemed fascinated by what you had to say. That made me realize just how passionate you are. It thrilled me and frightened me. With you I'm in completely unfamiliar territory. It's like finding myself on another planet."

Once again, Sarah is struck by Jamie's willingness to share himself with her in such an undefended way. She needs to respond honestly.

"Since you put your arm around me, and I lay my head against you, I'm longing to make love with you," she tells him hesitantly. "This is the first time I've let myself feel what's probably been there since we met. I know we can't be lovers, but that doesn't stop me from wanting you. It's the truth. And if you need to stop what's happening with us, I understand. I don't have the strength to walk away. If you do, please go, Jamie. Please do what's best for you."

Instead of moving away, he cups her cheek with his hand and turns her face to his. He can barely discern her features in the starlight.

"I love you so much, Sarah." His voice is low. "I have no idea what to do about that. You deserve so much more. But, God forgive me, I can't bring myself to leave you."

He takes her hand again. The night deepens, moving inexorably toward the first morning of a new year. They sit at the edge of the lake, bodies touching, hearts and minds joined in the mystery of man and woman discovering a oneness older than time itself.

NINETEEN

Jamie and Sarah meet often to prepare for their classes in a library's study room, walk in Tilden, and have coffee and conversation at Holy Grounds. Jamie introduces her to the Wednesday regulars at their table in the cafe.

"Sarah can offer us a Scriptural perspective," he tells them. She laughs, "Yes, my knowledge is encyclopedic." She fits in well and enjoys the lively and competitive discussions. Her other interests in mysticism and world religions make her a welcome addition to the group.

"Well that was fun!" she exclaims to Jamie as they head back toward the library after a spirited argument about whether Greek philosophy had been a boon or a disaster in the way it shaped Christianity. "For a minute, though, I was afraid those two seminarians might come to blows."

"It's always dangerous to criticize Aristotle to a Dominican," he replies. "They think you're trashing Thomas Aquinas. When they get too wrought up, we remind them of their order's leading role in the Spanish Inquisition. Then they remind us of the Jesuits' involvement in trying to over-throw Queen Elizabeth I and blow up Parliament. The Franciscans keep quiet, so no one will bring up their own history in Venice where they sold property confiscated from heretics to enrich themselves. It's valuable to know our Church's illustrious history. There's a lot of useful ammunition."

"You are such an irreverent man, Father. But at the altar you were also one of the most reverent priests I've ever known. It's a bit confusing."

"The institutional Church has a history that's hardly edifying, Still, there's really great beauty in our tradition too." he replies. "I'm particularly inspired by the experiences I've had with small Catholic communities here and in the Southwest and Mexico that personify Jesus' core teaching of loving God and one another.

"To see a community gathered in the name of Jesus, people who may be poor to the point of destitution, yet at the same time they are generous, humble, and eager to love and serve their brothers and sisters. Oh, Sarah, it's so beautiful, the Body of Christ alive in this world. To be part of that is the meaning of my life."

Sarah regards him with a pensive smile.

"Sweetie, we really missed you at Christmas! How are you?"

The voice on the phone is warm. It still holds traces of the soft melody of Julianna Lombardi's Mississippi girlhood, although his friend Mark's wife long ago abandoned her Southern Belle persona—except when it suits her to use it.

Juli always makes Jamie smile. It probably has a lot to do with the contrast between the form and the content of this woman. With her long blond hair and big blue eyes, she looks like the Mississippi homecoming queen she was two decades ago. That look and the accent belie the steel trap of a mind behind them. Many an attorney has been seduced and disarmed by this apparent icon of Southern womanhood sitting at the opposing counsel's table. All too soon they find that Julianna Riley possesses a superb legal mind coupled with an eidetic memory. What appeared across the courtroom as just another pretty face has turned out to be Joan of Arc on steroids.

After Jamie and Julianna finish their pleasantries, she gets down to business.

"You owe Mark and me dinner with all the trimmings. You promised to cook for Christmas, then you disappeared into the north country. When are you coming to pay your debt?"

"I'm ready anytime you are. I'd like to bring a new friend if that's all right."

"Sure, bring him along."

"Actually, it's a her."

There's a moment of silence on the line.

"Really?" Julianna's voice rises with interest. "You want to bring a woman to dinner?"

"Yes, and can we please sleep over together in your guest room?" he teases with a laugh. "I believe priests are still allowed friends of the female persuasion unless the Pope has tightened the rules, and I haven't heard."

"OK, OK … but except for Rosa, you've never brought a woman here before. Is she a nun?"

"No, a single woman…you know, the bane of the celibate class. She teaches Scripture at PTU. You'll like her. Free Speech Movement at Berkeley, first anti-Vietnam War peace marches, a feminist women's collective in the Haight. She's just our type."

"I'm surprised, that's all."

"Well, I haven't proposed to her yet. I wanted you to meet her first."

Julianna can hear the smile in his voice. She's bursting with curiosity. They talk possible dates.

"Aren't you going to tell me how to behave...you know, warn me not to grill her or be too obvious as I assess her looks and personality?" Julianna asks.

"No, I suspect you'll meet your match in Sarah."

The second they say goodbye, Julianna jumps up and practically runs into Mark's study.

"Hey," she exclaims, ruffling her husband's hair as he bends over a medical journal. "I've got very interesting news!"

It's late afternoon. Jamie and Sarah have come to the office she shares with other adjunct faculty members to get her master's thesis and a book of Sufi poems to lend him. He would like to learn more about Islamic mystics like Rumi who have produced some of the world's most beautiful spiritual poetry. When Sarah told him the lyrical love poems of St. John of the Cross were inspired by Sufi works he encountered in the libraries of Moorish Spain, he wanted to read them.

And the few things she's mentioned about women in John's gospel make him eager to see her thesis on the subject.

He watches as she stretches to reach for a book on a top shelf, then notices her breast straining against the material of her blouse. It's almost perfectly round and full. Jamie can see the hint of a nipple. Suddenly, he's completely and obviously aroused. Startled and embarrassed, he drops into the chair in front of her desk. He feels the blood rush to his face.

"Here's the Rumi." Sarah turns toward him. She does a double take because his face is red and his expression strange.

"Are you okay? Is anything wrong?"

Feeling like a trapped animal, he returns her look and tries for a normal tone of voice.

"I can't tell you," he rasps.

She stares at him and without thinking, drops her eyes to his lap partially concealed by the desk. The priest sees the direction of her look, puts his head down on the desk and starts to laugh. The sound is deep and rich and infectious. In a flash, Sarah understands the situation, and a whoop of laughter bursts from her. She practically falls into her chair, breaking up.

It's like an explosion. Both try for control, but it's impossible. They howl with laughter. Every pause leads to giggles then guffaws. They are like children overcome by the ridiculousness of it all.

Sarah, being Sarah, can't let it rest.

"This is very romantic." she gasps, sending Jamie into more paroxysms.

"May I say I think you're beautiful?" he counters hoarsely.

"I'm sure after sixteen years of deprivation, you would think that!" she retorts. More wild laughter follows. Karen Smithson, a professor of ethics whose office is down the hall, comes to the door and looks at them.

"I'd love to have some of that; I could really use it today!" she exclaims.

"And I'd love to share it with you, but I can't," Sarah manages to get out. "It's one of those 'you had to be there' things."

"And if you'd been here, you'd have wished you were

somewhere else," Jamie adds, unleashing more sputtering across the desk.

Dr. Smithson smiles. "Well, enjoy yourselves," she says.

"If we only could," Sarah mutters, setting Jamie off again.

When the laughter finally dissipates, Jamie takes the book of poems from where she's dropped it.

"Now please turn away, so I can get up and hobble home."

"I promise not to look. Now go!" Sarah closes her eyes.

"See you soon." He stands reluctantly.

"Not if I see you first," she answers. They part laughing.

THAT NIGHT on his narrow bed, Jamie recognizes that what happened in Sarah's office is no laughing matter. The dam holding back his sexuality that he's carefully constructed over the past sixteen years is being breached. A passionate desire sweeps through him. He longs to hold her, kiss her, make love to her. He pushes the thoughts away, but his body vibrates with passion and will not cooperate.

He uses all his tricks of discipline. Nothing works; in fact his desire grows as night moves toward morning. Right now he wants to be Sarah's lover more than he wants any other thing in the world. Finally, there's nothing to do but give himself over to the feelings.

They are so powerful, he doesn't have to act. It's enough to lie there, think of Sarah beside him and imagine what it would be like to express with their bodies the oneness they're already experiencing in their hearts and psyches. As his body explodes into sensations beyond anything he's ever known, Jamie's eyes fill with tears.

~

"I ADORE HER! She's a superb woman. You and she are a good fit. But what in heaven's name are you going to do?"

Julianna puts her hand over Jamie's and gazes at her friend. They're sitting at small table in a north Berkeley coffee shop two days after the four met for dinner.

He sighs, and a flicker of sadness passes over his face.

"God knows," he says.

"Mark and I agree we've never seen you like this with a woman before. There's so much obvious affection. And you really enjoy each other and have such fun together.

"Frankly, the two of you remind us of our early days together...the sweetness and closeness which seems almost innate, that let you know, 'this is the one.' "

Jamie lowers his eyes and stares at the table. His free hand traces the rounded edge. "It's true," he tells her in a low voice. "I love her. And she loves me. The moment I saw her face, the connection was instant and overwhelming.

"We both have serious reservations, for obvious reasons. But, Juli, I might as well try to stop the tide from flowing over the beach. It's the same for Sarah. In just four months, we're a part of each other. It's as though we don't exist separately from one another. I carry her inside of me all the time."

Julianna has known this dear man for more than a decade. Mark and he have been friends since they were boys in Oregon. They've shared their lives in countless ways. They've laughed and argued and confided in each another. More than once she's told Jamie his being a priest was "a terrible waste of a good man because there's a woman out there you'd be perfect for and vice versa." Now, apparently, he's found that woman.

"Are you going to leave? So many good men have."

147

"I don't know. I can't imagine leaving. I haven't discussed this with Richard or Sam or anyone in the order. You're the first person I've shared it with. Sarah has told her best friend she's known most of her life, but no one else. We just feel the need to explore what's between us for a while. And frankly, Juli, I'm finding so much joy in having her in my life that I don't want to give it up yet, selfish as that is. As soon as I start talking to my brothers, the world's going to rush in and complicate everything. I do worry about not being able to give her all the things a man wants to give the woman he loves. She's worried she's going to harm my life. But the sheer pleasure of being together pushes the fear away. I know we're playing with fire. And we may get burned."

Julianna reaches across the table and strokes Jamie's cheek.

"Oh my dear, dear friend, I'll pray so hard for you and Sarah," she assures him. "And Mark will too. We'll pray every single day that you'll discover what God wants for you and that it will be something wonderful."

TWENTY

Today actually feels like winter in the usually-mild Bay Area. An icy wind howls through the streets. Temperatures have dropped to the low 30s. There was frost on the ground that morning.

Classes will be starting up again soon, and Jamie and Sarah are preparing for them in the dining room of Sarah's home. It's warmer and more comfortable than the library or their offices. They've laughingly promised each other they'll behave impeccably and chastely.

They labor in silence for the most part, but enjoy the companionship. It's fun to share interesting facts they come across or a new thought or insight.

"Wow, the Tibetan Buddhists keep the dead in their homes with their families until a lama determines the soul has successfully passed through what they call the bardo," Jamie says. "That's the sum of the stages a soul has to negotiate right after death and before it reincarnates into another human life. It can take days or even weeks."

Sarah looks up.

"We'd find that horrifying, having to watch the body of someone you love decay," she says. "It's fascinating how conditioned we are by our cultures."

"... the body of someone you love ..." Jamie tries to forget her words, put them out of his head. It's as effective as someone telling you not to think about your feet or an elephant. His mind grabs the phrase and won't let go. His body follows.

He keeps his breathing calm and measured as he waits for his physical response to pass. He pretends to keep reading, but all he can think about is Sarah so close to him. What would she do if he got up, walked over and kissed her passionately, pressing his body against hers? Would she respond in kind? Would she push him away?

The temptation to give in to his desire and see what happens is as strong as the wind outside, buffeting him toward a complete loss of control. Fear flashes through him. He has to get out of here. Now. He feels ridiculous.

"Sarah," he say softly, " I need to leave."

She regards him with a quizzical expression. Jamie just sits there. He looks around the room. His eyes dart to hers, then away.

"Why do you look so guilty?" she asks in a joking tone.

He blushes. He clears this throat.

"OK, I want to make love with you. I'm restraining myself but just barely. It's time for me to go."

Sarah looks at him and feels the strong pull of temptation. If she's not careful, they may do something they'll both regret. So she takes her normal way out of a tense situation.

"Is it Adam holding the apple this time?" she asks sweetly. "Is Adam going to offer Eve a big juicy bite?"

Jamie gazes across the table at this crazy woman he loves.

"Well, is Eve hungry?" There is amusement in his voice.

"She's not that hungry!" Sarah retorts. "If she takes a bite, you know who they'll blame, don't you? That evil temptress who seduced Adam into making her an offer. After thousands of years of abuse for what happened 'in the beginning,' Eve isn't biting!"

They laugh. The crisis is averted for the moment.

Sarah turns serious.

"Jamie, please talk to me about why you're a priest."

"For something so important to me, it's really hard to explain." Jamie suddenly feels self-conscious.

"One of my very first memories is when I was four years old and Grandma took me to Mass at a rustic little chapel on the river. The Mass was in Latin, and there was beautiful music. The priest came down the aisle beforehand and sprinkled us with holy water. The incense smelled wonderful.

"When it was over, I just sat there, like I didn't want to leave. I asked Grandma who the man in the shiny green clothes was. She said he was a priest, and I told her that's what I was going to be when I grew up. Grandma wanted to laugh because I sounded so certain and so solemn, not at all my normal personality."

"Somehow from then on I always knew. I was your typical boy, often getting in trouble. I did dangerous, crazy kid stuff, like walking through a tunnel on the railroad tracks. I played baseball and was on the track team. I swore and cursed like the others. The only thing that was different was whenever I thought about the future, I saw myself as a priest. I knew I needed to get good grades, so I did. I knew I couldn't do anything really bad, like get arrested, so I didn't.

"I prayed every day, and I thought about God a lot, especially when I was outside and it was so beautiful and interesting, the world God had created. Sometimes I'd slip into church after school. It was very peaceful. I felt a deep presence of Jesus was there in the tabernacle.

"Generally, I kept all this to myself. I didn't want my friends to think I was weird. Also, if I identified myself as a future priest, people would expect me to behave like one all the time, and I sure didn't want to have to do that!"

"And then, suddenly girls were exciting. And I thought, 'Well, I'm not a priest yet. It's important to know what I'll be giving up, right?' Great rationalization, huh?"

Sarah grins at him, and Jamie continues.

"When I was trying to seduce girls, I had to be honest. I'd tell them that I liked them, but I was going to be a priest."

Sarah dissolves into laughter.

"You did what? You said what?"

"Well, I thought it was the moral thing to do," Jamie intones sanctimoniously, trying to keep a straight face.

"I'm trying to imagine being a teenaged girl and having some guy tell me, 'Hey, Honey, I want to bang you, but don't get any ideas because I'm gonna to be a priest.'" She looks at him like he's certifiable.

"Bang? Bang you? Is that the word you use for God's sacrament of love?"

Sarah's chortles. "Ah, yes, I remember those teenage sacraments of love well, Father," she gasps. "Especially the ones that took place in the Church of the Back Seat."

They howl with laughter. When the merriment dies down, Sarah regards him with a wistful expression. "Do you still feel as certain you want to be a priest forever?" she asks.

Jamie looks into her eyes.

"I do," he says simply.

The silence stretches out between them, alive with feeling.

"Why?" Her voice is tender now.

"As a kid I noticed there was a special kind of comfort a

priest could bring to people," he answers in a voice so low she has to lean toward him to make out the words.

"There were times I saw that people experienced priests as bringing God to them in some mysterious, powerful way. Those who were grieving or suffering seemed to feel God's love coming to them through this ordinary man.

"Of course, people can argue—and with good reason—that the whole idea that a priest represents Christ is fraught with peril. It can feed a man's ego in dangerous ways and create a sense that the priest is somehow superior to the ordinary Christian. That whole mentality leaves the door wide open for abuses."

He's quiet for a moment, and Sarah watches emotions play over his countenance. He seems very vulnerable to her as he contemplates his vocation.

"It's hard to express why it means so much to me, but it does. Being with people in pain, being a comfort to them. And I know some people experience that more deeply when it comes from a priest.

"When I try to explain, it sounds like egotistical nonsense, but it's who I am. I can't justify it. I just know it."

He pauses and regards her.

"I don't think I could ever leave the priesthood, and where does that leave you? Part of me believes it's wrong to put you in this position. The other part is afraid you'll turn away from me.

"Sarah, Sarah, I feel so confused. What do you want? Please tell me what I should do that's best for you, and I'll do it."

It's time to speak what she's been contemplating for weeks.

"Look, I've never been a woman who thought she could only be fulfilled by being married or having children," she tells him. "It's probably because my Aunt Eugenia had such a happy single life.

"Still, seeing my parents together, I always hoped for man I could love with all my heart who could love me that way too. It's never happened for me. I've been infatuated and thought it was love, but, deep down, I knew it wasn't. There have been a few men who may have loved me, but I couldn't reciprocate. When they got serious, I backed off. I suspected it wasn't love so much as that they were ready to get married and I was their girlfriend at the time.

"It came to the point that I wondered if I just didn't have it in me to love a man completely. Maybe it was a psychic gene I'd been born without."

She studies Jamie.

"Now I realize God was saving me for you. If what we've had together in the past months is all we can have, okay. Yes, of course I wish we could be lovers, but I accept that your vows preclude that.

"You're not the only one with self control. At least I think I have enough. This is new for me. I can't promise I'll never change and need more, but I'll always be honest with you. I trust you'll be the same with me. We're already discovering it's a minefield. All we can do is negotiate it together with God's help."

Jamie wants to touch her, but even reaching for her hand seems risky at this moment. A phrase from Teilhard de Chardin flashes into his mind: "The human is matter at its most incendiary stage." The famed Jesuit philosopher could have been talking about the incandescence Jamie is experiencing right this moment. Fire can consume and destroy or it can provide light and warmth. Which will it be for them?

He stands up and looks at Sarah with a smile touched

with sadness. He walks to the door and opens it. He turns and blows her a kiss. One final glance, and he's gone.

She continues to sit there. The room seems so empty. A tide of loneliness washes over her powerfully, wave after wave. It breaches her heart and radiates out in concentric circles. This is what it will be like on the day Jamie leaves her forever, Sarah realizes. And she knows, by the very definition of their love, that day will inevitably have to come.

TWENTY-ONE

N ow they meet only in public places: the library, parks, cafes and classrooms. The winter quarter begins. It's a busy time. Yet hardly a day goes by without at least some brief contact. They also try to set aside Saturday afternoons for long conversations in which they share their thoughts, their feelings and what is precious to them.

These talks are intimate and revealing. They are learning about one another and from one another and are being changed in the process.

Sarah has found her understanding of the Mass transfigured and deepened by Teilhard's essay, "The Mass on the World," to which Jamie has introduced her. She's read it several times and been astonished by the power and beauty of his reflection on his priestly actions.

Finding himself at dawn on the steppes of Asia without bread, wine or altar, the famed Jesuit paleontologist and philosopher had transformed the Eucharistic liturgy into a cosmic event. Teilhard had chosen to make the whole earth his altar. He imagined his paten and chalice to be "the depths of a soul laid wide open." He invited to the ritual "the mystic presence of all whom the light is now awakening to the new day."

He described the moment of consecration in words that take her breath away:

> "I will this morning climb up in spirit to the high
> places...and there—empowered by the priesthood
> which you alone...have bestowed upon me—upon all
> that in the world of human flesh is now about to be
> born or to die beneath the rising sun, I will call down
> the Fire."

Those radiant words invoking Christ's presence have changed Sarah's perception of the Mass. Now mindful of its mystical potential for union of the Divine and the human, she feels a sense of awe at the mystery and possibility.

"Have you ever experienced anything like he's describing?" Sarah asks Jamie one day as they sit on a bench at the PTU campus on the hill. In the winter sunlight San Francisco shimmers across the Bay.

"When I first read that passage, it stayed with me for weeks," he replies. "Every time I celebrated liturgy, I thought of Teilhard's vision in Asia.

"One cloudy afternoon I was saying Mass here at school, and as we reached the consecration, the clouds outside must have parted. I was holding the host up and suddenly it was drenched in light, like it was on fire. I felt the whole universe converging, all history and the future rushing toward that bit of matter. It was like everything was disappearing into a vast presence. I couldn't move or speak for what seemed a long time but was probably just a couple of seconds. Then the overwhelming quality receded, and I could function again.

"That moment is still with me." Jamie smiles shyly at Sarah. "I've never told anyone this before."

"Thank you," she says softly.

"Does a person have to be an ordained priest to call forth Christ in that way?" Sarah asks after a long silence.

"The Church teaches only the ordained have the power, but that simply can't be true," Jamie says. "All I know and have ever experienced tells me God is infinitely accessible to all beings."

"I think ordination gave me permission to invite God to come into the moment in this special way. Before I was ordained, I didn't realize I had to ability to do that. But everyone has to have the power to make Christ manifest here and now.

"I mean, he's always present in his fullness in every place and every time. If Christ is real, he's everywhere. What I as a priest am doing at the consecration must be calling His presence into our awareness. Until we're aware of Him, in an important way He's not present...at least not to us."

"So does that mean I have the power to call down the Fire?" Sarah asks.

Jamie senses a vulnerability in her words, so he thinks carefully about how to answer most truthfully.

"I believe you have the power but only if you realize it and claim it," he says quietly. "When a person comes to that moment of realization, that's ordination, whether or not it's some official action by representatives of the Church.

"Wow, I've never really articulated all this!" he exclaims. "I'm not sure I even knew I thought some of these things."

"I am so glad you believe this, because I've felt that it was true for a long time," Sarah tells him, relieved.

~

SARAH, in turn, has changed Jamie's perception of the divine by introducing him to the Sufi vision of Allah as "Love, Lover and Beloved."

Perhaps because he was orphaned at an early age, Jamie has found the "Father" metaphor for God moving and heart-opening.

However, the erotic quality of the mystics' symbols for God appeal to a man whose vocation requires him to transcend sexuality.

Eros is the life force, after all. It's becoming more and more clear to him that the Church's attempt to control and even dismiss that force makes no sense at all. The Catholic mystics knew better. Jamie has been intrigued to discover these great saints, particularly the women but men too like John of the Cross, perceived their relationship with Christ in erotic terms.

He recalls a story of how, once in ecstasy, St. Catherine of Siena had a vision of Christ giving her a betrothal ring and promising her, "I will show Myself to you, and you will be one thing with Me and I with you."

Teresa of Avila described her encounter in the language of eros.

"When my mouth touched His I became invisible, the way the earth would be if the sun took it into its arms ... How does the soul make love to God?"

Jamie's body—whether he likes it or not—is awakening from a decade and a half of strict renunciation. There are times when a powerful physical force of aliveness bordering on rapture floods through him. It's like every part of his body is aroused.

The mystics offer a spiritual alchemy for channeling sexuality into love for God.

As a male, Jamie needs images of the divine feminine if he is to meld his spirituality with the erotic. He has found two very powerful female figures of divinity in Judaism: Holy Wisdom, She who was with God "in the beginning," participating and delighting in creation, and the Shekinah, the one who is God's presence the world.

In Christianity, although the Church has always denied this, Mary has been worshipped like a goddess by millions over the centuries. And Jesus has long been identified as Wisdom/Sophia, so the Cosmic Christ has a feminine aspect.

Jamie has begun to cultivate a relationship with the Divine in feminine form to turn his passionate longing for Sarah toward God. In the solitary hours of deep night when he awakens alone in his bed, his heart and soul reach out toward the Shekinah, giving himself over to a union that invites all of him, soul and body, to come to Her in love. It is a revelation and a grace.

TWENTY-TWO

"Would you like to meet my family?" Sarah asks Jamie in early March. "We're having a birthday party for my Dad next Sunday. He's turning seventy-five."

Jamie's eyes widen. "Do you think we're ready for this?"

"God knows, but I'd really like all of you to know one another."

"Let's do it." He sounds more confident than he feels.

Giulia Caffaro is pleased Sarah wants to bring a friend.

"Is it a man?" she asks hopefully. Sarah grins to herself on the phone.

"The good news is, yes, it's a man, and I like him. The bad news is, he's a priest."

"Well, Anthony will enjoy meeting him."

Sarah smirks to herself. She can't imagine two more different priests than Anthony and Jamie.

~

As they drive through the Valley of the Moon, signs of spring are everywhere. Orchards are like Van Gogh paintings with the trees' new green leaves and white and pink blossoms, sentinels on a carpet of yellow mustard flowers. There's a bit of fresh green on grapevines twining the hills.

"What a wonderful place to to grow up," Jamie exclaims, looking around.

"It was! Grandpa used to take me to the City when I was a little girl. I remember seeing all the houses so close together and feeling sorry for the kids who had to live there."

There is a tension in Sarah's stomach and her heart seems to be beating faster than usual. She's been looking forward to this day with both pleasure and trepidation. She's pretty sure her parents and Jamie will like one another. She also knows, based on prior experience with bringing men to the ranch, that her mother and father are going to be scrutinizing Jamie and her, wondering how this priest fits into her life.

"I promise to behave in a cordial but distinctly clerical manner," he says, reading her thoughts.

"You have your work cut out for you, Father. When it comes to detecting my relationships with men, my father is Sherlock Holmes and my mother is Miss Marple."

He smiles at her, reaches up and briefly puts his hand over hers on the wheel.

"I'm hoping loaves of my homemade bread will help deflect that kind of attention and ease me into the Caffaro clan," he says.

In the afternoon, at tables under the trees, they'd enjoyed a delicious dinner, toasts to Franco, and a cake with a tiny figure of a rancher in his orchard. When it came time for gifts, her father had grimaced at the adult diapers which arrived without the name of the giver. "Coward," he'd growled. "Everything is working just fine," he'd insisted in response to taunting remarks from several Italian males.

After the other guests left, Franco and Giulia had urged Jamie and Sarah to stay for coffee so they would miss the worst of the traffic back to the East Bay on a Sunday night.

Looking around the table in the family dining room where they'd moved at twilight, Sarah silently watches the two men she loves most in conversation. In response to her parents' questions, Jamie has opened himself and his life to them, speaking with emotion of losing his mother and father and his love for his grandmother and the sweet life she created for the children.

"Grandma was the wisest person I've ever known," he tells Franco and Giulia. "She had just a few years of school, but she was always reading. She enjoyed thinking about things and people and life."

"My father Oreste was like that," her father responds. "He was a deep thinker too. He never stopped learning. The day he died he was reading a book on the Berber people of Africa."

They are all quiet for a moment, remembering.

"Aren't we fortunate, to have been graced by people like these?" Jamie asks.

Franco regards the younger man affectionately.

"We sure are," he replies. "I am so grateful for my family...my beautiful wife...my kids and grandkids. I thank God every day...several times a day. I didn't do anything to deserve all this goodness, but I really appreciate it."

Jamie already likes this man.

"I suspect God enjoys our appreciation more than praise

or adoration," he says. "There's something so personal and intimate about being appreciated."

Listening, Sarah heart surges. She looks at her mother and notices tears in her eyes as she observes the men. What is Giulia thinking?

The sense of deep intimacy in the room is as warm as the candlelight. It's hard to break the spell but eventually Jamie and Sarah need to head home. Her father sighs.

"I wish you could stay longer."

Jamie insists on joining Franco in washing the last dishes. Sarah hears laughter. Her father is probably telling him about the reputed sex appeal of males working in the kitchen. Her mother is still at the table, uncharacteristically pensive.

"Mommy, what's going on? Is everything okay?"

"I think he's wonderful," Giulia says. "I want him for you. I'm sorry he's a priest. What a waste of such a loving man."

Sarah's eyes widen. "What are you saying, Mom? He's just my friend."

Her mother frowns. "Look, I can see what's between you. And it makes me so sad."

Sarah is shocked. She and Jamie have gone out of their way to be casual and humorous with one another. She clears her throat.

"Mommy, you worry too much. I don't know what you're talking about.'

"Yes you do," Giulia replies in a serious tone. "And when you're ready to confide in me, I'll be here. God knows how I can help, but I'll be here for you, my dearest girl."

Sarah begins to cry, and that's how the two men find them, weeping quietly at the empty table.

"We're just feeling nostalgic and sentimental," Giulia explains.

"Yes," Sarah adds. "Sometimes things are so beautiful, they hurt."

Her father's liking for Jamie is evident when he walks them to the car. He hugs the priest with an obvious warmth.

"Think of us as your family in the country," he tells him. "I hope you'll visit us often. Catholics can't have too many priest sons."

Jamie laughs in pleasure and kisses the older man's cheek.

"Thank you...Dad," he says with a smile that touches Sarah's heart.

Franco waves as they drive down the lane of trees.

"Wow, that was amazing," Jamie tells Sarah. "I feel like I've been adopted by two great people." He glances at her. "You look so serious. Does this bother you?"

"My Mom read our situation perfectly, and that's why we were crying. She wants you for me, and she knows it's impossible. I denied everything, but she wasn't fooled. She said when I was ready to talk, she'll be there."

Jamie reaches up and touches her cheek.

"So it begins ... the pain," he says softly. "Are you ready?"

"No," Sarah whispers, placing her hand briefly on his knee, "but I'm willing and hopefully able."

TWENTY-THREE

J amie is sitting in his office in late March with no idea
that the course of his life is about to change.

When the phone rings, he picks it up distractedly,
pulling his attention from student proposals for final projects.
It's Diego Rios. "Do you remember me?" the Jesuit asks.

"Of course," Jamie replies. "I've thought of you and your
invitation a great deal."

"There's something wonderful happening in El Salvador
I'd like you to see." Diego says.

The Salvadoran priest tells a remarkable story. A few
musicians in San Salvador had put on a free concert and
invited poor and even homeless children to attend. They'd
played music to appeal to the young, like Tchaikovsky's Peter
and the Wolf. When it was over, dozens of the youngsters
wouldn't leave the theater. They'd pleaded for music lessons.
Their passionate response surprised the concert organizers.

The musicians found as many old instruments as they
could, but demand far outstripped supply. They were

impressed at how hard the children who received instruments worked to learn to play.

"They were practicing every spare moment. Their friends started hanging around the local music school asking to be taught. There was a landslide of interest," Diego says. "The people who'd volunteered to teach were overwhelmed. All this in the middle of a war!"

An amazing thing had happened next. A brother and sister who lived near the city's massive garbage dump had started experimenting with trash, from old cans to pieces of metal and somehow managed to build a crude violin and a cello. They didn't have perfect pitch, but they sounded pretty good.

A man who made a living by picking salable trash from the landfill had been watching the children work. Baldemar had always liked to tinker and helped find the kids items that might be usable. And then he'd started to build string and wind instruments in a shack adjacent to his small home.

When a music teacher heard Baldemar's ham can violin, he was enchanted. The sound was as good as a normal practice violin. The same was true of his cello and his wind instruments.

Now the first children's orchestra is giving concerts around the city. Another is forming.

"This is changing lives," Diego says with enthusiasm. "For the first time these kids and their parents have seen they can have futures they hadn't imagined. And for awhile, they can forget the killings and the fear."

"It sounds incredible," Jamie exclaims. "But what could I contribute?"

"I'm not sure," Diego confesses. "Maybe you can see for yourself and tell the story up there." The Jesuit laughs. "I really can't explain. I'd like to show you around, introduce you to people. You've heard of a leap of faith? Well, think of this as a trip of faith."

Jamie glances out the window at the trees with their new leaves unfurling from the dormancy of winter. Like the leaves, his heart is opening in a new season. He's experiencing with Sarah what feels like the springtime of his life. He doesn't want to go away. He doesn't want to leave her.

Yet, at Diego's words, he experiences once more the mysterious force calling him South.

Jamie looks through his calendar. There's nothing that can't be changed.

"I'll come for a week during spring break," he tells his fellow Jesuit.

"My God, you know how dangerous it is down there! The stories I've heard from refugees who've spoken at church have given me nightmares," Sarah says. "No one is safe. In fact, the military and militias are targeting priests and church workers. They say liberation theology is Communist."

They're sitting under an arbor in a picturesque cafe on upper Shattuck Avenue. Jamie's face is lit by an inner light as he talks of the journey Diego has proposed. She loves his enthusiasm but fear overwhelms her.

"It's true. The war is still going strong," he admits. "It's a massive unfolding tragedy. But most of the fighting is happening in the rural areas. Diego says in San Salvador you'd hardly know there's a war, except for the refugees and the sound of distant bombardments and smoke from fires in the mountains."

Sarah looks at him.

"I have no right to say this, but I wish you wouldn't go. I

have a bad feeling about you in El Salvador. I'm sorry, but I do."

Jamie can sense how much she cares about him, and he loves her concern. What a gift from God! They become silent as deep feelings sing between them.

Then in a gentle voice he tells her about Abrilla and her children, and how his afternoon with them still haunts him. His story is so vivid that Sarah can almost see them in her mind's eye.

"She and her children changed my life. It's like I fell in love with them," Jamie says softly. "When Diego invited me to El Salvador, I felt a deep peace and a certainty that something important was happening. It was like when I first looked across the room and saw you."

Sarah smiles sadly.

"You love two women, and it appears Abrilla is going to get you."

His face is tender. "This will be just for a week. I couldn't go away for any extended period until next year anyway. We'll have time to explore what God is giving us in one another."

It is one of those days that make Northern California the envy of the world. The trees are pink and white torches of late spring beauty under a deep blue sky. There is simply no doubt: God is the consummate Artist.

Sarah's heart lifts. It's good to be here with her mother planting in the garden. They talk as they work—family news, friends, the state of the country and the world. Finally, Giulia asks what's on her mind.

"How is Jamie? How are things going with you and him?"

Sarah's expression is unreadable.

"He's in Central America for a week with a Jesuit friend. He's been drawn toward ministry in Latin America for a long time." She tells her mother the story of Jamie's meeting with Abrilla and her children.

"He's a very special man. I understand why you love him," Giulia says, as though they've discussed the matter, when in fact, her daughter has said nothing since the evening of the priest's visit to the Caffaro home.

Sarah sighs. What's the point of holding back?

"We do love each other, Mom. I've never experienced anything even close to this with anyone else. Neither has he. I don't know what's going to happen. He's made vows. He's a person of integrity. There are insoluble problems. We're both aware of them.

"Still, this love feels like a gift from God. Right now just being together when we can, doing ordinary things, is enough. I have an overwhelming gratitude in my heart when I get to be with Jamie. Already I feel like I'm his for life. " Sarah stops, embarrassed to enthuse further about a relationship her mother can't be happy about.

Giulia looks at her for a long moment, saying nothing. Then she surprises.

"Sweetheart, I'm so glad for both of you. What a wonderful thing."

She smiles at the shock on her daughter's face. "I'm a crazy old Italian lady and a hopeless romantic, OK? I've thought a lot about this since I met Jamie. And it's true that love comes in many forms. You can't legislate it. The Pope can't stop his sons from loving. Yes, you'll have big problems other couples don't, but I believe you can find your way to something beautiful. You're both special human beings. I have faith in you two."

Sarah rises, hurries over to where her mother is positioning bamboo poles and throws her arms around her.

"Oh Mommy, you're incredible!" she exclaims.

"You mean for someone of my ancient age and conservative heritage?" Giulia jokes.

Franco finds them, weeping in one another's arms.

"Should I be worried?" he asks with a grin. "Or is this just a case of my favorite strong women overcome by spring in their garden?" They all laugh.

"My family!" Sarah thinks, fondly regarding her parents. Still, she wonders what her father would say if he knew the subject of their conversation.

BY THE LIGHT of a full moon, Sarah follows a well-worn path through the orchard to the creek. She heads for a certain spot along the bank where the stream widens and flows quietly. Ancient trees, oak, bay and buckeye, form a canopy over the water. For some reason she can't explain, the sky through openings in the foliage burns more brightly with stars than it does elsewhere.

She lies down in the soft grass, feeling the earth holding her. This ground is so familiar it seems shaped to the contours of her body. For as long as she can remember she's come here to think about her life, sometimes to cry, at other times to feel a soaring happiness. Tonight she's pensive, thinking of Jamie thousands of miles away in the place so compelling to him and one she may never be able to share beyond some volunteer work with refugees.

She reaches out to him as if love had the power of radar. What is he experiencing as he moves through a landscape and among people to whom he feels a mysterious draw? It's an hour later in El Salvador. He is probably in bed. As he prepares for sleep in a sultry darkness, what is he thinking? Feeling?

Suddenly, her sexual passion for Jamie floods her. It's a torrent of sensation, and she's powerless to resist the fire that is flaming through her. Her body begins to move in the ancient rhythms. Lying there, Sarah imagines what it would be like to give herself to Jamie physically.

When it comes, the orgasm is shattering. For a moment, it's like she's disappearing into him, into love itself. After it's over, her body continues to pulse like some great heart.

Then a devastating guilt sweeps over her.

Psychically connected as they are, on some level Jamie will tune in to her sexual experience. What if she's violated some essential trust between them by making love to him in fantasy? Sarah sits up and leans against a tree. Her head hurts as her mind slams up against the reality that this man she loves has given his life to something larger than himself in a way she's never done and probably does not completely understand.

Jamie's vocation and the totality of the gift of self it requires causes Sarah to recognize her own lack of an all-encompassing intention for her life. Yes, she has aspirations for her time on earth: to be a kind and loving person, to do good work, to use her creative talents.

She's devoted to her students and her teaching and is starting to experience an excitement for the creative writing she's beginning to do. It's part of a very fortunate life that brings her many kinds of satisfaction.

But what would be like to have a powerful call like Jamie's?

Part of loving him, it seems to her, will be to enter into his life with sincere sensitivity to its realities and its demands.

What just happened suddenly makes Sarah doubt her ability to do this. God knows she wants to, but can she *actually* be faithful to her intention to help him keep his vow?

Now she is annoyed with herself. What a prima donna! How stupid to turn a six-month-old relationship into a great love worthy of the grand opera they'd joked about. Don't most couples go through a rosy haze of celestial bliss in the early stages of being in love? Heaven predominates in the beginning of romance stories, while hell takes more time to show itself. What hell awaits her for being hot for a guy who happens to be a priest, a man she's only known for a short time? It's nuts to make such a big deal of this, she decides.

But a nagging thought persists. Suppose she has, without even realizing it, passed beyond the power of choosing. Suppose that what is between the two of them is already irrevocable.

"Oh come off it!" she tells herself, more irritated. "That's a crazy idea that belongs to romance novels." Of course she has a choice. She's perfectly free to halt the relationship with Jamie, not to see him (except by accident around Berkeley.) It would be wrenching, true, but severing this new connection is certainly possible at this point.

Yet when she attempts to imagine ending their friendship, she can't do it. Yes, it's too soon, but already he's part of her. She suspects it's the same for her as it was for her mother and Chiara. Hours after meeting their future husbands, each woman knew she'd found the man she wanted to spend her life with.

And what of Jamie's needs and desires? As much as possible, Sarah definitely wishes to be the woman and the friend he apparently needs and longs for. If someone is going to cut off the relationship, it will have to be Jamie. If Jamie does have to break it off, she'll be resilient. Then she thinks of how long it's taken her to find a man she loves with all of herself. "Stop it!" she orders firmly. "You're hardly a romantic heroine who's going to waste away when her non-lover leaves her."

Now she notices how cold and hard the ground is. She gets up feeling stiff and aching. It's time to go back to the house and try to get a good night's sleep. Morning will come too soon.

TWENTY-FOUR

As the plane rises, Jamie gazes at the tall volcano brooding over San Salvador. The mountain is like a metaphor for this country whose people live in the shadow of a war that can erupt into tragedy at any time.

The aircraft arches into the clouds, and he settles back, awash in memories of the last six days. People and events flow through his mind like photos in a slide show. What a kaleidoscope of the spectrum of human experience!

El Salvador, the only country named for Jesus Christ, is being crucified. Jamie has witnessed extreme poverty in the past. He has never before personally experienced the reality of war. In the capital city, one can hear the pounding of distant bombing and see fire in the sky at night from the far mountains. Yet parts of San Salvador seem removed from the brutal conflict.

A visit to a hospital treating some of the war's survivors had made it real.

The large cement fortress with its huge cross emblem was

unlike the antiseptic, orderly hospitals back home. It's pediatric floor resembled a party, chaotic but subdued, with scores of guests of all ages. He was literally stopped in his tracks by the onslaught of sights, sounds and the smells of food, unwashed bodies and illness.

Jamie knows his dreams will always carry images of the children there. In one huge room filled with cribs and cots, relatives crowded on the small beds and spilled onto the floor. Visitors and the medical professionals had to make their way along narrow corridors between parents and children, grandparents, aunts and uncles, brothers, sisters and friends.

Slowly individual scenes came into focus. Some were terrible like the little bodies missing an arm or a leg or both. A small girl's face was a mass of open wounds. Several children had bandages covering their eyes, and he'd wondered if they'd been blinded.

At Diego's urging, Jamie was wearing his "priest clothes," something he hardly ever did in the States. "Dressed like this we're available to people as priests," his friend had explained. "Otherwise we're just strange men."

Certain experiences will remain with him forever. Like the white-haired woman who grabbed his hand as though it were a life preserver and drew him to a crib where a tiny girl lay sleeping. The child had bandaged stumps where her legs should have been.

"Please bless my *nieta*, my granddaughter, and pray for her, Padre," she said with pleading eyes filling with tears. "Her life is going to be so hard."

Trying not to break down himself, Jamie reached out and touched the girl's soft little cheek. Her eyes opened, and she looked at him with an expression he couldn't read. It was sober, more adult than child. "What is your name, dear?" he asked in a low voice. She did not answer. "It's

Miguela, Padre," her grandmother said, patting the girl's hand.

Speaking slowly and softly in Spanish, Jamie told the child what a good and beautiful girl she was and how much she was loved. He paused to let her take in the words, then reverently made the sign of the cross over her and spoke the ancient, familiar blessing. For a long moment the girl stared into his face. Then her lips curved in a half smile. He smiled back through wet eyes. He turned and put his arm around her grandmother's shoulder.

"Señora, thank you so much for asking me. It is my privilege," he said gently. She leaned against him. "Thank you, Padre." For a time they stood together looking down at Miguela, united by their prayers for her future.

So many sights of suffering.

There were the babies and children who lay listlessly, eyes vacant, unable to respond to those around them. Some bore the cruel signs of malnutrition, the stick limbs and lined faces making them look like little old people.

In their separate, sterile room, the burn victims were dreadful to see, because these were the worst cases in the country: faces and limbs partially destroyed or disfigured, livid scars over swaths of children's bodies. He blessed them tenderly, although part of him physically recoiled at the devastation. He felt ashamed of his reaction.

When one little boy with bandaged legs raised his hand toward Jamie, he took it gently. As he caressed the small fingers, the child offered him a tiny smile. He felt a tearing in his chest. He bent slightly and touched the boy's face, running his fingers along his chin. But instead of being comforted, the child let out a loud wail and began to sob.

A gaunt man standing nearby said quickly, "Oh please forgive my son, Padre. Men he didn't know hurt him, so he is afraid of strangers. But he smiled at you. This is unusual. It is good. I think he likes you."

Suddenly Jamie's knees felt weak. He grasped the crib with a trembling hand, then looked at the father.

"Señor, I apologize to you and to your son," he managed to say. "I did not think before I touched him."

He turned abruptly and made his way out of the room into an empty corridor. There was no chair or bench, so he slid down the wall to the floor so he wouldn't fall in his unsteady state. My God, a couple of hours face to face with the war's victims, and he couldn't take it. He would be useless down here! He didn't have the strength for this ministry. What could he have been thinking?

Sometime later Diego found him. He helped him up, and Jamie felt more shame at his weakness. "It's all right," the Jesuit reassured him. "These children tear at your heart and soul. Your reaction is from your caring. It is a good thing."

Jamie did not believe him.

That night on the campus of the capital's Jesuit university, the two priests sat together in silence for a long time. They stared into the night, each lost in his own thoughts. "It was too much to begin, a baptism of fire. I should have warned you," Diego said finally. "It's just that I wanted you to see, to understand the agony of our people. And there it is, clear, obvious, in a single place."

"It's all right, brother. I had to know."

What else could he say? He felt that hospital had changed him. He'd lost the innocence of every person who hasn't seen with their own eyes, in the flesh, the horror one human being can deliberately inflict on another. He'd also lost a basic confidence that he had anything of value to offer those who were suffering from this war.

In the tropical darkness, Jamie found himself yearning for

178

Sarah with an intensity that shocked him. He wanted to see her face. He wanted to lean against her and feel her strength flow into him. He would have given anything right then to feel her hand holding his. He'd allowed himself to sink fully into the comfort of his daydream. He was so lost in it that Diego's voice, when it came again, startled him.

"Tomorrow you will be able to feel the joy of El Salvador, and it too is powerful and unforgettable."

Jamie hoped that were true.

IN THE PLANE to Los Angeles, Jamie scans his happy memories. Diego had been right. He would always remember the joy.

He sees again the faces of other children, so many and so beautiful in their pride and enthusiasm for the music they were making. He will forever have with him how they looked when they played their strange but surprisingly sweet-sounding instruments, fashioned out of old cans and other trash from the city dump.

Whose heart could resist those dear little faces, serious and determined as they strummed or bowed or blew.

"When I play, I'm away from here, somewhere safe and beautiful," a girl told him.

"My soul smiles when the music comes from my flute," a teenage boy confided. "If I'm angry, sad or in love, I can say it with my flute. I take it wherever I go."

Baldemar's face comes to him now, its hills and furrows sagging with age and hardship and griefs old and new. Yet when the former garbage picker turned craftsman shook Jamie's hand and smiled, the priest could see the shy, eager boy behind the aged skin.

He'd felt blessed to be there when the man presented new cellos, violins and flutes to several aspiring musicians. If delight could be personified in flesh and bone and tissue, Jamie has seen it in the body language and expressions of the man and the children. A pigtailed girl had carefully placed her oil drum cello against a chair, then ran to Baldemar and hugged him fiercely. *"Oh abuelo, que regalo es! Gracias de todo corazón!"* she'd cried. "What a gift, Grandfather. Thank you from all my heart!"

But the faces he remembers most poignantly are those of parents seeing their children play music for the first time in a public concert. He'd watched from behind the worn curtains of the stage at San Salvador's musical institute. As the strains of a piece by Salvadoran composer José Andrino filled the auditorium, Jamie had observed those faces—many bearing the marks of lifelong struggle—transfigured in a way he will never forget.

He'd suddenly recalled a painting in a Milan gallery of the disciples who'd met the risen Jesus on the road to Emmaus. The artist had captured the instant when the two had recognized their Lord in the breaking of the bread. Their sheer wonder and amazed joy at the sight of Him had touched Jamie so deeply that the disciples' faces still live in his mind.

In the mothers' and fathers' responses to their children performing, he'd seen that same rapture. It was as though these men and women shaped by pain and poverty had suddenly looked upon Paradise. As he'd watched them seeing their sons and daughters enter futures filled with new possibilities, Jamie had fallen completely, irrevocably in love for the third time in his life. First, with Abrilla and her children, then with Sarah, and now with the people of El Salvador.

He can still feel the soft fabric of the old red theater

curtains, the ancient dust tickling his nose and the spotlights warming his face. And he knew he had been born to serve people like these and in turn be transformed and inspired by them. Any gift he could give would be returned a hundredfold.

Jamie dozes. He's jolted awake by a realization that's like a kick to the solar plexus. Sarah!

He's opened his life to this woman and drawn her deeply into it. Now, if his superiors consent, he'll leave her all too soon. And she will have have no part, no say, in the direction of their mutual future. Doesn't he owe it to her to ask her to help him discern God's will before he himself makes a decision? Oh Lord, everything is getting complicated, and it is not hard to figure out why. He has been behaving as if he were free to enter into a continuing love relationship with a woman. He isn't. In loving Sarah, he' s beating his head against the wall of his priestly commitment.

Fittingly, Jamie's head begins to ache. He closes his eyes and attempts to clear his mind. There's no point in letting his thoughts race in useless circles that take him nowhere. It's impossible to plan ahead in this situation. He'll have to live it out, step by step. He needs to pray for light on the path that beckons.

TWENTY-FIVE

Sarah looks at him sadly. "Jamie, I have no right to an opinion. The decision will have to be between you, your superiors and God. Period."

"Are you angry?" he asks, placing his cup down on the table of the almost-empty cafe. "I'm putting you in an impossible position. In your place, I think I'd be angry."

"I'm angry. I'm sad. And a lot of good that will do me. You come back from El Salvador and tell me stories that break and delight my heart. You're a good storyteller. We're connected. I can feel what you feel.

"At times I'm so frustrated by our situation, I want to scream. You should have seen me at the ranch one day while you were gone. My parents were in town, so I was the only one around. I was walking in the orchard, thinking about us and the old men who run the Church and their crazy rules."

She looks embarrassed. "I had a meltdown, a full-blown tantrum. I was lying on the ground like a furious little kid. I cried. I screamed as loud as I could—-and flailed my arms. I said very unflattering things to God. If you'd seen me, I would have scared you. I certainly startled myself.

"It was incredibly cathartic. I felt great when it was over. Maybe a woman crazy enough to love a priest has to be able to go completely nuts once in a while when she's alone. Or I could do it *in front of you* and solve the whole problem. It would certainly turn you off." She tries to laugh but it quickly fizzles out.

Jamie feels a stab of pain around his heart. He doesn't know what to say.

Sarah stares through the window at the street outside the cafe. Her body slumps.

"At this moment I just feel kind of depressed. I don't want to lose you so soon. You warned me. But now it's not just theoretical. You're a priest with commitments. My appearing in your life doesn't change any of that." She's quiet for a while, and Jamie still doesn't speak. He wants her to have the chance to tell him all she's thinking and feeling.

Finally, Sarah continues.

"I've looked at us from every point of view I can come up with. I've prayed myself silly. I've made a scene, even though only God and a couple of rabbits were around to see it. I've talked with Chiara and my Mom. And do you know what conclusion I've come to after all this?"

Despite the fact they're in a very public place, Jamie leans close and takes her hand. "Tell me," he whispers.

She shivers at his touch. Her mind flashes to the night on the creek when she'd allowed herself to have this man in fantasy. "It's simple," she says in a low voice. "I love you. So I want to support you. Whatever form that takes. It's all I can do." She pauses.

"This makes me sound like a saint, doesn't it?" Now she smiles with an exaggerated pious expression, her eyes raised as if to heaven. "I certainly hope you'll testify in my behalf during the canonization process!"

It's Jamie's turn to be amused. He's on the edge of wild laughter. Being with this woman is like riding a roller coaster! He loves it. God, how he loves her!

"If you don't stop it, I'll propose marriage," he says. "If you accept, we can go off into the sunset together so you can live miserably ever after with a defrocked priest."

"Defrocked? Hmm...that sounds interesting," Sarah jokes. "If that means what I think it does, I just may accept."

She sighs. "I talk a good game, but I'm as selfish as the next woman. I've never had to make the sacrifices other women do as wives and mothers, so I'm probably even more selfish.

"I have no idea if I have what it takes to live up to what loving you demands. I just know I want to with all my heart and soul." She grins. "My body's not so sure." He looks at her. Something in her voice sounds strange.

When they return to discussing his visit to El Salvador, Jamie confides his loss of confidence. "The experience in the hospital was traumatic," he says. "That little boy showed me my limitations. How arrogant and pathetic to be a privileged North American thinking I can help people like him."

"Jamie, what are you talking about? One of your great strengths is that you don't see yourself as some savior to the poor unfortunates. You're a man in love, and you're always aware that you receive so much more than you can give.

"It's love, not ego, that's calling you. You long to be of service. There's no doubt in my mind that if you go down there, you'll touch many lives in healing ways. Never underestimate the power of your loving."

"I can't believe I'm encouraging you to leave me for El

Salvador!" She shakes her head and crosses her eyes. They laugh.

Jamie walks her home. "We'll still have months together," he reminds her as they head up the steep hill above PTU. "Will you stay with me?"

Sarah brushes his arm with her hand. "Of course I will."

"WHAT A GREAT PLACE!" Sarah exclaims as Jamie ushers her into Casa de Nuestra Señora de Guadalupe. Before she can take in the colors, sounds and lively atmosphere of the place, two small dark children race up and throw themselves at Jamie's legs.

"Padre, Padre!" they plead in high voices. "Come play with us!"

The priest pretzels himself down to their level. *"Buenas dias, Tia! Hola,* Tomas!" He hugs them, then stands up and brings Sarah forward. *"Esta es mi amiga. Su nombre es* Sarah." Tia and Tomas look up at her, their eyes still dancing in pleasure. *"Estoy muy feliz de conocerle, señora,"* the little girl says. The boy glances at her shyly, tongue-tied.

She bends down and shakes two little hands. They regard her with brief curiosity, then go back to what's important. "Will you play with us, Padre? *Por favor!"*

"I can't today," Jamie says regretfully. Their faces fall. "But I'll be back next week and we can play then, OK?" They aren't going to let him off that easily.

"Will you play Burro Rodeo?" Tomas enquires with a mischievous smile.

"I will," the priest replies with obvious resignation.

"Yay!" the children shout. "Promise, Padre?"

"I promise!" Satisfied, they run away.

"Burro Rodeo?" Sarah's grin is wide. "Don't ask!" Jamie says.

"Forget asking. I want to be there! Where can I buy a ticket?"

A small energetic woman bustles up to them.

"Jamie," she says happily. "How wonderful to see you! And you've brought a friend!" She turns to Sarah, smiling. "How good to meet you, my dear. I'm Rosa, Jamie's unofficial sister."

"I'm Sarah, and I've heard many good things about you." Spontaneously, the two women embrace. In the moment Rosa takes in a great deal of information. First, she likes this Sarah; she's warm and appealing. Second, this woman is the reason for the positive changes she's seen in Jamie in the past few months. The sadness and depression are gone. He's the happy, vibrant person she's known. Third, there's love between these two.

Naturally, the Guatemalan woman is wildly curious. A short time later the three are drinking coffee at a table on the patio behind the building. "I just got back from El Salvador," Jamie says conversationally. "I went down there for a week."

Rosa can scarcely believe what she's hearing. Her body goes rigid.

"What do you mean?" she hisses. Her voice trembles. "Why in God's name would you go there, Jamie?"

At the intensity of her reaction, Jamie mentally kicks himself. What was he thinking, blurting that out to someone for whom Central America is a living nightmare that never fades? He takes her hands in his and speaks softly, his face close to hers. "Forgive me, *hermana de mi corazon*, sister of my heart, I didn't think what you'd feel to hear that! It was stupid of me, insensitive. I'm sorry!"

The little woman's face remains stony, impervious to his gesture and words.

"When you told me about being drawn to the South, I always thought you meant Mexico or South America," she says angrily. "That was the impression you gave me. I never dreamed you'd be crazy enough to go where some evil men have been given the power of life and death over the good people. No one is safe there! Stay away, Jamie!

Her face crumples and her body sags. "*Dios mio, Dios mio!*" she exclaims, overcome with emotion.

Sarah watches helplessly. Jamie has forgotten her presence, so focused is he on his friend. Instead of feeling left out, she loves him more for the depth of his concern.

Suddenly, Rosa recovers herself. She regards Sarah with chagrin. "Oh my dear, my behavior is unforgivable! What a welcome for someone my beloved brother loves so much. Please excuse me. I just..." Her voice fades out.

Now it's Jamie's and Sarah's turn to be shocked. How could Rosa know what no one had told her. Until today, she has never even heard Sarah's name. They look at one another. Then, without planning, both stand and move their chairs around the table so they're on either side of the small woman. They each put an arm around her. The coffee cools. No one notices.

Later the two women sit together as Jamie presides at liturgy. Thanks to her Italian and the Spanish she's studied, Sarah is able to understand most of the Mass and his homily. If she can't decipher something, Rosa will whisper a translation.

Jamie begins by saying that, until he visited El Salvador recently, he'd been rather proud of his ability to forgive those who had harmed or offended him. Now he realizes he knows nothing about forgiveness. There's never been anything in his life that requires the level of forgiveness Jesus was talking about when he told his community to 'love your enemies. Do good to those who hate you. Pray for those who mistreat you.'

"Before I went to Central America, I thought I was being a good Christian if I forgave someone who hurt me or insulted me or did something I really didn't like. In El Salvador I met people whose spouses and parents and children had been tortured and maimed and brutally murdered by other people who didn't seem to have the slightest remorse for what they'd done.

"Hearing their stories—terrible beyond my nightmares—I suddenly realized what Jesus asks of us. And I thought, 'that is unreasonable. That is unfair. He surely cannot be asking a dear little *campesino* mother whose husband and children have been murdered by militia members to forgive those evil men. It's too much to require of a human being!' "

Jamie tells of meeting such a mother who lost her entire family less than three years ago in a massacre at a small rural town.

"Maria Teresa escaped death only because she had gone to visit her sick mother on a nearby hacienda that day. She returned home to find her entire village in flames, her husband, her two sons and her three-year-old daughter dead."

When Jamie had met her in a refugee camp, she was helping mothers, many of them widows, care for their children in the stark and difficult environment. "She told me, 'Padre, these little ones I can hold and touch and kiss are saving my life and my soul. Without their sweetness, I would be dead in every way.'

"I was frankly at a loss for words. Finally, I asked her how in the world she could hope to let go of hate for those who had done unspeakable things to her family." 'Oh it is so hard,

Padre, because sometimes I want to kill them,' she told me. 'But every time a baby smiles at me or reaches out her arms...when I can comfort a child and feel his little body warm against mine, a bit of the hate leaves me. I know now that only love can save me,' she said."

Jamie is silent. He looks around, his eyes meeting the eyes of those in the congregation. "I know nothing about forgiveness, but I have discovered there are ordinary people in this world who are the living images of Jesus forgiving his executioners. They may even surpass Our Lord's forgiveness because the horror was not done to them, but to those they loved most.

"And I bow in reverence to all the amazing human beings —including some of you—who are teaching themselves to change hate into love. They are fulfilling Jesus' every dream for humanity. In these, his beloved sisters and brothers, his true disciples, he must rejoice and be glad."

If a heart can sink and rise up at the same time, that's what is happening in Sarah's breast as she listens to Jamie's words. How can it be that her imperfect, unremarkable self can inspire love in this man? She hasn't a clue.

She turns to see Rosa watching her.

"You are giving him new life," the woman says in a barely audible voice. "I see this, and *I rejoice*." Sarah grips the woman's hand and feels the warmth of the rough palm against her smooth one.

When the Mass ends, Jamie is surrounded by people wanting to speak with him, some privately. He'd told Sarah this would probably occur. Rosa leads her through the busy kitchen to a small table in an alcove away from most of the activity.

For a while, they chat about the center and the Sarah's

Biblical classes. Rosa is interested in the roles of women in Scripture. "I would love that class," she says wistfully.

"Well, if I were more fluent in Spanish, I'd teach some of the material over here," Sarah replies.

"Would you really? You wouldn't have to teach completely in Spanish. A lot of people would like to hear more about the Bible and most of them know some English. I could be there to translate the complicated ideas." Her voice is enthusiastic. "Between the two of us, I believe we could make this work."

Sarah had made the offer casually, never expecting it would be taken seriously. Now she thinks about what it would mean to teach in this place and for these people Jamie loves. Why not? It takes only slightly more than half an hour to get from Berkeley to the Mission on the rapid transit BART train. "I'd like to teach here," she says impulsively.

"Oh this is good news!" Rosa beams. "We will learn a lot about women in the Bible, and you and I can get to know each other."

They part warmly, with promises to be in touch. Jamie watches them with satisfaction. As they walk to the train station, Sarah tells him about the Bible class. His eyes widen and so does his smile.

"That's wonderful. I thought you two would like one another. I won't be surprised if you become good friends." Sarah experiences a rush of joy. God is giving her an opportunity to share in Jamie's life more deeply and even have a part in his ministry.

TWENTY-SIX

Jamie and Sam are in their living room preparing for their classes. "What are you doing Friday night?" Jamie asks.

"I'm sure I have a hot date," Sam replies. "But I'll break it if you have something better."

Jamie grins at his fellow Jesuit He usually enjoys his sarcastic approach to life. "I'd like to cook dinner and invite a new friend of mine, Sarah Caffaro. You know her."

"The Gypsy. I tease her about her weird clothes." Sam pauses and eyes his roommate with a quizzical expression. "Why is there something strange in your voice when you mention her name?"

"What do you mean?" To his great chagrin, Jamie feels himself blushing.

Now Sam pounces. "What's going on?" he demands. "Why do you look guilty?"

"Oh this is going really well!" Jamie thinks. "Well, we're

not having sex and don't intend to," he declares. "Does that relieve your mind?"

"Not particularly. You tell me you want to invite a new female friend to dinner and immediately mention sex. I shouldn't be worried?"

Jamie begins to laugh. What else can he do?

"I like Sarah. I want to invite her to dinner. The three of us. I tell you, and you immediately imply there's something nefarious going on."

"Is there?" Now Sam is serious.

Jamie sighs. He might as well come clean since his house-mate will eventually have to know. "I care about her. I've only known her a few months, but we have a really strong connection. I'm not running off with her or anything like that. But to be honest, I have feelings for her."

"My God! So this is where the mid-life crisis went! Here I thought you'd resolved it. Instead you've gone off the deep end."

Now Jamie is angry. "I really appreciate being considered a damned cliche! Do you have any other wise insights to share? I can hardly wait!"

The two men have risen and now face one another. The exchange threatens to become more hostile, the last thing Jamie wants. He stops himself from escalating the anger. He looks at Sam.

"I'm sorry," he says quietly. "It's just that your attitude upsets me."

When Sam speaks, his voice is intentionally more relaxed.

"Let's sit down, have a beer, and you tell me about you and Sarah. I'll listen and try to put aside my essential jerk-hood. OK?"

Haltingly, feeling embarrassed, Jamie recounts the story

of the relationship as honestly and openly as he can manage. It's clear from Sam's face that he's dismayed.

When Jamie finishes, Sam shakes his head.

"Oh Jamie, I don't have to tell you you're playing with fire, excuse the cliche. I never thought you'd get caught up in this kind of thing. You've always been so much in charge when it comes to women. This is such an old story, and I hate to hear you telling it. What does Richard say?"

"I haven't told him yet. I debated telling you, because I knew what to expect. Suspicion. Disapproval. A predictable assessment of the relationship."

"Then why are you telling me?"

"Because you're one of my best friends, we live together, and I can't keep something this important from you. We're not doing anything wrong, Sam. I don't know how well you know Sarah, but she's a very independent woman. She likes her life. She's not longing to get married. She knows all the limitations on any relationship with me, and she accepts them. And when she's no longer willing to abide by the rules I have to live by, she'll tell me. She's an honorable person, Sam. I trust her."

"I suppose you think you love her?"

It is pointless to argue or get defensive.

"I do."

Sam closes his eyes. He drums his fingers on the arm of the chair.

The uncomfortable silence deepens.

Finally, he speaks. "You're like my brother, Jamie. And I see disaster ahead if you go this way."

Jamie observes his blonde, bearded friend with affection. "Sam, I've prayed about Sarah and me for months. Every day, many times a day. Despite what it may sound like, I'm actively working to discern God's will in the situation. I admit I'm also looking at the signs—the birds, the butterflies, our meeting on the pier. I'm certainly not interpreting these as God's approval, but they are strange, positive incidents of synchronicity.

"And the peace, that deep, profound sense of peace I've experienced from the first moment I saw her face. I take that very seriously. I looked across that room, and it wasn't lust or attraction I felt. It was a peace beyond my understanding. It was like my life had been completed.

"Sam, it's not impossible that Sarah's a gift of God. I feel my capacity to love opening and expanding because of her. Maybe I can be a better priest through this." His friend looks extremely skeptical.

"I need you, a friend and a fellow Jesuit, to help me discern what God wants." Jamie continues. "It's not clear to me that the only right thing is cutting off the relationship. You know I normally wouldn't hesitate to do just that. But, Sam, there's something about what's happening now with Sarah that keeps me with her. I can't explain it, but it feels of God."

"What do you want from me?" Sam sounds impatient and unconvinced.

Jamie considers. "I'd like you to be our friend. I intend to keep my vow. You can help me. We need people who give us a space to be together as friends. We can't afford to be a secret couple. That's trouble in the making. Do you understand what I mean? Are you willing?"

"What if I say no? What will you do then?"

Jamie frowns. "I don't know. I don't blame you for not wanting to get involved. I just wish you'd at least give it a chance."

Sam goes to the window overlooking the street. He stands there, watching a few late-night cars passing. Finally he turns back to his friend.

"Oh hell...I'll try," he says in a resigned tone. "In return will you promise to talk with Richard soon?"

Jamie nods assent. "I will."

"Sarah seems like good people. I enjoy talking with her," Sam admits. "However, if you want a mellow, relaxed atmosphere on Friday night, you'd better find a way compatible with your vow of poverty to provide me with a whole lot of decent wine."

HAVING FINISHED a salmon dinner and a respectable amount of decent wine contributed by his friend Mark, Jamie, Sam and Sarah have moved to a sofa and comfortable chairs in the living room. The conversation has been wide-ranging, from stories of life at PTU to the state of the world to anecdotes of some of the stranger aspects of the Church.

"You may have noticed that Jamie cooked fish for dinner on Friday," Sam tells Sarah. "He's really a very conservative Catholic at heart. He's afraid the change in the Church's teaching about meat on Friday during Vatican II may not have been officially adopted in heaven."

"That was a good one, wasn't it?" Sarah grins. "Imagine, being taught that if you ate a hamburger on Friday and died before going to Confession, you would spend eternity burning in hell! And I believed it totally. Most of us did."

"When the Church changed the law, I wondered about the people who supposedly were in hell for having a steak on the wrong day of the week. I figured they must be really pissed," Sam counters. "I sure hope the divine tribunal reviewed those cases!"

They all laugh.

The subject brings to mind other Catholic peculiarities. "Do you remember those little magazines with stories of holy children?" Jamie asks. "They were all so appallingly perfect. Obedient. Sweet. Unfailingly kind. Self-sacrificing."

"I do, and I remember they always died very young," Sarah says. "I decided being too good must be hazardous to your health." More laughter.

"Don't forget ransoming the pagan babies!" Sam reminds them. "Those little cardboard houses we put our money in during Lent. How much did it cost to ransom a baby and get them baptized?"

"I think it was five dollars, and that was a lot back then," Jamie says. "If we raised and saved the cash, we got to name the babies, right?"

"Oh yes, indeed," Sarah replies. "And thanks to a certain Classics Illustrated comic book about ancient Rome and Egypt I read when I was nine or ten, there are two grown people somewhere in Africa named Marc Anthony and Cleopatra Marie!" The men guffaw.

"And considering the obvious infallibility of our Church's past teachings and customs, how can we possibly doubt that celibacy and chastity are God's expressed will?" Jamie says daringly.

"Stop that!" Sarah exclaims. "You're going to scare Sam. He's just giving you a hard time," she tells the other Jesuit.

Sam looks at her, perplexed.

"I simply don't know what to make of you," he says.

"It's all part of the mysterious feminine," she answers. "You celibate males need to contemplate her more thoroughly."

Sam watches the two, the easy flow of conversation between them, the fun and good humor.

"My friend, you are in big, big trouble!" he thinks. Yet at the same time he can't help envy Jamie for having a woman like this in his life.

The talk turns to Christian theology "Who is Jesus Christ for you?" Sam asks Sarah, seeking to understand who she is as a person and a Catholic. She is silent for a while, her eyes focused inward.

"Conveying the essence of great truth in words is the soul of the dilemma for those of us who study and teach religion, isn't it?" she says finally.

"I can't answer your question well, Sam, because who Jesus is for me is an experience, not a concept. I experience him with spiritual faculties...my heart...my spirit...inner silence...a sense of wonder...my capacity for loving.

"There's a poem to the Hindu deity Krishna that I've turned into a Christian prayer for myself. It speaks to what we're talking about. Would you like to hear it?" The men nod.

Sarah recites the words slowly and distinctly.

"As wing to bird,
water to fish,
life to the living,
so You to me.
Yet tell me,
Jesus, beloved,
Who are you?
Who are you really?"

The three exchange glances.

"I agree we've let doctrine and dogma obscure the

197

mystery of Christ," Sam says, liking the way Sarah's mind works. "And who he is for a person depends so much on where that man or woman is coming from. The Christ of the theologian and the Christ of the mystic aren't the same."

Jamie smiles to himself. His Jesuit brother is discovering Sarah is someone who thinks and experiences in profound ways.

"Well, you may be a heretic, but you're an interesting one," Sam quips. "Next time you can interrogate us about our beliefs."

"I look forward to that opportunity," Sarah says with laughter in her voice. "And perhaps we can start with the implications of the fact that the word heretic comes from the Greek '*hairetikos*' meaning 'able to choose.' " She sends them a look of delighted mock superiority.

This factoid is news to both Jesuits, and the evening ends in amusement and good feelings.

"Come again," Sam invites.

"Thanks for a wonderful time," she tells them, smiling.

Jamie walks her to her car.

"I think that went really well," he says happily.

"Yes, it went so well I suspect Sam's going to be even more worried about you and me than he was before. Please be open to what he has to say. He knows you; he cares about you. He can help you find God's will for you in our relationship in ways that I simply cannot."

Jamie looks at her, surprised.

"Even if he wants me to stay away from you?"

"If you're really open to discernment, you have to listen to all voices with an open mind," she insists. "You know I don't want to have to separate, but I do want what's best for you. Sam is part of the equation in your discerning what to do."

As she drives away, Jamie remains standing there. He feels humble and grateful and joyful and sad, all at the same time. "This is what it means to be truly loved," he thinks and his heart moves tenderly toward the woman giving him such a gift. "Lord, please let me love her as well and generously as she loves me," he prays.

TWENTY-SEVEN

Jamie laughs so hard that Sarah worries he might fall off the bench.

"Only once?" he manages to get out between bouts of mirth.

"All I can say, Father, is you must be very sought after as a confessor." she retorts, trying to keep a straight face.

This is his response to her confessing her sexual fantasy about him! She hadn't known what to expect from Jamie, but it wasn't hilarity.

Suddenly, the ridiculousness of the whole situation strikes her, and she begins to chuckle. Soon their laughter is uproarious. Fortunately, there's no one around to hear them in the secluded area of the PTU campus on a Saturday afternoon in April.

"Oh Sarah, do you know how many dreams I've had of making love with you?" Jamie asks. "I mean actual dreams. In my sleep you and I have a very passionate relationship. And not a single vow is broken."

"So it's your fault that I fell into sin, you cad!" she exclaims. "I try to be pure, and all those nights you're seducing me in your dreams? You should be ashamed!"

They regard one another with glee.

"Maybe you need to do cultivate your own dreams," Jamie tells her. "That's the only no-fault way for us to be lovers! Just think of me fondly when you go to bed."

"Well, if you can have dreams, then I can have fantasies. No vows to stop me." She gives him a merry glance, then her face changes.

"Jamie, what are we doing? What's going to happen? I don't know about your dreams, but the sexual feelings I had in that fantasy were so intense they scared me. Now, hearing about your dreams makes me wonder how long we can go on like this. Where's in God's name is it leading?"

It's Jamie's turn to be serious. He's glad they're in a public place, so strong is his own physical response to her words.

"I can't answer your questions, Sweetheart. I have no idea. I want you. You want me. We're not allowed to be together as a man and a woman. Every day I pray to know God's will. The only answer I get is more love and more confusion."

They sit, quietly and soberly contemplating the conundrum of their relationship. They both know there are good sensible reasons to end it now. Jamie believes his spiritual director would advise him to cut Sarah out of his life. Sarah is sure most Catholics, including her father and brother, would concur. And yet...

In loving this man, Sarah is feeling her heart expand. Opening herself so deeply to Jamie is also reaching beyond him. As they become closer, she understands that she can reveal all of herself to him, both the light and the shadow, and still be loved completely. For the first time in her life she's willing to be fully vulnerable to another.

This epiphany that's changing her. She's seeing more clearly the vulnerability of other people. Her annoying neighbor who's always forcing his right-wing political views on her she now comprehends as a lonely old man trying to connect by engaging her attention. An obnoxious teenager strutting down the street accompanied by loud music wants to be seen and appreciated for daring to be herself.

Last week, she'd seen Giulia in a new light, not just as her mother, but as a woman with a whole dimension of life beyond her children. As Sarah listened carefully, she heard a woman who was confronting the process of aging and her own mortality. Quietly and subtly enough that it would be easy to miss, Giulia was mourning her changing looks and waning energy and fearful of what would happen to her physically as her body began to fail.

When she responded to what she was observing more as a friend than a daughter, her mother seemed startled and uncomfortable at first. Then, as Sarah gently led her with genuine interest, Giulia talked and revealed her fears and concerns. It had turned into one of the most intimate conversations the two women had ever shared. When it was over, her mother had hugged her for a long time. "Thank you, my darling girl," she said, her eyes moist. "It did your old mother a world of good to be able to talk like this to someone who loves me."

Yes, loving Jamie is changing her in sweet ways, making her more the person she's always wanted to be. So it's hard to imagine that what they're sharing is not God's gift, sex dreams and fantasies notwithstanding.

Now she describes those experiences to Jamie.

"This is where my love for you is leading me. Could God really be asking me to walk away from you?"

"It's happening to me too!" Jamie exclaims. "I'm seeing people more compassionately. I definitely haven't turned into a saint with other people. Just ask Sam. Still, there is a difference in me and it's for the better."

"But isn't the whole purpose of chastity and celibacy to make you more loving to everyone? Isn't it to keep you totally available to God and all people?"

"That's the theory. It's what I've been taught. Having a personal love relationship with a woman would make me less giving and available as a priest. It's always sounded right. I've believed it, lived by it.

"Now here I am loving you. You're always with me. But when people need me or I'm called upon to perform my priestly functions, your presence seems to deepen my capacities to be with others and respond to their needs. I don't begin to understand the alchemy of it, but that's what's happening, especially lately as we've grown so close."

"And I have to wonder if my professors and the Church itself are wrong. After all, they haven't tested the theory. If a priest loves someone the way I love you and desires her sexually, his superiors give him a choice: cut it out or get out. So the Church *could be* way off base." He grins. "Nothing like a bit of chutzpah on a Sabbath afternoon."

"Jamie, surely there are priests in loving, intimate, even sexual relationships they've had to keep secret. You must know some, or at least suspect. What kind of priests are these men?"

Startled, Jamie realizes he knows several who have close friendships with women, often nuns. He's always assumed the relationships were platonic. Has he been wrong? Have these people wrestled with the same temptations and feelings as he and Sarah and succumbed? It's not something priests and sisters tend to discuss with one another. Calling the men in question to mind, he reviews his impressions of them. He has to smile, because, to a man, they're warm and giving individuals, caring and kind. It is interesting that if he were asked to name those he considers to be holy priests, priests he himself would like to emulate, those men would be on that list.

When he confides this to Sarah, joy spreads across her face.

"That's great to hear. Even if it doesn't prove anything, it seems like a good sign."

TWENTY-EIGHT

S arah often spends one weekend a month in Sonoma. When he's free, Jamie accepts her parents' open invitation and joins her for a day.

During his visits, Sarah watches, both amused and annoyed, as her father turns Jamie into the acknowledged expert on all things Christian. Never mind that she has a PhD in Biblical studies, which includes the history of the early Christian community that produced the founding documents. Never mind that she's an avid student of Christian spiritual writers. Franco, who hardly ever asks his daughter a question about her areas of expertise, is eager to hear what Jamie has to say on all these subjects.

Jamie the psychologist quickly notices what's happening and lets Sarah know he sees it and finds it humorous. "A scholar is without honor in her own country," he whispers as they pass in the hall. She gives him a playful slap.

"The women in my family can't stand that the Church

still makes them second-class citizens," Franco says. "Why do you think that is, Jamie?"

"Yes, Father, please tell us how people as smart as the Jesuits would explain such injustice," Sarah adds sweetly, gazing at him, eyes wide with mock admiration.

Jamie can't help it. He snorts with laughter. "Because those old men who run the Church are damned fools," he replies. "And because they're not allowed to have sex, they're scared to have women around."

Giullia applauds spontaneously and looks like she's about to jump up and kiss him. Startled by his candor, Franco stares at his guest.

"I'm sure there are more nuanced answers to your question, Franco, but I stand by my opinion. Please don't tell Anthony. He probably wouldn't approve if he knew what a flaming liberal has sneaked into his home under the clerical collar I hardly ever wear.

"Seriously, It's wrong and stupid to exclude women from the inner life of the church and its structures of authority. Sarah can tell you how prominently Jesus' female disciples figured in his life and ministry." He turns toward her with a deferential gesture.

"She's the scripture scholar, not me. And when it comes to the subject of Jesus and women, her academic work is impressive." Her parents faces swivel in her direction, obviously surprised at the notion their daughter knows more than a Jesuit.

Sarah smiles at this man who makes her love and like him more with every passing day.

"It's true," she says. "Jesus' relationships with women were completely countercultural. They're actually the most revolutionary aspect of his ministry. His contemporaries must have considered him a reprobate and a libertine because he had women disciples and allowed women who were not relatives to be part of his inner circle.

"Anyone who studies what we can glean from the New Testament about Jesus and women can't help but be amazed by his lack of sexism in a culture where women were little more than chattels of their fathers, husbands and sons."

In response to Jamie's respectful questioning, Sarah lays out the evidence of Jesus' egalitarian treatment of the female sex. Her parents listen, rapt.

"What happened? Why did it all change?" Giulia wants to know. A lively conversation follows. Sarah explains and gives examples of how Jesus having women disciples and treating them as he did would have shocked and horrified many of his contemporary rabbis. She goes on to tell how the early Christian community began to diminish women's status as leaders and apostles, reflecting not Jesus' teaching and actions toward them, but the sexism of the ancient Mediterranean cultures.

"My daughter is not only beautiful; she's brilliant," Franco brags at the end of the evening.

"You're only recognizing that now?" Jamie asks.

"I guess I didn't realize how much she knew," the older man admits. Sarah is warm with satisfaction.

Later, his arms around his wife and daughter, Franco stands watching the the priest's car disappear.

"I love that guy," he says enthusiastically. "It's really too bad he's not available for you, Sweetie," he tells Sarah.

"I know," she replies, turning to give him a kiss. "It's a shame, isn't it?" She glances at her mother. Emotions dance in the women's eyes, deep feelings floating on the breezes of the summer night.

❦

SARAH HAS DECIDED NOT to reveal the nature of her relationship with Jamie to her father, sister and brother unless they ask. Until then, they probably aren't ready to know, she reasons. And if she's honest, she dreads that future moment.

With Franco, that time arrives on Labor Day when Jamie joins the family for a holiday barbecue. Sarah has been there all weekend.

It begins when her father intercepts a brief but tender look between the two of them. He spends the rest of the day observing the pair closely and realizes his daughter and this Jesuit he loves like a son are more than just friends. After all the company's gone, he invites Sarah to walk with him to the creek. As they sit on the bank and watch the water in the twilight, he wastes no time.

"Are you and Jamie lovers?"

She is startled and suddenly afraid. She offers a silent prayer before replying.

"Not physically, Daddy, because he has vows to keep. But, yes, in the sense we love one another deeply... we're lovers in that way."

Franco is silent at first, taking in what she's told him, then explodes into anger.

"Why are you doing this? For God's sake, you know there's no future in it! And it's a mortal sin!" Sarah feels tears rush to her eyes. When she answers, her voice is choked with emotion.

"There's no rational way to explain it, Daddy. The love came. Nobody invited it. I feel things I've never felt before. Sometimes it's overwhelming and frightening. At the same time, I've never known such peace. It's like this great, unexpected gift from God has come to me.

"It's exactly the same for Jamie. He's a man who's guarded himself against this kind of love for sixteen years.

He's always been faithful to the spirit as well as the letter of his vow of chastity. And suddenly all the barriers he'd erected against just this kind of experience were swept away. He met me, and his life changed too."

Franco stares at her in the growing dark. His eyes are hard.

"I welcome him to my home and treat him like a son, and he does this! He betrays the Church and my daughter and my family. I thought I knew him, but I guess I have no idea who he is."

Sarah begins to weep quietly in the hostile atmosphere.

"Why didn't he tell me what was going on?!" Her father is almost shouting. "At least he owed me that!"

Now Sarah's anger erupts.

"What are you saying… what are you implying?" she cries. "We haven't committed some great sin! We haven't broken any church law! We love one another, and we're trying to live that love in integrity. He intends to keep his vow. I don't want to harm him, so I intend to help him keep it. He's a wonderful person, a fine priest, a very good man. I can' t bear to hear you talk about him that way!

"He thought we should tell you how we were feeling, but I said no. I said we should wait until you noticed yourself. I was afraid that, until you could see what was happening between him and me, you just weren't ready to know."

Her voice breaks. "Dad, do you have any idea what you mean to Jamie? This is a man who lost his father when he was nine years old. The first time he meets you, you tell him to think of you as a father. He does. He loves you too. He hasn't betrayed you. He hasn't betrayed anyone or anything!"

Now Franco feels confused and even a little ashamed. He wonders why he's so upset. His daughter and the priest have done nothing except fall in love. It's something that could happen to anyone. Even the Pope. Probably even Jesus himself.

"I'm sorry." He moves closer to Sarah and puts his arm around her, drawing her close. "Everything I know about Jamie, I love. I love him too, Honey. I don't understand why I got so angry. I guess I'm scared for both of you, and anger is easier to feel than fear.

"Does your mother know?"

"She knew the first time she met him. I'm glad you know too, Daddy. I hate keeping something so important from you."

"What are you two going to do? Is he thinking of leaving the priesthood?"

"No, and I don't want him to. It's who he is...it's all he's ever wanted to be."

"But what about you? This isn't fair to you. If you stay with Jamie, you'll never have children, a family of your own."

"Jamie worries about that, too, but I tell him that, at least for now, it doesn't matter to me. Look, I could be married if I'd wanted to. I could have married Brian. I could be engaged to Tim; he asked me. And as for children, it's getting a bit late, don't you think?

"Some people aren't the marrying kind. Maybe I'm one of them. Maybe I'm another Eugenia. There could be something genetic. I might have a spinster gene. "

They sit together on the creek bank. Darkness has fallen. They have no solution to the problem of a priest and a woman in love. Yet Sarah feels relieved she no longer has to keep such a secret from her father. It's like a great weight has been lifted from her spirit.

For Franco, it's not so easy. His doubts and outrage linger. He wants to trust in the goodness and rightness of what's between his daughter and this priest he considers like family. However, he simply can't shake his discomfort and vexation.

They flare in a fight with Giulia for not telling him what she knew. When she defends herself with the importance of keeping a confidence, he storms out of the house and wanders through the orchard in a rage. Later, he apologizes, and she accepts, but it's not over.

After Sarah tells Jamie, he makes a special trip to the ranch by himself to talk with her father. Speaking calmly now, Franco admits his alarm and anger.

"If you were free, I'd welcome you with the greatest pleasure," he tells the younger man. "I don't think Sarah could find a better husband.

"But you're not free, and I feel like I would if she was with a married man. You're married to the Church. By being with my daughter, you're stopping her from finding someone she could share all of her life with. It hurts me, because, whatever happens, Sarah's going to end up alone."

Jamie looks at Franco with a sorrowful expression. He feels the full burden of what he's doing to the woman he loves.

"You're right," he says in a voice laden with pain. "She could end up alone. I'll do everything in my power to show her I love her as long as I live. I can't always be with her physically, but in other ways I will be."

The older man is not satisfied. "That sounds very romantic, but it doesn't warm a person on cold winter night. Or take care of her when she's sick or hurt. What will Sarah have if you're sent somewhere else? A few letters and phone calls? As the years go by, and she gets older, what will you be able to give her?

"You're not your own man, Father!" he exclaims, using

the title to emphasize his point. Jamie has no answer. He stares at the ground.

"I've offered to go away. I've warned her that what I can give her is much less than she needs or deserves. There are times I lie awake and pray she'll leave me. Every time I bring these things up, she won't even listen! She says what we have together is enough for her, at least for now, that it's way more than she's ever had with anyone else.

"And, Franco, God forgive me, I stay with your daughter because I love her more than I can begin to tell you. I'm a priest. I can't imagine not being a priest. It's all I've wanted to be since I was a little boy. And…" he pauses, and when he speaks again, his voice is so low that other man has to strain to hear what he's saying. "I can't imagine my life without Sarah in it.

"Am I just a greedy, corrupt reprobate who wants it all and doesn't care who gets hurt in the process? Believe me, I've asked myself that question many times. I wake up to it in the middle of the night."

The two are sitting on a bench placed on a rise that gives a stunning vista of part of the Valley of the Moon. They gaze out over the rolling hills, turning green from early autumn rains. Orange and golden leaves hang on trees in the orchard.

Franco is silent for a long time. Finally, he looks directly into Jamie's eyes.

"I don't believe you're corrupt. You seem to be a good man, a moral man. That's certainly my impression from all I've seen and heard of you. And I can't deny that I've never known my daughter to be so happy in a relationship. She glows. Her joy warms me. And it's because of you.

"This is so confusing to me. I honestly don't know what I'd do in your place. I'll tell you one thing. I'm questioning the whole idea that priests can't be married and have families.

I've been doing some reading, and find that priests weren't absolutely forbidden to get married until the early part of the 12th century. And they made the rule was because some priests were passing church property to their children and heirs. Is that true?"

"Yes, but unfortunately, it's not that simple. I wish it were. Some priests were marrying and having families in the Latin Church. Then it was totally forbidden by the First Lateran Church Council in 1123." Jamie smiles. "Don't be surprised that I happen to know that date!

"But, Franco, being single and living in chastity has been a major value, and sometimes a requirement, all the way back to St. Paul. It's a very complicated history. Many of the Church Fathers considered that a life without sexual expression was a superior life. The body was considered the enemy of the soul. It dragged it down to the basest human nature. If a man could transcend the sexual demands of his body, he could be more holy and pleasing to God.

"The misogyny that's such a dark strain in our tradition comes out of this worldview. Women are tempting, so they're to be feared. And we know how easily fear slips into hatred."

"That was the old days, the dark ages," Franco objects. "Now we have psychology. We think differently. Why is the Church holding on to something so ignorant? It's just inhuman!"

"I can't answer that." Then Jamie grins. "But I can recommend some books in praise of celibacy and chastity. I've read them all.

"Franco, for me, the reality is that I've taken a solemn vow to be celibate and live in chastity. I chose to take it, and I made this vow publicly in the company of my Jesuit community. Since then—seventeen years now—I haven't been with a woman sexually ... not even a passionate kiss.

Franco regards the youthful priest. "My God, you know I've never really considered and imagined what it must be like for you guys. How in the hell do you do it?"

"Day by day with a lot of exercise and many cold showers."

The difficult moment passes, although Franco's negative feelings cannot be dissipated by any conversation. Yet the intimacy of their talk brings the two closer.

TWENTY-NINE

Permission for Jamie to work for a year with the Jesuit community in El Salvador is easy to obtain. His Jesuit superior has long known of his desire to serve in Latin America, and sympathizes with Diego Rios' desire to have north American Jesuits act as witnesses to the ongoing tragedy of the war. He's also aware more priests are needed to minister to its victims. Jamie's fluent Spanish and psychological training should make him especially useful.

His provincial superior in the Northwest promises to find people to take over Jamie's teaching duties and liturgical work with parishes. He leaves the province office in Portland with a backpack full of papers to fill out. Walking to the Jesuit residence where he's staying, Jamie thinks of Sarah, and his heart aches.

She is on his mind even more strongly than usual, because he has an appointment tomorrow with Richard, his Jesuit spiritual advisor. They'll discuss his plans to work in El Salvador, along with the state of Jamie's heart and soul.

He has to tell Richard about Sarah, and he's frankly worried. Will he be able to make his advisor understand that a love connection as intense as the one he and Sarah share can exist without threatening his priesthood? He'll have to admit the sexual temptation. Can Richard possibly believe the sincerity of their intention not to act on it? Or their ability to maintain control of their desires when even Jamie can't be sure of that?

He fears Richard will tell him that—under his vow of obedience—he must end the relationship. Then what? He can't even allow himself to think about it.

Despite the risk, Sarah is convinced it's time to tell Richard the truth. "You have to if you're going to be at peace with yourself," she'd insisted. "Jamie, I don't believe anything can take away what God has given us in one another. But we can't control the form. You have obligations that make that impossible. If you trust in this love, you have to trust that God will show us the way to continue to express it."

He's embarrassed that her faith is stronger than his.

"Hey, Stranger! It's great to see you!" Richard declares, reaching out to hug Jamie enthusiastically. He's a tall bear of a man with unruly white hair and a trim white mustache. His dark brown eyes shine with good humor and good will. "You're going to El Salvador. So that dream's coming true."

They meet in his book-lined office whose windows overlook lawns and trees. Oregon is garbed in autumn. Against the dark greens of pines and firs, birches and maples glow gold and scarlet in the rare but welcome late October sun.

The older priest grabs his jacket. He prefers to spend time with those he guides outdoors "in God's own home." As they walk, the two men talk at some length about what it will mean for Jamie to do ministry in El Salvador. They go on to discuss mutual friends. It's an easy conversation; it's hard to stay tense around Richard who seems to create an atmosphere of serenity wherever he is. Yet Jamie's heart is pounding.

Sitting at a picnic table set among tall trees, the Jesuit studies the younger man's face. "How *are you*, my friend?" he asks.

Jamie gazes at his longtime spiritual mentor. He breathes a prayer, remembering Sarah's words.

"There's a lot to tell you," he says.

His mentor's eyes are gentle. "I'd like to hear."

"I love a woman very deeply, and she loves me." Jamie looks into those eyes.

"Well, so far that is good news," Richard exclaims. "It's about time you fell in love. I was beginning to worry about you. Tell me about her. Is she going to take you away from us? Or is she going to make you a better priest?"

Jamie is so startled, his face turns red. He starts to laugh. "Well, for one thing, you and Sarah would make a great pair! I never know what to expect from either of you! I've dreaded this conversation for months. I should have known better."

Led by Richard's interest and concern, Jamie reveals the details of their relationship. They discuss everything, from Sarah's promise to support his priesthood to the sexual energies they struggle with, to Jamie's fears of harming this person he loves by the limitations he lives under. They talk for a long time, and Jamie is warmed and heartened by Richard's open and caring attitude.

"Were you afraid I was going to lay down the law and forbid you to see her?" the older priest asks him.

"Yes I was, and what really troubled me was that I didn't

217

know if I would obey you." His own candor makes him anxious. Richard is silent for a long time, looking into the nearby forest. Then, again, he surprises and shocks Jamie.

"I've loved a woman for almost thirty years," he says quietly. "What we have together is the wellspring of my priesthood. She's a Dominican sister. So far we've kept our vows, but we're lovers in our hearts and souls. I consider her one of God's greatest gifts to me as a man and a human being.

"Needless to say, I don't share this with everyone, because many people would disapprove strongly. But from my personal experience, I've come to believe I couldn't be a priest in the full sense of that call without Norah. I can't speak for every priest, but I know for myself that I *cannot* love as Jesus asks me to love his people if I have to barricade my heart. Maybe some can pull that off but not me. I need the divine, but I also need the personal. Since I realized you were dealing with many of the same problems I faced as a young priest before I met Norah...having to guard your heart...keeping emotional distance from women friends—I've been praying for you. A couple of times I actually dared to ask God to send the right person into your life as He has into mine."

Jamie is so moved he can hardly speak.

"Well, God has, and I'm grateful beyond words," he finally manages to say. "And I'm so relieved that I can have your guidance now. It feels like we're on such a dangerous path."

"There's no doubt it's challenging," Richard replies. "How do I love Norah without comprising my commitment to God, the people of God, the Church and the order? It's not something I can tell you. You'll have to learn through your own experience. Can a man hold all those commitments and do justice to each of them? What I have with Norah has convinced me it's possible.

"Look, I believe strongly in the values of celibacy and chastity or I couldn't live them. But I also realize this way of life has its own spiritual pitfalls. A Jesuit is supposed to be a man for others, but when you live without a truly intimate relationship with another person, it's easy to become self-centered and oblivious to your own failings. There's no one who knows you well enough to call you on them, no one to help you see your blind spots.

"Of course, that's supposed to happen in religious community, but it doesn't always work, especially in men's orders," Richard continues. "We can be superficial with the other guys. I know a lot of priests who relate chiefly around sports, gossip and religious politics. I've been to parties in rectories where the booze flowed freely, and I felt I could have been in a well-behaved frat house.

"Being with Norah has forced me to consider another person in ways that's keep me from living focused on myself. I have to think about her feelings, and that's extremely good for me. When I'm being a jerk, she'll let me know. We've had our fights and tensions. There's nothing like the abrasiveness of intimacy to wear away some of the rough edges, and I have plenty of those. I'm softer because of her. I'm happier and more content and at peace. That's why I'm convinced she helps me to be a better priest. I'm sure of it. Many of my fellow priests would say I'm rationalizing my behavior, and maybe I am. I'm trusting my own experience in something our vows don't specifically preclude."

"You've got to realize, Jamie, that mine may well be a minority opinion among Jesuits, although it's hard to know for sure, because people tend not to be forthcoming about certain things. I know I'm not alone, but I've no idea how

219

many of us there are. I have had some very moving conversations with priests and nuns involved with other people romantically, as Norah and I are, or even as lovers, which of course does happen."

Richard pauses to study Jamie, then goes on.

"I've always noticed you have a penchant for relationship, more than many of the priests I counsel. It can make you a wonderful priest or send you out of the priesthood because celibacy becomes unbearable. I've been waiting to see what would happen with you. I knew that someday you were going to fall deeply in love. I had no idea what the result would be, and I figured it would depend on who the woman was. If she wanted marriage and a family, then you'd be facing the the most difficult decision of your life. There was no way of telling how it would go.

"I thought you'd stay because being a priest is so integral to your identity, but I couldn't be sure. Now it looks like God has given you someone who will support you in your vocation. That's pretty damned rare for a woman who's not in religious life herself." Richard smiles. "It sounds like Sarah loves you very much. She's willing to make tremendous sacrifices for your sake. I hope you'll always appreciate that."

Now the tears flow from Jamie's eyes, and he doesn't try to hide them. He pulls a handkerchief from his pocket and wipes his face.

"I can't begin to tell you..." His voice breaks, and it's a minute before he is able to continue. "There's simply no way to express what it means to me...what she means to me. Every day I pray that I can be as much of a gift for her as she is for me. I don't know how that's possible, but all I want is for Sarah to have joy and peace and love and every good thing. We don't have the answers to how to be together. We'll have to live with the questions and see where they lead us."

The men fall silent. The wind is blowing the bright leaves in a kind of dance. The air has the tang of pine and wood smoke. James looks at Richard.

"I worry that someday I'll break my vow. We're both fighting powerful forces in us. We intend to be faithful to my commitment, but we're human and at times very vulnerable. Do you have any wisdom to share?"

"Every relationship is different, so it's almost impossible to advise another person," Richard replies. "From what you tell me, you're being careful in all the right ways. Beyond that, each individual has to find their own path as best they can. When God creates us, he or she didn't seem to plan for men and women to live without expressing their sexuality physically, even if our vow of chastity requires this," he adds. "Unfortunately, there aren't any books or articles to advise a priest or sister on how to remain chaste in a passionate love relationship."

"Maybe that tells us something," Jamie quips.

"Or it might mean there's an important book that needs to be written," the older priest retorts. "Perhaps you'll write it. Or Sarah will."

"What if we fail? What then?" Jamie asks. "Does that mean we'd have to separate, keep apart?"

"I can't answer a theoretical question like that. I don't know what to say. There's peril here, no doubt. And that's why I suspect most priests would advise you to end the relationship before you find yourself becoming lovers in all ways. I can't say they're not right, or that I'm not wrong to even suggest you and Sarah continue to negotiate your way.

"If I were you, I'd evaluate your relationship with Sarah by how it affects your ability to be a priest in the fullest sense of your call. To me that what's central; everything else is mere detail."

Richard grins. "I guess I could end up in hell for leading you astray, but I hope God wouldn't send me for what would be a sincere mistake. Anyway, hell's not something I worry about. At this stage, I only know the God of love."

"There've been so many moments of synchronicity in Sarah's and my relationship, like the meeting on the pier. This may be another one. I happen to have a Jesuit spiritual adviser who's a heretic when it comes to the subject of priests and women in love," Jamie teases.

"Just one more thing for you to thank God for," Richard declares with an ironic smile.

THIRTY

Sarah can still feel her shock.

Ensconced in her favorite place near Jewel Lake, she remembers how they'd stopped by her house to pick up a book she needed to work in the library with Jamie and had decided to stay there long enough for a cup of tea. Both of them were still basking in the relief that followed Richard's assurance that loving one another the way they did was not intrinsically wrong. The elder Jesuit's own experience with personal love had removed a weight from Jamie's heart.

"I didn't realize how heavy it was until Richard took it away," he'd admitted to her. "It's like I have a new freedom to love you."

They knew they couldn't stay at home for long. The sexual yearning was too powerful. When they're together in private, they avoid looking closely at bodies. They're ready to separate quickly. Sometimes only humor saves them. Jamie jokes that he always keeps his hand in the correct position to grab the doorknob.

On one of his recent visits, Sarah had suddenly jumped up, rushed into the bathroom and locked herself in. They'd dissolved in laughter on opposite sides of the door.

This afternoon they took their tea outside on the porch and from the swing, observed the beauty of the dying year. Asters and chrysanthemums glowed along the path, and they could see the bright gold leaves of a ginkgo tree beyond the wall.

Without warning, Sarah began to sob. Jamie wrapped an arm around her and turned her toward him. He took her chin in his hand and lifted it tenderly so he could see her tearful face. Pain seared through him, and he too began to cry.

"Have we reached grand opera yet?" Sarah choked, trying for a lightness that wouldn't come. Instead they just held one another, two people bound together by intense emotion. They cried for all the lovely things they shared and for everything precious they could never have together. But most of all they grieved for the parting that was racing toward them as the months slid by. The light faded into twilight as they remained there, scarcely moving, for a long time. When Jamie rose to leave for an appointment, it was dark.

Jamie drew Sarah close to him. She could feel the warm, enticing pressure of his hands on her back. Then he bent his head and whispered,

"What if I left the Jesuits and asked you to marry me?"

The words arced through Sarah with the force of a blow. Her knees had gone weak, and she'd grasped a railing for support. Her answer had been swift and emotional.

"Jamie, you can't leave for me!"

Without another word, she'd pulled away from him,

turned abruptly and quickly escaped into the house, slamming the door.

SARAH IS STILL PONDERING her strong reaction a day later, trying to understand why she'd been so upset. Even remembering his words makes her angry. There was no joy in her response. Why?

She knows one thing for certain. She has no intention of being the catalyst for his abandoning his vocation. Just the thought frightens her. What a heavy burden it would for any woman to accept the responsibility of having a man leave the priesthood for her. Especially if the man in question loved being a priest as much as Jamie. What if he later regretted the decision? What if not being a priest plunged him into depression? What if his life was diminished for him in painful ways?

Sarah realizes she needs time before they talk again to examine her own reactions to his proposal. Then she'll be ready to hear where he was coming from in making it.

IN TILDEN PARK, Jamie is running along a muddy trail. He's cold and wet and aroused. Unable to subdue either his emotions or his body this afternoon, he's out here hoping the wind and cold rain will be even better than a cold shower. It isn't working.

He wants to laugh at the ridiculous spectacle of some sex-crazed guy tearing through the park trying to outrun his desires. In the past, the ridiculousness of the situation would have cooled his passion. It's not exactly breaking news that at times his penis will not submit to his will.

Today his desire is all-consuming, similar to the wild surges he fought so hard as a young priest and has struggled with all his life. Until now, though, even the most powerful sexual attraction has been casual, more or less tempting, depending on its object, but nothing in which he was seriously invested.

Now there is Sarah.

He wants to dismiss what he's experiencing with her as simply another example of the male brain leaving the head to take up residency in the sexual organs. This need to thrust and pound and enter is nothing special, he's tried to assure himself.

"You're just sanctifying raw sexual craving with pretty thoughts," he thinks often.

However, lately, secretly and somewhat embarrassed, he's hidden away in the stacks of the Berkeley city library reading love poetry. He wants to know how the poets describe this torrent that is threatening the man he thought he was.

At times he seems like a stranger to himself. It can be lonely, because he's afraid to tell his friends, even those closest to him, just how big is the force that's taking him over. Somedays even his prayers seem to distance him from God, leaving him spent and sad.

Sarah is his beloved, but he's unwilling to put the burden of his constant struggles with his vow on her. It's clear she's going through her own battles. He's seen desire flare in her eyes and watched her turn her away when it happens. He's felt the incandescence of her longing for his body. The other night, overcome with love, he shocked and alarmed himself by asking her if she'd consider marrying him. He had no idea he was going to say it. The question simply poured out of his mouth.

Sarah had been so startled she'd almost lost her balance. When she'd exclaimed, "You can't leave for me, Jamie," her voice had sounded scared and angry. She'd pulled herself away from him, then hurried into the house. They haven't talked since, and that makes him anxious. What's happening with her?

In the middle of this turmoil, the great poets of love bring him unexpected comfort. He's read Elizabeth Barrett-Browning's love sonnet to her husband Robert a dozen times, and been deeply moved by it.

"How do I love thee? Let me count the ways.
I love thee to the depth and breadth and height
My soul can reach, when feeling out of sight
For the ends of being and ideal grace.
I love thee to the level of every day's
Most quiet need, by sun and candle-light.
I love thee freely, as men strive for right.
I love thee purely, as they turn from praise.
I love thee with the passion put to use
In my old griefs, and with my childhood's faith.
I love thee with a love I seemed to lose
With my lost saints. I love thee with the breath,
Smiles, tears, of all my life; and, if God choose,
I shall but love thee better after death."

When he'd first encountered the poem, the lines had fallen over him like warm sunlight. From across an ocean and through almost a century and a half, it was as though Barrett-Browning were reaching out to him, a kindred spirit *who understood.* A bit of research had shown what she'd had to sacrifice to be with Robert Browning. When she'd married her fellow poet, her father had disinherited her, and the rest of her family had rejected her. She'd known personally how much love could cost.

Jamie is beginning to realize that the people of El Salvador, and the powerful attraction they hold for him, are probably what is going to keep him in the priesthood. The mysterious, compelling connection with those he met on his trip, and the ones he knows he will meet in the future, have come at a pivotal moment in his life. If he hadn't made the visit to El Salvador, all the work he's been doing as a priest in the last years would not be enough to stop him from leaving to be with Sarah if she'd have him. Just that thought shakes him to his core. Dear God, his whole world is being turned upside down!

He has finally recognized and been forced to accept the truth. The man in him wants to marry Sarah, share all her days, perhaps have a child together, and grow old in her presence. He remembers hearing John Denver's beautiful "Annie's Song" for the first time and feeling jealous that a man could love a woman *that much.* Now it could be his own theme song.

As John Denver wrote of his wife Annie, Sarah fills Jamie's senses like the loveliest experiences in nature: night in the forest, spring in the mountains, dramatic desert storms, the vast blue ocean. As the song says, Jamie wants to give his life to her and still serve God and other people too. He wants to always be with Sarah, drown in her laughter and die in her arms. That's just the nature of the love he has for this woman.

Yet Jamie feels certain he has promises to keep in El

Salvador. He believes he's been called by God to those people and that land. For how long, he has no idea. He will go gladly...and sadly. At some point, he'll return to his life in California and to Sarah. And then, who knows? He is moving into darkness and searching for the subtle light of stars.

THIRTY-ONE

The phone rings in the middle of the night, catapulting Sarah wide awake. Her heart pounds as she answers. This can't be good news.

Madeline's voice is so choked up, it takes a minute to understand what her sister is saying. "Mommy's had a heart attack. It's serious. We're at Queen of the Valley. Please come!"

Sarah cannot believe what she's hearing. It's December 30th. Five days ago at Christmas her mother was fine and in great spirits. Franco's gift had been a trip for the two of them to Tuscany in the spring. His wife had laughed and cried when she opened the envelope with the tickets, then kissed him passionately to the spontaneous applause of family and friends.

Half an hour after the call, hair uncombed, Sarah clutches the wheel of her VW to keep her hands from shaking. Tears obscure her vision, and she has to keep wiping her eyes. "Oh, Mom, Mommy," she pleads silently, "Please, please be okay! Oh God, please heal her. She's such a good person. She deserves a long life!"

Her mind fills with happy scenes of the past two weeks. Her niece Bella's visit had been so much fun for both of them. To her delight, her niece and her chosen little sister Gabriela had become instant friends. Sweet memories. The girls' eager faces in the colored lights of the Zoo as they tried to coax a little monkey to draw closer. Their giggles and giddy happiness at the holiday dinner in Berkeley, and Jamie's face watching them with a tenderness that made her chest swell. "Dear God, I'd love to have a child with this man!" she'd suddenly found herself thinking with a jolt of pure longing. Chagrined, she'd pushed the thought away.

Christmas, too, had been a cascade of joys: the stirring beauty of Midnight Mass, the pleasures of carefully-chosen presents, the good-natured teasing, delicious food and gales of laughter.

Now the trip to the hospital seems endless. Her thoughts whirl. Her father must be beside himself! She can't stand to imagine what he's going through. "How could he live without Mom?" she wonders. Painful images tumble through her mind. Giulia never waking up. Giulia dying. Giulia in a casket.

As she parks in the hospital lot and tries to steel herself for what she's going to find inside, she wishes Jamie were here. She needs him. His very presence is healing and hopeful. He'd called the ranch at Christmas from his sister's house in Maryland. Listening to her parents' end of the conversation, Sarah could have sworn they were talking to a much-beloved son calling home.

Her exchange with him had been quieter, punctuated by

silences in which each was feeling their deep bond. "I love you so much, Sarah," he'd whispered. They hadn't yet discussed his proposal but the tension seemed to have dissipated. Perhaps it would be best to forget it ever happened and consider it just a moment of weakness.

"I love you even more," she'd responded with a smile in her voice she knew he could hear.

Sarah finds her family huddled in a waiting room. Her father hugs her so hard it's painful. "Oh Sweetheart," he cries, "she's still alive, but it's touch and go. An artery was blocked, cutting off blood to her heart. Right now they're doing angioplasty, putting a ballon in the artery to clear it." Franco runs out of words. His face crumples. They join Anthony, Madeline and Paul in a group embrace.

"What happened?" Sarah asks. Franco relates how Giulia woke him to say she felt "like there was an elephant on her chest." She was having trouble breathing. "When she told me she needed to go to the hospital, we got here in twenty minutes. And thank God! They say that with a heart attack, time is everything."

Led by Anthony, they pray the Rosary, tearfully, and feeling shell-shocked and frightened, because the person who is the center and heart of this family is fighting for her life. It's impossible to believe all that joie de vivre, love and goodness could disappear forever.

"You should call Jamie," Franco says. "Ask him to pray."

"He's flying back tomorrow, Dad. I don't have his sister's phone number, and Sam's out of town." She recognizes there are many gaps in her knowledge of Jamie. She doesn't even remember his sister's married name.

"Well, it's only a day," her father replies with resignation. "And by tomorrow we'll be able to tell him more."

The door opens, and a tall balding man in a white coat enters.

"I'm Dr. Contreras," he says. "Mrs. Caffaro came through the angioplasty fine, but the temporary lack of blood did damage her heart. We can't tell how much. We're giving her medicine so she can sleep. Tomorrow we'll do more tests to find out how extensive the damage is."

"Can I see my wife?" Franco asks.

"Yes, but only you and only for a minute," the physician replies. He looks at the family. "Then I want you all to go home and get some sleep. Mrs. Caffaro is stable, and we'll call you immediately if anything changes." Franco follows him through the door.

Before they know it, their father is back. "All those tubes...she doesn't even look like herself," he says in a voice that wavers. Suddenly, Sarah realizes that Franco is getting old. Her heart clutches. One of these days, she's going to lose her parents. Even the thought is hard to bear.

"Come on, Daddy, let me drive you home," she says. "I'll stay with you."

"I will too," Anthony adds. Madeline and Paul will be going back to their children.

An air of impending grief hangs over them as they exchange hugs and kisses, then make their way out into the pre-dawn darkness.

JAMIE AWAKENS WITH A START. He reaches for the clock and sees it's almost 5 a.m. His heart is pounding and he feels strangely upset. Then his mind flashes to Sarah and he's gripped by emotions of fear and grief.

"Something's happened with Sarah," he thinks. "Dear

God, whatever it is, please help her!" Fully awake now, his rational mind takes over.

"It must have been a dream. You're not psychic." Then he realizes, "except with Sarah." He sits up, and starts to get out of bed. He decides to call her, but changes his mind. It's the middle of the night there. If he's wrong, he'll scare the heck out of her.

He lies back down and pulls the covers around his chin. He replays scenes of his visit with Ellen, her husband Todd, and his niece and nephew, Rosemary and Jason. There have been very happy moments and some difficult ones, too, like when he told them he was going to El Salvador. His brother-in-law teaches history at the University of Maryland, and has been following the situation in Central America closely, because one of his uncles works in Nicaragua with Save the Children.

"Oh God, El Salvador is a dangerous place, Jamie!" Todd had exclaimed. He and Ellen had pleaded with him to reconsider. It had been difficult and painful to refuse them.

"You're my only brother, the only one left in our family. I just can't stand to lose you," his sister had said. "Don't go. Please."

Jamie feels guilty. Maybe it's selfish to put himself in harm's way. His family *and* Sarah are all good reasons to change his mind. Then he sees again the worn faces of the parents at the concert, and he knows he'll go to El Salvador, at least for a year.

He had fully intended to tell Ellen about Sarah. She's a fairly open-minded Catholic. He thought she'd be happy to hear he has someone to love and be loved by, but he couldn't be sure. She might be upset. So he's remained silent and feels uncomfortable about that.

When they gather for breakfast, he tells Ellen he's has this premonition that something bad has happened to a family he's close to. She offers him the phone. There's no answer at Sarah's number. He calls the ranch. Nothing. When he's unable to reach anyone for hours, Jamie becomes very concerned. Obviously, something is wrong.

The flight home seems incredibly long.

THIRTY-TWO

S arah is packing a suitcase. The windows of her house are fogged, obscuring the weak sunlight of the last day of the year. She's going to the ranch for a few days. Thank God school isn't in session.

This morning, before driving home from Sonoma to get some clothes, she'd seen her mother. Giulia had been conscious but groggy.

"I love you, Mommy," Sarah told her in the brief visit she was allowed in the ICU. "Please get well. We can't live without you." The pale face on the bed smiled. Giulia looked exhausted, but she squeezed her daughter's hand.

"I love you too," she whispered. "And you don't have to worry. Only the good die young."

"Leave it to Mom to joke at the edge of death," Sarah thinks now. She keeps finding herself standing blankly in the middle of the room trying to figure out what to do next or what to pack. Finally, she stops and calls the hospital and learns mother is stable and more alert. Sarah feels both relieved and fearful. Restless, she goes out into the front garden. Unseasonably warm weather in the East Bay is causing spring bulbs to emerge from the bare earth a month early.

The sense of being lost and alone returns. She sits on the porch swing for a minute and regards the starkness of winter remaining in most of the trees and plants.

This is where Jamie finds her.

He opens the front gate gently. Seeing him, Sarah stands with a soft cry. He bounds up the steps and takes her in his arms. "Oh, love, I'm so sorry." He holds her close, one hand gently pressing her head against his chest. She can hear his heart beating.

"I couldn't reach you. I called the winery. Madeline told me," he tells her. Joy and pain fluctuate wildly through her. She is so happy to have him with her.

Although the air is mild, Sarah shivers. Jamie puts his arm around her shoulders, and they go inside. On the sofa, she nestles in his embrace. He strokes her hair tenderly. She tells him about her mother's heart attack and how it's affecting the family.

When she's finished, Sarah raises her face to his, and the love pours out—one to another—through their eyes. Without thought or warning, Jamie's mouth is on hers. The kiss begins like the touch of angel wings. It deepens as both of them gives themselves up to the ancient sacrament of connection.

It happens without reservation, beyond vows. Jamie can feel her fears and pain coming into him through her skin. A river of emotion and desire overwhelms him. His need to make love to Sarah sweeps away every defense he's built up over seventeen years. He presses his body passionately against hers.

Instinctively, Sarah begins to open herself physically to

Jamie. The desire to have him inside her, to know in her flesh the union she already experiences in heart and soul, is overpowering. She is losing control. Yet even in this intensity, she remembers her promise to him.

Her hands still touching his body, she moves slightly.

"Jamie, no." He lifts his head and looks at Sarah with a dazed expression. He takes her face in his hands and kisses her again, softly, his lips caressing hers.

"Thank you," he says. They lie in silence, his body against hers, for a long time. The rapid beating of their hearts is like music they're playing together.

Finally, Sarah says. "If you stay with me, someday it's going to happen. We're not super human. One of these days, we're going to make love. It's the way of life. It's what lovers do. We're no exception. Next time my brakes may fail, and yours are in very bad shape. We can't depend on them to keep us from going over the cliff. Jamie, unless you leave me, you're probably going to be my lover. You have to face it. You have to be honest with yourself and then decide if it worth the risk to stay with me. If you do, you're very likely going to break your vow, and I'll let you."

Jamie sits up. "You may be right," he admits, his voice soft.

Sarah stands. "I have to go to the ranch. Can you come with me? My Dad's been asking for you. He'd be really happy if you'd visit for a couple of days. Is that possible?"

"Of course. I'll meet you at my place. I'm still packed."

"Good. I'll finish here and pick you up. Oh Lord, I'm glad you can come. Everyone wants you there.

"May I say, Father," she adds wryly as he opens the door to leave, "that was an excellent kiss. And I consider myself something of a connoisseur."

Jamie laughs, then his face turns serious.

"Well, I won't forget what it's like to kiss you," he says. "I can still feel it, and that may turn out to be a big problem."

FRANCO RISES QUICKLY to meet Jamie, throwing his arms around him. The priest is shocked to see the change in his usually-animated and upbeat friend and father figure. He looks older, somehow smaller. His tanned face is etched with new lines.

"Oh, my boy, I'm so glad you're here!" he exclaims.

"Where else would I be?" Jamie asks, briefly caressing Franco's back.

Giulia is sleeping, hooked up to tubes and monitors. Her normally rosy face is wan. Franco leads Jamie to the bed.

"Sweetheart, you have company," he says softly.

She opens her eyes, sees Jamie and reaches out to him,

"Come and give me a kiss, my sweet boy," she tells him. "Have you been praying for me?"

Jamie bends down and touches his lips to her cheek. Sarah, remembering their own kiss, feels a wave of desire.

"We're all praying so hard, I hear the gates of heaven look like a truck crashed into them," he tells Giulia. They share a shaky laugh.

Giulia is doing well, Franco says, a tremor in his voice. "The doctor says starting treatment so fast limited the damage to her heart. Thank God."

The cardiologist has decreed a lifelong regimen of exercise, diet and stress reduction practices, along with medication to prevent blood clots.

"I'm going to have to be a very virtuous woman," Giulia

says with a weak grin. "I'll be an inspiration to the entire family." Her husband, daughter and honorary son exchange pleased glances. The woman they know and love is coming back.

∾

DURING HIS VISIT Jamie takes over the cooking.

"You're very good at this considering you're half Irish," Franco concedes after tasting his pot roast with vegetables that night. "Of course, Italian genes tend to be dominant over weaker ones from more northern countries," he teases. The atmosphere at the table is almost relaxed. It's just the three of them. Anthony's at the rectory in Sonoma. Madeline and Paul are at home with their children. Everyone had stayed at the hospital until Giulia was ready for sleep. She's improving and should be out of ICU in a day or two. They feel relieved and hopeful.

Sarah and Franco do the dishes. Jamie sits in the kitchen playing Anthony's guitar that's been gathering dust in his old bedroom. Her father is requesting songs from the 1940s when he was courting Giulia, favorites like "I'll Be Seeing You" and "I'll Walk Alone." Jamie is too young to know the music and lyrics for all of them, but when he falters, Franco takes over; he has a good voice, and he knows it. Jamie follows along.

"I'll be seeing you in all the old, familiar places," her father intones,

"That this heart of mine embraces all day through
In that small cafe, the park across the way
The children's carousel, the chestnut tree, the wishing well.
I'll be seeing you in every lovely summer's day

In everything that's light and gay
I'll always think of you that way.
I'll find you in the morning sun and when the night
is new
I'll be looking at the moon but I'll be seeing you."

"You can't find better love songs than the ones from World War II," Franco declares. "I remember once in New Guinea a band played that song at the enlisted men's club, and half of those tough G.I. Joes were crying."

He's especially nostalgic because tonight is New Year's Eve, and normally the Caffaros would be dressed in their best clothes, dining and dancing at the Verdi in Napa, a restaurant popular with the valley's Italian ranchers and vintners.

Now her father is telling Jamie about meeting Giulia.

"My friend Vic took me to a dance in Santa Rosa. It was just like that song. I look across the room and see this girl. Her hair is as black as a raven. Big dark eyes...oh those eyes."

This is a story Franco enjoys recounting. "I see her, and it's like I'm struck by lightning. Vic stops to talk to someone, and I bump into him. We almost fall on floor. Before I even met her, Giulia had my heart."

"I get that," Jamie says, glancing at Sarah with a smile.

"Oh great," she thinks, "all we need tonight in this house where I'm sleeping a couple of feet from you is a big dose of romantic memories." From the sly grin he flashes at her, she could swear he's reading her mind.

After Franco goes to bed, they sit together under blankets on the porch. The night is cold and exceptionally clear. You can see the Milky Way flowing across the sky.

"Our second New Year's Eve together and another amazing sky," Jamie says softly.

"Next year you'll be in El Salvador, so I want to enjoy this completely," Sarah replies. He takes her hand.

"It's going to be strange sleeping next to you with only a thin wall between us," he muses. So he's noticed the location of the beds in the adjacent rooms.

"Strange isn't exactly the word I'd use. I'd describe it as tempting."

"Well, obviously you're not as disciplined as I am."

Sarah sputters with laughter. "Yes, of course, Father, I'd forgotten the depth of your self control."

Jamie blushes in the darkness. "Can we please forget my lapse?" he pleads.

"Good luck with that," she retorts.

Later on the bed she slept in as a child, she finds Jamie's nearness disturbing. She wishes she hadn't felt the physical evidence of his passion against her body this morning. Right now, the phrase "to burn with desire" is more than just words. How are they ever going to get past that kiss? A line has been crossed. Can they really go back?

Jamie thanks God Franco is just across the hall. Remembering the softness of Sarah's body and how it fit with his, he can barely stand it. If they were alone right now, he's afraid he would try make love to Sarah if she'd have him. God has certainly fashioned a powerful incentive for man and woman to continue the human race.

"Happy New Year." he whispers, and knocks lightly on the wall. He smiles at the rhythm of her reply. At last fatigue and jet lag send him plummeting into unconsciousness.

It takes longer for Sarah to get to sleep. She worries she no longer has the ability to help Jamie keep his vow. This anxiety alternates with fears for her mother. Moving into her heart, she sends love out to both of them and prays for healing. Finally, she succumbs to exhaustion.

THE NEXT MORNING the two meet in the kitchen, take one look at each other and burst into laughter. It's one of those times when their situation seems completely absurd.

"What's so funny? Franco asks, coming in from outside, bringing a draft of cold air with him.

"The fact that a vow of chastity can make one of the most commons acts humans perform seem like the pearl of great price," Jamie tells him frankly.

"Well, it certainly can cost a lot," her father quips. "However, I can tell you from experience it's well worth it," he adds in a teasing tone.

"Daddy, I'm surprised at you. I didn't think you had a mean bone in your body."

"Come on, Honey, Italians invented the vendetta. We're not all love songs and great food." Then Franco's face turns serious. "My God, it must be tough to be in love and have a vow never to ever act on it," he exclaims.

"It's just the grace of God that you were across the hall last night," Jamie says, once again surprising Sarah with his honesty.

"And with my door open," her father adds mischievously. He heads to the stove and pulls out a large frying pan.

"How is Giulia this morning?" the younger man asks.

"She had a restful night and seems to be doing well. She should be finished with the tests by noon. I'll go in and have lunch with her." Sarah promises they'll visit later.

"I'll make you one of my famous omelets," Franco declares to Jamie, opening the refrigerator. "There are still great pleasures you're permitted to indulge in. And fortunately, my son, the members of your second family know their way around a stove."

Sarah glances at her father and feels happy. His words show how thoroughly he's welcomed her beloved into their lives. Jamie's expression reflects both delight and vulnerability. Franco sees this and reaches over to grasp his shoulder affectionately.

THIRTY-THREE

In the winter light off the Bay, Sallie Olds' eyes are like blue fire. They blaze with life and intelligence as she gazes into his face. It's the middle of January, and Jamie is here in her consultation room because he feels more confused and uncertain than at any time in his life. He can't see an acceptable way forward with Sarah, and there are only two months left before he leaves for Central America.

He's spoken frankly and in detail about their relationship. Sallie has listened with complete attention and interest. She's asked thought-provoking questions. It's the first time he's been able to confide in someone totally objective. He wonders if this warm and caring psychotherapist can help him with a problem that seems insoluble.

"My heart wants two different things that are impossible to reconcile," he says now. "I have two longings: to be with Sarah and to be a priest. The strange thing is that both of them feel like they're coming from my real self, Sallie. Am I wrong? Deluded?"

She looks at him. There is compassion in her eyes that causes a thickening in his throat.

"Jamie, I'm hearing your natural child in both your love for Sarah and your love for your vocation. You're in a difficult situation. You've told me you realize the rules of celibacy and chastity are man-made laws, that they have no basis in the gospels and the rest. You have all this information.

"However, chastity is an official requirement for being a Jesuit priest. You had to promise not to marry or act sexually. You say you took the vow freely, and even now it seems wrong to you not to keep it. Yet your love for Sarah is making it more and more difficult. This is what I'm hearing."

"Yes. And, to tell the truth, I no longer believe there's any good, healthy reason a priest can't love a woman and do ministry," Jamie says. "Two friends of mine are married Anglican priests. And, from what I can see, being married with families seems to enhance their ability to be parish priests. They know the complexities and demands of ordinary life from personal experience.

"Let's face it, Sallie, I live an unnatural life. Even before I met Sarah, I suspected my vow was stunting my emotional life and my response to people, especially women. I ask myself how a normal twenty-three-year-old man can promise he'll never in his entire life be sexual, that he'll live and die without expressing that part of himself. Hell, I'm not even supposed to entertain thoughts of sex. How many males can be that pure? I realize I'm in danger of rationalizing because I want what I can't have. But still, when you think the whole mandatory chastity thing through, it's almost crazy. It sure goes against how God made human beings."

He looks at her and smiles grimly. "Does this make me crazy too?"

"No, Jamie," Sallie replies, her eyes twinkling. "You're just deeply conflicted. Frankly, I'm amazed at the strength of your will. I sense a very passionate man. Can you tell me what it's been like to keep that vow of chastity for seventeen years?"

He speaks for almost ten minutes about the early years and how the nature of the struggle has changed over time. He tells her of his strategies for control and his rationale for keeping sexuality at bay.

"It's always seemed heroic for a man to offer God a sacrifice that big," he says, blushing. "It's embarrassing to admit the lengths I've gone to to keep that vow."

"Jamie, what does being heroic give you? What do you personally get out of doing something heroic?"

He looks at her, surprised, at a loss for words.

"I don't know," he says, his mind whirling. It's a question he's never considered.

"Take your time," she says softly. "See if you have any words. It's OK if the words don't come right now. You'll find them when you're ready."

He closes his eyes. A slideshow of images dances through the darkness. He sees himself kneeling before his provincial at the end of his novitiate, reciting the decisive words. "I, James Michael Quinn, promise to Almighty God perpetual poverty, chastity and obedience." Simple, memorable words that had sealed his future.

He sees the flicker of the candles in the church and recalls the fragrance of incense. Once again he experiences the powerful feeling of love that suffused him in that moment of offering his sexuality to God. He was one with all his brothers and centuries of Jesuits who had come before, valiant men willing to give their all "for the greater glory of God."

He recounts the solemnity and richness of that experience to the therapist, then shuts his eyes once more. Now mental images of his mother and father appear, smiling and waving goodbye to Ellen and him as they walk to their car for that final, fatal vacation. As he looks at them, their smiles seem impersonal, like those of strangers acknowledging one another on the street. He feels a deep ache in his chest. He remembers how often he's wondered if his parents actually loved him.

"I'm seeing my parents," he tells Sallie. "Maybe if I'd been more special, they would have loved me more." His sadness is palpable. "As I told you before, they were so crazy about one another. My sister and I were always outside their magic circle. We wanted in so badly."

"Does Sarah love you because you're special, because you're a hero?" Sallie asks.

"No," he exclaims, "and that touches me so deeply. When we connected, she knew nothing about me. From the moment we looked at one another, there was love between us. Love for absolutely no reason."

"Are you telling me Sarah finds you lovable beyond any of your attributes or anything you say or do, Jamie?" Sallie's eyes seek his.

"I guess I am," he replies shyly. Suddenly the room begins to spin.

"I feel dizzy, really light-headed," he says, gripping the arms of the chair.

Sallie reaches out and touches his shoulder. She waits. Then she says, "Could that be because with Sarah, the pressure's off? You know, the burden of being special and a hero? That's pretty heavy stuff to be carrying around. If all of a sudden, all that weight's removed from your head and shoulders..." She regards him with an inquiring look.

Jamie breathes deeply, feeling strange and at sea.

"I don't know. I've never felt this way before. I just don't know." His voice is shaky.

Sallie places her hand on his arm.

"Sit with the experience. See what comes up," she advises. They remain quiet for a moment, but nothing comes to his mind.

At last Sallie speaks. "Jamie, you don't need anyone to tell you what to do. You have all the answers inside of you. It's a matter of discovering what they are. You may have to go through a lot of debris to get to them. It's a good thing Jesuits are so good at discernment," she teases.

"You're well aware human life is fluid, changing, here and now," she continues. "It's not about concepts and rules fixed once and for all, although we sure behave as though how we're supposed to live is set in stone."

"Are you saying nothing is absolute?"

"That's what makes life so interesting. When people use the phrase 'think outside the box,' I believe this is what they're talking about. We have a power of freedom to create our own lives that's beyond what most of us can see.

"What's your life going to be, Jamie?"

"Well that's the choice I have to make, isn't it?"

"Is it?" Sallie's gaze is piercing.

Jamie feels as though his mind is exploding. He can't think. Waves of emotion wash over him: fear, joy, an almost physical grief.

Sallie sees what is happening and remains silent, although her expression is affectionate and kind. Finally, she asks, "Do we have more to talk about, Jamie? If we do, I can see you next week after the retreat you're making."

"Oh yes, yes please!" he replies.

"Good. I have some homework for you. Spend time with those two deepest longings of yours, to be a priest and to make love with Sarah. Close off every voice except your natural child. Listen only to him—and to God through him. See what he has to tell you.

"And we haven't even talked about your going to El Salvador. That's a very important step. What do you imagine working in El Salvador will give you? You might want to consider that, too.

"I like your heart, Jamie. It's a wise heart." Sallie's face is tender.

BACK HOME IN BERKELEY, Jamie considers when to tell Sarah about the process he's engaged in with Sallie. She has to know soon, but what can he say to her now? He's leaving tomorrow for a four-day silent retreat in Big Sur. Richard has recommended a period of private discernment to help him prepare for ministry in Central America. Sallie has, in effect, seconded his spiritual guide's suggestion. Thinking about days alone with God in a hermitage on the edge of the Pacific Ocean, Jamie is anything but pacific. Instead he feels poised on the edge of a bottomless chasm, about to fall into the unknown.

Sallie has made it clear that—to find his way into a future true to his real self—he needs to close the door to all influences, to allow only the Divine Being into the sacred meeting place in his soul where his real self resides.

He decides to wait to talk with Sarah until after the retreat. Maybe he'll have a revelation that makes everything clear. In the silence of Big Sur Jamie will simply give himself up to the beauty of God's world and the love that created it and holds it in being.

THIRTY-FOUR

G iulia and Sarah are enjoying a mild winter day in the ranch garden. Camellias are in full bloom with masses of flowers from deep scarlet to bone white.

"I wasn't sure I'd ever see this beautiful place again," her mother says as they relax on a carved bench. "I felt myself drifting in and out of consciousness and thought, 'maybe this is it.' "

She raises her face to the sun, and her features radiate a peace and contentment that both comfort Sarah and elicit a pang of fear. Just the thought of losing this beloved person is unbearable. Thank God she is healthy again.

"What was it like, Mommy, there between life and death? What were you thinking? What were you feeling?"

"No one's asked me that." Giulia touches Sarah's wrist, then sits back and gathers her thoughts.

"There was one night. Your Dad was sleeping in the chair. This weakness went through me. I felt I could die at any minute. My body was ready to shut down. I didn't think I had the energy to push death away.

"You've heard about your life flashing before you at the end?"

Sarah nods, her face rapt.

"Well that happened to me. So many scenes and so many emotions. There was your father seeing you, our first child, just after you were born. He was a man amazed at how much his heart could feel. It was right there in his eyes.

"I saw our wedding, how Franco looked at me when we were kneeling at the altar. I could feel all we gave each other that day and what it was like to make love for the first time." Giulia smiles at the memory, then regards Sarah.

"There's nothing on earth like coming together in love with your bodies. It has to be one of God's greatest gifts." She sees sadness rise in her daughter's face but doesn't comment on it. She has more to tell her.

"I saw myself sitting with Eugenia when she was dying, and she told me I was the sister of her heart. And being with my mother and father in their final hours.

"There were small things too, touching moments you never forget. I remembered my Grandpa introducing me to the owner of his favorite Italian deli in North Beach. He said, 'This is my granddaughter. Isn't she beautiful?'

"You know what? Every single part of my life that I experienced at that moment was about love. And it went beyond that.

"In my near-death time God showed me the universe is only love. Love created it and not a single thing in it isn't made of love...stars...that flower...a baby's fingernails...a killer's gun.

"Sarah, Sarah, my darling girl, when it comes to the end,

nothing matters but love. Everything else is like dead grass. And while I was drifting toward death, there was something very strange. I knew for sure that even the things we think are ugly or evil—like people who hurt children and dirty decrepit buildings—aren't apart from love. I could see inside of everything. And this light of love was in the center of each thing, even old rags and broken bottles and so-called bad people. Oh, there's just no good way to describe it, no words." Giulia lapses into silence.

"Mommy, that incredible experience has changed you, hasn't it?" Sarah's voice is soft. "I've felt it, but it scared me because I thought it might be some pre-death thing. You seem at peace in a new way...more loving."

"You think I'm preparing for sainthood, getting in the final grooming?" Her mother laughs, then becomes serious.

"If I'm different, it's because I want the time I have left on earth to be about love in small ways and big ways. That's my prayer every morning, 'Dear God, let me show love to everyone I meet today, and let me be open to receive it.' "

She grins. "However, yesterday I told Anthony he was talking like a jerk. This morning I told your Dad my life would have been so much better if I'd married Randy Scarpetta instead of him. So you don't have to worry I'll become so holy God will have to snatch me into heaven right away."

"Well, that's a relief. Be sure to say at least one mean thing a day so I can relax."

Giulia falls silent again, then reaches over and takes Sarah's face in her hands. She looks into her daughter's eyes.

"Okay, I'm going to say it, even though I may have to face God soon. I want you and Jamie to have what your father and I had on our honeymoon," she declares. "I see what's between the two of you and my heart aches because it's so beautiful, so good. You should be able to make love, and he should be able to stay a priest and marry you. And if he can't marry you, and you're all right with that, some promise he made when he was just a kid shouldn't keep you from being lovers."

The shock is so great that Sarah jerks away from her mother's touch. Her eyes widen and her mouth falls open. Her mind is reeling. The words she's just heard from Giulia's lips simply do not compute.

She begins to laugh helplessly.

"I can't believe my Italian mother is telling me to have sex outside of marriage, and even worse to have sex with a priest! There's a certain hot place that has just now frozen over, that's for sure. And you'd better hope it stays frozen, Mom, so you don't fall into it."

"Sarah, stop! I mean what I'm saying. Jamie is going to a very dangerous place. Suppose, God forbid, something happens. Will you always regret what you didn't have with him because of some rule? I hope you don't think I'm being cruel to raise the possibility. But I'm sure it's in your mind, whether you want it there or not."

"Mommy, everything you say is already haunting me. I'm going be worried every day he's in El Salvador. Of course I want to make love with him, but there's not a thing I'm willing to do to make it happen. I said I'd help him keep to his vow, and I have, and I will. There's only a few weeks before he leaves. I know I can do it at least that long."

"What if he changes his mind? Suppose he asked you? What would you do then?"

"I haven't let myself even think seriously about that possibility...so I don't know." Sarah pauses lost in thought. Finally she says, "Well, I'd have to be damned certain it was an actual change of heart and not just a momentary weakness."

She smiles, looking dreamily at the late-winter flowers. "Anyway, that will not happen." She pushes away the thought of his marriage proposal.

Giulia's voice is firm. "Jamie has become like a son to me. And a mother's intuition tells me right now he needs more from you than either of you can imagine."

Sarah sighs. "I just pray I'll do what's right for him."

Her mother smiles. "And I'll pray that you'll be open to all possibilities."

THAT NIGHT, walking along the Bay, Sarah mentally berates her mother for the ridiculous advice that has opened wider the door to temptation. "Damn it, Mom, how could you do this to me, make it even harder for me to be faithful to that blankety-blank vow?" she mutters.

She remembers a hot day last fall when her Giulia had sent her with lemonade for the season's apple-pickers. As she approached through the orchard, she'd seen Jamie, who'd volunteered to help pick, on a ladder, shirtless, wearing cut-off denim shorts he must have borrowed. It was the first Sarah had seen so much of him, and she'd stared. His body was olive-skinned, smooth and sculpted with defined muscles. He took her breath away, and she'd stood there transfixed.

When she made her presence known, Jamie had hurried down the ladder and quickly donned a shirt. They'd looked at one another sheepishly. She'd grinned. He'd blushed. Imagine, a man his age blushing because she'd seen him without a shirt!

Looking toward the Golden Gate, Sarah sighs.

Suppose Jamie did come to her wanting to make love before he left for El Salvador. How in the world could she refuse him? Yet how could she say yes, knowing that decision could harm him and take away so much that is precious to him?

Sarah sighs again and, with a final look at the dark Bay waters, turns and heads for home.

THIRTY-FIVE

The vastness of this place where the continent meets ocean is the perfect setting for a spiritual retreat, Jamie thinks. From a hill on the California coast under a sky that goes on forever, he feels intoxicated by the grandeur of creation.

The rush of an afternoon wind sweeping off the Pacific is invigorating. Endless vistas flood his eyes. The rough music of surf and seagulls fills his ears. He can smell the fragrances of beach sage and the tang of salt air. Every sense is alive and praising God. His body, too, is alive with feeling, aroused by the beauty around him and memories of Sarah.

Seated on a bench near the Benedictine hermitage, he lifts his face to God's heaven. For a long time he remains motionless.

"With all that I am, let me do your will," he whispers into the vibrant air. "Please show me the way, and I will follow."

He is both exhilarated and frightened by Sallie Olds' counsel to close off the voices of authority in his head, to listen only to his real self and divine inspiration. She's assured him that inner part of him will be able to distinguish the voice of God from all the others that will come.

"You'll know," she'd said.

How can he prepare himself for El Salvador? How is he to be with Sarah in the weeks before they separate?

These are the questions Jamie is bringing to this very private discernment. He won't consult even the wise spiritual guides at the retreat center. Instead, he'll make an effort to put aside everything: church regulations, the opinions of his Jesuit brothers, his friends and family, and the powerful draw of Sarah herself.

He is awaiting an epiphany, and it must come from within.

As afternoon stretches into evening, he leans against the bench and watches the patterns of his mind and emotions. He imagines Sarah's face and body and is piercingly aware of how much he wants her. The majesty of the dramatic coast intensifies the sensuality of the hours.

He lets himself experience fully the emotion he identifies as love, what it is for him before thoughts or words. He watches it begin as an outward movement from the vicinity of his heart. It expands, and he sees those he loves in his mind's eye. Each face is vulnerable and revealing. It is as if he knows and feels the entirety of the person, and is known by him or her in the same way. He breathes out, and the breath carries his love.

Every part of Jamie seems to be awakening. Flashes of pure sensation streak through muscles, organs and skin. He can feel blood rushing in arteries and veins. He is pulsing with the force of life, longing to give it with yearning so powerful he is almost overwhelmed by it.

Inevitably, Sarah comes to him in vision. Her arms are

wide, ready for him, and he goes to her in fantasy. Who he is, his history and all his roles, seem to disappear like night dissolving into dawn. This is what it means to be a lover, he realizes, to give to another and hold nothing back. It is to allow himself to be so undefended and porous to his beloved than she can penetrate him fully. In turn, he can receive all of her because his love has room for the mystery she is.

In the silence he lets emotion have him.

"Take me where you will," he prays. The words have hardly slipped from his mind, when all seems to stop, and Jamie is floating in a timeless space.

Gradually, like distant music, he senses a presence. At first it is ethereal, light and barely noticeable. It shimmers softly just beyond his sight.

Invisible waves are coming nearer. Something in his chest opens. The silence is so deep he cannot reach thought. Fear grips him. The impulse to fight his way back to his mind is strong.

The presence softens, becomes tender. Comfort flows around him accompanied by rapture so sweet he is ready to die into it, surrender completely.

Now he is lying on the ground, held by the earth itself, with no idea how he got there from the bench. The presence deepens. It holds everything that is and has ever been. Within its embrace, Jamie knows he is connected to the whole universe through all time and all space.

The presence takes voice.

"My beloved child, choose love."

JAMIE AWAKENS SHIVERING. The sun is a scarlet gash on the horizon. The ocean wind is cold, the slab of rock his head is resting on, hard. He starts to get up stiffly but quickly lies back down. His mind feels dense. How long has he been sleeping? What is he doing on the ground?

His thoughts unwind backward. He sits up so quickly it makes him dizzy. What happened before he fell asleep? Was it simply a dream?

The experience washes over him, compelling even in memory. What or who was it that came to him in a tide that swept away everything else? It's hard to recapture that moment the presence enfolded him so totally. He knows it was centered around his heart but coursed through all his being. In the end, "it" alone existed, and he disappeared in a kind of ecstasy beyond anything in his own spiritual history.

Jamie's eyes widen. He has never considered himself a mystic, but what he's just been through certainly resonates with some of the mystics' writings. The essence of it fits with their halting attempts to describe what has come upon them.

He hesitates to call the presence God. Yet its completeness, its complexity, the sense that it was much more "real" than what we call real; these soaring qualities make it impossible to dismiss the idea.

Suddenly, out of the darkness of forgetting, the voice emerges. "My beloved child, choose love." Before he realizes it, Jamie is weeping.

That voice. How strange it is in recollection. It wasn't a man's voice, but it wasn't a woman's either. The closest he can come is that the voice was perfectly balanced between male and female, if that makes any sense. It was soft enough to permeate him, so soft it could pass through any physical or mental barrier.

"What a strange idea, the power of softness," he muses.

"My beloved child..." He feels a warmth spread within and around him. He sees his grandmother's smile, tender and playful, directed toward two very lonely children. To hear those words and to understand the fullness of their meaning for the first time in his forty years is indescribably moving.

"Choose love." The heart of the message.

"You'll know," Sallie had told him, and she was so right. He knows. These are the words the Presence spoke to him, his challenge, his call into the future. However, immediately his mind rushes back with practical questions. Choose which love? The love for God he professed publicly in making his vows? Or his love for Sarah?"

Jamie looks up into a cobalt sky where a crystal white evening star shines in the West. The message is certainly ambiguous. How is he to discover the divine will unobscured by his oh-so-human longing for physical connection with Sarah?

With the mind's endless capacity for rationalization, how can he ever be certain a choice to become her lover would be anything but instinct rearing its head?

THIRTY-SIX

T he next days deliver more confusion and less clarity than Jamie had hoped. St. Ignatius gave his spiritual sons guidelines for making decisions, but even they aren't helpful, because of course they were never intended for what he is considering.

The Jesuit founder stated that any discernment begins with "indifference," an ability to step back from one's initial biases and approach each decision with an open, fresh mind. It is necessary to enter the process as free as possible.

"That's basically what Sallie told me, isn't it?" Jamie reflects.

Jesuits recognize that when emotions are involved, detachment is difficult to achieve. Ultimately indifference requires God's grace. Walking in the hills, Jamie looks up into the sky.

"I'm waiting," he prays, laughing.

In Jesuit discernment, an individual prayerfully weighs options as impartially as possible and seeks reasons that seem to support a wise choice. A decision that brings peace indicates a person is in accord with God's will. A lack of peace, agitation and conflicted feelings indicate he is on the wrong path. In what would have been unthinkable to him a short time ago, Jamie is actually considering that God might be leading him to go against everything he's been taught. He can almost hear the roar of disapproval from 450 years of Jesuit tradition.

A Jesuit may not even consider a choice that Ignatius called "manifestly evil." And there's no doubt in Jamie's mind that a decision to remain a priest and make love to a woman would fall into this category, at least in his spiritual father's world view.

Hour after hour, he slams up against this reality. Everything he's accustomed to is telling him it's wrong even to consider this. He has to choose between his vocation and Sarah. He cannot in good conscience have both. To remain a priest and be Sarah's lover would be to commit a sin serious enough to send him to hell. Or that was what the Church asserted.

Why in God's name is he doing this? He doesn't have to struggle so hard. He knows he has the self-discipline to control his sexual impulses until he goes to El Salvador. He is with a woman who cares enough for him to help him be faithful.

The thought of Sarah invokes her presence. He's filled with happiness the two of them can share their lives and spiritual journeys.

"For heaven's sake, isn't that enough?" Yet, tuned into Sarah now, he also feels her longing for him and the deep sadness she keeps mostly hidden for his sake. If he's honest, he has to admit Sarah wants to be his lover with all her passionate nature. Only love holds her back.

Jamie is surprised by his dogged refusal to quit beating his head against the wall of this impossible dilemma. The inner voices are getting louder, are telling him to stop his nonsense, that he's an arrogant fool, even an apostate in the making.

One voice says, "Just put this off and when you get to El Salvador and start doing some real ministry instead of spending too much time mooning around in a retreat center, things will be much clearer."

Another says, "Look this is damned good advice. You'd be smart to take it." Still indecisive, unable to stand more thoughts, he heads back to the hermitage to offer his services for whatever manual work needs to be done at the place.

A HAUNTING BIRD call awakens Jamie. He listens to the pure notes, and then to the silence as it falls back over the night. In the wordless reverie as he drifts back into sleep, the voice returns.

"Carry love with you into the dark." Fully awake, he lets the words reverberate through his mind. "Carry love with you into the dark."

"Dear God, another riddle. I've known you have a sense of humor from all those wild-looking creatures You designed, but do you have to inflict it on me now?" Jamie complains. "No wonder the Bible has caused such problems. Well, I do have chutzpah, teasing God at a time like this. Maybe Job should have tried it."

He's surely going to carry the love between him and Sarah to El Salvador. That war-ravaged place may be the dark. A realization hits with an almost-physical force. "I could die there."

He's known the possibility mentally, but suddenly it's real to him in a new and vivid way. The danger he's heading toward is palpable. The moment of his death, violent and swift, rises in his imagination. He can almost feel the bullet with the force of premonition.

"I could be killed. It's happened to men and women a lot more valuable to this world than me. I'm not immune."

If he dies in El Salvador what will he regret? At first he denies the answer that streaks like a meteor through the sky of his consciousness. What comes is not what the Jesuit priest in him wants to hear.

If he dies in El Salvador, his most poignant regret will be that he passed from this life without making love to Sarah.

Missing the ultimate experience of physical unity with her would be a great loss, but that's not it. The heartache will come from not giving himself entirely to Sarah, from denying her the depth of intimacy that comes with sexual love. He will deprive her of the fullness of what can be between a man and a woman who love and hold nothing back.

"A nicely done, a well-crafted rationalization if I do say so myself," a part of him declares mentally. "Yes, it's almost persuasive enough to convince anyone."

Suddenly the inner voice is back, softly now.

"What are you willing to sacrifice for Sarah?"

This new question brings with it a deep and surprising calm.

"What am I willing to sacrifice for you, my love?" He is asleep before an answer comes.

IN THE MORNING as he prays in the candle-lit chapel, the words "carry love into the dark" turn him powerfully toward El Salvador and the land and the people where he will soon journey. He realizes even more clearly why he is being called to this ravaged country. His psychological training and clinical practice give him practical knowledge. While he could not help the little boy in the pediatric hospital, there are others, traumatized and suffering, who may benefit from what he knows. He can carry the healing love of Jesus he is consecrated and commissioned to bear. And his love for Sarah and hers for him will also sustain his work. He feels a surge of joy and certainty that working in El Salvador is in alignment with God's will. Grace will be with him, expanding his own poor abilities to console and to comfort. He can go with confidence that Christ has called him.

THE BEACH RIMS steep sea cliffs. Jamie is wandering its rocky terrain. This stretch is usually empty, and he often stops here on his way back to Berkeley. He had left the hermitage this morning, reluctantly because the clarity he'd hoped for in the situation with Sarah is still eluding him. Walking along the ocean where he always feels close to God, he carries the pregnant question within him like a child waiting to be born. "What am I willing to sacrifice for Sarah?"

A flock of seagulls is fighting over something up the strand. Their raucous calls and combative flying draw his attention. Now a large gull lands a couple of yards away from him. She looks old, a bit frayed, but she strides in his direction with a firm step leaving little claw prints in the sand.

"You're one fearless old lady," he tells the bird as it draws near. Somehow he knows it's a female. She stops a couple of feet from him and looks directly at him. Her gaze is piercing, and he's surprised to feel tears welling as their eyes lock.

"Will you sacrifice your honor for Sarah?"

He hears the words in that same other-worldly voice. He

hardly has a chance to register their meaning before the gull utters a loud screeching cry and lifts effortlessly into the air. She soars out over the ocean as Jamie, dazed, watches her flight.

"What does my honor have to do with it?" Then it hits him forcefully. In essence what is holding him back from loving Sarah is not fear of displeasing God or his superiors. It's not because he's afraid being her lover will make him a less effective priest. What he really fears is losing his image of himself as an honorable man, a person of integrity.

"How terrible that would be!" Just the thought makes him feel sick.

He sits down on a rock and gazes mindlessly out at the ocean. He's close enough to feel the spray on his face and see the many colors of blue-green water and white foam swirling together in graceful patterns. Time passes, but he doesn't have the energy to move. He feels suspended. Thinking is useless, and he's numb inside.

"Dear God, please help me." He repeats it like a mantra.

Suddenly, in the doldrums of his spirit, the voice comes again.

"Love will cost you everything."

IT'S MARCH, less than three weeks before Jamie is to leave for Central America. Incredibly, he has still not made a decision about his relationship with Sarah, despite another visit with Sallie and much prayer and reflection. "I'm the Hamlet of sex, if Hamlet and sex could be both tedious and boring," he says to his face in the mirror as he shaves.

Worse, he hasn't shared with Sarah all the things that have been happening with him, and on some level she can feel it. Lately there's sometimes a puzzled expression on her face when she looks at him.

That damned vow is such a part of him now. Even though his intuition and emotions and something fundamental within him seem to be calling him away from it, he's still uncomfortable at the prospect of relinquishing what he's always considered essential to his integrity. Part of him says it's nothing but ego. Another part can't believe he's even considering breaking his solemn promise.

He had almost pleaded with Sallie to help him, to tell him what he should do, but she had gently refused. She'd moved her chair closer to his, taken both of his hands, and looked into his eyes.

"Jamie, you *know what the higher good is in this.* You received extraordinary guidance in those experiences at Big Sur. Now you need to discern the authenticity of that voice from the deepest part of you, where the truth that's yours alone resides. Your answer will come from that place. *You will know. And there will be peace.*"

In the midst of this intense inner conflict, his ministry in El Salvador is taking shape. He will work in a medical program affiliated with the Archdiocese of San Salvador. Besides priestly ministry, he'll use his clinical skills at a church-run refugee camp in the city and small community clinics in the countryside. He'll be part of a team guided by a Jesuit who has worked for years with survivors of trauma and torture. He should be a valuable mentor.

Considering the suffering of the people he hopes to serve, his other problems are trivial. Yet he senses that what happens with him and Sarah in the next weeks will shape the kind of man and priest he'll be in the future. Such ideas aren't even reasonable, but reason is failing him badly.

At the very least Sarah deserves to know what's going on.

To keep it from her until now is both inconsiderate and a sin against the intimacy of their connection. What in the world is stopping him?

For one thing, he recognizes, it seems unfair to spring on her some last-minute decision to abandon the restraints they've been living under. What a burden to place on her shoulders when she's been so good in supporting his determination to be faithful to his promise. She has never intentionally committed one act or said one word to tempt him away from it. She has been more vigilant than he himself.

Not to mention how cruel it would be to become her lover, then leave her almost immediately. His mind circles endlessly, despite the fact thinking is obviously getting him nowhere. Yet, he seems paralyzed to do more.

THIRTY-SEVEN

From the sofa in her living room, Jamie and Sarah watch the shadows of afternoon turn to sunset and then twilight through the western windows. It's Sunday evening.

They have both known parting would be difficult but are surprised at just how wrenching it is. They try to push back the sadness when they're together. They may succeed for a time, but it soon returns like a chilly cloud.

Now, though they don't talk about it, the sexual tension is building. They recognize he's going to have to go home soon, yet neither has the heart to make the first move.

"I feel like I'm about to have something amputated," Jamie says, looking grim. Sarah hates the depressed note in his voice.

"If you want to solve all our problems, I can suggest what to amputate," she retorts. "You can leave it with me for safe-keeping, and we'll both be happy." He tries to smile but doesn't quite reach that expression.

"I can't believe how much this hurts," he says.

"Well, it's your choice." She's angry now. "The hero priest is going across the world for 'the greater glory of God.' " She flings the Jesuit motto at him in an instant of pure rage. The energy of her anger feels good.

Yet looking into his stricken face, she regrets her attitude.

"Oh Jamie, I'm sorry. I'd never want to keep you from people who need you." Her words are the right ones, but she can't shake the resentment. He can tell from her body language. Their mood turns bleaker. They sit in silence, subdued, staring out the windows.

Finally, Jamie gets up to leave. Reluctant to go with things so unsettled between them, he stands by the hearth staring at the logs turning into rainbow flames. Sarah moves to stand beside him.

"Don't go yet; I promise to be good," Sarah says spontaneously. "Sit with me in front of the fire."

For a while they sit shoulder to shoulder on the hearth rug watching the burning logs and enjoying the physical contact. Then, without planning it, they are lying stretched out face-to-face, separated by a foot of carpet.

Sarah's heart reaches out to this complex, vulnerable man who is so dear to her. She intentionally sends her love to wrap around him like a protective blanket. In the sweet descending darkness of the winter night, she offers all of herself that she is able give him. His eyes widen in response, then close. He reaches out and touches her face briefly. Her eyes close too.

The minutes pass. Although he can't see her, Jamie can still feel her. Never before has he realized how much love is an energy. The firelight glows through his eyelids. He feels Sarah's love enter his heart. There's a radiance in his chest. It grows until it fills his body. He knows she's offering her entire being to him in this moment. He allows his own love to permeate the air around them and flow to her. Without words he conveys to her all she is to him and gives himself too in every possible way.

He hears a soft laugh.

"Wow," she whispers.

"Wow, indeed," he says quietly, marveling at the closeness they share on so many mysterious levels.

Desire courses through Sarah. Their bodies in the luminous light seem incandescent. If she moves physically toward Jamie, she knows she can have him. A spark is all it would take. If she caresses him now, they will make love. With what seems like superhuman effort, she reaches over and ruffles his hair, then quickly rises to a sitting position. "Jamie, if you don't leave now, I'm going to seduce you. I won't be able to stop myself. I want you so much."

"I want you too. You can't imagine…"

"Unfortunately, I can," she says, then sighs. "You are just so beautiful."

"I bet you tell that to all the priests you lie with on the floor of your living room," Jamie jokes in that rapid-fire change of mood they use to control passion. But humor proves inadequate tonight.

"Sarah, you're part of me. I'm part of you. Always. Any distance between us can only be geographical."

"I know, Jamie."

He reaches his hand out to her, and suddenly everything he's been holding back pours out: the meetings with Sallie, the mystical experience at the hermitage, the strange compelling voice and its words, the reasons he's kept these secrets from her.

Jamie watches the spectrum of emotions that play over Sarah's face: shock, confusion, wonder and fear. Obviously stunned, she listens to the onslaught of his confession.

"What are you saying, Jamie?" Her voice is sharp with

anger. "After a year and a half of struggle keep your solemn damned vow of *chastity, now* you're suggesting we change the rules at the last minute? That's just crazy!"

She stares at him. His face is a pallet of his feelings: guilt, fear, uncertainty, concern. But he does not know what more to say. The silence deepens.

"Jamie, you're under a lot of emotional stress. You're going into a war zone, and leaving everyone and everything you know and love. You're not thinking clearly!" Sarah's tone is more neutral, but her distress is evident. In her words, and even in her anger, Jamie hears her love for him, her desire to protect him.

It is then the peace comes over him, an all-enveloping cloud of divine comfort. This must indeed be "the peace of God, which surpasses all understanding," because it brings with it a certainty and a clarity that defy logic and conventional ideas of a morality. Jamie marvels at what he is experiencing. It is so complete, so total, so free.

Like lightning illuminating the dark, the words of the poet he knows through Sarah enter his mind, a verbal counterpart to the truth flooding him now.

"Out beyond ideas of wrongdoing and rightdoing, there is a field," he says softly. "I'll meet you there."

He sees her surprise turn to comprehension and then the shine of her tears in the flames' glow. He kisses them and tastes a salty tang. "Sarah, before I go, will you please let me make love with you?"

"What just happened, Jamie?" Her voice is hushed. "Something changed for you, didn't it? Her eyes widen. "Everything's changed, hasn't it? I can feel it. Oh my God, you really mean what you're saying, that you want us to be lovers!"

"I mean it with all of me, Sarah. Right now, though,

the important thing is what you want. What you feel. What you need. Any decision on this has to come from the deepest part of you. And if it doesn't match mine, well, so be it. *Please!* You *have* to be true to yourself! *That's* what I *need from you* above all else. Please don't do this *because I want it."*

Sarah studies Jamie, and her need to be physically joined with this man she loves, let loose by what he has just told her, threatens to dissolve all her resistance. It takes every bit of self-control she possesses not to reach out her hand or her lips to him and unleash all the longing and desire.

Only love stops her.

"Jamie, are you certain this is the right thing for you to do?" she asks finally. "Are you sure it won't harm your relationship with God or your priesthood to come to me like this? I'm afraid for you."

Again he is moved and humbled by the extent of her care for him.

"After all I've experienced around this, I'm certain for myself. But what about you, my love? Can this possibly be good for you? Let's face it, I'm inviting you into a strange secret relationship that won't be fair to you. We'll have to sneak around. If we're discovered, I can't lie about it and stay a priest. I have no idea what would happen then. We'd probably have to part. Please be really clear. I have nothing to offer you but a life in the shadows."

Suddenly Sarah smiles mischievously. "Well, here's something to put into the decision-making process. My Mom thinks we should have what she and Dad experienced on their honeymoon. We should make love. She told me so last week." She has to laugh at the astonishment on his face.

"Giulia said that? You *can't be serious!"*

She relates the conversation and enjoys his expressions.

"This may be the ultimate sign we should go ahead," she jokes. He can only shake his head in amazement.

Jamie returns to his concerns for Sarah.

"You'll be cut off from so many of the ordinary pleasures of being in relationship. You can't bring me into your life publicly except with a few friends like Julianna and Mark, and I guess your mother! You'll have to live with knowing that a lot of people, most Catholics, would think we're doing something sinful."

Sarah regards him gravely. "Jamie, what Mom said turned my head around. For the first time I let myself consider what it would mean to me and, more importantly, to you, for us to come together physically. I've thought about everything you're saying. The secrecy. The disapproval. The likelihood I'll lose you. The idea of breaking rules doesn't particularly bother me, especially since I'm convinced the Church is just plain wrong, even warped, in its teachings on sexuality.

"I don't mind keeping our relationship secret from most people. It's how we've been living anyway. I don't need to show you off to friends as a trophy that increases my status, although I'm sure it would." Her eyes smile at him.

"Still, you're shocking me, because I never thought you'd come to the point you'd actually make an intentional decision to abandon your vow. I always thought if we did this, it would happen because we lost control.

"Even with what you're saying now, I'm worried because you'll have to live with the burden that you're not who people think you are. In effect, you'll be living a lie. You can't know for sure what going against all your training and your history is going to do to a man as moral as I know you are. Is it really worth it?"

Jamie looks at Sarah. "I'll admit that's been the hardest

struggle. In the end, though, I simply don't believe coming to you in love will turn me into an immoral person, someone lacking in integrity. I will be a man who has broken an important promise. For you, for us, I can live with that."

A quiet peace moves into the room, and both of them rest in it.

"I love you. I love God and other people in loving you. I want to give myself to you without holding anything back. I believe I'll be a better priest if I do. The voice asked what I'd sacrifice for you. I'm willing to sacrifice my ego. But isn't that what love always asks us to do?"

Sarah pauses, gathering her thoughts.

"Jamie, making love with you would be so much more than just having sex, as wonderful and pleasurable as I expect that would be. I want to know you in that way a man and a woman can experience only by being lovers. I feel inseparable from you in my heart and my soul. Joining our bodies would complete the love. For me, it would be a holy act."

"That's *how I feel!*" he exclaims. "We already have that mysterious, almost mystical unity in every other way. Completion is the perfect word."

Suddenly Jamie grins and looks embarrassed. "It's probably a bad idea to use soaring language to talk about making love with me."

"Why?"

"Sarah, let's face it, you're dealing with a man with the sexual sensibility of a nineteen-year-old boy. My short history with girls ended at that age. So I'm bringing you all the sophistication and technique of a teenaged male, someone who hasn't had sex since he was just a kid."

Sarah giggles. They regard one another with laughter in their eyes. Yet they both feel shy and tongue-tied. A moment they never expected has arrived.

Neither knows what to do. Each watches the other, wondering.

Sarah breaks the silence. "I love the idea that you'll be able to take the memories of us together to El Salvador. You'll be there seeing and feeling all the suffering of people. It's sweet to think that when you're in bed at night you can remember us. Maybe it will be a comfort."

"Oh Sarah, Sarah," Jamie says, tenderness filling his voice. "On the last day of my life, I'll still be thanking God for you. Going to El Salvador as your lover, I'll bring so much happiness with me."

Now Jamie is at a loss. "What next? I don't have much experience with these things."

Sarah laughs nervously. Her heart is pounding. They are making a decision that flies in the face of sacred vows and long tradition, a choice that so many people they love and respect would find sinful, even disgraceful. Jamie's expression tells her that, for him too, the reality is sinking in. She smiles encouragingly.

"Jamie, just come here tomorrow night. It would be our night with Sam if he weren't out of town. I'll pray. I know you will too. Just come. We'll see what happens. Nothing is fixed. We can change our minds."

THIRTY-EIGHT

The moment he awakens, Jamie's chest clenches with anxiety. Then he remembers. Today could be the day his life changes. He's glad Sam's away. He sighs, anticipating how hard it will be to tell his best Jesuit friend he's broken his vow and done it deliberately.

Jamie takes a cup of coffee out to a small balcony that overlooks a steep hillside overgrown with vines and wild plants. A couple of moths flutter above a flowering weed. He remembers the two butterflies that lighted on him by the waterfall.

He sees Sarah's face in his mind's eye, and peace comes over him. He rests in it, sinking into prayer. "O Lord," he whispers into the quiet morning "I'm going to do something I never thought I'd do. I'm going to break a solemn promise to you. Please forgive me." The silence returns like a loving presence.

"Dear God, let me bring all the love in me to Sarah. May our coming together increase our capacity for loving. Please give us the grace to carry that love into every aspect of our lives." Is he committing a form of blasphemy praying like this in the circumstances?

He takes a breath, and allows himself to feel what it will be like to be with her in the most intimate way. He can hardly take it in. Emotions swirl around in him. There's fear he'll be clumsy or inadequate, but that passes quickly. Whatever happens, there will only be love, and very likely laughter. How great to trust someone as much as he trusts Sarah.

Just thinking about her, Jamie is aroused. For the first time since he was a very young man, he doesn't have to fight the powerful energy surging through him. His body throbs with desire and need, and he can allow himself to experience the sensations, completely ordinary for most men but a rare forbidden luxury for him.

A sense of wonder grows. Tonight or very soon, unless they change their minds, he and Sarah will come together! He feels like a virgin bridegroom about the enter the nuptial suite where the woman he loves is waiting, longing for him with the same intensity he yearns for her.

Remarkably, guilt seems far away this morning. The voice that invited him to "choose love" has led him to this moment. He will follow it to Sarah, whatever the ultimate cost. Today Jamie is not heroic or special, but simply ordinary. In that realization, serenity seems to emanate from everything: the sky, the plants, the air and his own heart.

SARAH SMILES at Gabriela's excitement over a new rabbit at the Little Farm in Tilden Park. It's a stately animal, pure white except for a black patch of fur encircling one eye. The child's face is pressed against the mesh of the hutch. "Hi,

Bunny," she calls softly. It reminds Sarah of her own over-
tures to wild creatures at the enchanted creek of her
childhood.

She's trying to focus on what's happening, but her mind
keeps turning toward Jamie. When she permits herself to
envision what it will be like to be with him, desire blazes
through her. Moments of uncertainly come too. Does she
really understand what it will mean to do what they are
contemplating?

She's not actually afraid anymore. Their relationship has
always centered around their mutual love for God. So will
their lovemaking. The Divine as Love, Lover and Beloved will
be with them, in that field "beyond ideas of wrongdoing and
rightdoing." When she and Jamie meet in that field, the world
will be so full that words like you and me will fuse into something new.

Sarah realizes Gabriela is talking to her.

"He looks so soft, even more than Betsy. I wish I could
have a bunny of my own." She regards her chosen big sister
hopefully, but Sarah only laughs and runs her hand through
the girl's hair.

"Honey, think how jealous wild Betsy cat would be. She
likes being the only pet."

The child looks up at her with big eyes, "But then both of
them would have a special friend to love. Wouldn't that be
nice?" She is the dearest little girl. Suddenly, Sarah imagines
having a child with Jamie and is suffused by a need
completely new to her. She pushes the feeling away.

Gabriela leads her toward the other farm animals, chat-
tering happily as Sarah tries to regain her equilibrium. Later,
driving home, she gingerly revisits what just occurred. In all
her life she's *never* longed for a baby. She's used birth control
for years, despite the Church's prohibition.

On impulse she stops at St. Mary Magdalene. The church is surprisingly warm. In the dim, incense-perfumed light, Sarah prays for Jamie and herself. "May whatever we do be good for him. Please help me to give him as much joy and peace and love as I can to take with him." The red light of the altar candle, signifying the presence of Jesus in the Eucharist, fills her with calm.

"Oh dear Lord," she sighs, not knowing what else to pray for.

THE LATE AFTERNOON sun is casting long shadows in the garden as Sarah opens the door to Jamie. For a moment they simply look at one another, both gladness and questions in their eyes.

She reaches out for him. Without warning, he bends down, sweeps her up into his arms and carries her into the house. She's startled but doesn't miss a beat. "Oh Rhett, y'all stop or Ah swear ah'll faint," she croons, in a terrible imitation of Vivienne Leigh in *Gone with the Wind*. He begins to laugh and staggers. He manages to lurch to the couch where they make a bumpy but accurate landing. Sarah regards him archly.

"You're breathing hard. Is it passion or exhaustion?" she asks. They break into laughter and find it hard to stop. Finally, she recovers sufficiently to get up and close the door.

A silence follows as they savor the sight of one another, rosy and breathless, soft with happiness. Jamie fondles Sarah's hair. His hand moves to her face. With a gentle touch, he strokes her cheek. She presses her face against his hand.

"Sarah, love, something occurred to me this afternoon. Tell me what you think. We have eight days before I leave.

That means we have time, even though it's not much. I thought it might be good to go slowly, not to rush. I've never wooed you physically. We've only had that one kiss.

"What about if we just kiss and hold and touch one another tonight without making love? I'd like to tell you what I'm thinking and feeling and hear those things from you.

"It's almost embarrassing how big this is for me, Sarah."

She smiles into his eyes and goes to him, then puts her hand behind his neck and draws him toward her. "What you're thinking sounds perfect to me." She can feel Jamie's face against her cheek.

"But will you let me rhapsodize without snickering?" he asks. Sarah giggles.

"That may be a problem," she admits. "We've developed that hair-trigger sense of the absurd to protect ourselves. Now it always kicks in just when I'm most moved by what you're saying, so I don't throw myself at you."

"Not having to rein in our feelings is going to be really strange, isn't it?" His expression is serious.

She nods in agreement. "Just remember, a snicker or snort is my way of expressing profound emotion." They regard one another with laughter in their eyes.

This gives way to shy, hesitant smiles. As Jamie watches, Sarah collects pillows and a blanket and places them on the carpet in front of the fireplace. She looks at Jamie. "Come," she invites.

Lying close, face to face, they silently appreciate this extraordinary moment. For the first time, they are free to go where their desires take them. Sarah experiences a sense of awe at the prospect, and not a little apprehension.

"Why is sex considered a hindrance to spirituality in most religions?" she says to hide her nervousness. "In many traditions, the most spiritual people don't indulge their sexual natures. It's not obvious why. Why shouldn't making love be the ultimate sacrament of union with God?"

Sarah laughs. "Only with a Jesuit would I be lying here contemplating the conundrum of sex and spirit."

"Well, what would you be doing with a Franciscan or Dominican?"

"This." She brings her lips to his. At first it is a light lingering, then a flood of sensations as the kiss deepens. There is a dream-like quality. As his mouth explores hers, they risk being swept beyond control. Jamie lifts his head and studies her. He has never seen such naked, defenseless longing on a face. And she's longing for him.

For Sarah, it's like the first time she has ever been with a man. "I feel like a virgin who's been asleep all her life." Her voice sounds amazed. "And now you're waking me. To be with you like this, Jamie, when I never thought it was possible...I can't begin to tell you..."

They lie together for a while in silence alive with emotion. Finally, Sarah sits up and invites him to follow. When they are face-to-face, her hands move to the buttons of her blouse. Slowly she opens one after another. She's wearing nothing underneath. When she spreads the fabric back to reveal her breasts, Jamie gasps. His eyes widen and move from her face to her chest and back again.

"So beautiful...and the colors of you," he murmurs. "Pink and rose and cream and brown. Oh Sarah, how lovely you are."

So moved by his response, at first she can't speak. She looks at him and sees something that stirs her beyond words. This man has the innocence of a boy. It's obvious from the wonder in his expression. He doesn't move, simply gazes at her.

"Jamie, love, you can touch me. I'd like you to."

He blushes, and she laughs softly. He seems to be holding his breath as he reaches out and cups his hands over her breasts. His eyes close as he caresses her. As she watches, becoming aroused herself, she is struck by the fact he is handling her body with the same reverence she saw in his movements in the liturgy. She bends toward him and opens his shirt. She strokes his naked chest, feeling the contrast of soft skin and firm muscles. His breath catches.

"I have something for you." He reaches into a shirt pocket. He opens his hand to reveal a ring, a fiery white opal set with small dark blue stones in a platinum band. "This was my grandmother's engagement ring. I'd like you to have it." His voice is shy.

"Being with you is the closest I'm ever going to have to a marriage. This ring is one of the few material things I treasure. Grandma gave it to me because I love opals. Ellen has her wedding ring. When she took this ring off and handed it to me, I said, 'It's beautiful, Grandma, but I won't be able to use it as it's intended.' She winked at me and said, 'Honey, you just never know.'

"Well, she was right, wasn't she, bless her?" His smile is tender with memory.

Sarah's face is radiant as he takes her hand and places the ring on her finger. The fit is close enough to wear it. Holding him with her eyes, she shrugs off her blouse. She reaches for Jamie and slips off his shirt. Soon they're stretched out again in front of the fire burning in the hearth. They can feel its warmth. They lie against each in the silent music of skin moving against skin. They experience a passion both deep and slow. They are blissfully in no hurry, totally in love with this moment and unwilling to let it go. They speak what language cannot say with eyes and hands and lips. The intimacy is sweet beyond belief.

"Heaven must be like this," Sarah whispers.

"It must be, since God is love," Jamie murmurs.

As time passes further into the winter-spring night, it is as though the burning stars in the pre-dawn sky have fallen to earth, now, in this place. Surprisingly few words are exchanged in the passing hours. Touches and kisses bring intimate revelations of one to the other. They are lovers in all but the final act.

"Do you feel it?" he asks softly.

"I do. Oh, Jamie, surely now you know this is God's gift to us." He answers by leaning his head against her breast to listen to the sound of her heart beating. She runs her fingers gently through his hair.

They fall into sleep, and peace and rapture follow them into their dreams.

THIRTY-NINE

Sometime in the early hours, they wake and make their way to Sarah's bed. They cuddle together in the sheer joy of this new closeness...laughing softly...sinking back into slumber.

Jamie opens his eyes, and for a moment is startled to find himself entwined with a warm soft body. He moans softly, the pleasure so great he can hardly contain it. He smiles into the dawn light. He has never spent the night with a woman. Imagine—a man in his fortieth year who has never shared a bed with a lover.

He watches Sarah's sleeping face, smooth and peaceful, lips curved slightly upward, lashes dark against her cheek. His heart swells with love. Her breathing is quiet. He notices her appealing fragrance; she smells like bread.

Without waking, she snuggles against him, sending shock waves of desire through him. He tries to slow his breathing to calm himself, but it is impossible with her skin against his, creating points of fire at every place they touch.

As his body rises, Sarah's eyes fly open. Happiness suffuses her face.

"You're here with me. Oh, Jamie."

"I love you," he says. Sarah grins.

"I can tell," she replies. They laugh, then look at each other with a question in their eyes.

"How about having coffee and doing our ablutions? Then we can come back to bed and make love."

Jamie experiences the shock of her words. They are really going to do this!

"Make love. Right here? That soon?"

"Yes, Sweetheart, after all this time and all the inner struggle...we're going to lie down here this morning and give ourselves to one another." Her face turns serious. "Unless you have changed your mind. Please be honest, Jamie!"

"I haven't changed my mind."

HAVING SHOWERED, Jamie is sitting on a bench in the secluded backyard, barefoot, shirt open, face raised to the sun. Sarah emerges from the house in a dark-blue Japanese kimono strewn with birds and peony blossoms. Her auburn hair is a wild halo, tips glowing red in the light. She sits down across from him.

They regard one another with the delight and shyness of children.

"You are so dear. Such a good man. I am the most fortunate woman to be here with you like this."

Jamie stands, comes over and takes her hand.

"Arise my love, my beautiful one, and come," he says softly. "For, lo, the winter is past. The rain is over and flowers appear. The time of singing birds has come, and the song of the turtle is heard in our land."

"My beloved is mine, and I am his," Sarah replies, glad to show him that she too knows parts of the Song of Songs by heart.

"Upon my bed by night, I sought him whom my soul loves." She rises and puts her arm around his waist.

"When I found him whom my soul loves, I held him and would not let him go." She draws him closer and leads him into the house.

Light through the closed curtains turn the room into a glow of rose. Sarah and Jamie lie without speaking, eyes exploring each others bodies for the first time. Jamie's heart is pounding and he can hardly breathe from the thrill of seeing her this way. She reads his feelings in his expression. They match her own.

"God couldn't have made you more beautiful." His voice is husky with emotion.

"I've never considered myself beautiful." Her tears well up.

"Look in my eyes, and you'll know the truth of how lovely you are." He reaches and strokes the curve of her body. "You're exactly what I dreamed you'd be, lush and wonderful, like a painting." His gray eyes radiate desire.

Now it's Sarah's turn to study him. He's tall, firmly muscled. His body looks powerful. Her breathing quickens, and he responds in kind. Yet neither moves toward the other, content simply to let the waves of sensation and emotion sweep through them.

"I can actually make love to you." Jamie's tone is incredulous.

"Yes, you can. Now." Sarah slides toward him and opens her arms. Jamie moves into them.

Desire unites them in what feels like a living sacrament, ancient and timeless. Words and thoughts seem far away. This moment itself is a prayer, unspoken but filled with a profound thankfulness and a fervent hope that their journey has led them to a place of God and an act of blessing.

They come together in passion and sweetness beyond even their imagination of what it would be. This is all the longing of the past eighteen months made flesh, expressing the union that has been there from the beginning. Sarah's body welcomes him, and moving within her, Jamie knows what it is to be in paradise.

They flow into one another with wild grace, like ocean meeting land on every lonely shore. She rises to offer herself, and he pours his life into her. In a soaring, burning moment, it is as though Sarah and Jamie cease to exist as individual beings, lost in a oneness where there is space only for the Divine. Two bodies joined in love are now, in the words of Teilhard de Chardin, "the incandescent surface of Matter immersed in God."

As they return to their separate selves, they continue to hold each other. So close that each can feel the other's heartbeats, they are reluctant to open any physical distance between them. The stillness stretches out as the energy of connection passes from one to another in a continuation of the act of love itself. After a time, Jamie moves his head slightly so he can look into Sarah's face. His smile is beatific.

"This is 'the birthday of my life,' " he whispers. "I've always loved that line from Christina Rossetti's poem. Today I know what it means."

Again they slip into a wordless rapture and, still touching, drift into sleep in the golden light of evening. Serenity permeates the room. The only sound is a soft pulse of breathing that seems to be coming from a single source.

SARAH AWAKENS to see Jamie studying her.

"My love, *my lover*," he exclaims softly.

"Are you happy?" she asks.

"Happy doesn't begin to describe it."

"I'm so glad. Part of me worried you'd be full of regret today."

"Sarah, I will never be sorry for loving you, body, heart and soul. As for the good people who condemn what we've done, well, God bless them. They may be right. But what happened with you yesterday was mystical...for a moment it was as if we disappeared together into Love itself." He trails off as he gazes into her eyes.

"Jamie, I felt that too."

They rest together in the quiet of the morning whose brightness is just beginning to show itself.

FORTY

Surprisingly, Sarah and Jamie do not indulge in unfettered love-making now. Instead, they spend much of their time together simply savoring the freedom of being able to express affection physically: embracing, kissing, caressing each other. Their passion seems to join them without the need to act on it. There is something sacred in simply experiencing the source of life moving between them as the energy of love.

"I'm still, well, 'awed' is the only word that seems right, by what it was like to make love with you," Jamie confides. "The emotions keep playing inside me like music so beautiful it can't be expressed in lyrics." They are entwined on the sofa in Sarah's living room at twilight the next day. Venus, the evening star, is glowing in the western sky. His head rests on her breast.

"What a beautiful way to describe it." Her voice is warm. "Part of me is longing to make love with you again. Another part is still absorbed in our first time. I don't need to reach for more right away."

Jamie strokes her hair. "Well, my love, let's enjoy our private honeymoon as long as we can. Tomorrow we face the world." Sam will be home the next day. The following evening Mark and Julianna have invited them to farewell dinner for Jamie. Rosa is coming. Under the circumstances, it promises to be an emotional gathering.

"You're going to tell Sam?"

"Yes, I owe him that."

"Wow, that will be painful. It's going to be really tough for him to come to terms with us. He won't be surprised, but it will hurt him."

"Yes, It will. I'm praying to find the best way to tell him."

Sarah takes his head in her hands and raises it. She kisses his lips, not lingering long enough to let the fire take hold.

"I'm praying too."

JAMIE IS PACKING his personal belongings into storage boxes to make way for a visiting Jesuit who'll share the apartment with Sam while he's gone. He doesn't have much to stow—clothes not suitable for the tropics, letters, official documents, a few "treasures" like the scrapbook his grandmother made of his youth and gave him when he was ordained. There are musical instruments—two guitars, a keyboard and an electric violin.

As he tapes the last box, there is the sound of Sam's key in the door. "Well here it comes," he thinks, feeling tense. His housemate calls his name.

"I'm packing." Jamie steps into the living room. Sam

glances at him, and drops his duffle bag, which hits the floor with a thud.

"You've done it, haven't you?" His voice is hard. Jamie is shocked. He didn't expect the confrontation to come this fast.

"How do you know?"

"You look different." Sam's body seems to sag, and he drops down onto the sofa. "Oh, Jamie, Jamie," he groans. "How can you radiate whatever, call it happiness, bliss, when you've broken your solemn vow to God?"

Jamie sinks into a chair. His face is grave as he registers his friend's obvious distress. Sam's eyes are glistening with what appear to be tears, and this brings moisture to his own.

"I wish there was something I could say or do to make this easier on you. At least I'm leaving, so you won't have me in your face. I hope that will help."

"I don't even understand why I'm so upset. It's not a surprise and really not my business." Sam sounds depressed. "I knew it was coming. What gets me is the joy in you. You're so calm. Guilt and shame should be pouring out of you, and they're not. That scares me."

Jamie is at a loss. He looks down at the floor and thinks of Sarah. He prays for guidance, the silent words emerging from a deep sorrow that he is hurting this man he loves.

"You know I like and care about Sarah. I want both of you to be happy." Sam's tone is angry. "Part me wants to ask you what it was like to make love with someone you love so much. I've never had that. If I'm honest, I'm feeling envious, and that really disturbs me. It's like you've upset the equilibrium of our lives big time."

"That's true, and God knows what the repercussions will be," Jamie acknowledges. "But, Sam, I'm not sorry. I *don't* feel guilty. I *have broken a solemn promise*, and I'd do it again in heartbeat. I may be delusional, but no one in this world could convince me God wasn't in what Sarah and I did.

"It makes absolutely no sense in the moral universe I've lived in all my life, but till the day I die, I'll believe loving this woman is right and good."

Sam can only stare at him. Finally, he utters a harsh bark of laughter. "Well, one of us is crazy, that's for sure."

"The party tomorrow. If you don't want to go, if it would make you uncomfortable seeing us together, feel free to be sick. We'll miss your presence, but I'll certainly understand."

His housemate's hesitation is only momentary. "Are you kidding? I'm baking Irish soda bread in celebration of the better part of your heritage. How it's going to go with the pesto from your depraved Italian side, I don't know, but it's what Juli asked me to make. She does have eclectic tastes.

"If only you were a 100 percent fine, upstanding and sexually-repressed Irishman, we wouldn't be having this conversation."

"In that case I could have succumbed to the temptation of Demon Rum, the Irish trap."

"Well, it's saved many a 'foin Father' from those wicked daughters of Eve. Besides, we'd be able to keep you inside, so you couldn't scare the sheep."

Still hurt and angry but seeking solace in humor, Sam regards Jamie with a wry smile. "Since I've avoided the booze and women pitfalls so far, my friend, get working on those canonization nomination papers."

Jamie feels relief wash over him. There may be difficult times and hard feelings ahead, but eventually he and Sam will be okay. Their long history will save them.

Sam is nowhere near as sure of the future of their friendship. But what can he do now when Jamie is about to leave for one of the most dangerous places on earth for priests? He says nothing more, determined to keep the peace for the present—whatever that takes.

A GLORIOUS SUNSET is forming in the West as Sarah and Jamie walk slowly along the pier at the Berkeley Marina. They are alone this far out, though they can see other people closer to shore. They reach the end of the weathered structure and pause to look toward the Golden Gate. They are holding hands, both aware of the sharp sweetness of the contact.

"I keep remembering what it was like to be with you, and not just in my body, although that feeling is pretty intense when you're within touching distance," Sarah says shyly. "There's a different quality to the love inside me too that I can't quite put into words. I think I'll need to find poetry.

"And something new is happening for me spiritually. When my heart opens and reaches out to God, it goes through you. You are so totally present. Am I making sense?"

In answer, Jamie turns and takes her in his arms. The wind is rising as he kisses her mouth, softly at first then with growing passion. Sarah responds in kind. She feels some essence of herself pouring into him and an essential part of him coursing back into her.

They are disappearing together in a vast brightness. With a shock of recognition, she knows that in a minute everything that separates them could disappear too...inhibitions, sanity... right here in the sight of God, the pier folk and the seagulls flying overhead.

Sarah pushes Jamie away gently but firmly.

"Do you come here often?" she asks wide-eyed. He

regards her with a slightly-dazed expression, then begins to laugh at the reminder of their first encounter on the pier.

"Thank you, *thank you!* Those wild sunset colors were shining through my eyelids, and I lost myself for a second there."

"Right, blame the sunset!" She bats her fist against his chest.

He drops to a sitting position and draws her down to him. She nestles between his knees, leaning against his chest. His arms go around her as they watch the sun rainbowing clouds in the sky.

"When you said what you did just now, I realized you were almost describing what happened to me earlier today," Jamie murmurs into her ear. "I was in Tilden Park in that eucalyptus grove across from Jewel Lake, and suddenly I fell into what I guess you'd call ecstasy. It was like being plunged into the heart of God. You were there, but the feelings were so strong, I couldn't sort out exactly what was going on.

"Then, when you said what you said, I knew just the thought of you and us was the gate into that experience. It was a flood, and you were the wave that carried me. You're right about needing the language of poetry."

"I love you with everything," Sarah whispers. They sit quietly as the earth turn toward the night.

At last Jamie speaks into the silence.

"My deepest spiritual experiences have been around the Eucharist. At the consecration, I've loved leading the community in the transformation of ordinary things into Presence. It's always been a very intimate act for me.

"Today I thought about Jesus' words a priest says, 'This is my body given for you,' Sarah, for the rest of my life, you're going to be part of that. I'm going to think of you, and feel you, in those words. I have a completely new understanding of what it means to give one's body for love."

Moved by what he's just revealed of himself, she nestles closer. They remain so until the first stars appear in the cobalt sky.

"Please come to me tonight." Sarah says softly when she finds her voice again.

"You are all fair, my love," he whispers in response. "Until the day breaks and the shadows flee, I will go my way to the mountain of myrrh and the hill of frankincense."

"You've been memorizing!" She glances back at him with obvious pleasure. Jamie smiles, his expression tender. He stands and helps her to rise.

"You have ravished my heart, My sister, my spouse," he says. "You have ravished my heart with one look of your eyes." Sarah laughs. Arm in arm, lost in one another, they begin to make their way home.

FORTY-ONE

Her hands full, Sarah rings the bell with an elbow. She can hear an operatic aria. The door flies open and Julianna appears, cheek smudged with flour. She grabs one of the grocery bags and leads Sarah into a large, bright kitchen. Fragrances of meat and onions perfume the air, while Maria Callas sings from La Bohème on a tape player.

Sarah begins to rummage in the bags, putting off the emotional moment she knows is coming. "I've brought the pesto and avocados for the salad. I hear you've asked Sam to make Irish soda bread—a strange combination, but what the heck?" she babbles.

"I wanted to celebrate both parts of Jamie's genetic heritage, and I hate corned beef *and cabbage*. What else do the Irish have?" She turns toward Julianna, and their eyes meet. In a flash they are hugging, weeping and laughing.

"*O Dio mio,* two *paesane* emoting." Sarah manages to choke out the words. "We'd better wring ourselves dry now before the others come."

Her friend examines her face. "*Povera donna mia*," she begins, then stops abruptly, her eyes penetrating.

"Oh Lord, Sarah, my God, you've made love with him, haven't you? Yes, you have! I know it! Tell me the truth."

Sarah's features register shock.

"I can't believe this!" she exclaims. "Sometimes it's hell having intuitive friends. Sam took one look at Jamie and knew instantly. This has to be a secret, and it's pretty scary that we're obviously so transparent. What did I do? How did you know?"

"I can't say exactly. There's something different about you and I can feel it here." Julianna strikes her chest creating a floury imprint on her blouse. "It's like a silent singing, and I'm hearing it."

Sarah blushes and turns away. Her companion is remorseful. "I'm sorry. You know me, from brain to mouth in a nanosecond. But the other night Mark was saying it was such a damned shame, Jamie going off into danger without you two ever being together like that.

"Now tell me everything! Hurry, we only have an hour before my husband gets home."

"I'm telling you nothing! For heaven's sake, Juli, Jamie's life and reputation are at stake here. "Please, please don't tell anyone, I beg you!" Sarah leans against a counter and puts her hands over her face. On cue, her friend changes the subject.

"I'm making espresso. Would you like a cup?" For the next half hour, the women work together to finish the meal preparations. They chat. Then Julianna puts her pies in the oven, dusts herself off and motions Sarah into the garden. At first they sit under the yard's large walnut tree without speaking. At last Julianna can no longer contain herself.

"Sarah, I am so, so happy for you and Jamie. I cannot tell you how happy. Just let me say my piece, and I'll shut up."

Sarah's face looks vulnerable. She sighs. "All right."

"Jamie has so much love in him, and he gives it away generously. We've all felt the gift of it, and returned it. It's been easy. He is one lovable man. At the same time, he's been so existentially alone. Mark and I have wanted someone for him, a woman with a love big enough for a man in his situation.

"When we met you, it was obvious you were ideal. Even my laconic Mark got excited. The first time you came here, after you left, he said, 'Juli, she's the one. If only he can see it. If only he can reach beyond all that Catholic conditioning.'

"So while you two have been fighting your heroic battles with passion, some of your friends have been praying you'd lose. And what do you know, God has answered our prayers!"

"We're struggling so hard, and you are praying we'll fall? With friends like you, as they say, who needs enemies?" Sarah looks incredulously at the other woman.

"So you're 'fallen' are you? Wicked sinners? Is Jamie going to confess to Sam and ask for absolution?"

The opera is still playing through the open door, and now a tenor's voice soars into some great drama. It's all too much. Sarah starts to laugh. Soon they are both laughing so hard, the two family cats come to stare at these crazy, noisy humans.

That's how Jamie and Mark find them. Jamie grins.

"I guess I didn't need to worry you'd be overcome with grief at losing my charismatic presence. Don't stop for us. It's the perfect send-off."

"Can you share the source of this hilarity or did we have to be there?" Mark looks curious.

"Sorry, but you had to be there." Julianna regards him

with a wicked glint in her eye. She is dying to stare at Jamie and monitor exactly how he is with Sarah but resists temptation. Instead, she stands and hurries into the kitchen muttering about pies in the oven.

Sarah's heart is pounding as she raises her eyes to Jamie and tries to force her voice into a friendly but casual tone. Instead, it emerges high and nervous, and Jamie sneaks her a delighted glance.

"Hello there." His voice is artificially deep and calm. It almost breaks them both up. Mark comes to the rescue by bending down to give her a kiss and suggesting a glass of a new wine he's discovered.

"OKAY, YES I STILL LOVE YOU," Sam whispers into Sarah's ear as she answers the door to let him in. "But I'm very pissed off, disapproving and envious. Don't mind me."

"You're a good person." She hugs him.

"Well, better than some." He sounds teasing and chiding at the same time.

"You're right of course. What can I say, Sam? There's nothing, is there?"

"Do not judge lest ye be judged," he retorts. "That's my mantra these days."

Mark appears with perfect timing.

"Did you bring the soda bread?"

"Of course, even a Jesuit can remember something that simple."

REPLETE with good food and conversation spiced with laughter, a dozen friends relax around the large round table that is one of the Mark's and Julianna's prized possessions. It's been a sweet and heartfelt evening, saved from mere sentimentality by the caustic wit of those gathered. It's late, but no one seems to want to move to end their last time all together for a year. A sharp, bell-like sound calls their attention as Mark taps his knife on a wine glass.

"We are here to bid adios to our good friend here." He touches Jamie on the shoulder. I can speak for everyone when I say, 'Jamie, we love you. We'll miss you. We'll be praying for you.' "

"Here, here," the others call out.

"I love *you all*." Jamie's eyes are misty. He looks around the table at each one. "I'm sure going to miss *you*. I know our prayers will help keep us close."

"You're our hero," Rosa proclaims. He reaches over and pulls her hair.

"Oh, of course, the saintly priest going off to save the people. Give me a break, Rosy! If Rome comes sniffing around with canonization papers, all I ask is that Sam be the one to write my holy biography." Sam snorts loudly.

"That was a fine snort, my man," Julianna declares. "You don't often hear a snort of that caliber these days. It's a lost art. Yours, though, had real resonance." Laughter.

As it fades, Jamie looks directly at Sarah, his expression naked with love and longing. Shocked by his non-verbal candor, she manages to return his gaze steadily. Silence falls. Their friends watch both of them as the moment stretches out. Without a word he's making clear the nature of their relationship.

When he finally speaks, his voice is husky. "Sarah is going to miss me most. I hope each of you will help make sure she has a lot of happy times while I'm away."

Now everyone is talking at once, assuring him that will happen.

"Well, love, now they all know. I hope you've done the right thing being so open," Sarah thinks, her expression solemn.

∾

IT'S A GLORIOUS MARCH SUNDAY. Purple wisteria and golden honeysuckle perfume the air as Sarah walks down the hill to the seminary chapel. The Catholic community at PTU is gathering for a liturgy commemorating the fifth anniversary of the assassination of Archbishop Oscar Romero, killed by a single rifle shot as he celebrated Mass in the chapel of a hospital in San Salvador.

Because Jamie is about to leave for El Salvador, he's been asked to preside. The sun is warm, yet Sarah feels a chill. The valiant archbishop who risked and lost his life for the sake of his people reminds her that church workers are still being kidnapped and murdered down in that country. It's a very dangerous place.

She remembers how the passion with which she opened to Jamie this morning was tinged with a piercing fear. As she held his body to hers, she thought how vulnerable the human body is. It could be destroyed in an instant.

During the night, waking together in the darkness, they'd said things to one another that will be with Sarah always.

"I'm still awed by how profound this is for me," Jamie had said. "Making love is so total, so all-encompassing. It's not just my body. It's everything I am. I didn't expect that."

He'd traced her face with his finger. "Once I had a dream of making love to you. Your body was an altar where I could worship God in the Divine Feminine. That's how it is to be with you."

Sarah looked into his eyes. "It's adoring God with our bodies," she said. "Making love with you is surrendering to the God of life, opening myself totally to the Divine through you."

In the darkness, they rested in the feelings their words evoked.

Then, silently, in unspoken communion, they'd moved together into the ancient sacred ritual. An ordinary room in an ordinary house became for a time, a mosque, a temple, a cathedral of love. As it was in the beginning, is now and ever shall be, world without end.

MOVING AS THE LITURGY IS, for Sarah it brings a cloud of dread. Jamie recalls the story of the archbishop who, despite threats, continued to speak out about the murders and torture of innocent civilians by the Salvadoran army, police and government-sponsored militias.

He reads from Romero's last sermon in which the archbishop had spoken feelingly of ordinary civilians who'd been killed in the past week. His final appeal was to young soldiers and policemen:

"Brothers, each of you is one of us. The peasants you kill are your own brothers and sisters. When you hear a man telling you to kill, remember God's words, 'thou shalt not kill.' No soldier is obliged to obey a law contrary to the law of God.

"In the name of God, in the name of the suffering

people whose cries rise to heaven more loudly each day, I implore you, I beg you, I order you in the name of God: stop the repression."

As the liturgy continues, Sarah finds she cannot separate the priest from the lover. Jamie's graceful movements call to mind the ways he touches and loves her body. When he reverently speaks the words of consecration, "This is my body given for you," their eyes meet. Passion and sacredness collide inside Sarah, leaving her breathless.

Permeating everything, though, is her fear for him. She wants to protect him from pain and hurt and the possibility of death. But all her love is powerless to shield him. After Mass, Sarah doesn't have the heart to listen to the goodbyes and good wishes.

She walks home dispiritedly.

The reality is here. Jamie is leaving for a place much further away than the distance in miles, to be among people whose lives and experiences are so different from hers that she can scarcely imagine how it feels to be them. He'll be in the midst of a terrible war waged by men who consider priests their enemies.

In the bright spring day, she suddenly feels the darkness and pain of all women and men who send their beloved ones into great danger. Like a cloud of witnesses, they surround her—those who have reluctantly opened their arms to give those they love most over to the senseless destruction that war is.

Here and now Sarah has to face the cruel truth: Jamie may die in El Salvador. Pure pain cuts through her. She can see her garden wall ahead. Hunched over, her arms wrapped around herself, Sarah staggers toward it.

FORTY-TWO

Jamie and Sarah say goodbye in the early morning after a night of loving.

They part in the garden with the hopeful beauty of spring all around them in the green leaves and blossoms like God's promises for the future. A cascade of lavender-hued wisteria over the wall is perfuming the soft air.

They've decided this is more intimate and private than the frenzied atmosphere of the airport. Jamie is flying to Baltimore to spend a few days with his sister Ellen and her family on his way to Central America.

Silently, they hold each other enveloped in feelings so powerful that speech is impossible. Her head is against his chest, and she hears the beating of his heart. They remain motionless for a long time.

When they finally move apart, Sarah's smile is mischievous.

"Forgive me, but I can't resist." She begins bravely to sing in a voice that, while pleasant, only occasionally reaches the tune.

"Now the hacienda's dark
The town is sleeping.
Now the time has come to part
The time for weeping
Vaya con dios, my darling
Vaya con dios, my love."

Grinning, Jamie raises his arms in a dramatic gesture, and adds his deep, trained voice,

"Wherever you may be, I'll be beside you
Although you're many million dreams away
Each night I'll say a prayer
A prayer to guide you
To hasten every lonely hour
Of every lonely day"

"Vaya con dios, my darling
Vaya con dios, my love."

They break into the free, uninhibited laughter of children. It is a moment filled with so many emotions.

"Sarah, I love you with all my heart and soul, but I beg you, please don't give up your day job." They laugh into each other's eyes. Then Jamie kisses her tenderly. Watching her face and releasing her hand reluctantly, he opens the gate behind him, and disappears into the street.

～

As he walks down the hill, despite his sadness, warmth radiates from his heart. It reaches out to the people and animals he passes, and they respond. Children smile shyly or offer big grins. Adults give him friendly hellos and smiles and sometimes expressions so vulnerable they seem to allow him into the secret depths of other hearts.

Jamie feels suffused with love for everything, the sparrow sitting on a branch over the sidewalk, tender blades of grass fighting their way through a crack in the pavement, a crossing guard whose surly face softens when she looks into his.

In the early hours, the last time they made love, it was as though he could not get close enough to Sarah. He yearned to fuse with her, to be one body holding two souls. Strange thoughts that powered his passion, a longing she too experienced.

"Is there any way I can *be you and me at the same time?*" she'd breathed. "It's not enough anymore to be just me. I want to see through your eyes and feel with your heart too."

He gazed at her face alive with love for him, and could find no words to express what he was feeling. Instead he gave himself to her completely, telling her with eyes, and lips, hands and body how well he knew and shared her desire. As they lay together in the stillness afterward, he spoke softly.

"You and I are one being."

Remembering, Jamie is incandescent with joy. "It's wonderful to see someone so happy on a beautiful spring day." An elderly woman in a dress with a pattern of flowers, holding a cane, is walking toward him. He stops and regards this person, whose features show the marks of time and life.

"What a sweet thing to say to a stranger. Thank you for sharing your love with me."

She is obviously surprised yet pleased by his remark.

"That's what we're here for, isn't it, to share love?" She smiles as they pass on the sidewalk.

"I believe I just met an angel," Jamie thinks, walking on. What just happened is what he is hoping for. His prayer is to carry this powerful love he and Sarah share wherever he goes and to absorb her best qualities into himself. He's asking God for her generosity, her capacity for caring, her overflowing empathy, her sense of fun and so much else that delights him. He prays to bring the best in both of them to the people of El Salvador.

SARAH'S CLASS on John's Gospel ends in a lively conversation as students examine the text word-by-word, searching for clues to what the evangelist was trying to convey through the symbolic language in the account of Jesus' resurrection.

As she gathers her books and papers and sets out for the library, her mind turns to Jamie. He's been gone for almost two weeks now. He'd called from Maryland the night before he'd left for Central America. "Why don't you just leave your profession and come with me?" he'd teased. "You can be my housekeeper."

Sarah had chuckled. "In your dreams, Father."

"Too late, you're already in those." There had been a smile in his voice.

He'd warned her his letters might take weeks to reach her. "So we'll have to do a lot of communicating beyond words, Sarah. I feel you with me. I hope you feel that too."

"No worries there, Jamie. You're part of everything I do. You're with me night and day. Like you said, one being."

Now, pausing on the hill over San Francisco Bay, she looks into the vast blue dome of the sky. Far away in a place very different from this one, Jamie is offering his love and his life to people she will never meet. "I love you." She says it silently, her heart lifting up beyond herself. "I love you so much," Sarah tells God, Jamie and the people of El Salvador all at the same time.

FORTY-THREE

S an Salvador, April 3

Dear Sarah,

"I write your name in this hot tropical night and see you in my mind's eye the last time we walked along the Bay with the breeze blowing your hair into a halo against the setting sun. And the way we came together later that night at home. Memories wash over me. As you hoped, I smile.

I wonder what you're doing right now. I'd like to imagine you're sitting in the garden thinking of me.
As we left the plane I asked the friendly pilot how far San Salvador was from Berkeley. He looked at me quizzically, then went back to the cockpit, returning to say we were now 3,159 miles or 5,083 kilometers from our town. Somehow it's a

comfort to know the actual dimensions of our physical separa-
tion. In my daydreams I can travel down those miles in no time
at all.

San Salvador has changed since last year. Even more young men
with assault rifles were stationed around the airport, and most
looked tense. I offered friendly smiles as I passed them, but no
one responded in kind.

Diego met me with a hug and a bouquet of small sunflowers.

It was reassuring to see him, my brother in Christ and my
friend. He'd borrowed a Jeep from a Catholic charity to take us
into the city center. The road from the airport includes lonely
stretches with no signs of habitation. When Diego pulled off
the highway and stopped near a grove of trees and I saw the
flowers, I knew where we were. It was where Ita, Maura,
Dorothy and Jean were stopped and kidnapped. People have
planted a little garden with four carved wooden crosses. The
other day there were iris and narcissus and a few red poppies.

It was a very emotional experience to be in the place made sacred
by the sacrifice of those brave and loving women.

We knelt down, and in the stillness the presence of God was
palpable. I prayed for the Salvadorans living so very precariously
and painfully in their own land. I asked Our Lady of
Guadalupe to keep you safe and well and to fashion us into
effective instruments of God's love and compassion.

Oh, Sarah, I feel so inadequate in the face of the pain one can
sense everywhere.

I am staying in an old convent. They gave me my own room, and I feel guilty because some women religious are shoehorned two and three to a room. My protests were to no avail. "Padre, I do not think the sisters want you in their rooms," Pablo, the custodian, joked to shut me up.

It's interesting to arrive during Holy Week. In the middle of so much turmoil, there's also an air of expectation of the upcoming feast. On every corner people, including young kids, are selling holy pictures and posters, medals and pamphlets of saints' lives. Pictures of Jesus crucified and risen and the Holy Family (looking very holy indeed with their eyes raised to heaven) are occasionally interspersed with posters of Rambo and Superman. I laughed out loud the first time I saw this strange combination, to the delight of the boy salesman. "But Jesus is stronger than Rambo or Superman, right Padre?" he said, I guess to reassure me. (I was wearing my collar because I was on my way to the chancery to get my "priest credentials.") Walking in one neighborhood I heard the bleating of lambs and tried not to think what would happen to the poor little creatures later in the week.

On Easter I'll be helping out at San Marcos, a vibrant parish on the outskirts of the city. I spent yesterday evening with Ricardo, the pastor, and like him a lot.

It's been a long couple of days getting to know my way around and meeting people. I will close now, sending you my love. I promise more details in the next epistle. God bless and keep you, Sarah."

Yours,
Jamie

BEFORE SEALING THE LETTER, he places his hand on it as though trying to imprint his love onto the paper. Leaving it on the small desk, he heads wearily for bed. He sighs, feeling adrift and alone in an alien world. He sits on the edge of the cot, too tired to undress. "My God, my God," is the most he can manage before his mind simply shuts down. He is asleep as his head touches the thin hard pillow. His dreams are dark visions of children whose bones pierce through their skin, pleading with him from among fields of dead bodies.

When he opens his eyes in the morning, the reality of where he is assaults him like a hard punch to the solar plexus. This is a place of agonies beyond his ability to imagine. The bleak images of his dreams flood his mind. Pushing them aside with great effort, he remembers lying beside Sarah in rosy light. His mind savors the details of their loving. His body feels again the rapture of their first coming together. Jamie's breathing deepens, and the tension begins to ebb.

"I love you," he whispers into the dawn.

Energized, he gets out of bed and kneels before a crucifix, the room's only adornment, surrendering to God and offering himself to all the day will bring. Depression threatens again, but he concentrates on Sarah's face in his mind's eye. Diego has warned these first days in this crucified land will be difficult. "God will give you the strength, but it takes time to grow it," the priest had told him. "It's like a muscle that gets stronger as you exercise." He hopes his friend is right.

Riding into San Salvador three days ago, he had been struck by the smell. It was like being tossed into the middle of a dump of rotting garbage. The humid air and the heat made it worse. Diego saw the reaction on his face and smiled. "Don't worry, you'll get used to it. Soon you'll hardly notice it at all."

As they'd driven toward the neighborhood where he was

to stay, he'd seen that shanties had sprung up on every bit of vacant land. Pieced together from cardboard, wood and tin, they looked more like sheds for animals than homes for human beings. Narrow lanes wound among them, many not wide enough for a car. The flimsy structures were laid out in chains of misery.

"Refugees from the countryside," the Salvadoran Jesuit had explained. "The army is forcing then out of the rural areas, so the rebels won't have any civilian support or sources of food. They call it 'draining the sea.' They figure if they do that, the fish, the guerrillas, will die out. They've depopulated large areas of El Salvador."

They'd stopped at San Marcos Church, part of a complex that included a rectory, a community center and the convent where Jamie would stay. It was obviously a busy place, with classes going on, and cooks preparing food in a large kitchen. In two spacious rooms men and women were manufacturing hammocks and tortillas—small businesses that helped support the parish. Diego had introduced him to the pastor, Ricardo, a tall, hearty man with a shock of gray hair and lively eyes. He'd showed them around.

That evening by candlelight (because the electricity was off), the two men sat on a porch to catch the occasional breeze. At first the conversation was light, the usual getting-to-know-you talk. Then Ricardo turned to the American priest with a serious expression.

"My friend," he said. "You have come to a country that is in hell, even though traces of heaven can be found here too. Nothing in your life in North America has prepared you for this monstrous war in El Salvador."

Both were silent, lost in their own thoughts. Finally Jamie spoke, his voice soft. "Ricardo, how can I help? Will I be able to do anything useful for people?"

The other man regarded him soberly. "You are going to see and hear things that will test your faith to the utmost. I can promise that. You will think, 'What kind of God created men who can do such horrors? What kind of God could design such monsters and let them have their way?'

"And yet most are only young boys who have been trained and manipulated and coerced into savaging their own. They are lost souls, and you will be called upon to find the light of Christ in them too, no matter how deeply it is hidden, no matter how obscured by fear and hate and blood lust." They were grim, dramatic words, and Jamie felt them in his gut.

"What will wear you down, day after day, hour after hour, is the pain everywhere you turn your head, so much of it deliberately inflicted," Ricardo continued. "There are times you will forget that somewhere there are children who have food to fill their bellies, decent clothes and real homes instead of shacks cobbled together from whatever their parents can find.

"You will forget there are women who are young and pretty instead of worn into old age by their twenties, women who do not have despair and fear lurking in their faces. You will forget that somewhere there are confident men able to make good livings for their families who live on peaceful streets."

"Everything you think you know of God and those supposedly created in His image will be tested, Padre." The older priest had sounded sad. "You will have to seek a new God, and there is no guarantee you will find it."

He'd reached out and placed a hand on Jamie's arm. "As to what you can give, my brother? Most of all, simply your presence and your love. You will fail in this every day, often fail badly, but these are what you have to offer. Is there enough love in you to survive here? Tell me that, *mi hermano.*" His sharp black eyes had peered into the younger man's.

A bolt of fear had shot down Jamie's spine and he'd felt his spirits sinking. Suddenly, Sarah had been there in a powerful flow of feeling that enveloped him. He'd closed his eyes for a moment and let her have him, heart and soul. He'd opened them and gazed at Ricardo.

"By the grace of God, I have been granted that love," he had replied.

FORTY-FOUR

The next night three nuns in the convent invite Jamie to dinner. During silent prayer before the meal, he looks around the table at the women, their faces honed by the suffering of a life shared with the poor in wartime.

Monica and Francine are American Dominicans who've been in El Salvador since 1981. Francine, a nurse practitioner, trains local people to provide basic health care and education out in the community. Monica teaches in a Catholic school for refugee children and holds literacy classes for their parents. On weekends both sisters use the protection of their American citizenship to drive priests into rural areas and outlying towns to say Mass. The third woman, Sister Dorothea, a fellow Oregonian and Maryknoll missionary, is a nurse midwife taking a break in the relative safety of San Salvador after months in the much more dangerous district of Chalatenango.

The four share a simple meal of tortillas, beans and cabbage salad seasoned with salt. While they eat, the conversation centers around practical things Jamie needs to know about the city, what neighborhoods are especially dangerous. Places to get decent cheap food. Sights to see. They laugh at the women's stories of the difficulties some priests have had getting used to a new culture.

"The Salvadorans are crazy about their children. Nothing is more important than their kids' happiness," Monica says. "Sometimes this means the little ones are allowed to run around and play during Mass. An Italian priest I know was incensed to see all this during the first Mass he said down here.

"He stopped the liturgy and told the parents in no uncertain terms to make their children behave or leave the church. There was a moment when nothing happened. Then, as one, all the adults gestured to the children, and every single person walked out the door. They stood outside looking in, waiting patiently for my friend to continue the liturgy. He stood there with his mouth open. He had no idea what to do next."

They all chuckle. "What did he do?" Francine asks.

"He went out and humbly invited them back in. Then he gathered the children at the front of the church and solemnly asked them if they would please not run or shout during Mass. Equally solemnly, they agreed to his request, and things were a lot better, at least for a while. That day Vittorio learned the value of treating everyone, including misbehaving kids, with respect."

"Then there's the whole matter of time," Francine says gleefully. There's a burst of laughter among the woman. "Either you'll learn to go with the flow down here when it comes to time, or you'll need blood pressure medication," she tells Jamie.

"When he first arrived, my Maryknoll friend Tom was asked to say the 5 p.m. Mass at a church about ninety miles

319

from here. Tom is obsessively punctual and will do almost anything to be on time, but on this trip he encountered a military convoy, animals on the road and some construction. He was a nervous wreck and drove like a maniac where the road was empty. He was certainly not going to be late for Mass! He pulled up to the little church sweating, with his heart pounding, but blessedly on time. He got out of the car and hurried in. There was no one there. Finally a man wandered in and exclaimed, 'Padre, you're early!'

'But I thought they said Mass was at 5 p.m.'

'Yes, that's right, but go have a rest. We won't begin until later. I'll call you.' Jamie joins in the laughter.

"Thanks for the warnings," he says. "Unfortunately, I'm sure I'll do plenty of things to add to your collection of insensitive and clueless priest tales."

"Be sure to let us know," Francine requests. "We're working on a book."

After they finish the meal, tea is served and the conversation becomes sober. "There have been days I've felt like death was battering me from all sides," Dorothea confides. She recalls a morning that began with a sixteen-year-old trainee of hers being blown apart by a mortar that struck near where she was working in the family cornfield. Later that morning, Dorothea and a colleague were riding in a truck with a tiny casket of a two-year-old boy who'd died of leukemia, and passed the headless corpse of a dead guerrilla. The same afternoon she'd gone with her friend Gloriana to search for her son among a dozen bodies that had been exhumed from a mass grave.

"I will never forget her face when she saw what was left of her boy."

"How do you bear it?" Jamie exclaims.

"Not very well," she admits. "I'm a mass of wounds.

Sometimes I think that's all that's left of me, a hide of wounds and anguish around the empty space of the person I used to be."

"But you endure. You're still here?"

Dorothea is silent for a few minutes. When she speaks, it is almost a whisper. "They are so incredibly dear, these women and their children and the good men who care about them. The little ones are unbelievably sweet. Some still have the innocent eyes of babies. Others look like very old people with tiny faces.

"I love them more than I've ever loved anyone or anything and sometimes that includes God. They've captured my heart and my soul. I am theirs until I die. Serving them is my purpose, my meaning." She bows her head and blushes. "I'm embarrassing myself."

Jamie reaches out his hand and places it over her slender fingers.

"Thank you," he says.

AS FRANCINE DRIVES, Jamie looks down into the steep ravine. Along the banks of a muddy stream a kind of village has sprouted. A few dozen buildings of brick, tin, scrap wood panels and materials he doesn't recognize, some only yards from the water, nestle along the shore and back into the hillside. A slab of concrete serves as a kind of public plaza. Clothes are drying on makeshift lines.

The people are refugees, many of whom lost everything when the military swept through their towns and farms. The rainy season is beginning. Soon the shacks will flood regularly, polluting the entire settlement.

Children are everywhere, playing with a ball in the plaza,

splashing in the water, sitting on a stone wall dangling their feet. A small girl is chasing a little pig around in the stream. Another is filling plastic jugs with the water. A few women wearing aprons notice the visitors first. They stare curiously as the two make their way down the hill.

"*Buenos dias,* Señoras," Francine calls with a friendly wave. "*Hola, Hermana* Francina," the women respond with big smiles. "Welcome."

"Who is your handsome boyfriend?" a large woman in a blue dress demands, causing laughter all around.

"You are wicked, Eva," the nun tells her. "This is Padre Jamie. He has come all the way from America to be with us."

"And now I know they are true, the rumors of how beautiful the women of El Salvador are," the priest says, joining in the spirit of the banter. The residents of the little shantytown gather around them, delighted.

Soon everyone is sitting at the "plaza" in old chairs and on a wall. They want to know all about the priest, his family, where he lives, his work in California. They have never met a psychologist and want to know what one does.

"I talk with people about problems they are having," Jamie says.

"How does talking help?" a woman asks. He explains that the job of a psychologist is to listen carefully and help the person discover how to help herself.

"Most of the time all of us, deep inside, have the answers we need for our lives. If someone listens to us and draws us out, we can often find those answers. Usually people will try to tell you what they think you should do. A psychologist helps you find your own way." The women's faces are alive with interest.

"Padre, sometimes I get angry with my children for no reason, and it hurts them and me too," Maria-Marta, a young woman with hair already graying, says softly as the others lean forward to hear. "Just this morning, I don't know what happened to me. My nerves got out of hand. My boy Carlos asked for another tortilla and I slapped him. Why did I do such a thing?"

She is weeping silently, although her voice is composed. Those listening nod. They have experienced the anxiety and helplessness of not being able to stretch a small amount of food to meet the needs of growing children. Now they remember the many times their own nerves betrayed them. Moisture comes into Jamie's eyes. The women see this and look at him and one another with soft expressions.

"My dear sister," he says haltingly, "You and these other good mothers here live with anxiety and fear that would be hard even for Our Blessed Mother. I think you struck Carlos because you love him so much and can't bear to see him go hungry. You do all you can to get food, yet your children do not always have enough to eat. Isn't that how it is with you?"

Several heads nod, including Maria-Marta's.

"Even Mother Mary would be frustrated in your place," he consoles. "We are human. When things go hard, we lose control of our feelings. We can't help it. But when we get angry and hurt someone, we can also make things right," he continues. "What happened after you slapped your son?"

"He looked so shocked and sad, and then he ran out of the house," she replies. "I didn't have a chance to do anything to make it better."

"When you see him again, what would you normally do?"

"I'd be nice to him and pretend like it never happened."

"Is there anything else you could do?" Maria-Marta regards him for a long moment.

"Maybe I could let him know of the love in my anger, how worried I am when there's no food, because I love him

323

and my other children so much." She falls silent, and Jamie can almost see her mind working behind the furrowed brow.

"If I do this, I think he will see my anger is not at him. He is a good boy. I will tell him how glad I am to have a son like him." Suddenly, she smiles. When she speaks again, her voice is more confident. "That is what I can do," she says, turning to the priest.

"Thank you, Padre. You have helped me very much."

Jamie laughs. "My dear sister, I did nothing but ask you a few questions. I just made a way for your own wisdom to come out."

"Do you see Maria-Marta has inside her the understanding to know the best thing to do?" He looks around at each of the women.

"Si, Padre," a few say, and the others voice or nod their assent.

"Well, it is the same for all of you. The wisdom is in you. If you ask questions like I just asked, you usually will find a wise solution to a problem.

"You can ask yourself or one another questions instead of giving advice. But you need the patience to go inside and wait for the answer. It may not come at once. Sometimes you have to think many thoughts, feel many feelings and wait. But when it comes, you'll know it's right. It will be very clear to you."

"If we ask questions, will we be psychologists like you? Can we make money?" the woman in the blue dress asks with a twinkle in her eyes. Everyone laughs.

"I THINK you'll be a gift for the people here, Jamie," Francine says as they walk back toward the jeep. "You seemed to find your place with those women so easily. Starting out by teasing and complimenting them at the same time was just the perfect thing. They definitely warmed up to you. When Salvadorans tease you, you can be sure they like you."

"I really like them too. I wish I could offer them more than a few psychological platitudes. They're such gallant women. Here they are holding onto a sense of fun and enjoyment in living conditions many people from our part of the world probably couldn't survive in."

"Are you falling in love like Dorothea?" the nun asks in amusement.

"I believe I am," he answers. "That didn't take long, did it?"

"Please don't think you'll find this lightness in everyone," she warns. "There's grief and heaviness too. You'll meet people who've lost their entire families or their husbands and wives and a couple of children. It's all they can do to keep on living."

"Thank you for reminding me," Jamie says quietly. "I pray I'm up to this."

FORTY-FIVE

P adre Laurens is around Jamie's age, but with his gray hair and wrinkled face looks ten years older. His expression is melancholy except when it lights with pleasure or humor. He walks with a stiff gait. His Dutch Jesuit order sent him to El Salvador as a missionary in 1972. Thus he is an unwilling historian of the country's brutal conflicts that have shaped his ministry for so long.

Laurens' church is in a town ringed by hazy blue mountains, a pretty white and yellow building with a graceful bell tower. Jamie has come here curious to meet this fellow Jesuit, because it is whispered that he ministers to the guerrillas who dominate these hills—and sometimes even travels with them. It is a secret known only to a very few. If it were revealed, Laurens would be dead in days. Diego, a good friend of the priest, has written a letter of introduction.

Sitting in the parlor of his small rectory, the priest tells Jamie he'd expected poverty in Central America but was unprepared for the reality. Death by starvation was common, and malnutrition stunted children's development. Peasants wore rags sewn together with other rags. Many lived in hovels, some fashioned from branches and leaves. If the crops on their little plots flourished, they could live. If the crops failed, they could die.

It was worse in the cities where refugees from rural areas were already flocking, even back then. Militias and army units regularly rampaged through the countryside and its towns and villages, particularly in the districts of Chalatenango and Morazan. These were singled out, according to Laurens, because they were the places with the most vibrant Christian communities that embraced liberation theology and influenced the people to seek better lives.

As poor *campesinos* and shopkeepers began to discover in the Bible that God wanted justice for the poor, their eyes were opened. Laborers on huge plantations started to organize into bargaining units. Schools for both children and adults sprang up all around. Priests and nuns of the "popular church" invited teachers and health care workers to come. And the young and the idealistic did come, eager to be part of a movement of persons discovering that joining together in community gave them bargaining power. The Dutch priest's expression brightens as he remembers those hopeful days.

"But all this threatened the power and control of the handful of wealthy families for whom El Salvador is their personal fiefdom filled with serfs to work their land and do their bidding," he says.

Laurens had been in El Salvador for five years when General Carlos Romero became President in an election marred by blatant fraud and voter intimation. "They didn't even pretend to run a fair election," he says. "Romero had the military in his pocket, so he could do anything he wanted."

A week after the vote, a huge crowd gathered peacefully in downtown San Salvador to protest the election fraud. "I was there when the security forces opened fire on us. I saw men and women and even children mowed down by the bullets. A few feet away from me was an overturned stroller, the baby spilled onto the street. The little one was crying hysterically. Nearby its mother was crumpled on the ground. I tried to reach them, but frightened protestors blocked my way. Soon the plaza was literally running with blood. People were screaming and crying in pain and terror. They tried to escape, but the crowd was too thick.

"It was a massacre, the most horrible thing I had ever experienced." The priest shakes his head. "I couldn't believe what was happening. I stood there and got ready to die. I said a prayer for the people of El Salvador. I asked God's mercy on them and on me. Any minute I expected to feel bullets tearing into my body." He shudders. The memory is vivid. "I still wake up shouting in the night."

His anguished eyes seek Jamie's.

"Then something hit me in the back of the head and I passed out. When I woke up, I was in a makeshift hospital with a concussion. I never found out what happened to the mother and her baby. I think of them often, and I wonder."

Jamie wants to reach out a hand to the priest but it's as though he's paralyzed. He'd read about the massacre, of course, but books can't begin to convey the energy of emotion that is passing from Laurens to him. For a moment it's like he himself is in that plaza experiencing the nightmare.

The Dutchman looks down at his feet and continues.

"From what I heard, when the people had fled, the army rushed in with trucks and took away the bodies. We'll never know just how many died, but some 1300 men, women and children disappeared that day and were never seen again. President Molina, whom Romero had defeated, blamed the protest on foreign Communists. He said they had to be stopped or El Salvador would be lost to them."

"And that was before the war started," Jamie muses.

"Yes, that was what passes for peace in this country," the other man responds.

Now Laurens changes the subject abruptly. He says that his Masses for the guerrillas are often broadcast live over Radio Venceremos ("We Shall Overcome" Radio), the underground station that moves constantly to thwart the government's desire to find and destroy it. Jamie has heard its broadcasts which many Salvadorans depend on for "real news." It is known for its leftist slant, commentary and pointed ridicule of the government, but it also provides spiritual sustenance through liturgies and inspiring talks, many religious.

"A few months ago, the army started bombarding the town where we were holding and broadcasting our Mass. On the radio in the background listeners could hear loud explosions. Meanwhile, our guerrilla choir is singing 'When the poor seek out the poor, and we meet in organization, then will come our liberation, the hope that Jesus gave us.' I can assure you, brother, no one was bored during that liturgy!" His face lights in a mischievous smile. "I love that the military and the government murderers have to listen to my homilies telling them the truth about themselves."

When Laurens goes out on the road with the *compañeros*, it is understood he will never shoulder a rifle. He's there to preside at Mass, perform sacraments, offer spiritual support and use the skills he learned in a year of medical school before joining the Jesuits.

"You wouldn't do it even to save someone's life?" Jamie asks.

"Only in that moment will I know," the other Jesuit replies.

It's clear Laurens loves and admires the men and women he calls freedom fighters and willing martyrs for the sake of their people. "In America you hear awful things about these guerrillas, that they are scheming Communists out to take over the whole hemisphere, that they kill and rape and pillage their own people," he says. "Those are lies and government propaganda. Not that they're perfect. Some of them have killed and destroyed property. Some groups have kidnapped people like mayors and held them for ransom to finance the armed struggle.

"But what I see all the time is their incredible bravery and willingness to sacrifice their very lives for the good of the poor and oppressed. I would like to introduce you to some of them."

Laurens bends close to Jamie and says quietly, "The day after tomorrow I'll be celebrating Mass in a community near the hills. Why don't you come with me and see the heart of this revolution first-hand?"

The implications of accompanying the priest flash through Jamie's mind.

There's the immediate physical danger, of course. And if anyone connected to the military or the government finds out, he could easily become a target of those who routinely kill church workers. Finally, he might also become a danger to those he works with in the future. Guilt by association can be a death sentence down here. He says all this to Laurens who seeks to ease his fears.

"I know these people well. They can be trusted to keep

your visit secret. However, I can't guarantee your physical safety, because attacks from the air come suddenly."

"I need more time to decide. May I tell you tomorrow?" Jamie asks.

"Take your time. But decide to come, Padre," the priest says with a smile. "You'll be glad you did."

IN THE SOFT warm air of the tropical night, Jamie lies in a hammock under the sky. Banks of clouds and fields of stars alternate above his head. The darkness is alive with sounds, chiefly insect conversations and bird calls, and the occasional shrieks of creatures he can't identify. The perfumes of flowers and blooming trees envelop him. It is deceptively peaceful. Because of the heat he's only wearing shorts and can feel a humid breeze caressing his chest and legs. His senses wide open, he experiences a moment of piercing joy at being alive in God's beautiful world.

"Sarah," he whispers, and suddenly she's with him. His body surges, and he lets the fire have him. He falls into sleep still undecided.

Waking early, he stares into a blue sky swirling with rose-colored clouds. He gives himself over to the dawn stillness and to the presence of God. Gradually a sense of warmth and intimate closeness steals over him. In the peace that now enters and surrounds him, Jamie prays for discernment.

He envisions himself standing outside the church watching the other priest leave without him. He feels a pang of deep regret and wants to run after Laurens, but it's too late. In his imagination he feels forlorn. He has the impression he's missed something important.

Now Jamie examines the other possibility. In his mind's

eye, he sees himself setting out with the priest. The man's old jeep bounces on the rutted road as they head into the hills. He feels a sense of well-being and exhilaration and thinks, "This is a risk worth taking."

He allows his mind to move back and forth over the two scenarios. His feelings remain the same. He rolls out of the hammock and goes to find Laurens.

~

APRIL 15
    The Countryside

DEAR SARAH—

"A new priest friend and I are camped in a ruined village on the road to a town whose name I won't mention in case this letter falls into the wrong hands on its way to you. We've passed many gutted villages where the homes are rubble.

We went by a corn field this afternoon, but most of the land is vacant, the people driven away by the army in an effort to starve out the guerrillas and rob them of the support of the campesinos. (The guerrillas call their members "compañeros" or companions, comrades, so I'll use those words most of the time.)

This evening after dinner, just before the sun went down, L led me a few hundred yards from the buildings to a place where the soil was mounded higher than the rest of the land. He knelt down and began to dig with his hands. The hair rose on my neck as I watched him. The first thing he unearthed was a bone that was clearly a human femur. Next came a skeletal hand. Digging deeper, he uncovered the roundness of a human skull. As he brushed the dirt away, we could see how small it was. Obviously a child's.

Without warning, I dropped to my knees and threw up.

I began shaking. L grabbed my shoulder and pulled me away so I wouldn't fall into my own vomit. I lay on the ground, over-come by what I now knew was hidden beneath us.

I've never felt anything like I felt that moment—despair so deep I was drowning in it and grief far beyond any in my life.

The tsunami of emotion lasted only minutes but will probably haunt me for a long time.

I can't begin to convey the fullness of that experience, Sarah.

It was as though I were absorbing all the horror that had happened in that place. (I only write about this because I promised you honesty. Sometimes the truth will distress you, but I know it's what you want from me.)

"What happened here? How many are in that grave?" I asked L after he led me back to our camp. "The army came or a mili-tia. Who knows? How many? Dozens? Scores? I can't tell for sure. This isn't one of the 'official massacre sites.' It's something I discovered the first time I camped here. Later I brought a shovel to probe," he told me. "If it were only a few people, perhaps I could bury them with dignity. But everywhere I dug, there were human bones. I had to give up."

(I am keeping a journal I will eventually send you recording the words of some of the people I talk with about things which seem particularly important. I plan to ask the Jesuits for a small tape recorder to carry with me.)

As we sat there, it was hard for me to think of anything to say to L who has seen so much. Finally I asked him how he endures the realities of human suffering and depravity like those he found in the field without sinking into negativity and even hatred of the perpetrators.

His answer reminded me of the need to stay close to my Jesuit roots. Every day, L told me, he meditates on the passion of Jesus as Ignatius taught us to do in Spiritual Exercises. He prays intensely to be able to join himself with Christ and learn to suffer his way, in love and forgiveness and even compassion for those who are killing him. "This quality of Jesus' love is the deepest spiritual root of our impulse to work for peace and justice. Anything less would be an unworthy motive," he told me. "Jamie, the Exercises—especially those on our Lord's passion —will carry you through anything God lets you encounter in El Salvador."

He's right of course. Our Jesuit tradition offers most of what I need to serve the people here...all the people, even those who torture and murder. It sounds impossible, but in the order's history many have gone before me and met that challenge. Knowing this gives me hope. And don't forget, I have a personal secret weapon in the struggle to love.

And please don't underestimate how powerful she is!

We are traveling in an old Jeep, the ubiquitous vehicle in these parts because it's reasonably comfortable and also capable of crossing streams, climbing mountains and making it over roads that are only tracks. This is hilly, barren-looking country, mostly tufts of grass in rocky soil, with stands of ragged-looking trees.

It's the end of the dry season and water is scarce. The sun is like fire. It's a new experience to feel so thirsty your tongue seems fused to the roof of your mouth and you know you can't have water until you come to a well. The only moisture for miles lies in foul mud holes. Oh, Sarah, the things we take for granted in America!

I'd been uncertain about taking this trip for many reasons.

After the experiences of today, my accompanying L seems both right and inevitable.

Good night, my beloved. May God bless you and keep you."

FORTY-SIX

"A lot of the campaneros used to come to Mass but not take communion," Laurens says. "They had scruples because they had killed soldiers or militia. I told them not to worry. I said because they are willing to give up their lives for others, they have every right to come to Eucharist. Jesus would want them to. He is longing to embrace them."

He looks at Jamie with as if he's expecting to be challenged or censured. The two are preparing a rough wooden table as an altar in a large open shed that once held sugar cane before the civil war pushed out most of the area's agriculture. It's in a field surrounded by trees and rising into hills in what seems like the middle of nowhere. "We can turn any place into a church," the Dutch priest had told him earlier. "A tree stump, a cloth on a flat stone. It's all Jesus requires to feel at home."

Now Jamie looks at him with obvious interest. Encouraged, Laurens continues his impromptu homily on the sacraments.

"I don't encourage personal confession anymore," he declares. "Before Mass I say let's make a sincere act of contrition together, to acknowledge the pain we have caused, and that God loves us despite whatever we've done. I tell everyone to receive communion without any qualms. That's how I understand Jesus. He is the one who welcomes all to himself, every single one."

Jamie smiles at his fellow Jesuit, wondering what Pope John Paul II would think of him. "Please tell me more."

"Take Baptism. I make it clear we're not baptizing a child for fear the little one will go to some limbo if it dies without being baptized, because a loving God would never do this. I hate that people have been taught to fear God.

"Baptism is for us to recommit ourselves so this child will have in us a true Christian community to belong to. It is up to us to awaken the child's conscience and courage, so he or she will always work for the good of our country and our people." He speaks while arranging a vase of wildflowers for the altar.

Now Laurens goes to a large storage bin near the back. He removes the top revealing an empty box the size of a military trunk.

"What is this for?" Jamie asks.

"All will be revealed," the Dutchman says in a teasing tone. He looks up and grins broadly as a few people appear from around a bend in the road.

"*Hola*, friends, *Bienvenidos!*" he calls, waving enthusiastically. Turning back to Jamie, he exclaims, "Our Mass is a party, a real celebration! You'll see!"

The next hour is a blur of being introduced to dozens of people arriving, many carrying plates or baskets of food. Some cart crates of bananas and watermelon to sell at stands they are setting up. Women are bringing homemade tortillas and cold drinks. A group of youths is fashioning tables from boards and sawhorses. It's Salvadoran potluck! Jamie is surprised at how much laughter he hears.

A number of people are dressed in their best clothes, a rainbow of colorful blouses and shirts. Most are fraying and obviously have been been mended many times, but they are clean and neat. Others wear jeans and sturdy dark-colored shirts. He wonders if they are fighters.

There is much interest in Jamie as a new padre from North America. He shakes so many hands his own feels numb. He's touched by how open and friendly people are, although their smiles often cannot overcome the sadness in their eyes. A number are shy in their greetings; others are hearty and outgoing. His finds his heart filled with affection as he looks into their strong-planed faces.

Some, like the legless boy who arrives in a chair to which bicycle wheels have been attached, and the adults and children with obvious wounds—missing limbs or fingers, a mangled ear, scars and burns—make him want to weep, but he holds back. He intuits that simple friendliness is what they want from him. Tears of compassion could be mistaken for pity.

By the time Laurens rings a large hand bell, the place has indeed been transformed into a festive space with booths and tables and children playing. Jamie sees three men and a woman with guitars and a flute. There will be music! The crowd must be close to fifty people, Jamie estimates. He has chosen not to join Laurens in celebrating this Mass. He prefers to act in the role of server and give out communion, so he'll have more opportunity to watch and to listen.

The music begins. The tune is definitely upbeat. Everyone seems to be singing with spirit and gusto. It's the first time Jamie has heard the hymn. Later, he will learn it's one of the songs at the spiritual heart of the revolution.

"You are the God of the poor,
the human and simple God,
the God who sweats in the streets,
the God with the weathered face;
that's why I speak to you
just like my people speak,
because you are God the laborer,
Christ the worker.
"Hand in hand you walk with my people,
you struggle in the fields and the city,
you stand in line at the construction site
waiting to be paid your day's wages.
You snack on shaved ice there, at the park,
with Eusebio, Pancho and Juan,
and you even complain about the syrup
when it doesn't have enough honey."

Now Jamie's eyes *are* wet. The manner in which these people identify with God in the most tender and down-to-earth ways is like nothing he has ever heard. How he wishes Sarah could be here to share this.

"I have seen you at the corner store
standing behind a counter,
I have seen you peddling lottery tickets
unashamed to do so.
I have seen you in gas stations
checking the tires of a truck
and even laying tar on highways
wearing leather gloves and overalls.

"You are the God of the poor,
the human and simple God,
the God who sweats in the streets,
the God with the weathered face;
that's why I speak to you
just like my people speak,
because you are God the laborer,
Christ the worker."

As Laurens begins the first prayer, Jamie notices a group of men and women approaching, dressed in camouflage or khaki clothing and carrying rifles. He watches as they carefully place their guns into the large box. So that's what it's for! Removing hats and caps, they slide silently into the congregation.

The Mass is simple and joyous. It centers around the Scripture readings and people's reflections on them. Today's Gospel is Jesus' well-known homily about how God cares for birds in the sky and the flowers in the fields.

An older woman in dark green blouse reads the text with practiced skill. Jamie looks around and is impressed by how enrapt each person appears to be; even the children are listening intently.

"Now if that is how God *clothes the wild flowers growing in the field which are there today and thrown into the furnace tomorrow, will He not much more look after you, you who have so little faith?"* she proclaims.

"So do not worry; do not say, 'What are we to eat? What are we to drink? What are we to wear?' It is the Gentiles who set their hearts on all these things. Your heavenly Father knows you need them all.

"Set your hearts on His kingdom first, and on God's saving justice, and all these other things will be given you as well.

So do not worry about tomorrow: tomorrow will take care of itself. Each day has enough trouble of its own."

The woman returns to her seat, and there is a pause as if to give people the chance to fully take in what they have heard. When Laurens speaks, his voice is challenging, almost angry. "How can Jesus say these things when there are so many among us who cannot feed our children, who starve and die because we are so poor?" he demands. "I ask you, where is God's care in El Salvador?"

Jamie's breath catches. How many priests would dare to confront Jesus and his words so honestly and directly to an audience like this one? What will people say? His heart is beating faster as he waits to hear. For what seems like a long time, no one speaks. Then a grandfatherly man stands up.

"When I plant my seeds and watch them grow into food for my family, I feel God's care. What a wonderful design! A tiny seed grows into a plant that gives me many squash or ears of corn. It's like a miracle, but it's how God made things. Surely this shows His care for us."

"God wants us to have enough to eat and give our children," a young woman cuddling a tiny baby says. "He created a world with *so much food*. If we share it, there is enough for all people and for the animals too."

A boy who looks to be about eleven or twelve rises. "Why does God allow the rich people and their military to do what they do to us? Why does God permit them to push us down in the dirt and kill us while they enjoy their lives in big houses? Are they more powerful than God? Or does

God care for them more than us?" His tone is tense and angry.

"*Mi hijo*, you are asking the great questions that religious people have asked since forever," Laurens tells him. "Many turn away from God because terrible things happen, and God doesn't stop them. They see this and say to themselves, 'What good is such a God?'"

There is a silence which stretches out until, at last, a gray-haired woman stands. "God created us free to be good or bad," she says. "If He controlled us and forced us to be good, we would not be human. We would be like those mechanical people. What is the name for them?"

"Robots," a young girl calls out, beaming that she knows the answer.

"Yes, robots," the woman continues. "Who would want to be a robot?"

One after another, the speakers reflect on the scripture in fresh, insightful and wise ways. It is clear these listeners have imbibed Jesus' words deeply. For them, the gospel is *personal*.

"It is very hard for me to take up the gun and fight," a stocky young woman dressed in fatigues tells the group. "It is not my nature. When I hear this story about God's care, I pray that Jesus knows I am doing the things I'm forced to do because I care for my people. I want them to have the food they need and clothes and homes. If I don't fight, they won't have them. I hope God understands and will forgive me if I have to kill someone." Her voice breaks.

As he listens, Jamie is moved, inspired and—he is embarrassed to admit it—astonished.

"What an arrogant, ignorant ass I am," he thinks. "Talk about underestimating a category of people!" No wonder supporters of liberation theology rejoice in the potential of the poorest and least educated. No wonder they see the *campesinos* in communities of liberation as the future of the Church and maybe of humanity itself. Suddenly he realizes Laurens is talking to him.

"Padre Jamie, have you anything you'd like to contribute to our conversation?"

He looks around at the faces regarding him curiously. He reaches inside for the depth of his own sincerity. An image of Sarah speaking about scripture comes to him. Finally he says, "In my years as a student and a priest, I have heard so many discussions of this teaching of Jesus. Yet I have never heard these words of our Lord considered with as much wisdom and heart feeling as I've heard from you today." He pauses; his voice is husky. "I am honored to be among you. You have a great deal to teach me."

Jamie suddenly feels shy and dips his head. When he looks up, he sees many looking back at him with affectionate eyes. Laurens radiates his pleasure.

"It is almost a miracle to find a Catholic priest who is willing to learn from you, isn't it, friends?" he teases. There is laughter.

Excerpt from a letter to Sarah:

"Giving communion was a very emotional experience for me at my first liturgy in the countryside with the campaneros. Sometimes back home this has an automatic, routine quality.

I've often wondered what people were thinking and feeling as they accepted the host.

In Chalatenango I was struck by the reverence of these Salvadorans as they opened their hands to receive the Eucharist. Each one looked me in the eye. It's hard to describe their expressions. All I can say is those faces conveyed that something important was happening for them. I wish I had your gift with words to better explain. Even the movement of their hands was deliberate and careful. There seemed to be tenderness in the way their fingers touched the host. Many kissed it. I felt I was witnessing an intimate embrace."

∼

AFTER MASS, the fiesta begins. Jamie wanders around the stalls, and people insist he try every kind of food. He soon finds himself with two heaping plates. To his chagrin, no one will allow him to pay. So he accepts the beans, tortillas, corn, salsas and fruits humbly and with gratitude. Balancing one plate on each hand, he attracts the amused attention of a boy and girl who giggle at his awkward position.

"Help me, please, friends, to eat all this, *por favor*," he implores. "It would be a kindness." Eagerly, they each take a plate and lead him to a fallen tree that serves as a bench. The girl runs off to get forks and napkins. Her name, she tells him, is Lupe. Her brother is called Pepe.

"Our names rhyme, Padre, isn't that funny?" the boy says.

Jamie chuckles. "Your parents are poets."

Their mother is a teacher in a nearby town. Their father works somewhere in the hills, possibly among the campaneros? They live nearby with their grandmother. Lupe tells him how much she loves school, and Pepe announces how much he hates it.

"I will be a doctor someday like my auntie Trina," the little girl says looking at Jamie with a determined expression. "That's a wonderful ambition," he replies. "Why do you want to do that?"

"I want to help people not to die." Her little face is sad. "When the bombs and the guns hurt people, I will be able to fix them. My friend Rodrigo died from a bullet when the army came. There was no doctor to help him." She pauses. "I miss him so much. Since we were babies, we used to talk and play every day."

Jamie gently puts his hand on her thin shoulder. "Rodrigo is lucky to have such a good friend as you. When you are a doctor, you can remember him every time you save someone or make them well. You can say, 'Rodrigo, my friend, I do this for you.' Then he can be with you in his spirit all of your life."

Lupe regards the priest thoughtfully. "That is a good idea, Padre," she tells him, then, with the lightning resilience of a child, she says, "Let's get some dessert." As the two walk away carrying the now-empty plates, Jamie notices Laurens sitting on a stump writing in a notebook. A line of people is waiting for their turn with him.

Having finished dinner, the guitarists are tuning their instruments. Jamie makes his way to them and sits down to listen. The music is lively, and a few people begin to dance, making up in enthusiasm what they may lack in skill. More join in. Soon all ages are dancing in every combination imaginable. A grandmotherly woman is twirling, her hand held by a handsome young *campanero*. Old couples, young couples, children together, it's a lively scene. Jamie cannot believe he is in the middle of a war zone among people who have lost family members, their homes and the lives they once knew. Suddenly, Laurens is beside him.

"You're surprised?" he asks. "So am I when joy suddenly breaks out among the people. It used to happen all the time. Now not so much. Rejoice when you see it, Jamie. It may not come again soon."

"I noticed you writing in a book with people waiting," the younger priest says.

His companion sighs. "They tell me the names of their dead, their wounded and those who have gone missing so I can offer a mass for them. 'Write down the name of my mother, my father, my uncle, my brother, my daughter,' they say. I take a notebook wherever I go. Many have been killed in massacres, army raids, by bombs, or simply found dead on the road or in a field. Others have disappeared, and their loved ones fear for them. I can show you pages and pages, and only a relative few have died from natural causes or accidents." His face is grim.

Then he playfully cuffs Jamie on the arm. "And look at them!" he exclaims, gesturing dramatically toward the dancers. "Just look at them!"

A large handsome woman wearing a turquoise-colored blouse strides up to him. "I saw you signaling me to dance with you, Padre," she declares with a grin, reaching for the priest's hand. He smiles and allows her to lead him into the swirling melee. Jamie watches them with a bit of envy. "Wouldn't Sarah love this!" he thinks with a pang.

He turns his attention to the musicians as their fingers fly over the strings. One of the men notices his interest. "Do you play, Padre?" he asks.

"I do."

The musician stops, gets up and comes over to Jamie. He hands him the guitar. "Please play for us, Padre Jamie."

Even though he doesn't know the music, it seems familiar, and he's skilled enough to follow the others with some mistakes. When the set ends, he feels exhilarated, thrilled to be even a small part of this remarkable celebration of life and love.

Two musicians approach him. "Padre, will you play some *música* Americana for us?" one requests with a smile.

"I'd be honored," he replies in Spanish, "You know how

we guitarists love to show off." Their faces brighten with suppressed laughter.

"Of course, we know you will only play holy music, you being a priest," one man teases.

"Oh certainly," Jamie counters. "Anything else would be undignified." They grin mischievously at one another.

When it is announced the priest from America will begin the next set, there is friendly applause. Jamie starts with a rousing hymn by the St. Louis Jesuits, a musical group that had revolutionized Catholic liturgical music in the '70s. His voice rising in the warm air, he sings:

"Lift up your hearts to the Lord,
praise God's gracious mercy!
Sing out your joy to the Lord,
whose love is enduring.
Shout with joy to the Lord, all the earth!
Praise the name above all names!
Say to God, "How wondrous your works,
how glorious your name!"

By the end of the piece, people are clapping and dancing.

"Mas, mas, por favor, Padre!" voices call out. He plays and sings a few St. Louis Jesuit favorites translating them into Spanish as well as he can on the fly. With "The Cry of the Poor," the group becomes quiet as the words engage their hearts.

"The Lord hears the cry of the poor.
Blessed be the Lord.
Let the lowly hear and be glad:
the Lord listens to their pleas;
and to hearts broken, God is near,

who will hear the cry of the poor."

He ends the impromptu concert with Paul McCartney's "Let it Be," which speaks of Mother Mary coming to him in times of trouble with her words of wisdom.

It is obvious from how many join in the song that Beatles music is popular even in rural El Salvador. Who knew? He remembers John Lennon's assertion that the Beatles were "bigger than Jesus" and wants to laugh.

The applause, smiles and laughter reassure him that he hasn't made a total fool of himself. The musicians are effusive in their praise. "Bring your guitar and join our band, Padre Elvis," one jokes. "You are welcome to play with us any time."

As he goes looking for water, a slender young man in khaki stops him and draws him aside.

"Padre, would you come sometime and visit my brothers and sisters up there?" He gestures toward the hills. "We do not see priests often enough." He smiles. "And we have guitars." Jamie realizes he is being invited to a guerrilla camp. The dark-eyed campanero regards him with a wistful, hopeful expression. "It would be a grace, Padre, if you would come to us."

Pushing aside common sense and all the reasons this is a very bad idea, he makes an instant decision. "It would be my privilege," he says. The man's face lights up. He shakes the priest's hand vigorously.

"When you are ready, Padre Laurens can show you how."

Jamie walks away in a bit of a daze, wondering just what he has gotten himself into. He heads into the trees away from the group. Alone, he sits on the ground and looks up into the night sky filled with a million stars. "Dear Lord, I hope this is the right thing to do," he prays. "If I weren't a Jesuit intellectual who knows better, I'd ask for a sign about now." He hopes God appreciates his humor.

Later as they prepare to sleep awhile under the stars before they head back to town while it is still dark, he tells the Dutchman about the invitation.

The priest looks thoughtful for a few moments, then says, "Now may be the best time for you to do this. Once you're settled in and officially working, people will notice the new North American priest and know you're around. The military and their minions will be keeping tabs on you. Right now you're traveling under the radar. It will be easier to slip away."

"Will you help me?" Jamie asks.

"Of course," comes the answer.

"My brother, I don't know whether to thank you or curse you at this point."

The other Jesuit laughs. "It's too soon to tell," he says.

It's a clear night, and Jamie can see the Milky Way in all its grandeur. Awe and wonder at this vast universe surge through him. A wave of love for its creator floods his heart.

Suddenly Sarah is beside him, against his body in a close, tender embrace. It is so real he's almost certain she's feeling something similar at this very moment. A sliver of moon has risen in the sky. He likes knowing it is looking down on both of them.

FORTY-SEVEN

A half moon shines above the canyon, and Jamie is grateful for its pale light as he stumbles along a narrow trail following a teenager who must have been sired by a mountain goat. He is drenched with sweat in hot, humid darkness. As the distance between them lengthens, the boy stops and turns.

"Are you okay, Padre?" he whispers.

"I am," the priest whispers back, trying to hide his breathlessness, a macho posturing that makes him laugh to himself. "It's only that you, Carlito, are an Olympic champion trail runner." A quiet chuckle comes through the darkness.

"You are doing very well for a man your age." There is a teasing quality in the voice. "Don't worry. We will be there soon." "Soon" proves to be an encouraging fabrication. More than an hour later, the boy stops and waits for Jamie.

"Padre, we are near," he says. He puts a finger to his lips and whistles a bird call. In a minute, the same call is repeated through the darkness. "They have heard us,"

Carlito tells him, "and someone is saying it is safe to come in."

He turns off the path into what at first looks like impenetrable brush. Jamie finds himself in a natural tunnel formed by branches and leaves of tall shrubs and trees. He begins to hear muted voices and other sounds. Suddenly, the tunnel opens into a clearing almost hidden beneath an overhang of the mountain. They are in a field of packed earth with several tents on the perimeter. A couple of few dozen men and women are engaged in tasks or sitting around a fire. It must be for cooking and light. They certainly don't need more heat. Two men are washing dishes in large plastic drums. A few women are making what look like thick tortillas. All the faces turn toward them, and a lively curiosity rises in shining eyes. A handsome woman emerges from the shadows and hurries toward Carlito. She embraces him with kisses on both cheeks.

"*Mi hijo*," she exclaims. "You are back safely, *gracias a Dios.*" She turns to Jamie and extends her hand. "I'm Leta," she says. "A hundred welcomes, Padre. We are so glad to have you with us."

Before long, the priest and the youth are seated on a log with tin plates of tortillas and beans. Jamie, hungry from a long day of hiking with little to eat, is tempted to wolf down his food, but a look at Carlito stops him. The boy takes small bites, obviously savoring each one and chewing it carefully. Jamie, too, restrains himself, realizing that for people like these, food is precious and to be appreciated. The *compañeros* continue working and talking with one another to give the new arrivals a chance to finish their meal.

By the time they're served hot "coffee" made from roasted maize, everyone has gathered around them. The questions begin. Where are you from, Padre? What is the pueblo of Berkeley like? How long have you been a priest? What do you think of El Salvador?

"Why have you come to our country, Padre?" a young woman wants to know. Jamie pauses and looks at the attentive expressions.

"It's a long story," he says, reluctant to reveal his heart's history to strangers.

"Wonderful, Padre, we love long stories," a bearded man in camouflage calls out. There is laughter. "Please tell us."

Putting aside his hesitation, Jamie smiles and begins. "A long time ago, when I was young, I was sent to help build and repair houses near a *basurero* in Tijuana, Mexico."

He speaks honestly and openly with deep emotion as he tells of the experience. "… so for these many years after I met Abrilla and her children I have felt God calling me to the people of South," he concludes. "I believe you have much to teach me. And I hope to find ways to serve you."

He looks around. "My country is supporting the ones who are hurting and killing you," he continues softly. "That's another reason I am here." A solemn silence falls over the group.

"I'm with you to hear your stories and bring them back to the citizens of America so they will know what is happening in your country. I'm here to listen and to learn." He decides to lighten the mood. "Now, I realize Catholic priests willing to learn from lay people are as rare as white armadillos." There are hoots of laughter and grins all around.

Someone brings out a guitar, and the evening moves into music and singing, from upbeat patriotic tunes to haunting ballads of love and loss. These are subdued so as not to draw attention to the camp's presence in this remote canyon. When a man sings softly of looking for the north star because that's the way his beloved went when she left him, Jamie thinks of Sarah with a pang of longing.

He finds it difficult to keep his eyes open and is relieved when the musicians stop playing, and people begin preparing for bed. Carlito directs him to a place to spread his sleeping bag. Exhausted, he lies down in the warm darkness and falls almost instantly into sleep despite the hardness of the ground.

He is awakened before dawn by singing. Feeling a bit bleary, he quickly recognizes a Spanish version of *The Internationale*, the hymn of the socialist movement.

"Stand up, victims of oppression
For the tyrants fear your might,
don't cling to your possessions,
You have nothing without rights...

...Let no walls divide the people,
walls of hatred or walls of stone,
Come greet the dawn beside us,
We'll stand together or die alone."

At breakfast, maize coffee and warm tortillas, Jamie understands why Laurens called this plain food the most delicious meal in the world when it's eaten at the front.

A tall, wiry man with a luxuriant mustache comes and sits beside Jamie and introduces himself as Alejandro. From Laurens, Jamie knows he's one of the commanders of the military force this group is part of. Last night he' d been struck by the man's natural authority as he walked around the camp and talked with people, frequently touching a man or woman affectionately on the arm or shoulder.

"Comandante Alejandro," Jamie greets him, reaching out

his hand. "It is such a pleasure to meet you. Laurens thinks the world of you."

"Padre Laurens is a superb friend to our people," the man replies in a mellifluous voice as he grasps the priest's hand firmly.

Jamie has already heard the man's tragic story. Alejandro and his wife Luisa were high school teachers in San Salvador, and he was an officer of the teachers' union. When the killings and disappearances of teachers and labor leaders began to accelerate in the capital, the couple sent their three children aged four to nine to live with Alejandro's mother in a small city, Santa Teresa de las Rosas, where it was still peaceful. The town was close enough that the couple could visit their children on weekends and far enough away from the conflict that residents felt safe.

But one day a paramilitary unit (one of the many that roamed the countryside with the tacit approval of the government) showed up in Santa Teresa. They burned the church and then attacked the school, firing hundreds of bullets into the building before setting it on fire. The couple's older son and only daughter died in the attack. His mother was at the market for medicine. The younger boy had a bad cold; she'd left him home with a neighbor. High-powered bullets sprayed through the open-air marketplace had ripped through her leg, pulverizing the bones to the point it had to be amputated.

Alejandro's heartbreaking experience is the kind of human catastrophe that has devastated tens of thousands of Salvadoran families in the six-year war. Killings, mutilations, rapes and torture still take place routinely at the hands of the army, right-wing paramilitary groups and certain elements of the police. Although larger cities are not immune, the lion's share of the atrocities are committed in rural areas, towns and villages. These days, almost no one is safe in huge swathes of the country like the Chalatenango and Morazan districts where the guerrillas are a significant presence.

Jamie studies the man's face sculpted by suffering with its large, expressive eyes that are pools of pain. Alejandro and other civilian-soldier leaders interest the priest. He is very curious about several things.

Why, for example have the Salvadoran army, militias and death squads been unable to defeat the *compañeros* after years of trying? Government troops have powerful American weapons and have been trained by elite American forces. They receive millions of dollars in aid from the United States.

Yet this shabby little band, the Farabundo Martí National Liberation Front (FMLN), has refused to be conquered. The army has launched countless offensives in the last five years but can claim few military victories. Jamie read an article by a military expert who reported the kill ratio in actual battles averages twenty to thirty government soldiers to one guerrilla. This is nothing short of astonishing. How is it possible? After they talk for a while, he poses the question. Alejandro smiles broadly. His eyes sparkle.

"I wish I could tell you it's because we are great warriors," he says with a grin. "But we survive because the Salvadoran army is unbelievably inept. We are surrounded on land, and they vastly outnumber us. They have the latest American weapons and helicopters to bomb us.

"We have only old rifles, machine guns, anti-tank artillery and some outdated surface-to-air missiles. Not to mention that we're practically starving half the time and have thousands of peasants and other civilians to try to protect. Yet again and again, we outfox the army. Little David beats the hell out of Goliath. If it weren't for American weapons and aid, we would have already won this war.

"Despite what's really happening, the Salvadoran government-controlled media reports massive enemy casualties, many guerrilla leaders killed, and numerous caches of weapons destroyed. We know it's all lies But their propaganda makes the American officials very happy. 'See,' your Mr. Reagan can proclaim proudly, 'we are making great progress against those godless Communists.' " Alejandro's tone is cynical.

Jamie also wants to know more about what he has heard from Laurens and others that, with few exceptions, the guerrillas conform to the Geneva Conventions. They do everything possible to avoid civilian casualties. Looting is forbidden, and any food they take from local farmers must be paid for.

In addition, Dr. Charlie Cross, a British doctor Jamie'd met who'd spent more than two years with FMLN, had sworn that—in stark contrast to the Salvadoran Army that tortures or kills most of the guerrillas who fall into its hands—the *compañeros* treated their prisoners of war humanely. They are usually fed whatever their captors have to eat and sometimes even housed in the homes of families.

"I know, I know, it sounds incredible, especially when the government military has been so vicious and heartless," the physician had said in response to Jamie's disbelief. "But I've witnessed this with my own eyes." Jamie remembers Cross's assertion as he regards the man beside him. This is a chance to find out more.

"Comandante, I've heard you treat your prisoners well. This is hard for me to believe considering the savagery of the other side. How do you enforce good behavior by your troops?"

Alejandro looks him in the eye. "Padre, most of my soldiers are devout Christians. These people did not choose military careers, and it is difficult for many to kill or harm.

Any priest who's spent time with us undoubtedly could tell you how many confessions he has heard from those who have killed in battle and feel guilty. Imagine the dilemma of our officers who must turn good Catholics into soldiers who will kill when necessary but not fall into blood lust that leads to torturing or murdering the unarmed. I assure you it is a formidable challenge!"

"*So how in the world do you do this?*" Jamie persists.

"It helps that often the 'enemy soldier' we capture is a peasant like many of our *compañeros*," the comandante answers. "He may have been rounded up by officers who seize those they want, including young boys, force them into the army and threaten their families if they do not comply. Or he may have been brainwashed into believing we are evil.

"I will never forget a young prisoner who confessed he had killed babies and little children. He had murdered the small ones, he told us, because he'd been taught they were the seeds of an evil force that would destroy everyone and everything. But now he had seen us up close; he'd had a chance to observe our school and clinic and cooperative. He'd never experienced anything like our community and its hope. He was only a boy himself, and he started sobbing.

'How could I have been so stupid to believe those lies?' he'd cried out. 'In the name of God I am so sorry.'

"There was a silence. Then the people sitting next to him at the camp meeting put their arms around him and held him while he cried with the force of an infant's wails. Later he asked to join us and was accepted." As he gazes into the priest's face, there is a flash of pure joy in the eyes of this man who has lost his own children so brutally.

"Padre, these are the things I hold inside me," Alejandro says simply.

"Of course we're not angels. Far from it," he admits. "I

strongly disapprove of some things other *companero* groups have done, like kidnapping for ransom. And there have been instances of wanton cruelty and unwarranted killing by our side. What's surprising is how rare this is."

Then his expression and voice change. It is almost like another person has taken over his body. "I have to fight my own hatred and desire for revenge," he says grimly. "Do you know my story, Padre?"

Jamie nods. "I do."

"I lived for weeks so choked by rage and hate for those who murdered my Rosaria and my Felipe and their friends that sometimes I could hardly breathe." Alejandro's voice is harsh. "I wanted to kill and torture the men who'd done this, including the rich landowners behind so much of the violence. Day and night I let myself fantasize what it would be like to take my pistol and machete and sneak into the neighborhoods where the army officers and government officials live. I would kill the evil scum in front of their own children, just mow them down and spill their blood.

"There were times Luisa my wife had to hold me physically to keep me from leaving the house to do something awful. Oh, Padre, this good woman, this mother whose heart has been crushed, now had to watch her husband turning into a beast."

The soldier's face is a mask of agony that makes Jamie want to turn away. Instead he puts an arm around the man's slumped shoulders and draws him closer. Eyes closed, the comandante surprises the priest by leaning against him like a child. The morning sounds of the camp seem far away. Feeling constriction in his own chest, he spontaneously reaches out to Sarah with his heart.

"Help me to touch this man with my love," he asks

silently. He notices tears on his companion's cheeks, and bends his head toward his.

"Oh my dear man," he whispers. Neither moves as the silence stretches out. Minutes pass. Finally Jamie asks, "What stopped you from acting on your desire for revenge?"

After a pause, Alejandro straightens and reaches into a pocket of his shirt. He draws out a photograph creased and darkened with time and sweat. It shows three children with bright eyes and wide grins. The youngest, a toddler, has his arms around a black and white puppy who seems to be grinning too. The three radiate the essence of childlike delight. He passes it almost reverently to Jamie, whose own eyes fill as he examines the little faces.

The soldier places his finger on the image of the smaller boy. "It was my Nando who stopped me from doing something that would tarnish the memory of my daughter and my son. His full name, Hernando, means 'ardent for peace.' He is well-named.

"About a month after they died we were spending the weekend in the home of my mother's brother in a city far from the danger. It was very hard for me to be around people. My anger was so great. Anything could set it off. One day at lunch I yelled at my poor maimed mother for no reason. Then I couldn't stand the hurt in her eyes caused by my mean words. I pushed away from the table so hard the dishes rattled. I almost ran into the bedroom, slammed the door, and flung myself onto the bed. I felt about to explode. I wanted to die too.

"A while later I heard a gentle knock I recognized on the door. How could I ignore my little son? Reluctantly, I told him to come in. He was quiet as a mouse as he climbed up on the bed and lay down beside me. I was turned toward the wall.

"After a few minutes a small hand crept onto my neck; it slid into my hair and ruffled it. Finally a small voice said, "*Pobrecito*, poor little Daddy. You feel bad, don't you? Come outside and play with me and Churro like you used to. I think you'd feel better.'

"He led me into the garden. We played with the dog and a ball. Nando was laughing and running around. The dog was chasing him and barking. I saw life and the future right there in front of me. I smiled, my first smile since that terrible day.

"Healing will take much time, if it ever comes fully, but it started that afternoon." He offers Jamie a soft look shaped by sadness. "My heart has broken open, and spilled out the hate," he says. "The goodness of my children is my moral compass. I keep them with me. When I am tempted to act in revenge, I look at this picture. It is like a conscience in my pocket."

As they spend a few peaceful days, the fighters keep fit with an hour of calisthenics each day. They rest and read, mend clothes and cook. Jamie joins the exercise and, though he'd thought he was in good shape, these *compas* make him look like the ninety-seven-pound weakling in the old body-building ads. They are still doing pushups effortlessly after he has collapsed on the ground. A young man teasingly suggests he pray to the patron saint of strong priests "although we have never heard of one." Everyone laughs. While he has already experienced emotional heaviness in many Salvadorans suffering in this terrible upheaval of their lives, he relishes their natural sense of fun.

He wants to do his share of the physical work but is asked

instead to be available for people who would like to speak with a priest. Priests are rare in many areas of El Salvador. He has heard, for example, that in northern Morazan there are only six priests for some 160,000 Catholics. Thus it's no surprise that people seek him out. He gets the chance to know some of these men and women with a deep intimacy as they willingly share with him their lives in war.

FORTY-EIGHT

Excerpt from journal written to Sarah by flashlight:

"It's late, my last night in a companero *encampment. All around I can hear the sounds of people sleeping… snores, occasional moans and cries, and once in a while someone talking in their sleep. There is the constant drone of insects. Do insects ever sleep?*

My bed is a plastic sheet on the ground with my backpack as a pillow. These compas, *young and old, live this way for months and even years.*

(Getting a good night's sleep can be a serious problem at the front, according to a doctor who's spent two years with the guerrillas. He told me tranquilizers—for sleep and stress—are prized like gold.)

Sarah, I am among people who are sacrificing everything in the hope their children and all the young of this country will someday be able to have the quiet miracle of ordinary lives. I've heard this—in different words—from everyone I've spoken with this week.

And then they turn to me with sad and puzzled expressions.

Why, they beg to understand, does America, this great universal beacon of freedom and opportunity, send money and weapons to a government and an army that kills and tortures and destroys to keep the poor people of El Salvador from having everything that America stands for?

'Your President Reagan, surely he doesn't know what the army does to us,' a young woman said to me with a question in her voice. 'He must be a good man to be chosen by your people. If he knew about the killings, the massacres of women and children and old folk, and the way the soldiers destroy our towns and villages, surely he would make them stop, wouldn't he?'

I was totally at a loss. What could I tell her? In the end I said some of us were in El Salvador to learn the truth and take it back to America. When she grabbed my hand and kissed it, 'Oh thank God for you and the others, Padre,' I wanted to weep. Oh, Sarah, I wish I had your gift with words to tell the stories of these gallant Salvadorans.

I met a young couple, both guerrillas. Although obviously strong, she is painfully thin and reminds me of Abrilla. Their story is a microcosm of this war's effects on the innocent.

They were small farmers in the Chalatenango area who watched with growing fear as soldiers and militias did dreadful things in communities all around their few acres. When the wife became pregnant, they were more afraid than ever. How could they protect a baby in such danger?

Once their son was born, they lived in constant dread. One day a contingent of soldiers came to their village, rounded up everyone in the central plaza, then ransacked their homes and stole anything of value. They shouted, threatened the campesinos, and fired their guns into the air. They warned the people that helping the 'guerrilla devils' in any way would mean death to them and their families.

From that day, every time they looked at little Benito, they imagined what could happen to this child they loved. After many sleepless nights and much prayer, they came to a decision. The woman had a childless cousin in New Mexico, and they asked her and her husband to adopt their son. They accepted the offer with joy, traveled to El Salvador and took the baby home with them. The memory of the last time they saw Benito, held up to the window as the taxi drove away, was written on their faces as they shared their story with me. 'It is for the best, Padre,' the young father assured me in a quiet voice. 'Our boy is safe now. He will have a happy life.' 'But we miss him so much,' the young mother confided. 'We did not have him long, but even so, it is like the light has gone away. We have joined the campaneros for him for and the other little ones. If we live, maybe God will grant us other children. If we are killed, we can die in peace.' Oh Sarah, already I know how ordinary this sad story is in this crucified land.

I've met a few younger men who still consider war an adventure. But most of the guerrillas I know are older and wiser. A sweet-

faced woman who must be in her late 60s gestured to silver streaks in her black hair.

'I didn't expect to be an old lady warrior,' she said with a laugh. 'Here I am sneaking down trails on night maneuvers when I should be sitting on my porch in a comfortable chair knitting and watching the world go by.' She sighed, and I could hear the depth of her longing.

'I'd give anything to be home with my cat, working in my garden and cooking for my children and grandchildren when they visit.

'But Padre, we have lived as slaves here. Now we have learned to know this is not God's will for us. Even the old ones like me who will not see the victory trust their children and their grand-children will enjoy the fruits of our sacrifice. We fight so we can hope for them.' Later I wrote down her words and cried. If you ever lose faith in humanity, dear Sarah, come to El Salvador and meet people like Marcellina. In only a few weeks they have transformed my heart and mind.

It's been a surprise and delight to discover that in peaceful lulls these compañeros *like nothing more than spending hours talking about God, the meaning of life and what may happen after death. I listen and am amazed at how deeply they think about the great questions.*

You would love these conversations. And how much I'd like having you here to share them! At times you feel so far away. Then I close my eyes, and I'm back in your beautiful house, sitting beside you and watching your face in the firelight. The love and joy I feel are indescribable. Often I am swept up into

prayer in those moments. And I marvel how you and I have
become gates to the sacred for one another."

～

IT IS A FRIDAY AFTERNOON, the kind of perfect spring day that seems to bring the world a new intensity of life. Sarah is walking home up steep streets, pausing to catch her breath. She uses each stop to notice the artistry of spring flowers decorating gardens: pink and purple hyacinth, yellow daffodils and rainbows of tulips. Their fragrances waft up to her, opening her senses to the beauty of God's world. Suddenly she is suffused by the memory of lying with Jamie in late afternoon light. Her body surges with the sensual vision so powerful her knees feel weak. She laughs in surprise and knows she is actually blushing.

"Are you feeling this too right now?" she asks him silently. "I think you must be. Our energies of desire are meeting through space." Yesterday she'd received a letter mailed almost three weeks before it arrived. The time it took for it to travel from San Salvador to Berkeley reminds her how far apart they are geographically and culturally.

Tonight she'll be helping with a fund-raising dinner and program for Sanctuary West, an organization of churches and synagogues that helps refugees from Central America. Before she goes, Sarah lies down on her bed to rest. Her contribution to the dinner, a rice and bean dish, is ready to go. In the restful dimness, she experiences a special Friday afternoon peace and imagines Jamie beside her. Wouldn't that be sweet!

She's going to the ranch tomorrow for the first time since Easter. Teaching and Sanctuary activities have kept her busy, so she's really looking forward to seeing her family. Her parents are well, thank God. Giulia seems to have recovered fully from her heart attack, and the healthful lifestyle she's adopted has been good for both her and Franco.

She plans to make an important proposal to Franco and Giulia this weekend, and it won't be easy to convince them to do what she's asking. For a couple of weeks now she's been formulating passionate pleas, gathering information and praying fervently. She's even written to Jamie for his psychic assistance.

Drifting toward sleep, she thinks about Sam's phoning yesterday to read her a new letter from Jamie. It told of his meeting a Jesuit psychologist—an expert on post traumatic stress, a diagnosis gathering the symptoms suffered by many who have experienced traumas—at the University of Central America. The priest had promised to show him around and introduce him to residents of a large refugee camp on the outskirts of San Salvador. There he'll be part of a pastoral ministry team that works with displaced people and also travels to smaller towns and communities in zones of conflict.

"The camp is where they bring some of the most traumatized people. The UN reps who run the place hope the relative safety of the capital, still free from aerial bombing and direct army attacks, will give them some relief from the constant danger of a war zone and so be conducive to healing. My new mentor, Martin, has warned me treatment options for those with forms of post-traumatic stress are limited. There aren't enough psychologists to provide long-term therapy for folks who need it. And the numbers of those experiencing PTSD are increasing so fast.

The result is that counselors must rely less on sophisticated psychological expertise and more on simple therapeutic techniques

that provide support and relaxation and depend on empathy,
kindness and love. These are basic tools whose effectiveness our
chaplains know well. And the great thing is that ordinary
Salvadorans can be trained to use them.

'Everything we do is to build internal strength in the person,'
Martin told me. 'We make use of their natural resilience and
desire to survive and thrive. Our experience is teaching us how
deeply God has placed in each human being powerful and effec-
tive capacities for self-healing. In effect, our task is to draw
them forth.' "

Both Sarah and Sam are wondering how Jamie will be affected by being face-to-face with the tragedies of the brutal war.

"He's so emotional. I've always hassled him about being such a 'girly guy' when it comes to feelings. Now I think all that sensitivity is going to be a big liability for him down there," Sam had confided to her. Sarah remembered Jamie's intense response to being at the massacre site.

"I'll be rough for someone like him," she'd admitted. "But Sam, he has an inner strength and peace. And his faith is so strong. I believe he'll be okay," she'd added hopefully.

THE WIND IS a dark torrent whipping Sarah's hair and sending cold blasts of sand from some nearby beach through her clothing and against her skin. She welcomes the physical discomfort. It distracts her from the painful emotions that propelled her away from tonight's Sanctuary event. Perhaps a hundred people had gathered in the spacious church hall to raise money to buy medicine and medical supplies for clinics in El Salvador. A large banner with a photo of Salvadoran children in indigenous clothing hung on one wall. They looked like kids everywhere, reminding those attending that the people under threat in that part of the world were just like them and their own children.

Sanctuary West is an organization led by ministers, rabbis, priests and women religious who've opened their churches, convents and synagogues to Central American refugees in the country illegally after fleeing murderous regimes. Most have lost everything and have heart-breaking stories to tell. They provide vivid accounts of the terrors they've been forced to endure in their homelands. Often their audiences know virtually nothing of what is happening to ordinary people in those countries and of their own government's role in the violence. Generally, those who hear the refugees' stories are either horrified and want to help or refuse to believe them, unable to face the idea of America colluding in such evil.

Sitting at a table with Julianna, Mark, Sam and three Jesuits she'd never met, Sarah had listened to the conversation about recent events in El Salvador. When it moved to Jamie, she had remained silent, letting the others talk about what they knew from his letters. Noting she wasn't participating in the stories about him, one of the Jesuits had asked if she knew him.

"I do," she'd said, her voice casual. "I'm a member of his prayer chain," she'd added with a tight smile. Suddenly the room had seemed so hot and stuffy Sarah had found it hard to breathe. She'd felt a growing tension as the mayor of Berkeley, who'd recently returned from a trip to El Salvador, talked about the terrible conditions there. When a man and a woman each told of murdered children and destroyed homes in hesitant English and choked voices, Sarah had found herself trembling and realized she was about to start sobbing. It was a visceral reaction she couldn't control, but she'd managed to rise and excuse herself.

Now she was here at the edge of the Bay letting the cold and cutting wind dry her tears. This emotional storm had been building all week. Yesterday she'd been in the Mission with Rosa, teaching a scripture class at the center. Jamie's presence was palpable in that place and with the Guatemalan woman with whom he shared such a warm, deep love.

She'd been almost overcome by sadness several times. She could barely hold back tears when she'd played house with three little Salvadoran girls who'd pleaded with her to join them in their happy fantasies of family life, so different from the stark reality in their native country.

"My Pepita is going to go to college when she's big," a small girl with thick pigtails and glasses had told her seriously as she rocked and kissed a well-worn, much-loved doll with brown skin and black hair. Their innocent joy in describing the pretend meal they were serving had made Sarah want to cry at the thought of starving children.

"Your *pupusas* are delicious, Señora Rojas," one tiny girl had complimented another. "What do you put in the filling?" She'd spoken in an adult tone that forced a grin to Sarah's face. They were just adorable.

She'd been on an emotional roller coaster the entire visit. Even the insights her students had come up with while discussing the Parable of the Prodigal Daughter (she'd changed the gender to provide a fresh point of view) had evoked an element of sadness as she'd remembered Jamie's description of a similar sharing of scripture at a liturgy in the Salvadoran countryside.

Rosa hadn't been her normal ebullient self either, and at times Sarah had found the woman watching her surreptitiously. Finally, she'd put her hand on Sarah's. "I didn't know whether to tell you this, but Cruz Rodriguez just found out his youngest brother, the one he was trying to bring up here, was killed this week by a death squad."

"Oh no!" Sarah had cried, picturing the sweet, sensitive Cruz in her mind's eye. "What happened?" Rosa's face had been harsh. Her eyes had blazed.

"Manuel was walking home from school when a jeep with four soldiers in it drove up and forced him into the car." Her face had sagged into despair. "They found his body thrown beside a road the next day. He'd been shot in the head and had forty-eight cigarette burns on his body. His mother counted them."

Grief stricken, Sarah remembered how Cruz had shown her a photo of Manuel, a cheerful-looking teenager with a mischievous grin. In addition to going to school, Cruz had been working two jobs to save enough money to return to El Salvador and bring his brother back on the "underground railroad."

"Manuel is the smartest one in our family. He wants to be a doctor," the boy had confided with a touch of pride. Sarah had given him a hundred dollars toward his trip. He' d thanked her profusely and promised to introduce her to his little brother "when he comes."

Now Manuel would never come. She'd felt a sharp pang in her heart. "Is there anything I can do? Does Cruz need anything?"

Rosa had sighed sadly. "At this point there's not much anyone can do. He's distraught. He's staying with Father Domingo at St. Peter's." She'd squeezed Sarah's hand across the small table where they were sitting. Neither had spoken for a while. Finally Rosa'd offered a prayer.

"Dear God please bless Cruz and Manuel and their

family and comfort them with your peace," she'd prayed with emotion. "And, if you have time left over, dear Lord, please take care of Jamie, that crazy gringo priest who doesn't have sense enough to stay where he belongs. Please keep him safe even if he doesn't have the brain of a chicken in some matters."

An involuntary smile had flashed through Sarah's dejection. "Amen!" she'd exclaimed fervently.

TONIGHT HERE ON the edge of the midnight bay, Sarah is filled with despair and depression. And she feels guilty for feeling bad. There are billions of people who, finding themselves in her life at this moment, would think they'd died and gone to heaven. She often remembers something a priest who worked with homeless children in Africa had told a Bay Area woman who was complaining at length about her difficulties with a building contractor. "Ma'am, that's a first-world problem," he'd said.

Yes, her angst is a first-world problem. She realizes that, but the pain is still there. A seagull flying through the dark utters a poignant-sounding cry. Sarah gives herself over to her grief and fear. "It is what it is," she thinks. "I'm human."

Lifting her heart, she consciously sends her love out to Jamie and the people he's with. In her imagination, she draws it around him like a warm, soft blanket, mentally kissing him as she does so. At the same time a shiver runs through Sarah as she recalls the passage in Jamie's letter to Sam, revealing that he will be part of team traveling to "zones of conflict." She has not been able to shake those words from her mind. They haunt her.

FORTY-NINE

Although the weather in the Valley of the Moon is mild today, Sarah perspires with nervousness as she drives toward the ranch. There's so much at stake. She has to find the right words and arguments to convince her parents to give work and a home to a family of Salvadoran refugees she has befriended.

Her father's right-hand man, Enrico Torres, is about to retire. He'll be leaving the house on the ranch where he's lived for almost thirty years and moving to Ukiah to be closer to his daughter and grandchildren. She can visualize Eduardo, Josefina and their two children in the tidy cottage while he works in orchards, and she helps with the house and garden. All she needs now is to persuade Franco and Giulia to take in someone who is in the country illegally. It won't be easy.

～

"WILL you please just meet and talk with them before you decide?" Sarah pleads.

"Honey, you're being unreasonable," her father argues. "You're asking us to break all kinds of laws. You're asking us to risk going to jail. Hell, maybe the immigration people could even seize the ranch."

She pauses, trying to control her anger. Franco doesn't react well to verbal attacks. Taking a few deep breaths, Sarah stands up and goes to join him on the sofa. She puts her hand over his work-roughened one.

"Daddy," she says softly, "if you meet this family and hear their story, you won't care about breaking some unjust laws. I can almost promise you that. I'm not going to tell you what they've been through. You need to hear it from their own lips. That's why I'd like to bring them to the ranch, so you can meet them and see for yourself."

"You'd be wasting your time," he says stubbornly. "If you don't like a law, then get it changed. But while it's the law, we have to obey it if we're good citizens."

Giulia remains silent, looking from one to the other. She's hardly said a word. Sarah is becoming annoyed by her mother's silence.

"So what about your father and your uncle during Prohibition?" Sarah asks her father pointedly. "They went on making wine from their grapes. And they kept the hidden winery and the roadhouse in Vallejo open until the feds shut them down."

"Well, they were forced to break the law because it took away most of their livelihood," Franco counters. "They had no other way to support their families.

"And I don't condone what they did, even if I can understand it," he adds with a hint of self-righteousness in his voice.

Sarah gazes at him as she mentally counts to ten to keep her temper. Suddenly Jamie comes to her mind, and she remembers him saying how he loved her compassion and empathy. The anger dissipates, replaced by a sense of tenderness. "Please help me," she prays silently.

"Daddy, it's true that you'd be taking a risk," she says gently. "But it's not that big a risk. The Sanctuary lawyers can reassure you. Hundreds of people all over the country are helping these refugees stay here, knowing they face death or prison if they're deported. The Salvadoran death squads came after Eduardo and his family because he organized a cooperative in his valley so the farmers could get better prices for their crops. They said he was a Communist. They know who he is, and they'll also know the minute he arrives back in El Salvador. It's a small country."

"I just can't ... " Franco begins, but Sarah cuts him off.

"Dad, right this very minute Jamie, a man you consider a son, is risking his life to serve the people down there. Think about that! You're a man of deep faith. That's how I see you. Please, please pray about this before you give me a definitive no. You need to ask Jesus what he wants you to do. You need to trust in God."

"Sarah, I'm sorry but I'm not going to change my mind," Franco insists. "Jamie's a great guy, maybe even a holy man. I'm just a plain old sinful rancher. As far as I'm concerned, the subject is closed."

Now Sarah's frustration boils over. She turns to her mother.

"You haven't said a word," she says in an accusatory tone. "What do you think about all of this?"

"I don't know," Giulia says. "It's a lot to take in. I just don't know what I think. I can see your side. I can see your father's. You want me to agree with you, but I'm not sure."

"How can you possibly be neutral?" Sarah demands. "The right thing to do is just so clear."

"Well, I'm sorry, but it's not clear to me," Giulia retorts. "You've made your case, but you can't force people to do what they don't want to do. You tend to bang your head against a wall when you can't have your way. Stop now."

Sarah wants to leave in a huff and head back to Berkeley, but that would be the most counter-productive move she could make.

"Jamie, help me not to give in to my stupid anger," she implores, then thinks wryly, "I'm praying to you like you're a saint. Don't get a big head," she mentally teases and feels better.

"Have you brought Jamie's new letters?" her mother asks, like she's reading her daughter's mind. "Will you please leave them for us to see?"

"Sure, Mom," Sarah says. After all, she's read them so often, she practically knows his words by heart. She follows her mother out of the room, pointedly ignoring Franco.

A FEW WEEKS LATER, Sarah is in the courtyard of the Sonoma mission. It's like being whisked back to early California. Ancient olive trees frame a stone cistern that served the needs of the Spanish padres and native American residents of Mission San Francisco Solano. Sarah has always found the garden both charming and haunting. Solano is the smallest and last of the twenty-one California missions, opened in 1823 as an outpost to keep the Russians who had settled in Fort Ross on the coast from moving inland.

From when she was a little girl trying to crawl into the old adobe oven in the courtyard, she has spent many hours here daydreaming of the past. At times she can almost hear forgotten voices whispering on the breeze: Native American converts forced to work in mission industries, who died in droves from foreign diseases and cruelty; Franciscan friars, some pious and sincere, others ruthless and ambitious; Mexican soldiers from the adjacent barracks.

Today she is here with Gabriela and her best friend Maresol. The two girls have been almost inseparable since they met at a Sanctuary picnic. Both are excellent students in the fifth grade and share a love of animals and Nancy Drew mysteries. Both have known hard times and suffered great personal losses.

Gabriela grieves for her dead parents. Maresol's fourteen-year-old brother was kidnapped and murdered in El Salvador.

Sarah knows from the girl's mother that Javier, a boy who loved soccer and was shyly beginning to notice girls, had failed to return from an errand to the store. Late that night, the child's body was found by relatives behind an abandoned factory only blocks from their home. He had been shot in the head, and four of his fingers severed. His agonized parents never were able to find out if they'd been cut off before or after he was dead. Traumatized by the horror, the family had found themselves unable to resume normal life. Maresol's mother, Soledad, had risked the dangerous journey to "El Norte." Her father Damian had joined the guerrillas in the hills, and they have not heard from him in months.

Today the girls seem light-hearted and enthusiastic as the three explore the mission with great interest.

"That painting looks like water, sand and flowers," Gabriela says, pointing to a colorful band along the walls of the quaint chapel.

"I've always thought that too," Sarah replies. "A number

of the mission churches have interesting paintings of things from nature."

Later, they make their way to the gracious early 19th-century home of General Mariano Vallejo, a prominent military commander and landowner in Spanish California. The house itself in Sonoma is furnished as it was when the Vallejos and their large family resided there. The dining room table is set for a formal dinner.

The girls can hardly contain their excitement at a bedroom with beautiful dolls and a doll house that includes a miniature kitchen with cups, plates, pans and utensils around a child-size metal stove. Watching their happy, eager faces and remembering all these two have been through, Sarah loves being part of this joyful moment.

They share a picnic under old olive trees and next to a moss-covered cistern fed by a spring on the property. A pair of ducks float by on the water. Dragonflies hover above. When a hummingbird hovers down to sip, Maresol sighs blissfully. "I think heaven must be like this," she says.

"IS THIS YOUR BROTHER?" Maresol asks as she studies Anthony's handsome face in a collection of family pictures in the living room of the Caffaro home. Giulia has invited them for tea as part of their Sonoma excursion. The girls have just finished a short tour of the ranch with Franco. Some frogs at the creek and three new kittens in the barn have evoked animated conversation. Sarah confirms that the photo is her brother Anthony.

"I miss my brother," Maresol says. "He used to teach me futbol."

"Is he still in El Salvador?" Franco asks.

"No. He's dead. They killed him." The little girl's voice is without emotion.

"Oh Honey, I'm so sorry. What happened?" Giulia asks.

"It was the army. He went to the market and never came home. The soldiers shot him and cut off his fingers." Maresol's tone is eerily matter-of-fact. The elder Caffaros sit in stunned silence.

Then, feeling she has to say something, Giulia asks, "What was his name? How old was he?"

"He was fourteen. His name was Javier. He was a very good brother, because he would play with me sometimes." She turns to Sarah.

"Is Anthony still alive?"

"Yes, He's a padre."

Maresol's face lights up, "Oh good, maybe he will pray for Javier and say the Mass. I know he's in heaven, but it's still good to pray."

"Yes, my dear," Franco says in a hoarse voice. "It is very good to pray."

DRIVING home to Berkeley as the girls chatter about the day from the back seat, Sarah feels alternatively hopeful and anxious. She'd promised herself to stop pushing the refugee family on her parents. The trip to Sonoma with Gabriela and Maresol had been planned before her confrontation with her Dad.

"Oh you have to bring them by here; we have kittens," Giulia had insisted when she'd mentioned the outing to her mother in their weekly phone call. When they'd arrived, she'd introduced Maresol simply by name. The girl had mentioned El Salvador only in response to a question from her father.

Sarah has left the matter in God's hands. And God has come through big time! She knew her parents had been shaken to the core by Maresol's innocent comments. Would the little girl's tragic loss change her father's mind? Right now she knew a major battle was taking place between Franco's stubborn mind and his tender heart. Which would win? Well it was back in those divine hands again.

FIFTY

The woman's long black hair is scraggly and unwashed. She huddles in a chair, arms wrapped tightly around her chest. Her eyes are closed in a face that sags with anguish and fatigue. A year ago Antonia and her husband Gonzalo had five children. Now two are gone. Their eldest disappeared on her way to her aunt's house a year ago. Their youngest girl was killed when a bomb destroyed the town library.

Twelve-year-old Gaspar was shot in the shoulder, caught in crossfire outside the family home. Although he survived, when Antonia found her son bleeding in the street, she had stopped speaking. Since then she has not uttered a word or touched or looked at Gaspar, her daughter Bibiana or five-year-old Donato.

At the request of her family, Jamie's mentor Martin visits the bereaved woman regularly, to pray and perform what he's described to the younger priest as "simple, healing acts."

"Come with me. I think she is close to a breakthrough,"

he'd told the younger man. "There have been small, subtle signs of increased responsiveness, movements and changes in her facial expression. You'll learn to recognize them. Last time she started fingering the rosary Gonzalo always places in her hand. That was new."

Jamie's reaction had been trepidation. What could anyone offer a mother who'd endured such loss?

Today the two priests, along with Gonzalo and Antonia's mother Pilar, are sitting around Antonia, praying the rosary in low voices.

"*Dios te salve, María, llena eres de gracia, el Senior es contigo.*" The familiar words are like hushed music in the room lit by candles on a small altar to Our Lady of Peace. Antonia has not moved; her face is a sculpture of grief set in stone, rosary beads fallen from her passive fingers.

As the prayer continues, Jamie has a sudden idea. His heart starts beating faster. Does he dare do what he's thinking? Suppose it makes things worse? Should he ask Martin first?

"Please help me," he prays fervently. In his mind's eye Sarah's face appears. He feels a surge of love and confidence. He begins to sing softly,

"A la puerta del cielo
Venden zapatos
Para los angelitos
Que andan descalzos
Duérmete niño
Duérmete niño
mete niño
Arrú arrú
Duér."
"At the gates of heaven,

They sell shoes
For the little angels
That go barefoot.
Sleep baby,
Sleep baby,
Sleep baby,
Hush now. Sleep."

It's a lullaby he'd first heard at the center in the Mission. Now his voice, sweet and tender, carries the song into this house of sorrow. He doesn't look to see Martin's reaction. He focuses completely on Antonia, directing the love he's feeling straight to her heart.

"A los niños que duermen
Dios los bendice
A las madres que velan
Dios las asiste
Duérmete niño
Duérmete niño
Duérmete niño
Arrú arrú."
"The children who sleep,
God bless them.
The mothers who watch,
God helps them.
Sleep baby,
Sleep baby,
Sleep baby,
Hush. Hush."

One by one, the others join in, voices only slightly above a whisper. Soon the little room is filled with lullaby.

Long minutes pass. Then a single tear slips from Antonia's eye and rolls down her cheek. Slowly, she reaches out a finger and touches her husband's hand that's been resting on her knee before drawing her own hand back. The response is fleeting, and she quickly returns to her almost-catatonic state, but those gathered exchange glances and tentative smiles. It is a beginning.

~

DRIVING BACK to the university in Martin's old rattletrap of a car, the men are silent, each lost in his own thoughts. Jamie is marveling at how the image of Sarah had turned him into a channel of love that flowed out toward Antonia. For a time, as he sang, he'd seemed to disappear to himself. There had been only the force of love passing through an empty gate. He doesn't begin to understand exactly what happened. He is just grateful.

As if reading his mind, Martin says, "Love is the great healer, and we're all only conduits. The love in your voice as you sang, Jamie...we all felt it. It reached a deep part of that dear grieving woman that I call 'the cave of the heart' where God's spirit dwells. The 'cave' holds the beautiful capacities we are all born with—aliveness, joy, love, and the ability to experience and endure the pain of being human and go on. With the grace of Christ, we can help people open that cave, even if it has been slammed shut by tragedy. Because it is always there, filled with the soul treasures each one needs to live fully.

"Your instincts are good," the elder Jesuit continues with a glance at Jamie. "Somehow you knew the lullaby was a risk worth taking. You have a sensitivity that will serve you well here and make you an instrument of healing. Put aside any doubts about having something to give, mi hermano. God will work good things through you while you are here."

Jamie can only look at his mentor for a moment, so deep is the emotion the man's words evoke in him. Finally he says, "Thank you. Coming from you, that means so much. I'll pray every day that what you say will be true."

When they arrive at Jamie's convent home and Martin has stopped the car, he has one more counsel. "Don't be discouraged when there is only a fleeting moment when the soul place is reached. From my own work with the traumatized, I promise you that even a brief time can be powerful for the person. For an instant, they know themselves as whole and have access to the center of their being."

He looks into Jamie's face. "It's also important to recognize that someone like Señora Antonia, who's endured this level of trauma and tragedy, won't be able to find total healing by herself. She'll need a loving community that can sustain her to complete the process.

"As a priest, your role will be to nurture and inspire these communities gathered in the name of Christ. And there are many of them in El Salvador. They seem to flourish best in the areas where the war is most intense. Among them your priesthood will flourish as well."

Martin smiles encouragingly at his American brother. "And remember, I'm here for you in any way I can be. Shall we meet every two weeks, at least at first? I can be a sounding board. And besides, I'll be very interested to hear what you are doing. What do you think?"

Jamie is overjoyed. "It's a wonderful idea," he says. "Thank you so much!"

DEAREST SARAH,

*"You were truly here with me, so much a part of what happened
in that small room. I know we talked about being resources of
love for one another that would make it possible for each of us to
love with a power greater than we possess as individuals. At
times I wondered if we were just caught up in the passion and
happiness of what we were discovering together and creating a
satisfying fable to justify the fact I was breaking a vow we both
considered sacred. Today I experienced our dream made real here
in El Salvador.*

What we imagined is coming to pass in my ministry.

Are you having similar experiences?

*I miss you very much. Often in the hot, humid nights I lie on my
cot filled with longing. Other times I rest in the pleasure of
memories—and you know very well what they are. Do you
realize we actually have made love only seven times? (OK, I
counted!) Yet I am a different man because of you. Next time
we're physically together I will count the ways as Elizabeth
Browning did.*

*Pablo Neruda expresses what I feel much more eloquently than I
ever could:*

*"I want you to know one thing.
if I look
at the crystal moon, at the red branch
of the slow autumn at my window,
if I touch
near the fire*

the impalpable ash
or the wrinkled body of the log,
everything carries me to you,
as if everything that exists,
aromas, light, metals,
were little boats
that sail
toward those isles of yours that wait for me."

Is it the same for you, Sarah? Does everything
bring you to me?""

FIFTY-ONE

D earest Sarah,

"*Every morning I walk through the Calle Real Refugee Camp on the way to work. It gives me a chance to meet the people who live here. They, in turn, are curious about the new priest in town. (The collar is now a permanent part of my wardrobe.) These women, children (lots!) and some men have fled army operations and indiscriminate bombings of towns and villages in areas dominated by the* compañeros. *Most have lost every-thing they owned.*

Some have managed to save a few precious photos that may be all they have left of children, husbands, wives, parents, or brothers and sisters who've been killed or disappeared. They show the pictures to me shyly, handling them like sacred relics.

"This is my Carlos. Wasn't he handsome?" a woman with a face etched in sorrow said to me as we sat outside the barrack

*where she now lives. "He was a good husband. In spring he
would pick wildflowers and bring them to me. He called me his
'little flower.' She looked up at me with such a vulnerable expression that it was hard not to take her in my arms and cry with
her. For a minute I considered following my impulse but was
afraid it might shock her.*

*One woman stopped working on the hammock she was weaving
to talk with me and offered me the photograph of a pretty young
girl smiling in that sweet, innocent way of children.*

"My Benita was muy intelligente,*" she told me with pride.
"She loved school so much that sometimes I had to force her to
go and play. 'I have to study,* Mamacita,*'" she would say.
"Can you believe a girl like that? She was always telling me
about what she had read. 'Mamacita, did you know…?' Oh
Padre, I can't tell you how much I miss that one." Her grief
was so intense I could feel it in my body. I put out my hands
and she took them. We sat exchanging many feelings through
those joined fingers.*

*Remember how it was for us, Sarah, how we discovered what
hands by themselves could convey?*

*In poignant ways they bring some of their old homes with them.
In the narrow space in front of her large cubicle with a tin roof
Señora Alfreda has a small garden planted in empty cans. A
tomato plant, carrots and lettuce. One can holds pansies and
another, a bright red geranium. "Oh Padre, you should have seen
my garden in Guarjila. It was so beautiful, I confess I
committed the sin of pride." She smiled mischievously. "Imagine, Padre, these days I get pleasure out of remembering my
sins." I couldn't help laughing out loud.*

389

Thank God, there are instances of delight. Those are the times I especially wish you were with me.

Yesterday I saw a boy leading a black chicken down the road on a string "leash." It was like he was walking his dog! His name is Chico. He calls her Chicka. I invited him to have tea with me. (I carry a thermos around for occasions like this.) Sitting in a small plaza, this kid with his bright eyes and cheeky attitude told me he found the future Chicka running loose outside the camp. He used a piece of bread to lure the bird close enough so he could capture her. "At first she did not know we were meant to be together," he told me with a grin. "She pecked me good." He still has the scars from their first meeting on his wrist. "But now she loves me," he added happily. And indeed Chicka shows him an impressive amount of affection, at least for a chicken. She sits on his lap and clucks softly while he pets her. It's the cutest thing. His Mom has threatened to cook her if Chico doesn't behave and get good grades in school. "Chicka is making me a good boy, Padre," he said. "So she is a very holy chicken," he added with a look that seemed to dare me to challenge this religious assertion.

"Chicka is obviously a servant of God," I agreed, eliciting a big smile from Chico. "And you are her holy protector. It's your duty to make sure she doesn't end up in a soup pot." "Oh don't worry, Padre, my gallina *will live a long life." The two made my day."*

Outside in a hammock in the hot damp air of early evening, Jamie tries to rouse himself to join the sisters for dinner. He wonders if he even has the energy to get to a standing position. He's glad it's not his night to cook.

The past few weeks have been an immersion into a hell of human making. He has seen and heard things far beyond any of his previous experiences. In a dilapidated hospital in an urban refugee camp, he has come face to face with the results of the evil forces that live within us. Nothing has prepared him for what men can do to children, women and old people.

There is Ramira, a teenaged girl stopped by militia on the way to market with her grandmother. Forcing the older woman to watch, the men raped the girl over and over, then rammed a rifle barrel into her body. They shot the grandmother in the head and left both on the road. Though there is no residual physical damage to explain it, Ramira cannot use her legs and is confined to a wheelchair. She is part of a group of traumatized teenagers Jamie plays and sings for. His music seems to comfort them, but he cannot sit near Ramira because she is terrified of being physically close to a male.

Paco is eight years old, the only survivor of a massacre in which his mother, father, grandparents, brother and sister were shot to death in their home in a village near Las Vueltas. He survived because he had been outside going to the bathroom when the soldiers came. But he witnessed it all from behind a tree. Now he is experiencing what appears to be a fear-induced blindness. Jamie spends time holding and rocking the little boy who often trembles in his arms. When Paco sobs uncontrollably, Jamie soothes him with lullabies.

A woman named Tecla was badly burned when the Salvadoran military set fire to the house in which she was hiding with her family members. They shot at anyone who tried to escape. Tecla lost her mother and eight-year-old daughter to the gunfire. She is well enough to join what is left of her family now living in the camp, but her face and chest are a mass of scar tissue.

She is so deeply ashamed of her appearance that she refuses to let her husband, her son and her remaining daughter see her wounds. She covers all but her eyes with scarves. Those eyes hold such depths of such agony that it is hard to look at them. Tecla likes Jamie to pray the rosary with her, and so he does, reciting the familiar words, *"Dios te salve, María, llena eres de gracia, el Señor es contigo."* As they share the simple prayers, and his hand occasionally rests tenderly on the woman's head, her expression sometimes reflects a sense of peace, temporary though it may be.

Most of his psychological training is of little use now. Instead his body is the conduit for this ministry: singing, touching, holding, praying, speaking. How strange that giving his body and his heart over to love, rather than all his studies in religion and psychology, may have been the essential preparation for this work.

His relationship with Sarah has afforded him an ease and comfort with the physical he did not have before. Until he allowed himself to be with her in the ultimate intimacy, he always felt it necessary to withhold his body from others in countless ways. He was armed against touch and contact. Now he is free to touch, to embrace, to caress without the fears that held him back in the past. Tired though he is, he smiles into the dusk.

AT THE TABLE with three of his housemates, Jamie tries to be alert and upbeat as they eat their meal, but he doesn't fool these El Salvador veterans.

"My friend, you look like hell," Sister Francine tells him

frankly. "It's a known fact that after just weeks in disaster or war zones, people will be traumatized to some extent. It's happening to you. I can see it."

"She's right," Sister Monica declares. "You're picking up the trauma from those you're working with."

"God, please don't say that!" Jamie exclaims, covering his eyes with his hand. "If I'm already falling apart after only three months in El Salvador, I'll soon be useless. Isn't it possible I'm just tired and adjusting to a very different world?"

"Jamie, you're obviously not sleeping well. You seem to be losing your appetite and there's a bleak expression in your eyes at times," Francine says. "Look, it's not some lack in you. It happens to everyone. Suffering from post-traumatic stress is actually a sign of how completely you're giving yourself to the people you're ministering to."

"As a psychologist you must recognize how counterproductive it is to deny what you're experiencing," Monica adds. "You've got to deal with the effects of this stress day to day. Otherwise you'll be a basket case before you know it. You simply have to take care of yourself. It's time for you to meet Ariana."

Dearest Sarah:

"I've joined a support group for people like me who have come here with the intention of helping the Salvadorans through ministry and personal involvement. It's hard for us helper types to admit we're vulnerable to absorbing the trauma of the people we're working with. The old ego gets in the way. There's still an unredeemed part of me that believes I'm supposed to be the strong one, who sweeps in to rescue the weak and suffering. Please pray I can let that part go.

The group is one of several created by a woman called Ariana, a nurse midwife who's been in El Salvador since 1979. She's a sharp, very competent and insightful woman our age, feisty (you two would like each other) who cuts through any BS that comes her way with the subtlety of a machete. When I met her, she immediately made it clear to me that macho posturing and aspirations to be the self-sacrificing "hero priest" (her phrase… I believe someone else I know once called me that!) are nothing but "f-ing bullsh-t." (She has a way with words!) and need to be abandoned totally "if you want to be any damned good to anybody." Ariana is bracing!

It's not surprising that the same nurturing techniques we ourselves use with traumatized people are beneficial to us as well: relaxation practices, physical movement, massage, music, prayer and frank, open conversation. Each of us is assigned a more experienced "partner" we can confide in and come to for support when things get tough. Mine is Alain, a medic who worked with an ambulance crew in his native France before coming to El Salvador after watching a TV show on the war that mentioned an urgent need for medical care in dangerous conflict zones. He'd seen the face of a little girl in pain crying in her mother's arms, and 'she called to me so strongly, I could not resist her. So here I am,' he told me. He's been in the country two years.

We had dinner together to get acquainted. Alain is forty-five, divorced with no children. He's a humorous, outgoing man. I like him. We talked about our lives with surprising intimacy. I debated telling him about you—our talk was that free and honest—but thought it best to wait until I know him a bit better."

Jamie puts his pen down on the bedside table and heads for his cot. It's so damned hot and sultry. He'll never again take cool, fresh air for granted. Images of the Golden Gate at sunset flood his mind, and with them Sarah comes, her hair and eyes reflecting the light. He remembers those eyes alive with love for him. His body vibrates at the memory.

Her latest letter came today bringing a sense of home. She's hoping to convince her parents to hire and house a refugee family on the ranch. Knowing Franco and Sarah, Jamie has no doubt where he's placing his bet.

What she writes to him is generally upbeat and loving, but there's also an undertone of frustration that she is doing so little good in the world. In response to his account of meeting some traumatized children, she'd asked, "How can I help? What do they need? What would comfort them?"

He wonders if Sarah understands how powerfully her love sustains him in his ministry here. He suspects she doesn't recognize the extent to which he depends on that love. He wishes he could find better ways to explain the power of their connection in his life and work.

Jamie's mind drifts toward Sarah and the beautiful Bay Area.

Ariana believes sensual pleasure is an important healing tool for PTSD. Jamie smiles, remembering what it felt like to join his body with Sarah's. He gives himself over to the emotions and sensations of loving this woman. He realizes he doesn't feel at all guilty at what he has done and is doing. What would his spiritual guide Richard have to say? O God, this is not the best subject to contemplate when you are trying to go to sleep.

FIFTY-TWO

The phone rings as Sarah is leaving her house for the library to work on a new course for the fall. "Good News for the Poor" will focus on the stories and teachings of Jesus as viewed through the lens of liberation theology.

She's finding deep satisfaction in creating the class. Can privileged people like most at Pacific Theological Union comprehend what the gospels can mean to the poorest Christians? Will she be able to help students get a real sense of a world and points of view so different from their own, when she herself only knows that world second-hand through Jamie, the refugees with Sanctuary and the media? It will be a challenge. She will invite refugees and nuns and priests who have lived and worked among Christian liberation communities in Latin America to speak to her students.

"Hi, Honey," her father says when she answers. "You're coming Thursday, aren't you?"

"Dad, when's the last time I wasn't at the ranch on 4th of July?" she responds with a touch of the exasperation she's still feeling at Franco because of his stubborn refusal to consider her proposal.

There is a pause.

Then he says, "You know that guy you wanted me to hire for Rico's job?"

"Yes?"

"Well, why don't you invite him and his family to come Thursday?" His voice rises. "Now don't get the idea I've changed my mind!" Sarah smiles to herself but remains silent.

"I'd just like to meet them, okay? No promises. Don't get their hopes up. I mean it! Just invite them to join your family to celebrate the Fourth if they don't have plans. Got that?"

"Loud and clear, Dad. No promises. Just 'come and have dinner with us.' Maybe Josefina will bring her homemade tamales."

"No, don't let her go to all that trouble, because nothing may come of this."

"I understand, Dad. Don't get their hopes up. But Josefina probably will want to bring her tamales. She's very proud of them."

She keeps her voice calm and even. "I'll find out if Eduardo and Josefina are free. If nothing else, they'll have a chance to see an American ranch up close. With their farming background, they'll enjoy that."

"That sounds good. Love you, Honey."

"I love you too, Dad."

Sarah puts the phone down and begins to laugh and dance around the room. When her tender-hearted father meets the dignified Salvadoran farmer, his vivacious wife and their sweet kids and hears their story, he'll be a goner. He'll be begging Eduardo to accept the job.

She grins and her mind turns to Jamie, and she sends all the joy she's feeling out to him. "This is for you too, my love."

~

THE AIR IS rich with the fragrance of peaches, and the orchard is in full summer glory as the two men walk among the trees. "It is a wonderful place," Eduardo says. "I can feel years of work and devotion in this rancho. It is beautiful, what you and your family have made with God's gifts." Franco feels a glow of satisfaction.

"To my father this property was like a living person. He called it *la nostra madre terra*, and he taught me to love and care for it," Franco replies with pride. "Now my twelve-year-old grandson, Charlie wants is to be a rancher, and he has so many ideas. He's pushing me to make the ranch organic, you know, without artificial pesticides and fertilizers."

Eduardo smiles. "Charlie and I will have to talk. As poor farmers in El Salvador we use nature's ways to keep down the bugs and weeds."

"Until the soldiers came, and the helicopters." His happy voice turns sad.

"In one afternoon it was gone...everything we had made, I and my parents and grandparents.

"Our whole community, the little ones and the old, had to run to the hills. We hid in caves. We came back to a nightmare." He looks directly at Franco, his face full of pain. "Almost every home was nothing but piles of burned stones. They killed all our animals, our cows and pigs, even our cats and dogs. They left them to rot in the sun. They even chopped down our fruit trees. It was not for military gain. It was to destroy our lives."

Franco looks around at the lush trees and vines and his

lovely home in the distance. He tries to imagine it all wantonly ruined. Involuntarily he shudders, moisture pooling in his eyes. The men walk on, examining small green grapes and the pear crop. They speak of fruit and farming practices. It's clear Eduardo knows fruit growing.

Impulsively, Franco makes a decision. "Eduardo, amigo, will you come to work for me?" he asks. "My right-hand man has retired, and I need someone to help me run the ranch. There's a house where you and your family can live. I think we could work well together."

He grins at the astonishment on the Salvadoran farmer's weathered face.

"Señor, do I understand that you are offering me work and a home?" Eduardo asks, his voice incredulous. "You do not even know me, the kind of man I am. Or what I can do on a ranch."

"Maybe it's foolish to act so soon," Franco admits with a sober expression. "But you're obviously experienced with fruit trees and vines, which is what I need. And I already like you. I sense you' re a man I can trust. I may be wrong. Time will tell.

"Besides," he adds, "hiring you will make my daughter very happy."

"What about *la migra*, the immigration police?" Eduardo persists. "Won't you get in trouble? We have no documents for America."

Franco ignores a trace of fear along his spine. "If I can't take a small risk to help you and your family, what kind of person would I be?" he asks.

Eduardo nods solemnly. "We will trust in God," he replies quietly.

"*QUERIDA MADRE de dios es un palacio!*" Josefina exclaims from the doorway as she looks into the front room of the modest house. Two eager children brush by their mother and run into the room.

"Stop. Behave, now!" Her tone is sharp. Ten-year-old Teresa and seven-year-old Celino skid to a halt. Giulia laughs.

"Let them go. They want to see everything." When the woman nods at the pair, they take off like race horses out of the starting gate. Soon the air is filled with excited voices.

"*Venga, Mamacita,* come and see this!" "There are so many rooms." "Will we live here alone or with other people?" "*Mira!* Mama, look at this!"

Accompanied by Giulia and Sarah, Josefina walks slowly through the house, her eyes bright. The rooms are filled with light shining through windows onto cream-colored walls and newly-refinished hardwood floors.

"Our friend Enrico worked hard to get the place ready for whoever came after him," Franco says, trailing the women. "We were fortunate to have a man like that."

"It will be much to live up to," Eduardo says coming to stand beside his wife. He takes her hand. "*Que pienses, Querida?* What do you think, my dear?"

"What do I think? I think I've died and gone to heaven. *Mi amor,* promise you will take care of the children now that I've gone." Everyone laughs.

Sarah can hardly contain herself as the unofficial tour continues. She walks up to Franco, throws her arms around her father and gives him an enthusiastic kiss.

FIFTY-THREE

It's a rare hot day in Berkeley. Mark, Julianna and Sarah
are drinking wine in the shade of the tall walnut tree in
the couple's backyard. Sarah sighs happily. "I sure like being
with you two," she says. "You feel like family."

"We feel the same," Julianna says, raising a glass of scarlet
wine to Sarah. "*Cugina!*" she exclaims with a wide smile.
"Dear cousin."

Now Mark looks at Sarah, beaming. "I have some news,"
he says. "I've applied and been accepted to spend a month
with an international group of Quaker doctors and nurses.
Guess where I'll be?"

Sarah's eyes widen. "Not El Salvador?"

"You got it!" Mark exclaims. "Physicians for Peace are
focusing their efforts on Central America these days. There's
so much need. I read about them in a medical journal."

"Tell me everything." Sarah says.

"I'll do pediatric surgery in San Salvador," he tells her,
then grimaces. "It'll be very different from what I do here

because many children have horrendous wounds. "We're talking amputations and trying to put mutilated little bodies back together. I'm studying surgical techniques I never learned in medical school.

"I'd also like to go out in the refugee camps to see what's happening with children there. And I have a friend who makes children's prostheses. I've promised to look around for him. He'd like to work in El Salvador if he can do enough good to make it worth the risks. I'll report back to him."

Sarah's face radiates joy.

"Oh Mark, that's so great. To be able to help the children!" Her expression turns wistful. "You might see Jamie. It's a little country, the size of Massachusetts."

"We have an idea," Julianna says. "Why don't you go with Mark?"

"For heaven's sake, I have nothing to offer!" Sarah protests vigorously. "They don't need Scripture classes. I'd be like some kind of war tourist."

Julianna pats her hand. "We've been thinking about this. Mark will be going after the holidays when PTU is on break. Why not spend the next couple of months gathering medical supplies, then go down with Mark to help distribute them? Physicians for Peace has guidelines on what's needed and how to get the things into the country. And I'll bet there are people in Sanctuary willing to donate money to the cause. Our Salvadoran contact sent word the supplies they received from our fundraiser are almost all used up."

Sarah shakes her head. "I don't have the right to barge in on Jamie and demand his attention by my presence. I would never do that."

Julianna gets up and goes into the house. When she returns, she's holding a letter with familiar handwriting.

"Juli," Mark protests. "Don't. Jamie told you what he did in confidence."

"I realize that, but it feels like the right thing to do." She opens the letter, turns to the second page and begins to read.

"I am simply in awe of these women, men and children who are enduring the unendurable and often bearing it with a grace that makes me ashamed of my own weakness.

This morning Nohemi, a nursing assistant at a camp clinic brought me a cup of tea. She is always doing little kindnesses for the staff and the patients. She buys candies out of her own small wages and gives them to children who are upset or in pain. These are such rare treats that many of the little kids who get one can actually forget for a moment all the 'bad stuff,' like injections, going on.

Nohemi has a garden behind the shed where she lives, and will often slip flowers or a few vegetables to some of the poor women who come for treatment. I've seen sad, tired faces bloom with the sweetest smiles at her gift of a tomato or a handful of poppies.

She has such a sunny personality that I was completely blown away to discover the Army had killed her husband, her daughter and her mother-in-law in one of the dozens of massacres that go unreported to the public. The nurse who'd hired Nohemi confided this to me.

'Please don't tell her I gave away her secret, Padre,' the woman said. 'She doesn't like people to know. I tell you because you can say Masses for her. She is very strong, but everyone needs prayers.' I understand she has two living children, a daughter and a son. The boy is off fighting with the companeros.

Now I notice Nohemi with particular attention. How in the world can a human being go through what this woman has and be the kind of person she is today? Poor tortured El Salvador needs the balm of its hidden saints like Nohemi. May God bless and keep them and shed their grace on all of us.

In contrast, I'm discovering just how weak I am. Only three months into this work and I'm already feeling its effects… trouble sleeping…occasional blinding headaches. I feel like a total wimp. Veterans who've been here awhile tell me I'm exactly like anyone else from an easy life in a safe country who is dropped into a cauldron of agony like this.

"Yep, you're just another guy, J," Ariana, my nurse-midwife mentor, declares. "You're not St. Ignatius, St. Francis or another Christ as the Church used to refer to you clerics." I like this woman a lot. Sarah and she would be instant best friends.

Please don't tell Sarah, but I fantasize about her being here with me. I imagine her seeing El Salvador with her perceptive vision and compassion, then writing stories that let people back home know on an emotional level the horrors being done here in their names and with their tax dollars. However, I'd never ask her to come, because if I did, I'm afraid she would, and I have no right to bring her into danger. That's the last thing I'd want to do!

I'm very glad to hear you're well and happy and doing important work in California. It's great you're treating the refugees, Mark, and you're offering your legal expertise to the Sanctuary folks, Juli. I pray for both of you every day. I said a special prayer at Mass on your anniversary, remembering that wonderful

404

day we shared. It was such a joy to be part of the marriage of a man and woman I love whose love for one another was obviously so deep and generous. (And who could ever forget that reception party!)"

Julianna looks up from Jamie's letter. Sarah's eyes hold the beginning of tears. "He *wants* me to come to him," she says softly. "It even sounds like he *needs* me to come."

FIFTY-FOUR

With Ariana behind the wheel, the jeep tears along a winding road as Jamie prays fervently they'll make it to Guazapa. He's supposed to say Mass there tomorrow morning, but this woman drives like she'd trained with NASCAR, and he wonders if they'll get to the place in one piece.

They'll stay the night in a convent in the shadow of the local volcano. Although it's only a day's walk from the capital, Guazapa is a conflict zone. You don't travel around there after dark.

Ariana is telling Jamie how, when she had set up neonatal and pediatric clinics and trained dozens of health care workers, all her work and success were wiped out because she chastised a Salvadoran trainee in public. She glances at him.

"I was riding high. The American heroine was going to bring good health to the poor." She laughs wryly. "Then one day we had a party. And this guy who hadn't come to work all week turns up for the festivities. I made a snide comment about how nice it was he could make it to the party but not to work.

"Everyone thought I'd treated him badly. He was part of them. I was the outsider. On the basis of that one remark, people started to drop out of the program. They didn't want to work with me anymore. They started to interpret everything I said negatively and referred to me as 'that pushy *gringa* who comes in and tries to run everything.' "

"What did you do?" Jamie asks.

"I apologized to him...to everyone, but it didn't help. I had to turn the project over to someone else. It was a hard way to learn to treat every Salvadoran with respect. With all the stress people are under, they can't take more negativity, especially from a foreigner." She chuckles. "I'm happy to share my Salvadoran street smarts with you, Padre. The first rule of life here is 'Practice humility.' "

"Thanks, Ariana, I needed that. Lesson taken."

Rounding a curve, they see a military roadblock ahead.

"Welcome to the real El Salvador," she whispers as she slows, then stops the jeep. "Be cool," she warns quietly.

His pulse speeds up, but Jamie is not very worried. American passports are considered reliable guarantees of safety these days in rural areas controlled by the military. The Salvadoran army doesn't want to offend its American patrons by killing U.S. citizens. They know the murder of the four U.S. churchwomen in 1980 had created a worldwide firestorm of protest.

A tall man in fatigues who sports a luxuriant mustache strides up to the vehicle. He looks angry.

"*Pasaportes, rápidamente!*" he barks, his face close to Ariana's. "Hurry up!" She quickly removes the document from her purse. Jamie opens his backpack to retrieve his.

The Salvadoran lieutenant (his bars are visible now) studies both passports. Then he looks at Jamie.

"Who are you and what are you doing here?" he growls.

"I'm a psychologist."

"Who is your sponsor?"

Jamie hesitates then says, "I'm a Jesuit priest. I am in your country to help your people." The man's eyes harden.

"Get out of the car," he orders gruffly. Jamie complies. The officer grabs the priest's arm roughly.

"What are you doing? You have no right!" Ariana says loudly. "The Americans won't like this." Despite her words, Jamie feels a jolt of anxiety.

"Shut up and get out of here!" the soldier commands. He pulls Jamie toward a military jeep by the side of the road. As his companion continues to protest, he is shoved into the car. He doesn't resist.

"It's okay. Don't worry, they wouldn't dare harm me," he calls to Ariana.

When the lieutenant gets into the vehicle, the priest reaches out his hand as though they were meeting under normal circumstances. "I'm Father James Quinn, Sir," he says in a friendly tone, hoping to diffuse the situation. The man looks at him likes he is an idiot. He ignores the gesture, slams the car into gear and takes off, engine roaring.

They race past sugar cane fields and tin-roofed adobe huts and within minutes pull up to a large walled compound with an iron gate guarded by four soldiers with rifles. On the wall is a huge painting of a black and white skull pierced by a yellow lightning bolt. A sign proclaims "Barracks of the Army of El Salvador Guazapa District."

As the jeep approaches, the gates open. The car has hardly rolled to a stop when the lieutenant shoves Jamie toward the passenger door.

"Get out!" he snaps. Exiting the vehicle, he propels the priest forward by a rough hand on his back. Realizing the man is trying to intimidate him physically, Jamie assumes a serene expression.

"Please let me feel your peace," he prays silently and imagines Sarah's face filled with love.

The lieutenant marches him quickly down a hall to a closed door and knocks firmly. "Enter," a deep voice commands. The door opens into a large, sunny room dominated by an imposing wooden desk. Behind it is a tall, stocky man with close-cropped white hair and piercing black eyes.

"My colonel, I found this Jesuit on the road to Guazapa," the lieutenant says. The officer rises abruptly. A tight smile on his face, he reaches for Jamie's hand and grabs it with a bone-crushing grip.

"I am Colonel Rogerio Monterrosa. Please sit down." He gestures to a chair and resumes his own seat. "To what do I owe the pleasure of your presence in my district?"

Ignoring the sarcasm in the colonel's tone, Jamie smiles sweetly and introduces himself. He speaks of his affinity and admiration for the Salvadoran people, his desire to be of service to those traumatized by war, and his coming here to do a liturgy. Monterrosa listens without comment then asks, "You are American?"

"I am."

The older man regards the younger one cooly. Then he smirks. "It must be boring these days in *los Estados Unidos*," he declares. "No wars…no ways to have part in the great adventures of men. So you come down here to to play in our war.

"You priests arrive claiming you want to do good, then you run around making revolution, convincing the poor that God wants them to be rich. Priests from everywhere are coming." He chuckles. "Of course, since they don't let you have sex, you need to find excitement somewhere—to get the chance to feel and act like real men."

To his chagrin, Jamie laughs out loud. He can't help it, and it takes him a minute to rein in his spontaneous laughter. The colonel first looks startled, then breaks into laughter himself.

"You have nerve, Jesuit. I like that. But I don't like you rampaging through my country, making trouble, stirring things up. Without people like you brainwashing the *campesinos* and turning them into Communists, this war would have been over a long time ago.

"Instead it drags on and on, and more innocent people die. Can't you understand that? You are hurting the poor. You're not helping them."

Jamie looks at him. "Sir," he says quietly. "I want no trouble. I'm in Guazapa to say Mass for the Catholic people here. You would be very welcome if you want to come."

The colonel guffaws.

"There's nothing like a trouble-free Jesuit," he says. "We need more of them. They're too damned rare around here."

Jamie smiles amiably. "May I leave now?"

"Certainly. In fact, I will have someone drive you to the church. It is a long walk and you could encounter some hostile Salvadorans. Have you seen this?" He reaches for a flyer on the desk. "*Be a Patriot. Kill a Priest*," it proclaims.

The colonel shakes his head. "I remember when priests were loved by everyone."

As Jamie reaches the door, the colonel has the final word.

"Be careful whom you treat, Señor Sacerdote. Anyone who aids the Communist dogs is an enemy of the state."

Dearest Sarah:

"Mass today was a lively affair. The church was packed, and there must have been fifteen musicians, including an accordionist. At times the church rocked with music, but around the Eucharist the songs were gentle and heartfelt. At the end of the liturgy, there was one particular piece sung with obviously great emotion and even some weeping.

Later I learned the The Blue Hat is the song that expresses the heart and soul of this revolution. As a woman with deep lines in her face and sad eyes told me, 'Singing El Sombrero Azul gives me the strength to continue this hard fight. When I am in despair, I listen to it and believe again.' I wish you could have been there to hear the spirit of these gallant Salvadorenos come forth through their music.

"The Salvadoran people have the sky for a hat. With great dignity they search for a time when the earth will flower over those who have fallen, when happiness will replace all this pain. Come! The march is slow but still a march.

By pushing the sun, the dawn draws closer.
Come! Your fight is pure like a girl when she gives herself in love with a free soul.

Come now, Salvadorenos, there's not a single bird which after taking flight stops in mid-air.
Brother and Sister Salvadorenos, long live your blue hat.

Let your clean blood spread across the sea
And become an enormous rose of love for all humanity."

It's always amazing to feel such an upwelling of joy in this place of constant sorrow besieged by war. The army attacks frequently, from the air and from the ground. There are free fire zones where soldiers have permission at certain times to kill anything that moves.

An elementary school teacher told me the first thing kids are taught is how to survive an air raid. They need to know where the underground shelters are and how to get to them quickly when they hear the sounds of approaching planes. Many times after a raid, the young teacher said, some children, especially the littler ones, are terrified to come out. They sit in the dust, trembling, until an adult carries them back into the light.

Yet here these people were, singing and dancing, their bodies and faces radiating gladness.

While we were in town, Ariana showed me the small hospital she and her health promoters use. It's an old three-room adobe house. The living room that serves as a ward has six beds. Another room is for examinations and simple medical procedures like stitching wounds or setting bones. The kitchen doubles as an office. Patients wait to be seen on a covered porch.

We are training local health promoters to help traumatized persons with the simple techniques I've mentioned.

We're also forming support groups in towns and rural areas for those who've lost family members and/or their homes. The campesinos who are already doing medical work are very intelligent and eager to learn. With some education in mental health, they'll be able to lead these groups. So we can utilize the love and wisdom already in a community for people to help one another. It might seem simplistic, yet it could become a healing tide spreading out to places where there are no psychiatrists or psychologists (almost everywhere down here). We'll have to wait and see, but having been among the Salvadorans for only this long, I'm convinced they have the potential to do great things, including building a society that could be a shining example to the rest of the world.

FIFTY-FIVE

T he sun looks misty, its edges softened by filmy clouds, as
it slides toward the horizon. The flowers and green
leaves in the small private garden outside the hotel room are
lit with heightened color.

Jamie's eyes are soft as he gazes into Sarah's face. She in
turn studies each of his features lovingly. The longing they've
felt in the months apart makes the joy of finally being
together indescribably sweet.

He can hardly believe she is actually here with him. Her
arrival with Mark had been a total surprise.

Mark and Sarah had laughed at Jamie's expression when
he'd seen her walking up behind his old friend. Sarah wishes
she had a photo of his astonishment—so great that his mouth
and eyes formed circles—like a cartoon character. "I may
faint, but it will be a good faint," he declared with a booming
laugh.

"Jamie, you remember my wife," Mark said, drawing
Sarah forward and making them laugh so hard that people

nearby stared. (Jamie was wearing his collar, so it seemed like a prudent strategy. They'd agreed in advance to do it.) Recovering their composure, Sarah and Jamie gravely shook hands, avoiding each other's eyes, while Mark held her arm like a proprietary spouse.

Tonight Jamie and Sarah are alone in a private patio of the small Spanish-style hotel where she and Mark are staying in San Salvador. In the quiet they savor the peace they find together, peace with a completeness almost palpable in the growing twilight.

Suddenly Jamie's expression turns merry. "Do you come here often?" he asks. Sarah dissolves in laughter.

"No wonder you're celibate!" she manages to say.

Then she is in his arms. She feels his heart beating against hers. The silence deepens into what is beyond words and flows between them. Time passes unnoticed.

"I can't begin to tell you how much I love you," Jamie says. A sunset sky glowing with many colors adds to the beauty of the moment.

As he speaks, Sarah experiences waves of pain radiating from him. Then his pent-up grief bursts forth. His tears fall onto her cheek, and he cries so intensely that the sheer physicality of it reverberates along her own body.

Sarah grasps his hand.

"Come," she says. "I want to be able to hold all of you with all of me."

He is quiet as she leads him inside and to the bed in the modest room.

Lying with her in the growing dark, Jamie's tears continue to flow, shining in the deepening tropical night.

"Sarah, Sarah, I guess I've needed you with me to dare to feel the agony of the people here."

His grief pierces her own chest like an arrow.

"Dear Jesus, may I be what he needs right now," she prays. Her arms bring him closer until his weeping stills.

He sighs. Haltingly, in a voice often thick with emotion, Jamie tells her stories.

He had been in a small town for a liturgy and baptism in the Morazan district when four little boys were killed by a grenade they'd found in a field and mistaken for a toy.

Hearing the explosion, Jamie had run and knelt beside them, only to hold and caress their little bodies helplessly as they'd bled and screamed in the dust and weeds. A passing nurse frantically did what she could for children whose hands had been blown off and whose faces were ruined by shrapnel. Later he'd prayed over their small broken forms as their mothers held his hands tightly and joined their tearful voices with his own.

Another time Jamie had been called to give last rites to Marianna as she lay dying on the outskirts of San Salvador. She was someone he'd met and talked with, a friendly, bright-faced woman, a member of a teacher's union and a leader of an organization that helped battered women.

Marianna had been dragged out of her elementary school classroom in the middle of the morning by men who drove her to the edge of the city, threw her to the ground and poured acid into her face, then riddled her body with bullets. Her husband had been there when Jamie arrived, unable to embrace his dead wife because of the dangerous acid. The man's keening cries still haunt his dreams.

One day as he walked near the military academy, a young boy lined up with scores of "boy soldiers" had grabbed Jamie's sleeve. With tear-filled eyes, he'd whispered frantically, "*Mi madre* doesn't know where I am. They took me while I was on my way to *mi abuela*'s. *Mi madre* is Marita Robles in Calle Berlin. Please tell her!"

A grim soldier had approached and pushed him away roughly. "Get out of here, or this guy will pay," he'd threatened.

"I found his mother and gave her his message," Jamie says. "She cried with relief, because she'd thought her son was dead."

Finally, Jamie tells her of visiting a poor woman, badly crippled, whose seven-year-old grandson was taking care of her: cleaning, cooking, washing her clothes, putting wet towels on her swollen legs.

"He had such sweet little face, and the loveliest smile. I gave him some candy and he was thrilled. The first thing he did was offer a piece to his grandmother."

Sarah's own heart breaks open as she listens to tales that unfold through Jamie's voice. "Thank God for the goodness," she says softly when his words run out.

"Oh yes. Thank God!" he replies fervently.

They lie on their sides, face to face in the dark. Feelings and sensations arc between them. Right now Jamie's actual physical presence with her is so affecting that words don't come easily. It's the same for him. A light goes on in the garden. It's still dim, but she can see him again. He smiles at Sarah with more tenderness than she has ever experienced directed toward her.

Her touch begins as a way to comfort this man she loves, but it soon catches fire against his skin. He responds with caresses of his own that start gently then intensify as the need to give himself to Sarah sweeps away everything else. Jamie pauses, raises his head and seeks her eyes with his.

"We are a prayer of love," he murmurs.

"This is worship, isn't it," she breathes. "God loving God through us."

Later Sarah will find words which come close to

describing what it was like to make love with Jamie that night. They are not her own words. Instead they come from a mystic describing a spiritual experience of union with the Divine Beloved.

In the infinite mystery
Of knowing You,
as my own Self,
I surrender everything,
form and essence,
what has been...
what is...
what could be.

I let it go—sweetness, struggle,
oneness,
even the connection
of my true heart.

And still this love surges
like sea overwhelming shore,
and what once filled the world
now floods from universe to universe
and beyond.

Tonight in this room, a sanctuary from the war outside, Sarah is certain the body is an essential part of the most profound spiritual experiences our lives can hold. Those who attempt to wrest the physical away from the spiritual dimension are doing violence to the human person. She knows this beyond any doubt. Making love is the ultimate human connection, the act designed by God to bring all life into the world. It is at the very center of the Holy.

"We were part of something vast," she will write later in her journal, reflecting on the experience when she was back in America. "Jamie and I were motes of dust in the light of a boundless sun. All the love in the universe was gathered there in that moment, and we simply disappeared into it. Yet we were part of it, too, creating its substance in being together."

SARAH AWAKENS to a chorus of birds greeting the approaching dawn. Jamie is sleeping on his side facing her. Free to observe him fully, she sees the traces this tragic land have etched into his body.

Back home, there had been a boyish quality to him. His youthful energy and the aliveness of his face had made him appear younger than his years. No longer. He is thinner now, almost gaunt, and there are new lines around his eyes. Her heart twinges to see that his beautiful dark hair is being infiltrated by gray.

Even more disturbing is how he is sleeping. In their nights together in Berkeley, she had marveled at how peacefully he slept, still and silent with a serene expression.

"You look like a choir boy when you're asleep, as innocent as an angel." She'd told him.

"You've never witnessed the sleep of the just before?" he'd quipped.

The choir boy is gone. During the night Jamie's restlessness had movements awakened Sarah several times. He could not seem to get close enough to her. At times she's felt almost claustrophobic as he'd pressed against her body. The man who in the past slept so quietly she'd had to check to be sure he was still breathing now moaned and had even cried out once. He may have slept, but he certainly didn't rest.

Studying him, she sees a new jagged scar on his right wrist. It strikes her as emblematic of all the deep wounds he's carrying from what has happened to him in El Salvador. In only a few hours together, she already knows he has changed. It grieves her to realize the immensity of the pain in him.

"Dear God, if there's any way for me to comfort Jamie, to share his pain, please show it me how," she prays, caressing his cheek with the softest possible touch.

His eyes fly open. He looks surprised, then his expression floods with joy.

"You're really here," he whispers. "I thought I'd dreamed it."

As SARAH and Sister Francine unpack the medical supplies from America in the small-town clinic, the Salvadoran nurse's face resembles a child's on Christmas morning. Her eyes sparkle at the sight of the bandages, splints, surgical tools, antibiotics, pain medication and sedatives.

"Madre Dio, do you know what treasures you are bringing us?" she exclaims. "My rag bandages have been washed so many times, I can read a book through them." The women laugh.

Francine is escorting her through the Chalatenango district to distribute the supplies to clinics run and operated by local people, some trained by medical professionals like Francine and Ariana.

"Profesora Sarah is a friend of Padre Jamie," the nun says. The woman shakes her hand enthusiastically.

"Padre Jamie is here every Tuesday to say the Mass and talk with us and listen," she says. "He is a good friend. We are grateful for both of you, Profesora. Will you please join us for coffee?"

Soon Sarah is seated on the ground under a tree with spreading branches, surrounded by friendly women extremely curious about this norteamericana whose presence is turning an ordinary day festive. Glad for all the effort she's put into studying Spanish, she easily answers questions about her home, her family, her unmarried state (a cause for amazement and concern) and her opinions about El Salvador and those she has met here.

When they learn she teaches the Bible, and especially its stories of women, they beg her to teach them. For a second, she has a fantasy of coming and doing just that. There is something so appealing about these Salvadorans; she understands more of what draws Jamie to them.

As they talk, everyone is busy with some task. Two are weaving hammocks. A woman appropriately nicknamed *La Abeja* ("the bee") is buzzing around, picking up bits of litter and sweeping the packed earth around the clinic. Others are grinding dry corn or preparing tortillas. Sarah has observed that most Salvadoran men, women and children are very energetic, even a number who look worn and malnourished. Jamie has told her of watching whole families happily trekking to sugar cane fields at 3:30 or 4 a.m., delighted to be able to do something to bring in a little money.

This reminds Sarah of driving along the road earlier and being puzzled to see trees with strips of paper, rags and trash hanging from their branches. When she'd asked Francine, the nun had laughed, explaining the *campesinos* did that to embarrass trees that didn't bear fruit that year. "They hang these things to make the tree feel ashamed in front of the other trees, so it will be more productive next season. Even the trees are expected to work hard here."

"You are the most industrious people I've ever met," Sarah exclaims to the busy women around her. "Everywhere I go, people are working, even many of the little ones. I come from a place where we often sit around doing nothing much. Here I feel guilty, because I am a worthless woman compared to you all."

The women grin and chuckle.

"If that is true, then now I know where I want to be when I die and go to heaven," declares a gray-haired lady with braids twined around her head. "I'll say to St. Peter, I've been a very good person on earth, so send me to Berkeley, California for my eternity." Everyone laughs good-naturedly.

Jamie had suggested that when the opportunity arose in conversations she focus on people's strengths and the positive things in their lives.

"The tragedies are always with them, weighing on their hearts," he'd told her. "You have such a radiant spirit, and that's part of the gift you bring here. Fun and enjoyment are so important for people living on the edge of hell."

Sarah had glimpsed that hell on trip here. Bombed-out villages lay abandoned, their homes and small shops already being taken back by jungle-like vegetation or simply collapsing in areas made barren by modern versions of Agent Orange.

Francine had stopped to pray in a ruined chapel, its altar still intact, though its bell tower had fallen and the sanctuary was open to the sky.

"I used to drive priests to this church for Sunday Mass," she'd said. "After liturgy, we'd stay for lunch and the weekly market. I made many friends." She'd led Sarah through the abandoned town, pointing at rubble where houses had stood, silent witnesses to the ongoing tragedy of El Salvador. Francine had looked at Sarah with grief in her eyes.

"When I'm in this place I can still see and hear them too. Luz, Ximena, Trinidad, little Angelita and Violeta. and so many more." Her voice had trailed off. "I can pretend that Basilia is hurrying toward me, calling out a welcome. That Caridad is giving me some flowers her small hands have picked. That Ercilia is telling me, 'Wait till you taste my new recipe.' For a moment they still live on this earth with me. They still have the promise of the future they had hoped for at the end of the war."

The two women had wandered silently through the haunting, haunted landscape with its poignant artifacts of a past life: broken plates, a child's shoe, a shattered chair.

Then Sarah had seen something terrible for a rancher's daughter. An orchard had been hacked to pieces, each tree lying near its stump.

"Oh no," she'd groaned. Soldiers had gone out of their way to destroy a few dozen mature fruit trees. She'd thought of her father's pride in his trees and his meticulous care of them. Her mother used to tease that they were his mistresses.

"You're just jealous of how I much I love my girlfriend Peaches," he'd once joked, throwing his arm around a trunk. "She gives me nothing but sweetness, unlike some people we could mention." Her mother had cuffed him playfully.

Now Sarah imagined this Salvadoran orchard's previous life: children climbing the trees, people eating ripe fruit with enjoyment and laughter, just like at home. Francine had touched her shoulder.

"They want to extinguish the future too," she'd said sadly.

FIFTY-SIX

Sarah finds Mark alone in the small dining room of their hotel. He sits at a table with his head in his hands, the dinner in front of him untouched.

"Mark, what's wrong?"

Startled and disoriented for a second, the pediatrician raises his head and stares at her.

"The world is wrong! The American government is wrong! All these starving and maimed children!" The normally-mellow Mark's voice is angry. "And it's all so goddamned unnecessary." He pauses. "What sheltered lives we live in the good old USA, the f-ing land of the free and the home of the brave. People should see what America the beautiful is doing down here!"

He gestures to a chair. "Sit down and join me, sweet Sarah. It's true what they say. Misery *does* love company."

She takes a chair across from him. "Tell me."

Mark grimaces, then begins to speak in a weary monotone. "A British nurse, Susan, took me on a field trip today to show me medical conditions outside the hospital and also give me a break from non-stop surgery. At a shack in one of the endless shantytowns, a young woman met us at the door. She looked frightened.

" 'I'm afraid Amado is going to die,' she told me. She lifted what looked like a bundle of rags from a hammock. A tiny baby was wrapped in them. He was like a skeleton. Lita —that's her name—explained that Amado is the child of her sister who'd died giving birth to him.

"The baby's father is so weak and sick from TB he can't walk. Lita is trying to nurse both Amado and her own son, Donato. She said Amado was born sickly and suffers from diarrhea. We gave her medicine for him and enough formula for a month. Poor little guy...there's hardly anything left of him. I'll stop by next week, but I doubt he'll make it. Poor Lita, trying so hard to keep him alive.

"And malnourished kids are everywhere with their little distended bellies and stick arms and legs. I've never before seen children lying on the ground or sitting propped up against walls because they're too wasted to move, let alone play. Then there are the kids who can hardly breathe from the asthma they've gotten from the polluted city air and open cooking fires inside the houses. Susan tells me people are always getting burned too."

He lets loose a blast of four-letter words and curses, then glances sheepishly at Sarah.

"With all I've seen in the operating room, I don't know why this got to me so much. Maybe because I know Lita and her dying brother-in-law and starving nephew are like tens of thousands of others in this country. They're human beings just like us. She even looks like a friend of Juli's. The resemblance really hit me.

"And you know what?" A vein is starting to pulse in

Mark's forehead. "Most of the arable land and wealth in El Salvador are owned by fifteen families. FIFTEEN f-ing families! All of this horror—this war, the torture, the killing, the ruined lives—is happening mainly to protect the goddamned interests of THOSE FAMILIES! Can you believe that? Because for these rich Salvadorans to share their obscene wealth with the ordinary people would be a triumph for Communism, according to that bastard in the White House!"

Sarah reaches out and puts her hand on his. "I know, Sweetie, I know. It makes me want to shoot some people . Or better yet, hack them to death with a machete."

"You want to do what?" Jamie is standing at the door. "Four days and you're ready to commit murder? Obviously, it's not safe to let you out alone down here." He laughs, but the sound is jarring.

"Ah, it's none other than the holy Father," Mark quips with an edge to his voice.

Jamie turns quiet, watching the faces of these two so dear to him. "I know I'll sound like a pious jackass," he says finally, glancing from one to the other, "but a wise old priest who's been sharing the life of the people here for a decade warned me against outrage and making anyone my enemy.

"Please listen," he continues, seeing their indignant expressions. "I was seething with rage after less than a week. It got to the point I couldn't even pray without being overcome with fury at the rich, the military, Reagan. I was fantasizing assassination!

"But Laurens told me any amount of rage and hatred would close parts of my heart. He said I was going to need every bit of that heart to meet the suffering of the people." Mark looks at him angrily, obviously not convinced. "OK, OK, I'm being annoying as hell, insufferable and whatever you want to call me," Jamie tells his friend. "But dammit. What he said is true."

He looks at Sarah. "He was right, because even my whole heart and my love aren't enough. I'm always drawing on your heart and your love to get me through the pain." Her face changes from irritation to tenderness, and she reaches her hand out to him. He goes to her, bends down and kisses her gently.

Watching them, Mark longs for Julianna. Suddenly, he shudders as he thinks of the dangers here and how vulnerable his beloved childhood friend will be in the ministry he's committed to. Jamie and Sarah do not notice.

SWEAT POURS down Mark's face as he uses a bone saw to sever the lower portion of a ten-year-old boy's right arm. The child's hand and forearm were burned when a spotter plane sprayed white phosphorous on him while he was playing near his village. By the time his father carried his boy into the hospital in San Salvador, the limb was a shredded mess that made the pediatrician want to vomit. Thank God the child had passed out from shock. "Please help us, Señor Medico," the man had pleaded, his eyes pools of fear and misery. The lower arm was beyond saving.

As Mark works quickly, afraid he may find the upper arm irreparably damaged, he keeps glancing at the boy. Tomaso is a small skinny kid whose own destiny is to work in the fields like his father and grandfather before him. What will happen to him now? How will a one-armed man make a living in this ravaged place? Tears are mingling with the sweat as he imagines the child's future. He won't even be able to have fun playing ball with his friends, or any other makeshift game that requires two hands.

He sighs with relief, because the humerus bone is intact, so he can save the elbow, making it much easier for the boy to use a prosthesis. He'll have to find a way to keep in touch with this family, so his friend Bill, the artificial limb builder, can contact them if and when he comes to El Salvador. With the number of child amputees Mark has already seen, there's great need for his services.

Washing up after the operation, his last of today, Mark wonders if he can survive a full month here. He's a pediatrician with a specialty in surgery, but until this week he'd never amputated a child's limb or fixed a jaw shattered by shrapnel. He'd never had to cut into a little body to see if organs slashed by bomb fragments could be saved.

He'd never dealt with a little girl who'd stepped on a land mine only to watch helplessly as she died, despite his best efforts. He's grateful he'd studied up in preparation for the kind of surgery war might require. But all the books and videos in the world couldn't prepare him for the little kids who'd been hurt deliberately by people who intended to kill or maim them.

After their tense conversation earlier, he'd gone back to talk with Jamie seeking guidance. Already he was hating those who harm children and wanting to hurt them in return. Explosive rage was gripping him to the point he was afraid of losing control. Yesterday he'd found himself about slap a nurse who'd dropped a scalpel, and that scared him.

His priest friend had no words that could solve the problem, but he'd given Mark a massage and played some gentle music for him. They'd talked quietly, shoulders touching, for a long time before Jamie went to be with Sarah for the night.

"That's the best all your psychological training can do for

me?" he'd mocked Jamie. Yet he did feel better and more relaxed afterward. His friend's practical acts of love had soothed him. Now Mark wishes he'd taken Jamie's advice and asked Juli to come with him. He definitely longed for her loving presence now. He had called home to hear her voice, but the call took almost six hours to go through and the connection kept breaking up.

He understands Jamie's intense need for Sarah more clearly. Observing the power of their connection and watching it deepen, he wonders what's going to happen to these precious friends. How in the world can they have a future together?

After speaking with Jamie, Mark knows he has to come to terms with his limitations. He'll do what he can in this month he is committed to being here. He'll help some children. He'll even save some lives, as he probably saved Tomaso's today.

But it's like trying to empty a lake with a spoon. And when he returns to California, the lake of children's tragedies will continue to fill from the ugly river of war that feeds it. All his work will leave only a ripple in the surface, and that will soon disappear. He rubs his hand over his eyes. It would be great if he could cry and find release in tears. Instead he feels numb inside.

THE HALL IS FILLED with people crowding benches on both sides. The Salvadorans waiting are quiet and sober, most slumped in their seats, their eyes focused on something beyond this place. There must be thirty people here, Sarah estimates, mostly *campesinos*, identifiable by their sun-marked faces and roughened hands.

Ariana leads her to a desk outside a closed door. A gray-haired man rises and comes around to hug the nurse-midwife.

"Maria Julia is expecting you," he says in a friendly tone. She introduces Sarah as a writer who is here "to bear witness to what her government is sponsoring." His handshake and greeting are warm.

"The good people of America need to know these things," he tells her.

Sarah is nervous to be meeting Maria Julia Hernandez, legendary human rights lawyer and devoted advocate for victims of government and military violence. Sponsored by the Catholic Archdiocese of San Salvador, Hernandez and her team have spent years gathering evidence of massacres and individual killings. They interview survivors and record their experiences. They've also compiled a book of photographs of the dead and disappeared.

Hernandez' struggle for justice has made her enemies, and there' s reportedly a price on her head. She's known to begin each investigation with a prayer. "Well, God, I'll either see you in person today or you'll give me more time to keep fighting."

The door opens. A small round woman with short dark hair gently ushers out a couple. The man's arm is around the woman. Both have traces of tears on their faces. "*Vaya con Dios, mis queridos*," the small woman who is obviously Hernandez says quietly. "I will do all I can to find justice for your son, may he rest in peace." The two regard her with looks that border on reverence.

"We know you will, *Doña*," the man says in a choked voice before they walk away. Hernandez watches them in silence, then turns to the two women.

"Ariana, a hundred welcomes, and to your friend also. Please come in," she invites them. Sarah is struck by the penetrating eyes in her broad face. It's like the lawyer can see her from the inside out. This is somewhat intimidating, as though she is being evaluated with a single glance.

The room is sparsely furnished with a table, chairs and file cabinets. The only decorations are a crucifix and two photographs of Archbishop Romero, Hernandez' friend who worked closely with her until his assassination.

After Hernandez offers cookies and coffee from a large dispenser, she comes right to the point. "El Salvador is doing the redemptive work of Central America. The people's struggle here is a remarkably pure, just war on behalf of the poor and the desperate. It is a true liberation movement," she tells Sarah, her voice filled with passion.

"So many of those who come to us started out with nothing and were treated like dogs their entire lives by the rich who run this country." The attorney's eyes snap with anger. "They were starved and beaten and forced to work in unbearable conditions. They endured every kind of abuse.

"When they finally rose in protest, the powers-that-be declared war on them. They've attacked them and bombed them. They've raped and tortured and killed them by the tens of thousands. Your government supports this genocide and finances it. The weapons come from the U.S. And most Americans have no idea what is happening in Central America, what is being done in their names. Worst of all they don't bother to inform themselves, because they don't really care."

Sarah nods and drops her head in shame. Then she looks up at Hernandez. "I care," she states with conviction. "I've worked as a journalist and my intention is to write the truth of what I am learning here. When I get back to the States, I plan to submit articles to publications like *Newsweek Magazine* and *The New York Times*.

"I'll do my best to communicate the reality of the experiences of ordinary Salvadorans. I want to help readers feel what it would be like if they and their children were caught in a war designed to destroy them and their future."

Hernandez regards her intently. "Our work here, our sacred task, is to listen to their stories," she says. "We record everything they tell us, each word. Many have come from long distances and made sacrifices to get here. There are five of us in this building who spend seven hours a day, six days a week, listening with our minds, hearts and souls as well as our ears.

"Come spend time with us, *mi hermana*, and you will understand. As people tell us how their children died or their parents, or their husbands and wives, and they see how we listen, something changes. You can hear it in the timber of their voices. You can see it in their posture and their expressions.

"They arrive beaten down, hunched in their chairs, often with heads bowed, unable to look us in the eyes. They show all the signs of victims of vicious oppression and abuse...shattered by the atrocities and savagery they have gone through. It is in every line of their bodies and in the hesitancy of their speech.

"Then we encourage them to tell their stories. And we listen. And listen. And listen. They look up and they see how completely we are listening and truly hearing what they have to tell us.

"Señorita Caffaro, we often witness a transformation right in front of us. They raise their heads. They sit up straighter. Their voices become firmer, more confident. By listening, showing that what they have to tell us is important, we give them back their human dignity and their hope. It is an alchemy I do not fully comprehend. Yet I see it happen before me.

"People who bring us their stories trust they are bearing witness to a truth that will lead El Salvador to a positive future. So all their suffering...all the pain and the losses...will not be in vain. They believe when the terrible acts of the government and the military are exposed, things will change for the better.

"You see, dear American friend, the only way you can live with so much suffering, your own and what you have witnessed, is to believe it has a redemptive value. Otherwise, all is meaningless, and life is absurd, a cruel joke by a heartless God."

Sarah's face is grave. "If you allow me, I will come and see and hear for myself," she promises.

FIFTY-SEVEN

J amie watches Sarah's face, noticing each expression and nuance of feeling that passes over her features as she reads what she has written.

"Señora Elvira is a small woman with a face made for laughter. Even in repose it has a jovial cast. The laugh lines and naturally upturned lips remind me of my Italian grandfather, one of the happiest people I have ever known.

"Today, however, as the aging Salvadoran woman begins to tell her story, all the signs of past joys are erased. Her normally-cheerful eyes are bleak. They gaze out at a landscape beyond this simple office in San Salvador.

" 'A soldier pulled my Jesus from the group of young men they had rounded up in the plaza,' she says in a voice that breaks at times during her narrative. 'I don't know why they picked him. Maybe it was his red shirt. He was so proud of that shirt.

'What's your name, Boy?' the man shouted. When my son told them it was Jesus, he laughed. 'Perfect,' the soldier declared. 'We can play Good Friday.'

"Bravely, this little woman has come here today to bear witness to the horror: How they nailed a board to a tree like a crosspiece. How they ignored the tearful pleas of Jesus—'Please, please don't hurt me.'—and his mother—'For the love of God, please don't hurt him!' How they nailed the sixteen-year-old boy's hands to the wood as he screamed, and his mother tried to frantically to rush to his side, only to be held back by a soldier who grabbed her roughly, encircling her neck with his arm. How one of them split Jesus' chest open with a single blow from a machete. She remembers the blood sprayed like a fountain, then pooled around his feet.

"In her dreams she still hears them laugh. She sees one carelessly raise a rifle and pump two bullets into her boy's head and neck.

"Elvira recalls how—after they let her loose—she clasped his ruined body made so slippery by his blood that she slid down to her knees. How she wept clinging to his legs as the soldiers turned and walked away. How her family and friends stood paralyzed, afraid to move to help her or Jesus until the killers had driven off.

"Her words bring the scene to life, a living Pieta of flesh and blood—a horrific irony here in the only country in the world named for Jesus Christ—El Salvador—The Savior. Even to listen to this mother tell what happened to her child is almost unbearable.

"One would expect Elvira to be hunched over in agony as she recounts the crucifixion and murder of her son. But no. Instead her spine is straight; she sits upright in the chair. At first her voice quavers, but it soon grows strong.

She tells the human rights interviewer the essential facts. 'This happened in _____ on 25 March 1983. The soldiers were from a company of the _____ battalion. The man who shot my son was tall with a big belly. They called him Sergeant Rambo.'

"The woman falls silent. She regards the man who has been listening intently and with deep interest to her story. There is compassion in his eyes—and respect. 'Please, Sir, I ask justice for my Jesus and all the others,' she says with a simple dignity apparent to each person in the room. 'Will you help us?' "

Sarah pauses. "That's all I have so far," she says, looking at Jamie with a touch of self-consciousness. "It needs work. I want to make Señora Elvira and her terrible experiences even more gripping and vivid for a reader."

Sitting beside her on a sofa in their small hotel room, Jamie reaches over and cups Sarah's chin in his hand, raising her face to his. "I love what you're doing," he says gently. "You're going to be a channel for the Salvadoran people to speak to the people of America. Your writing can make what's happening here real to ordinary Americans."

She smiles, but her eyes are sad and her face is strained. "What I write won't change anything for anyone," she says. "At least you can do some tangible good."

It's clear to Jamie his beloved Sarah has already lost the innocence and naïveté that seem to be the birthright of Americans.

"I'm so glad you're here, and I'm also sorry, because experiencing all this suffering directly is going to hurt you and change you in ways you can't know." He frowns. "It happens to everyone who comes to help or bear witness. It's an inevitable consequence of touching catastrophe."

She stretches out her arms out and draws him close. Together they sink into the silence of their deep connection.

"If I hadn't come here, I wouldn't know who you are now, who you've become in this place," she says at last. "When I made love with you later back home, it would have been with the man you used to be. And he doesn't exist anymore. I realize that.

"And Jamie, how can I be a true part of the Church, the Mystical Body of Christ, if I'm ignorant and immune to all this suffering? Is that even possible?"

"I can hardly imagine what it will be like to go back to the way it was for me in Berkeley," he replies. "How will I ever be able to enjoy one of Sam's great dinners without seeing those little-old-people faces on starving babies? How will I be able to run in Tilden without seeing the girl I met today dragging herself along the road on a plank with wheels because her legs are gone?"

Sarah leans against him, her head on his shoulder. He

touches her knee and lets his hand linger there. What else is there to say? The truth is like a juggernaut pushing against their defenses. Nothing will ever be the same for Jamie. And what about her?

"Go home," he says abruptly. "Don't stay longer. Francine can finish giving out supplies. Please go. Don't let El Salvador take you away." Sarah hears the love and concern beneath the words. But what he is saying is canceled out by the intensity of his longing for her. It rushes toward her through her senses and her spirit. She lifts her eyes to his, and he knows she understands what he is not saying. His breath catching, he clasps her hand and raises her to her feet. He looks at her.

"Arise, my love, and come," he says, smiling in an attempt to dispel the bleakness.

"In the Song of Songs the bride sought her lover but didn't find him. so tonight we're rewriting Scripture," Sarah replies, trying for humor.

Yet there is nothing light or humorous in the lovemaking that surprises them by the sheer, raw power of their need to give themselves to one another.

The force of it leaves them both shaken.

"Well that's a completely new level of physical sensation for me," Jamie says, feeling himself blushing in the dim light from the lamp in the garden.

"Nothing in my past even comes close to what I just experienced with you," Sarah responds. Remembering her total physical abandon, she feels suddenly shy.

They rest together in a quiet peace. Then she says, "What do you know about sacred prostitutes?" Jamie's answer is a gust of startled laughter.

"Woman, you're never boring! I don't know much. Why do you ask?"

"The Sacred Prostitute is a very ancient figure," Sarah

answers. "She's mentioned in Sumerian poetry 4,000 years old. What makes her wonderful to me is her healing power. It was said that a man coming home from war injured and broken in his heart and spirit could go to a sacred prostitute, usually in a temple.

"She would prepare a lovely, sensual ritual space—flowers, incense, holy images. She would invite him in, and ultimately into her life-giving female body. By embracing her, he could surrender his pain into her keeping. She was the symbol of the goddess of love. Coming to her sexually, the wounded soldier would go through an initiation that enabled him to return to his former life healed of war.

"That's what I'd like to be for you." Sarah whispers.

Jamie's body quickens at her words and the images they evoke—his beloved opening herself to him as a goddess of love and healing. He reaches for her with passion and with hope.

Later, as Sarah drifts off to sleep with her head against his chest, she tries to imagine a future back in California in her pleasant life, but she simply cannot find it. Jamie remains awake for a long time, enjoying the feeling of her body touching his, soothed by the soft rhythm of her breathing. It's too sweet to leave for sleep.

He wonders about a world where people like Sarah and himself can be so protected from the untold anguish of millions of their fellow human beings that even brief contact with the reality has traumatic effects.

⁓

As the plane rises up from San Salvador, Sarah peers down intently at the rapidly diminishing city as though she could still glimpse Jamie in the web of tiny buildings and streets.

Her heart is thudding in her chest, and she feels choked by fear.

Will she ever see him again?

When she, Jamie and Mark stood in the departure lounge, she'd suddenly felt a premonition that this would be the last time. Sarah is pretty sure her reaction is only natural. After all, she is leaving someone she loves beyond words in a very dangerous place. Her fear may be predictable and inevitable, but that doesn't diminish its strength.

As they'd embraced, she'd clung to Jamie, completely forgetting they were in a public place, letting her fingers savor the hardness of his muscles and the softness of the skin of his neck. When she would not stop touching him, he'd put his hands on her shoulders and gently moved her away. The love radiating from him was like a warm fire on a cold night.

"I promise you we'll meet again, Sarah," he'd whispered, reading her mind.

"Yeah, where, in heaven?" she'd demanded in a voice loud enough that Mark, who'd turned aside to give them privacy, glanced back.

Jamie had leaned in close and murmured, "The gallant missionary is bidding farewell to the only woman he will ever love. Do you think she's the kind of person to make a scene?" Then he'd smirked. "And heaven indeed! For a wanton priest seducer, you're pretty confident."

Sarah couldn't help herself. She'd actually chuckled. "Worry about your own soul, shameless vow breaker," she'd retorted softly, trying not to cry.

Jamie had grinned then and held her hands tightly. "Just like in grand opera. The hero and heroine part forever. The music soars."

Sarah had risen to the occasion. Raising her arms dramatically, she'd boldly belted out a line of Jamie's favorite

Italian ballad. " '*O sole mio sta 'nfronte a me*," she sang, causing the two men to laugh out loud and nearby Salvadorans to regard the trio with curiosity and amusement.

"She always leaves me with song," he'd told Mark.

"Making it a lot easier for you to let her go, right?"

Jamie had grinned at Sarah.

"That must be her intention, yes."

So they parted in good humor, but as she turned for a final look before boarding the plane, their eyes met, and Sarah felt like part of her was being ripped away.

"Please keep him safe, dear Lord," she'd prayed fervently. "Jamie has such love for your people in El Salvador. They need him too."

~

"MIO DIO!" Franco exclaims in a voice charged with revulsion.

Giulia's face reflects the horror of what their daughter has just read to them: Señora Elvira's testimony about the murder of her son. "*Dolce Madre di Dio, abbi pietà di noi,*" she moans.

"Is it too much, too graphic?" Sarah asks. "But these kinds of things happen regularly down there! Some of the men in the army and the militias are like mad dogs with absolutely no restraint. The cruelty is diabolical. It's hard for us up here to imagine what's become 'ordinary' in El Salvador." Her parents are silent for a few moments, obviously thinking seriously about her question.

"You've made the humanity of the Salvadoran people very real in your first article," her mother says finally. "Those stories show how much parents love their children, how humorous people can be, even in such dire circumstances, and how wise and insightful when they reflect on the gospels at Mass."

"And that wonderful tale about the little boy and his 'holy' chicken," Franco chimes in, laughing.

"This is going to shock and sicken readers," Giulia continues. "Especially since you've set the stage in such a way that people will be pierced to the heart by what happened to Elvira and Jesus. It makes me start to feel what it would be like to watch soldiers hurt Anthony that way." She shudders involuntarily. "Or see my daughters killed in front of me," she adds with visible emotion.

"This is powerful story-telling," her father says. "I think it will have the kind of effect you are hoping for. If your second article is about the suffering, will there be others?"

"I want to do an article about the situation through the eyes of foreigners, particularly U.S. citizens, who are there to help. I interviewed a number of them. I also hope to include what's needed right now in El Salvador, like medical supplies and protein sources, with detailed information about how Americans can contribute and assist the Salvadoran people from here."

"Do you think they'll be published?" Franco asks.

"I don't know, Dad; they're pretty controversial. The Reagan administration is always trying to convince Congress the Salvadoran government is making '*significant progress*' in human rights. To keep them voting money to finance the so-called struggle against Communism in Central America. That makes my articles intensely political. And now the Justice Department has started criminal prosecutions against two Sanctuary activists in the Rio Grande Valley.

"As soon as I finish the last piece, I'm going to contact *The New York Times*, *The Washington Post* and the weekly news magazines to see if they're interested. If not, I'll work to get them published wherever I can."

"I pray for Jamie every day," Giulia says, abruptly changing the subject. "It used to be just for his physical safety. Now, from what you tell us, I'm also praying for the wounds to his heart and soul."

Sarah's face is grave. "Please pray very hard," she replies.

"Honey, how are you doing?" her father asks. "You look terrible."

"Gee, thanks, Dad, just what any woman likes to hear."

He regards her soberly. "You just aren't yourself since you've been back. "You seem so tired and stressed. I worry."

"I'm still recovering. It was traumatic to be there, even for only two weeks. And of course I'm scared for Jamie," she adds. "Part of the time he works with *campesino* communities in the countryside where guerrillas are hidden in the hills. That makes him an enemy of the state to some people. His American citizenship is the only thing that gives him any protection. The Salvadoran government doesn't want the bad publicity it would get if the military or a militia killed an American priest. But it's really dangerous down there." Her voice trails off.

"He must have been so happy to see you." Her mother says brightly.

Her daughter's face is tender. "Oh, Mom, I can't begin to tell you."

They sit together quietly in the sunny room in the peaceful countryside, each lost in their own thoughts and feelings.

FIFTY-EIGHT

S *an Salvador*
  January 21

Dearest Sarah,

   This morning the convent rooster started crowing well before dawn. I decided his incessant 'Quiquiriquí' (that's Spanish for cock-a-doodle-doo) was a lament of longing for his hen lover and actually felt tears welling up. So I'm now officially crazy, driven to chicken romance fantasies by your absence after our sweet time together.

   I once asked Sallie Olds what she thought would come after death. She said, "Remember the time when you felt most connected to another person? I think it will be like that." Now I believe the wise woman is right. Heaven will be like the days you were here with me ...

   Training a group of campesinos *this week to lead support groups for other traumatized people, I was struck once again how wise and intelligent these ordinary Salvadorans are. They may have little or no formal education, but they're capable of deep thinking, and I really appreciate*

444

the freshness of their observations. You have experienced some of that, so you can understand.

Yesterday a middle-aged woman who's lost her husband and a daughter to the war, told us, "There is something that happens in me when I can talk about these sad things with people who know from the inside what it is like to lose the ones we love." (Fortunately, I was recording our session.)

"Their eyes give me something the eyes of others don't," she continued. "I do not have a name for it, but it spreads like a soft oil over my heart. And when I speak with these sisters and brothers in my pain, their voices sound the way I think Jesus and Mary would sound if I could hear them with my ears. I do not understand why, or exactly what I am trying to say, but it is true."

No one spoke for a moment, then another woman dealing with her own multiple losses said, "When your child or your wife or husband is killed or murdered, you go to a place where most of your friends and family cannot come, because they do not know the way. You are alone, like you have been dropped into a desert that is empty as far as you can see. The loneliness is so great, your are afraid you will die of it. It burns your soul."

For a while there was no talk, only quiet tears. Then the woman looked around the circle into each face. "Now in this desolate place I have turned and found each of you here with me. Your own pain has given you the map to here. I am not alone anymore." She smiled shyly. "This means so much to me."

O Sarah, I am filled with love and gratitude. Sometimes I'm so overwhelmed with emotion that I go somewhere alone, lie on the ground and open my arms wide. There are no words... just the infinite sky.

Love always,
Jamie

～

FEBRUARY 9

DEAREST JAMIE,

Life is interesting and strange these days. It's like living in two places at once, mysterious and disorienting, with a flow of love like an underground river.

I am here teaching a course in the gospels through the lens of liberation theology. At the same time I am there with you and the people I met in El Salvador as you all live out those gospels together and discover the true meaning of Jesus and his message in the middle of a war.

As I listen to my students discuss the texts and the theology, I realize how much we perceive in abstractions because most of us have no personal experience of the conditions that give rise to liberation theology. I wonder if we can actually understand the power of Jesus' 'good news' from lives like ours. Maybe that's why so much of Christian morality in the first world is obsessed with something as inconsequential as how and when people have sex. Of course rape and incest are terrible and destructive, but just how much of the horrendous suffering of millions of the poor and powerless has anything to do with sexuality? It's surely not central to the greatest sin of the world that Jesus spoke of.

It made me think about what you said my last night in El Salvador when I asked you if you ever felt guilty about our being lovers. You said, "I couldn't feel guilty about loving you, but I am still sad I thought it necessary to make a solemn vow that I would never give my body to a woman I loved." That you felt guilty for making that vow, and your punishment was that—if they knew—many people would consider you a dishonorable man for breaking your public promise.

You told me you realized most of your Jesuit brothers would condemn you for not leaving the priesthood because you're with me. "I'm living in contradiction," you said. "I have no defense to offer anyone. I've given up my honor for love."

And then you whispered, "Loving you is my prayer. It's how I come

446

to God." *Jamie, I am in awe of the mystery of us. Your words will resonate in me for the rest of my life. The fact the Church wants to deny its consecrated men and women this profound spiritual dimension simply cannot be the will of our God. After all, it is God Who designed us in such a way that physical union can be an act of the deepest worship... beautiful beyond imagination. You and I are so very blessed to know this from our personal experience.*

Jamie... Jamie... Jamie

～

THE SANCTUARY PEOPLE *are continuing to gather medical supplies for Ariana's clinics, as well as "necessary items" like toothbrushes and tooth-paste for a major shipment later this month. Two Berkeley pastors, Bob and Marilyn (a husband and wife team you will enjoy) will shepherd it down. I've been collecting donations of materials for the art therapy projects you want to start. So far the four big art stores in town have been very generous. You will receive two large boxes of art paper, pens and pencils, paints, brushes and crayons. Best of all, the managers of two of the stores say they'd like to contribute materials on a regular basis!*

～

MY PARENTS SEND *you their love and want you to know they are not only petitioning God on your behalf, but are also soliciting help from people they've known whom they believe are now in heaven. It is my father's opinion these 'local saints' are much more responsive to prayers because they don't have as many demands on them as the 'big ones' have.*

"Mary and Joseph must each have thousands of requests -maybe even millions- a minute to deal with," he told me with a straight face, although I detected a twinkle somewhere. "However, Mrs. Mary Margaret Maguire, our neighbor and a saint if I ever knew one, is prob-ably up there waiting eagerly for a prayer to answer."

447

It makes sense to me. Have the Jesuits ever considered the 'enhanced efficacy of unknown saints?' Anyway, if you're ever in need, St. Mrs. Mary Margaret Maguire is awaiting your call!

With all my love, Sarah

∼

CHALATENANGO DISTRICT
February 24

DEAREST SARAH,

We need more processions in the American Church. They have them all the time down here, and they're great. I was part of a celebration last weekend when the congregations of several small parishes walked and sang their way to the church in a larger town. There were guitars, cane flutes, maracas and a drum, not to mention many voices raised in song. One of the most loved is Victor Heredia's "We Still Sing," a strong declaration that "By the grace of God, we are here today together. We are still here."

Imagine, a couple of hundred people, women carrying babies or with bundles on their heads, children with banners and flags, men lifting statues of Mary and the saints high into the tropical air. More folks join the procession at every village and crossroad. And the music leads and supports them on their way.

They sing of still dreaming of the flowers of life that are hidden now. They ask God to give them hope and let them know the garden of their lives will light up again with the songs and laughter of those they love so much. They affirm that they will continue to sing and dream of a different, better day for their children, for all the people.

Oh the faces, alive with hope and joy in this perilous district, putting aside their fears to walk past the soldiers in their barracks and their trucks, looking forward, their 'eyes on the prize.'

When we finally arrived at the town we were met by a procession from that church (San Antonio) with people carrying candles, the statue and banner of the saint, tortillas, mangos and flowers, singing the same song.

We found the church in darkness, lit only by candles and late afternoon light through the stained glass windows.

After everyone was settled, a silence fell over our congregation. A woman and a man stepped into the pulpit and began "the roll call of the martyrs," the names of those who have been killed for their work organizing the campesinos, teaching the poor to read, or introducing them to liberation theology and other "subversive activities."

It is a very emotional ritual. One of the readers will call out a name, "Roberto Torres" or "Mercedes Portillo." Together the people gathered will answer, "Presente!" As someone explained to me, 'The martyrs are not remembered because they once lived among us. They are welcomed because they are present, here and now, in our midst... part of us. They are present to inspire and motivate us to continue the sacred work.'

By the time the liturgy began, people were overflowing with the Spirit, ready to be swept away in the mystery of Jesus's presence with his brothers and sisters in divine love. I felt so amazingly fortunate to be there and of course longed for you to be with us. Because you've been in El Salvador, it's much easier to imagine you beside me. In fact, even though you're not a martyr, (and definitely not a saint!), I whispered 'Sarah Caffaro' to myself during the roll call, and could swear I heard you say, 'Presente.'

Always yours,
Jamie

FIFTY-NINE

Sarah is enjoying the safety of being home in California. Of course, there's always the chance the "Big One," a massive earthquake, will strike. And even crossing the street can be dangerous. But when she'd awakened today to the sound of a helicopter flying over Berkeley, she didn't have to worry about bombs raining death from the skies. When she goes outside, she doesn't need to watch out for armed men prowling the streets.

What an incomparable luxury to live free from ever-present danger and fear. Americans simply do not appreciate how fortunate they are.

It's Sunday morning, and the winter light gives clear definition to every plant in the garden. Sarah wonders where Jamie is saying Mass today. She knows how much he loves liturgies in small towns and rural areas. With so few priests in conflict zones, some communities often go for weeks without a Eucharist. Mass becomes a special event, a small fiesta. It is a great combination: deep prayer as a community followed by a party. Jamie had taken her to one in Chalatenango, and she'd been moved and enchanted by the depth of the people's devotion and the liveliness of the celebration that followed.

Sarah marvels at the fluidity of time in the mind. She and Jamie were together less than two months ago, but it seems like it was only yesterday and also an eon in the past. She's restless, missing him, longing to connect in the mysterious way they are able to feel deeply into one another over distance.

Before liturgy at Newman Center, Sarah decides to walk the pier so special in their relationship. It's one of the places she's closest to him, where the beauty of the Bay and the beauty of love seem to merge into a mystical dimension of matter and spirit as one.

Today, however, the Bay is bleak and foggy, very different from her home in the sun-drenched hills. Wisps of fog drift round the bleached, ancient timbers of the jetty. It's almost deserted; only a few intrepid fishermen greet her as she heads out. She imagines Jamie beside her, holding her hand in public and laughing at his daring.

When she reaches the slatted barrier at the end of the walkway, she presses her face against the wood and looks out toward the Golden Gate. The estuary is a somber gray, matching the color of the sky. In contrast, the bridge is a smear of glaring orange. Sarah finds her spirits sinking. She drops to a sitting position and leans against the side.

Drifting with the mist, she remembers an old nursery rhyme that begins, "One misty, moisty morning." She hears the haunting call of a foghorn across the water.

Sadness envelops her, and she seeks a reason for the tide of feeling. "Jamie won't ever come back here to live," she thinks, realizing what she's been unwilling to face before now.

Suddenly, she *knows* it's true. The life they've shared in California is over.

The pain is sharp, and she lets herself experience it fully without trying to lessen its pangs. Part of her has known he wouldn't return permanently since she'd observed him with the people of El Salvador. At the liturgy in the countryside, she'd watched him offering communion to a little girl, both their faces tender and open to one another other. And she'd thought, "This is who Jamie is. This is the man he was born to be."

At that moment he was so beautiful and full of light. And as she'd recognized it would soon be time to relinquish him back to God, she had never loved him so much.

From the beginning Sarah has understood Jamie could not "belong" to her as Julianna and Mark do, for life and till death do us part. Yet that understanding does not quench her sorrow now.

Her eyes slowly scan the Bay for something. A sign? Comfort? As though in response to her unarticulated wish, a ray of sunlight suddenly streams down on a harbor along the Marin shoreline. Seeing the sparkle where light and water meet, she's suffused with gratitude.

They might not be together physically, but she and Jamie are on the same planet at the same time, simultaneously sharing all it means to be human at this period in history. When she looks up at the moon, it is the same moon he's seeing. She can imagine him living and laughing and serving the Salvadorans he cares for so deeply. Letters can be an intimate bridge between them. She'll know what he's doing, thinking and feeling, and they can share their inner lives.

On some future night, the man whose body is like a sacrament for Sarah, will be lying on a bed in a far place longing to make love with her. And there will always be opportunities to meet and touch and talk and laugh and love again. As long as they both exist on this earth, reunion will be possible.

Pensively, Sarah raises her face, her back against the rough planks. She almost welcomes the damp cold and discomfort as she gazes at the sky.

Doña Manuela's wrinkled face is solemn as she looks into Jamie's eyes and carefully presents to him the plate of bread for communion. Her gnarled hands tremble slightly. Her spine is compressed by age and heavy loads, yet she walks with a dignity that touches his heart.

"Thank you, *Doña*, and may God bless you," he whispers as he takes the plate. She smiles and turns, making way for the teenaged boy carrying the wine. The musicians are playing softly, and the singers' voices are muted for the part of the liturgy called the Presentation of Gifts.

The music is one of the Saint Louis Jesuits' hymns Jamie loves most, speaking the promise that, no matter what a person has to face, God is with us, and all will be well.

> "You shall cross the barren desert,
> but you shall not die of thirst.
> You shall wander far in safety,
> though you do not know the way.
> You shall speak your words in foreign lands,
> and all will understand,
> You shall see the face of God and live.
>
> Be not afraid,
> I go before you always,
> Come follow Me,

and I shall give you rest.

If you pass through raging waters
in the sea, you shall not drown.
If you walk amidst the burning flames,
you shall not be harmed.
If you stand before the power of hell
and death is at your side,
know that I am with you, through it all."

And blessed are your poor,
for the Kingdom shall be theirs.
Blest are you that weep and mourn,
for one day you shall laugh.

Be not afraid,
I go before you always,
Come follow Me,
and I shall give you rest."

He considers the trustful lyrics perfect for the plight of
these dear people.

The liturgical prayers continue in the old sugar cane shed
in the war-torn district where Laurens had brought him
almost a year ago. He is always happy for the chance to take
the other Jesuit's place for Mass here. It's his favorite place in
El Salvador. The people feel like family even though he has
only been with them a handful of times. They make him so
welcome and enjoy teasing him. He plays music with them,
even dances when invited. Moreover, his little friends Pepe
and Lupe, of whom he's grown very fond, live nearby.

As the Dutchman had shown him, Jamie has carefully
prepared the shed with its dirt floor as a place for worship.

There are candles and vases of early wildflowers on the altar. The large box is still in the back, and he has heard it open, meaning guerrillas have joined the congregation.

Now Jamie spreads his hands reverently over the unleavened bread.

"Blessed are You, God of all creation,
through Your goodness we have this bread to offer
that earth has given and human hands have made.
It will become for us the bread of life."

Out of the corner of his eye, he notices Lupe and Pepe under some trees. When a neighbor brought them here today because their grandmother was working, they'd pleaded to be allowed to play outside.

"No, *ninos*, you must go to Mass!" Señora Munoz had declared.

"Please, Padre, please!" Pepe had implored. "*Por favor!*"

"If Señora will give her permission, perhaps you may go out for a while, if you promise to stay close." He'd looked at the woman with wide eyes, and she'd relented.

"*Gracias, gracias,*" the children had shouted as they turned and raced gleefully toward the trees.

"Forgive me, Señora, but for the small ones, play can be their prayer," he'd said with a shy smile.

"Padre, sometimes I think you are just a very tall child," she'd told him with a grin.

"Bless me, Madre, for I have sinned," he'd replied ruefully. She'd laughed and cuffed him on the wrist.

A bell rings. Jamie takes the bread in his hands. He bows his head. Silently he remembers all who have participated in this sacred act through history.

With feeling, he intones the words of consecration. "On

the night before he died, Jesus took bread, and giving You thanks, he broke the bread ..."

His heart is full as he repeats the ancient words calling Love Himself into this moment. The bell rings once more. He straightens and slowly raises high the host now transformed into Presence. He places it on altar and reaches for the cup of wine.

Out of nowhere comes a sound like giant flapping wings. It takes Jamie a few seconds and the fear on the faces of the people near him to realize he's hearing helicopters approaching.

"To the cave! To the rocks!" voices cry. In a flash the shed is emptied. A man races back, "Come, Padre, Now!" Instinctively grasping the plate of communion bread, Jamie begins to run.

The noise is overwhelming. The sounds of explosions are coming closer. He feels heat. Suddenly, he hears a scream.

"Padre, help!" Lupe shrieks.

He turns toward the sound of her voice. The little girl is trying to reach the shelter of the shed. She is dragging the limp form of her brother.

"Pepe is hurt!" she cries.

Jamie's heart is pounding. The plate falls from his hands and the consecrated bread scatters as he dashes to the children and throws his arm around the little boy. Grasping the girl with his other hand, he pulls her with him toward the shed.

The helicopters are almost directly above now. The noise and the wind from the rotors are hellish, blotting out everything else. There is no time to head for the cave or the rocks. Holding the children tightly, Jamie dives under the altar table. As soon as he's on the ground, he tries to shelter the Lupe and Pepe with his body. Thank God, they're small kids.

"Dear God, please keep them safe!" he prays with all the energy of the adrenaline coursing through him.

Jamie is about to ask the children if they are all right, when something slams into the back of his neck. His chin hits the ground. Time slows.

First he notices the fragrance of the earth, deep, rich and loamy, so beautiful he wants to cry. "I am lying on the altar of life," he thinks.

He feels a sharp jolt of pain. Something wet and warm is running down his neck. He wonders if it is blood.

"Am I going to die?"

Images of Sarah flash into Jamie's mind. He sees the faces of people he's met and served in El Salvador.

"Please let me stay with the people I love," he pleads silently.

The next instant he finds himself above the room looking down on a scene of chaos. He sees an overturned chalice and bread strewn across the floor. The words "Jesus crucified" slide through his consciousness.

A body is lying half covered by the altar. "Those are my shoes," he realizes. "That's my body." He gathers his psychic strength and wills himself back down onto the ground to be reunited with the physical form.

"Please let me stay!"

Everything changes. Now time is a lazy river on a summer day on which he can drift through a panorama of his entire life, glimpsed—how can this be?—all at once. His parents holding hands. Police at the door with the terrible news they are gone forever. Sister Regina chiding him in front of the fourth grade class. His grandmother's tender expression as she sings bedtime lullabies ...

He is lying before the altar of the cathedral giving his entire being to God. Singing his and Sarah's love to a

457

sorrowing Salvadoran mother. Watching three little boys screaming and dying in the road. Laughing uproariously with Sam. Making passionate love with Sarah in the rosy light of late afternoon.

Every experience, large and small, arrives simultaneously. And he feels each one as if for the first time in a single cascade of emotions and sensations.

In that long, flowing moment Jamie surrenders.

"I am Yours. Thy will be done," he breathes into the air.

"Sarah." His spirit rises upward and he finds himself over San Francisco Bay, lifted on a fresh breeze blowing through the Golden Gate. Sarah is sitting on their pier staring at the sky. Her sweet face is filled with wonder and love. And laughter.

SARAH IS AMAZED to see a white pelican arrive out of nowhere and hover above her. Jamie's favorite bird. Its wings beat strongly to hold itself in place. What is going on?

"Jamie, oh Jamie, is that you?" she calls.

Her laughing face will be the last thing he sees. A force more powerful than gravity draws him toward her. Jamie feels himself disappear through Sarah into a Vastness where there is only endless Light and boundless Love.

For Sarah it begins softly, a tender warmth on her skin, the way her body feels under Jamie's hands. Her eyes close and she is with him so powerfully and completely that her breath catches in surprise.

Her mind and heart are a kaleidoscope of their times together. Feelings, words, thoughts, sensations shift in passionate and ecstatic patterns, always changing.

"This is how I would die into the love I have for you: as

pieces of cloud dissolve in sunlight." Rumi's words flood through her.

And Sarah knows.

Jamie is moving away, pure spirit now. With everything in her she tries to hold him.

"Please, dear God! Oh, please!"

Her uncontrollable cry reverberates along the pier and over the water into a world suddenly more empty than it has ever been.

As she falls into grief, Sarah hears a familiar voice.

"Do you come here often?" it asks. There is the sound of a smile in the question. "I do too," he says.

ACKNOWLEDGMENTS

It has taken a loving and supportive community for me to write *Song of the Turtle*, and those who helped and guided me and shared in the adventure of creating a novel are the best friends anyone could have.

A dozen of them read the manuscript in various versions and made it so much better with their insightful evaluations and suggestions for changes. You know who you are and I hope you realize how much I appreciate your efforts on behalf of a story you felt needed to be told. Jose Artiga, executive director of SHARE El Salvador, improved the book with a few wise observations.

Three dear collaborators, Paula Aiello, Pat Sullivan and Barbara Lodman, did major editing of the book and honed and enriched the words and the narrative. My gratitude to them is boundless.

Anyone who decides to publish independently could not find more talented (and patient) midwives for the birth of their book than Beth Barany of Barany Consulting, and her husband Ezra who designed the book's cover. Beth was always just an email away and guided me through the labyrinth of the publishing process with a skill and kindness I could not have imagined until I experienced it.

The beautiful cover photograph of the Berkeley pier at sunset is the work of Harold Davis, a Berkeley photographer whose photos everyone who loves the beauty and grandeur of our world will absolutely want to see. His online galleries will take your breath away.

https://www.digitalfieldguide.com/

Bill Collins provided me with a very fine website (songoftheturtle.com) and could not have been more generous with his time and considerable expertise.

Finally, of course, there is the Love that is the basis of *Song of the Turtle,* its life force and inspiration. I think of those dearest ones with whom I have shared this love. I feel a gratitude so vast it could not be expressed in a thousand novels, and I smile.

BIBLIOGRAPHY

Raymond Bonner, *Weakness and Deceit: U.S. Policy and El Salvador.* The New York Times Book Company, New York, 1984.

Laetitia Bordes, ed, *Our Hearts Were Broken: A Spirituality of Accompaniment.* Red Star Black Rose Printing, Oakland CA, 2000.

Beth and Steve Cagan, *This Promised Land, El Salvador.* Rutgers University Press, New Brunswick, 1991.

Susan Classen, *Vultures and Butterflies: Living the Contradictions.* Herald Press, Scottsdale PA and Waterloo Ontario, 1992.

Charles Clements, M.D., *Witness to War.* Bantam Books, New York, 1984.

Mark Danner, *The Massacre at El Mozote.* Vintage Books, New York, 1993.

Jeanne Evans, *"Here I Am, Lord": The Letters and Writings of Ita Ford.* Orbis Books, Ossining, NY, 2005.

Adam Kufeld, *El Salvador: Photographs. W.W. Norton and Company, New York and London, 1990.*

Gloria Leal, Marta Pineda and Michael Gorkin, *From Grandmother to Granddaughter: Salvadoran Women's Stories.* University of California Press, Berkeley CA, 2000.

Judith M. Noone, *The Same Fate as the Poor. Orbis Books, New York, 1995.*

Maria Lopez Vigil, *Don Lito of El Salvador.* Orbis Books, Ossining, NY, 1990.

_____*Death and Life in Morazan.* Catholic Institute for International Relations, 1989.

_____ *Oscar Romero: Memories in Mosaic. Partan, Longman and Todd, Ltd., London, 1993.*

ABOUT THE AUTHOR

Jesus's invitation to love and the world of nature have been at the center of Siddika's life journey. As a child, she explored her grandparents' northern California ranch, watching insects, aquatic creatures, and animals, fascinated to discover their intricacies and mysteries. In recent years, her spiritual wellspring has been a deep connection with the beauty and complexity of nature's gifts and secrets. The scientists' recognition that earth consists wholly of webs of relationships is for Siddika like uncovering fresh holy scriptures just now seeing the light of day.

Siddika is a former newspaper reporter who returned to graduate school at midlife for a master's degree in Biblical Studies and a Ph.D. in History and Phenomenology of Religion. She has taught courses in World Religions, with a focus on the spirituality of these wisdom traditions, at Bay Area colleges and universities.

Made in the USA
San Bernardino, CA
22 September 2018